JOURNEY
TO THE
END
OF THE
WORLD

READ MORE ABOUT JOEL GUSTAFSON'S ADVENTURES IN
THESE COMPANION NOVELS

A Bridge to the Stars

Shadows in the Twilight

When the Snow Fell

HENNING MANKELL

JOURNEY TO THE END OF THE WORLD

TRANSLATED FROM THE SWEDISH BY LAURIE THOMPSON

DELACORTE PRESS

Translation copyright © 2008 by Laurie Thompson
Cover art copyright © 2011 by Christopher Dessaigne / Trevillion Images

All rights reserved. Published in the United States by Delacorte Press, an imprint of
Random House Children's Books, a division of Random House, Inc., New York.
Originally published in Sweden as *Resan till världens ände* by Henning Mankell,
copyright © 1998 by Henning Mankell, by Rabén & Sjögren, Stockholm, in 1998.
This translation was originally published in Great Britain by Andersen Press, Limited, London, in 2008.

Delacorte Press is a registered trademark and the colophon is a trademark of Random House, Inc.

Visit us on the Web! www.randomhouse.com/teens

Educators and librarians, for a variety of teaching tools,
visit us at www.randomhouse.com/teachers

Library of Congress Cataloging-in-Publication Data
Mankell, Henning.
[Resan till varldens ande. English]
Journey to the end of the world / Henning Mankell ; translated from the Swedish by Laurie Thompson.
— 1st American trade pbk. ed.
p. cm.
Summary: In the late 1950s, fifteen-year-old Joel is anxious to finish school and leave the remote logging town in northern Sweden to sail to far-off places with his father, a former sailor, but the arrival of a letter giving news about his long-absent, nearly forgotten, mother, sends Joel and his father to Stockholm on a journey that will change their lives forever.
ISBN 978-0-385-73498-1 (trade paper)
[1. Fathers and sons — Fiction. 2. Coming of age — Fiction. 3. Mothers and sons — Fiction.
4. Single-parent families — Fiction. 5. Sweden — History — Gustavus VI Adolphus, 1950–1973 — Fiction.]
I. Thompson, Laurie. II. Title.
PZ7.M31283Jo 2011
[Fic] — dc22
2010022499

Printed in the United States of America

10 9 8 7 6 5 4 3 2 1

First American Trade Paperback Edition

Random House Children's Books supports the First Amendment and celebrates the right to read.

JOURNEY TO THE END OF THE WORLD

To the memory
of my parents

This is the fourth and final book in the series about Joel. The first part was *A Bridge to the Stars*. Then came *Shadows in the Twilight*, and *When the Snow Fell*. In this book there are occasional references to characters who appeared in the earlier stories. I have not always bothered to describe them in detail again—what they look like, or why they do what they do. Anybody who wants to can always catch up by consulting previous volumes in the series of stories about Joel. But it is not necessary, of course. Most of what you need to know is to be found in these pages.

—HENNING MANKELL

One night in March

The year when Joel will soon celebrate his fifteenth birthday, he wakes up out of a dream that has made him feel frightened. When he opens his eyes in the darkness, he doesn't know where he is at first. But then he hears his dad's snores rolling in through the half-open door.

That's the moment when his dream comes back to him.

He'd been walking over the ice on the frozen river. He didn't know why he was there. But he suddenly noticed that the ice was beginning to crack under his feet. He started running to the bank as fast as he could, but all the time more cracks opened out in front of him. He would never be able to get to the bank. Then, as if with the wave of a magic wand, all the winter ice vanished. Apart from the small floe he was standing on. Then he noticed there was something odd about the water. It wasn't black and cold like it usually was. It was boiling. And all the time the floe he was standing on was getting smaller. In the end there was nothing left of it. Fierce white crocodiles were snapping at him. And he was falling. Falling straight into their jaws . . .

He notices that he's covered in sweat. The hands of his alarm clock gleam in the darkness. A quarter past four. He's so relieved to have escaped from his dream. He pulls the covers up to his chin and turns to face the wall in the hope of going back to sleep. There are still a few hours to go before he needs to get up and go to school.

But he can't sleep. He lies awake. Persistent thoughts fill his mind. Three more months and his school days will come to an end. He'll get his final report. Then what will he do? Where will he find a job? What would he really like to do? The thoughts won't go away. Especially when he thinks about Samuel. For as long as Joel can remember, his dad has been talking about moving away from the little town they live in. As soon as Joel finishes school, Samuel will become a sailor again, and take Joel with him. But the years have gone by and Samuel talks less and less about the sea. And ships. And all the ports waiting for them out there in the wide world.

There's a lot to think about. Joel sits up in bed and leans his back against the wall. It's March already. Before long the snow will start to melt away. It will be his birthday next month. He'll be fifteen. That means he'll be allowed to ride a moped. And see adults-only films. His birthday will be the day he no longer needs to sneak into the cinema without being seen. He'll be able to walk past the caretaker with a ticket in his hand.

Becoming fifteen is an important event.

But he feels worried. What will happen?

• • •

In the end he manages to go back to sleep.

Outside a solitary dog runs past the house. It's on its way to somewhere only the dog knows about.

But Joel is asleep. In his dreams the spring thaw has arrived already.

And the ice is melting. . . .

— ONE —

Joel was halfway down the hill just past the vicarage when his chain came off. He was so surprised that he swerved and lost control of his bike. He crashed into the hedge round the horse dealer's garden and flew headfirst into some currant bushes. One cheek was badly scratched, and his left knee was bruised. But when he scrambled to his feet he was able to stand up and rescue his bike from the hedge. He'd made a big hole in it. As the horse dealer had a fiery temper, Joel rapidly wheeled his bike away and leaned it against the vicarage fence.

It was an afternoon in the middle of May. There were still patches of snow left in the shadow of house walls and on the verges. Spring had not yet brought any warm weather with it. But every afternoon after school Joel took his bike and rode through the streets of the little town. He felt worried and restless. What was going to happen shortly? When he left school?

A few days after he'd had that dream about the river with boiling water, he'd asked Samuel. He'd prepared himself carefully.

They usually had pork and fried potatoes on a Sunday, but as it was Samuel's favorite, Joel had made it for that night's dinner even though it was a Tuesday. Joel knew that the best moment to take up an important matter with Samuel was when he had just finished eating and pushed his plate to one side.

And that moment had come. Samuel put down his fork, wiped his mouth and slid his plate away.

"We have to make up our minds," Joel said.

Although his voice had broken now, it sometimes happened that things he said came out like a squeak or in falsetto. He spoke slowly and tried to make his voice as deep as possible.

Samuel was usually tired when he'd finished eating. Now he blinked and looked at Joel.

"What do we have to make up our minds about?" he asked.

Samuel seemed to be in a good mood, Joel thought. That wasn't always the case. Samuel could sometimes be peevish, and in that case Joel knew there was hardly any point in trying to discuss something important.

"What we're going to do when I've left school."

Samuel smiled.

"What sort of a report are you going to get?"

Joel didn't like Samuel answering a question by asking another one himself. It was a bad habit that lots of grown-ups had.

But he had prepared himself thoroughly. Joel's school marks were always important to Samuel.

"I'll get better marks than last autumn," he said. "I'll be in the top three for geography."

Samuel nodded.

"When are we going to move?" Joel asked. He must have asked Samuel that question at least a thousand times before. Nearly every day, year after year. The same question. "When are we going to move?"

Samuel looked down at the blue tablecloth on the kitchen table. Joel thought he might as well continue.

"You're not a lumberjack," he said. "You're a sailor. When I've left school we won't need to stay here any longer. We can go away. We can sign on for the same ship. I'm fifteen now. I can also be a sailor."

Joel waited for an answer.

But Samuel continued staring down at the tablecloth. Then he stood up without a word and put on the coffee water. Joel wasn't going to get an answer, that much was obvious.

He suddenly felt angry.

He'd made a big effort and prepared Sunday food even though it was only Tuesday, but still Samuel couldn't give him a sensible answer.

He thought he ought to swear and tell his father a few home truths. Tell him he had an obligation to answer now. Joel had no intention of asking the same question another thousand times.

But he didn't swear. He cleared away the plates, scraped the remains into the slop bucket and put the crockery in the sink.

"I'm going out," he said.

"Don't you have any homework?" asked Samuel, without looking up from the coffee water that was just coming to the boil.

"I've done it already," Joel said. "Besides, soon there won't be any more homework."

Joel waited. But in vain. Samuel said nothing else.

Joel took his jacket and went downstairs.

No answer this time either.

Joel thought about this the following day as well, when he was mending the chain on his bicycle. He hadn't put his question to Samuel again, but had the impression that his dad was thinking it over. Why that should be the case, Joel had no idea. But that was what he suspected, and the feeling was very strong.

It also worried him. When Samuel said hardly anything and seemed to be lost in thought, he could sometimes lapse into one of his phases. When he would just disappear, and then come home drunk late at night. It was a long time since that had happened last, but Joel knew it would happen again. Sooner or later. And that was something he always dreaded. Being forced to go out looking for Samuel, and then dragging him home when he was too drunk to walk without help.

Joel tried to wipe the oil off his bicycle chain using a sheet of newspaper that happened to be blowing past.

Let's hope it doesn't happen at the end-of-term ceremony, he thought. That Samuel turns up at church drunk.

Anything but that.

He turned round and gazed up at the church tower. The clock told him it was high time for him to go home and put the potatoes on to boil. He mounted his bike and started pedaling. On the graveled area behind the petrol station, some boys were dividing into two teams. Several of them were Joel's classmates. He pedaled even harder. He always needed to make the dinner: he'd always been his own mum. And Samuel's as well, sometimes.

When he left school he'd stop doing the cooking. If Samuel wanted to eat when he came home, he'd have to prepare the food himself.

Joel kicked open the gate and freewheeled to the side of the door where he could park his bike. Then he raced up the stairs and wrenched open the kitchen door.

And was stopped in his tracks.

Samuel was sitting on a chair at the kitchen table. Alarm bells started ringing. Samuel wasn't supposed to come home as soon as this. On the few occasions he had done so in the past, he'd either been ill or started drinking. But he didn't seem to be drunk. His eyes weren't red and his hair wasn't standing on end. He didn't seem to be especially ill either.

He looked up at Joel and seemed to be surprised.

"What's the matter?" Joel asked. "Why are you at home already?"

Samuel pointed to a letter lying on the table.

"Who's it from?"

"Take your jacket off and sit down, and I'll tell you."

Joel kicked off his Wellingtons and hung his jacket over the back of his chair. Then he sat down. He was very much on edge. What could there be in a letter that was so important that it made Samuel come home earlier than usual from his work in the forest?

He noticed that Samuel was very tense. His lower lip was trembling.

"I've had a letter from Elinor," he said. "I haven't heard from her for ten years."

Joel waited for what was coming next, but nothing did.

"Who's Elinor?" he asked, when the silence had been going on for long enough.

"Elinor used to run a bar in Gothenburg," said Samuel. "In the days when I was a sailor."

Joel sighed silently. A few years ago Samuel had met Sara, who worked in a bar in town. Samuel had sometimes spent the night at her place. But then the relationship had come to an end. Sara had broken it off. And Samuel had started drinking. Now he had evidently received a letter from another woman who worked in a bar. Maybe Samuel had spent the night with her occasionally, as well? But why was it so important?

Samuel can be odd sometimes, Joel thought. Just as odd as all the other grown-ups. They think backwards when they

9

ought to be thinking forwards. He gets a letter from somebody he hasn't heard from for ten years. And his lower lip starts trembling. But when I ask him how soon we can get out of this dump of a town and go to sea, I don't even get an answer.

Joel looked at Samuel, and thought that perhaps he ought to ask him something. Give the appearance of being interested.

"What does she want?" he asked.

"She's told me that she knows where Jenny lives."

It was some time before that sank in.

Then it seemed as if Joel had been caught up in an earthquake. He was shaking, and it seemed the house was about to collapse and fall down to the shuddering ground.

Somebody called Elinor had written a letter about Mummy Jenny. The one who had vanished ages ago and not been heard of since.

Samuel had put his glasses on.

"It says here," he said, "that Jenny lives in Stockholm. On a street called Östgötagatan. In a district known as Söder. And that she works as a shop assistant in a grocery store in a square called Medborgarplatsen."

Joel stared at Samuel.

"Does it say anything else?"

Samuel took off his glasses.

"It says that she's remarried."

"But she's married to you?"

"We never got round to getting married. So we didn't need to get divorced either."

Joel was confused. Had Samuel and Jenny never been married?

He was interested now. He wanted to know about everything in the letter. He held out his hand. But Samuel placed his own large hand over the white paper.

"The letter's addressed to me," he said.

"Jenny's my mum," said Joel.

"It's written by Elinor. Elinor was a friend of Jenny's. That's why she's written to me."

Joel tried to think straight.

"How can it say that she's remarried if she was never married to you in the first place?"

Samuel nodded slowly.

"A good question," he said. "But I suppose that's just what people say."

"Does it say anything else?"

"Elinor's suffering from back pains."

"Does it say anything more about Mum? I couldn't give a damn about Elinor."

Joel was surprised by what he'd just said. Samuel looked at him in astonishment. Joel felt scared. Samuel could sometimes fly into a rage. Even if he used to swear himself, he didn't like it if Joel swore.

"Elinor's a nice lady," said Samuel. "She's worked hard all her life. It's hard going, serving in a bar. Just think about how difficult it was for Sara, the trouble she had with her legs."

"That's not what I meant," Joel mumbled. "But does it say anything else about Mum?"

"No, nothing."

"Who's she married to?"

"It doesn't say."

The conversation petered out. Samuel put his glasses back on and read the letter one more time. Joel could see how his father's lips were forming word after word. All Joel could do was try to understand what had happened.

For the first time, somebody had been able to tell them where Mummy Jenny was living. Whenever Joel had asked about that before, Samuel had merely shaken his head and said that he didn't know.

But now, all of a sudden, everything had changed. Mummy Jenny had an address and a job. And unfortunately, a new husband into the bargain.

Joel started to scrub the potatoes. Samuel had started reading the letter yet again.

"Can't you read it out loud?" Joel asked.

"The letter's to me," said Samuel.

They ate their dinner in silence. Boiled potato and black pudding. They had no lingonberry jam left.

Joel had burnt the black pudding.

After dinner, Samuel went to his room. He switched on the radio and lay down on top of his bed. As he had closed the door of his room, Joel was forced to peep in through the keyhole. He could see that Samuel was gazing at the only photo of Jenny he still possessed.

Joel went to his room and also lay down on his bed. Grown-up people who had important things to think about often seemed to lie down on their beds to do so. As Joel was almost grown up himself, he thought he'd better join them. But he was too restless. He got up again and went to look out of the window. It was still light out there. He tried to imagine the house where Mummy Jenny lived. Then it dawned on him that he actually possessed a map of Stockholm. He'd found it in a rubbish bin at the railway station a few years ago. The only question was: where had he put it? He started searching. And finally found it right at the back of his wardrobe. He took it to the kitchen and spread it out on the table. Samuel's door was still closed. Joel could hear music playing on the radio. He bent down and took another look through the keyhole. Samuel was still holding the photograph of Jenny. But now he was staring up at the ceiling. Joel went back to the kitchen and pored over the map of Stockholm, trying to remember what Samuel had said. Mummy Jenny lived on a street called Östgötagatan. And worked in a grocer's shop in Medborgarplatsen.

Joel started running his finger over the map. He found Medborgarplatsen first. His heart started beating more quickly. Mummy Jenny seemed to have become more real, now that he had found the place where she worked. He kept on searching.

He had just managed to trace Östgötagatan when the door opened and Samuel came into the kitchen to join him. Joel gave a start, as if he'd been found out doing something that wasn't allowed. Maybe Samuel wouldn't want him to pin down Mummy Jenny's address? But Samuel just came to stand by his side.

"I didn't know you had a map of Stockholm," he said in surprise.

"I found it in a rubbish bin," Joel told him. "I thought I'd better see if she—Elinor, that is—was telling the truth."

"She didn't used to tell lies," said Samuel. "Not all that often, at least."

Joel pointed out Medborgarplatsen. And then Östgötagatan. Samuel went back to his room to fetch his glasses. Then he pored over the map and nodded.

"She doesn't have far to go, then," he said. "From Östgötagatan where she lives, to Medborgarplatsen where she works."

It suddenly occurred to Joel that there was something he had to say. Something he couldn't overlook.

"Can't we go and visit her?" he asked. "Now that we know where she lives."

Samuel sat down at the table. Looked hard at Joel.

"Are you serious?"

"She might be glad to see us," said Joel. "After all these

years. She might want to know what her son looks like. Now that he's fifteen years old and has got a good school report. In geography, at least."

Samuel looked doubtful.

"At least we can go there and take a look at her," said Joel. "Peer in through the window of the shop where she works. She probably won't be able to recognize me. And you can wear dark glasses."

Samuel burst out laughing. That was a surprise. It was always a surprise. Samuel didn't often laugh. He often smiled. But laugh? Joel could hardly remember the last time it had happened.

"You're right, of course," said Samuel. "As soon as you've left school, we'll go and look for her."

Joel wondered if he could believe his ears. Samuel realized that his son was confused.

"We'll go as soon as you finish school," he said. "I'll apply for a few days' holiday right away."

"Should we write to her and tell her we're going to visit her?" Joel wondered.

Samuel thought for a moment before answering. Then he shook his head.

"She didn't tell us when she left. So why should we tell her that we're going to pay her a visit?"

Joel had another question.

"She probably won't recognize us. But the question is: will you recognize her? She might look quite different."

"I'll recognize her all right," said Samuel confidently. "No matter how much she's changed."

That evening, when Samuel had gone to bed, Joel got up again. He hadn't got undressed. He picked up his shoes and his jacket, and tiptoed out. He knew which steps to avoid, because they creaked.

It was still light when he left the house. He wheeled his bike out of the gate, then got on and started pedaling for all he was worth. He raced down to the bridge and when he eventually pulled up he was sweaty and out of breath.

He'd arrived at Gertrud's house. Gertrud didn't have a nose, and lived in a strange house with an overgrown garden on the other side of the river. Joel felt that he really had to tell her about what had happened. Gertrud was his friend. He'd already told her about Mummy Jenny, who'd gone away when he was very small.

Gertrud had once undergone an operation that went wrong, and as a result she lost her nose. She didn't have many friends. Joel was one of the few.

As he leaned his bicycle against her ramshackle fence, she came out to greet him. She'd seen him coming, through the kitchen window.

"Long time no see," she said.

"There's so much to do for school," Joel said. "Lots of homework."

But that wasn't true. And they both knew it. Joel sometimes thought it was awkward, visiting somebody who didn't have a nose, and Gertrud knew that was what he was thinking.

But sometimes Joel felt he simply had to see her. Sometimes Gertrud was the only person he could talk to.

Like now, for instance. When a mum called Jenny suddenly appears out of nowhere, having been missing for so long that he can't remember what it's like to have her around.

Joel went with Gertrud into her kitchen, which was chaotic and nothing like a normal kitchen. That was the way Gertrud was. She did whatever she fancied with her furniture and fittings, made her own clothes, and paid no attention to what other people said or thought.

Joel didn't want to be seen with her in public, but it was all right to meet her here, late in the evening, in her kitchen. Besides, she gave him an opportunity to practice for the future. He'd read that when a boy became a man, the thing to do was to have secret meetings with women.

"We're going to Stockholm," he said. "Samuel and me. We're going to meet her. Obviously, I wonder how she's going to react."

Gertrud thought that over, while she fitted a new handkerchief into the hole where her nose used to be.

"I'm sure she'll be pleased," she said eventually. "She's bound to be."

But later, when Joel was cycling back home, it struck him that Gertrud hadn't sounded really convincing.

Seeds of worry had been sown in his stomach.

What if Mummy Jenny didn't want to see him or Samuel? What if she was furious about Elinor having written that letter telling where she lived and worked?

It was dark in the kitchen when Joel got home. The door to Samuel's room was closed. But he wasn't snoring. He was probably still awake, thinking about the letter.

Joel went to bed. But he found it hard to go to sleep. He could picture himself and Samuel walking down a street in Stockholm.

Samuel still hadn't started snoring.

We're both lying awake, Joel thought. In our respective beds.

But we're thinking about the same thing.

A mum who's suddenly come back.

— TWO —

When Joel raised the roller blind he found that it had been snowing during the night.

The ground was totally white.

He stared out of the window, scarcely able to believe his eyes.

It was the beginning of June. Today was his last day at school. At the leaving ceremony they would sing about sunshine and joy and "all things bright and beautiful." And the ground was covered in snow.

A thought struck him. One he'd never had before. Perhaps it was the snow, which could sometimes fall in June, that had driven Mummy Jenny away? Perhaps she simply hadn't been able to stand it anymore? All that cold and darkness and snow that wouldn't go away, despite the fact that it was summer already?

Joel shook his head in annoyance. It was a big day. His last day at school. And there was snow on the ground.

He got dressed and went to the kitchen. Samuel had

already drunk his coffee. He'd also shaved. Joel looked at him in surprise. Samuel hardly ever shaved in the middle of the week. Only if he had an appointment with the doctor, or had been summoned to the logging company's office for some reason.

Not only that, he had shaved himself thoroughly. Joel was often irritated by the careless way his father usually shaved. There was always some stubble left under his chin.

"It snowed last night," said Samuel with a smile. "You never know what the weather's going to do in these parts."

"But what you do know is that you shouldn't live here," said Joel, making no attempt to disguise his annoyance.

"I've taken the day off," said Samuel.

"Why?"

"So that I can go to the school-leaving ceremony."

Joel was buttering one of the three sandwiches he ate every morning. He looked at Samuel in astonishment. Had he misheard?

"Why?" he asked.

"It's a big day," said Samuel. "Your last day at school. I think I ought to be there, don't you?"

Samuel had never attended an end-of-term ceremony before. In the early years Joel had found it a problem. Being the only one in the class who didn't have at least one parent present for the occasion. Then he'd got used to it, and it didn't bother him anymore.

Joel tried to assess quickly what the implications were. Was it a good or a bad thing? He decided it was good, because Samuel had shaved properly for once. He actually felt pleased. Ever since that letter had come from Elinor, something had changed. It wasn't just that they would sit in the evening and talk about Mummy Jenny and the trip they were going to make in only a few more days' time. But Samuel knew that Joel wasn't thinking about anything else. And Joel knew that the same applied to Samuel.

"You shouldn't arrive before ten o'clock. We shall be rehearsing until then. And tidying up the classroom."

He ought really to have picked some flowers the previous evening, but he hadn't got round to it. Two cars had crashed at the corner of Kyrkogatan and Snällmans väg. Joel had been close by at the time, and watched with interest how the two drivers had started arguing. Joel walked over to the window and stood on tiptoe. He could see a few yellow flowers under a tree where they'd been sheltered from the snow.

Joel ate his sandwiches and brushed his teeth. Then he remembered that he ought to have put on his best shirt and a different pair of trousers in view of the forthcoming ceremony. When he returned to the kitchen he realized that he would have to hurry if he didn't want to arrive late.

Samuel was sitting at the table, looking at him.

"Perhaps we ought to take a present," he said.

Joel didn't understand what he meant at first. A present for whom? For the teachers?

Then he realized that his father meant a present for Jenny, of course. Joel hadn't thought about that.

"We must have something to take with us," Samuel said. "Get a move on or you'll be late for school."

Joel thundered down the stairs. Sometimes Samuel could surprise him. Of course they must take a present for Mummy Jenny.

He was already in the street before he remembered the flowers. He leaned his bike against the fence and ran back into the garden. Seven drooping cowslips would have to do. He added a few blades of grass to make the bunch look a bit bigger. On the way to school he thought about what they could give Jenny. But he found it hard to concentrate. He would have to get the school-leaving ceremony out of the way first.

He entered the classroom at the very last moment. Miss Nederström looked disapprovingly at him. But she didn't say anything. It was the last day. Then they would all go their different ways. Miss Nederström could just as easily become emotional as she could get angry. Today she certainly wasn't going to quarrel with Joel or anybody else.

By ten o'clock the classroom had been tidied up and decorated. The parents were squashed in at the back. Joel had noticed Samuel when he arrived: he was trapped in a corner now. Miss Nederström was in a good mood and only asked questions she knew her pupils could answer. Joel was asked a geography question. After the demonstration lesson they sang a hymn and then processed to the church, class by class. The snow had melted away by then. When they were all assembled in the church, the headmaster gave a speech, all the pupils were given their reports, and then it was all over. Miss Nederström had tears in her eyes when she shook Joel's hand. He felt most embarrassed.

"You ought to have gone on to college," she said.

"I've got other things I have to do first," Joel replied.

He'd been thinking about that for nearly a year now. If he ought to try and get a place at college. But the thought of four more years' schooling was too much for him. He wanted to get out. Out into the world.

Samuel was waiting for him outside the church.

"I'm pleased that you could give the right answer to the question you were asked," Samuel said.

"It's just as well she didn't ask me a question about history," Joel said. "I'd have been bound to get it wrong."

Then they went home. Just for once, Joel also had a cup of coffee. He still wasn't quite sure what it felt like, having finished school. Knowing that after the holidays, when autumn came, there would no longer be a teacher checking up on whether he got to school on time.

Now life was going to begin. Real life. And it would start with the trip to Stockholm he and Samuel were going to make. He wasn't at all sure what would happen after that. He'd been given a half promise of a job as errand boy at the ironmonger's. But what then? What would he do next? It all depended on Samuel. Were they going to move house, or weren't they?

Joel had worked out a plan. There was a big harbor in Stockholm. Ships from all over the world went there. It wasn't as big a port as Gothenburg, but even so: perhaps Samuel would finally make up his mind when he saw all those ships berthed at the various quays. Joel had made up his mind to take Samuel to see the ships as often as possible. Naturally, Samuel had forgotten what it was like to be a sailor. How could he possibly have remembered? Living for so long as a castaway in the depths of those enormous forests, where there was no sea, only gloomy little lakes.

Samuel examined Joel's report in detail.

"You ought to have learnt how to count better," he said. "But apart from that, it's good."

Joel said nothing. Samuel was right. Maths was the most boring subject Joel could think of.

Then they started to talk about the present they were going to take to Mummy Jenny. What should they give her?

"You're the one who knows her best," said Joel.

"She used to be very keen on hats in those days," said

Samuel tentatively. "But maybe she isn't anymore. Besides, how would I be able to go into a shop selling ladies' clothes and pick out a hat for her?"

Joel knew that Samuel and Jenny had once met at a dance.

"Maybe she'd like a gramophone record," he suggested.

"But has she got a gramophone?" Samuel wondered. "You can never be sure."

"Everybody has a gramophone," said Joel. "Apart from us, perhaps."

He regretted saying that the moment it had crossed his lips. Samuel didn't like to be reminded of the fact that they had so little money. It could make him very morose. Joel didn't want that to happen. Not now.

"Maybe she has the record already," he said.

"What record?"

"The one we were going to give her."

This conversation's getting very odd, Joel thought.

"Perhaps we could give her a gift voucher," he suggested. "Then she could choose for herself what she wanted to buy."

Samuel shook his head.

"No, it has to be something real. Something you can put in a parcel. If we had an elk steak we could have given her that."

Joel looked at Samuel in astonishment.

"Are you saying we should take her an elk steak? What if blood were to start dripping out of the suitcase? The police would think we'd murdered somebody."

"It's not the elk-hunting season now anyway. We'll have to think of something else."

It was afternoon. The sun's rays were streaming in through the kitchen window. Moving steadily across the wall. Until they reached the showcase containing the *Celestine*.

"Maybe she'd like to have *Celestine*," said Joel. "That would be something that we like as well."

Samuel spent a long time gazing at the model ship in its case before answering.

"I suppose it was on display there when she went away," he said. "You might be right. Perhaps we ought to give her *Celestine*."

They didn't make a decision. But now they had an idea, at least.

One more week before they were due to set off. They would take the night train on Saturday evening. They'd arrive in Stockholm on Sunday. Joel had asked Samuel about all the details. Not least where they were going to stay. Samuel had said that there were cheap hotels near the railway station. Joel was also worried that Samuel wouldn't take enough money with him. But that wasn't something he could very well ask about. Instead, he made a point of going through Samuel's wallet when his dad wasn't looking. Samuel had three hundred kronor. That was a lot of money as far as Joel was concerned. But would it be enough? He didn't know.

The days passed slowly. Joel tried to go back to sleep in the mornings after Samuel had left for work in the forest, but he was far too excited to stay in bed. He got up again, ate his sandwiches and went out. No more snow had fallen, and it had become warmer as well. He didn't just cycle around town, but went for quite long rides, exploring the logging tracks. Whenever he came to a clearing where the sun's rays managed to penetrate as far as the ground, he would find a biggish rock and sit down to think. Most of all about what it would be like to meet Mummy Jenny. But also about whether he would manage to persuade Samuel to make up his mind about moving at last. And what he would do if he didn't succeed. If they came back here and Samuel carried on going into the forest to cut down trees.

One day Joel had sat down at the kitchen table and made a long list of all the jobs he knew about. Then he tried to work his way through them all, and imagine what it would be like, doing each one.

Airline Pilot Captain Joel Gustafson
That sounded tempting, of course. Visualizing yourself in uniform. With nerves of steel. Making a skillful emergency landing in the middle of some desert or other. But there again, he knew that a pilot had to be able to do sums. No doubt his mark for maths wouldn't be good enough.

Surveyor Joel Gustafson
What exactly did a surveyor do? Look at things? Measure distances? Wander around by the side of ditches and logging tracks? Noting down how far it was between fences? That would bore him stiff.

He worked his way through his long list as he sat in those sunny glades, wondering what life would be like as a motor mechanic or a gamekeeper, a watchmaker or an actor. He also thought about what he had dreamt of only a year ago: becoming a rock idol. But he had accepted the fact that he couldn't sing well enough, and probably wouldn't be able to learn to play the guitar as well as was necessary.

Some of the jobs on his list he could cross out straightaway. What he wanted to be least of all was a lumberjack like Samuel. Anything at all but that.

In the end he concluded that there was only one thing he really wanted to do. To become a sailor. What Samuel had been when he met Mummy Jenny. He could become a deckhand or an ordinary seaman. Start at the bottom of the ladder.

Sailors worked with ropes and did lookout duty. They didn't need to be good at sums. He would never wake up in the same place as he'd gone to sleep in. The ship was always on the move. He would get to see everything that lay beyond the never-ending conifer forests. He wouldn't need to stay in this little town where there was even snow on the ground when school broke up for the summer holidays. He would only sign on for ships that were heading for warmer climes. Somewhere out there was also Pitcairn Island, and the women waiting for him in transparent veils.

Almost every day he thought about what had happened the previous year. When he discovered that Ehnström's grocery store, where he always bought food for himself and Samuel, had acquired a new shop assistant. Her name was Sonja Mattsson, and she wasn't going to stay in the town for very long. She was somehow related to the Ehnströms. Joel had made a hopeless New Year's resolution, that within the coming year he would see a naked woman. And one day he had caught a glimpse of Sonja Mattsson wearing nothing but a transparent veil.

Then it dawned on Joel that Sonja Mattsson had gone back to Stockholm: maybe he would be able to meet her there? She had said she'd like him to visit her if he ever went to the capital. But he didn't have her address.

That thought struck him while he was sitting in a woodland clearing, crossing out jobs on his long list of possibilities. He immediately jumped into action. Cycled back to town. He knew that if he went to the telegraph office he would be able to find out details of any addresses and telephone numbers he needed. He was a bit worried as he walked up the stairs to the office. A few years ago he had connected lots of lines at the switchboard one night when the operator had fallen asleep.

Nobody had realized that he was the one who did it. But you never knew. There were some people who seemed to be able to see straight into his mind.

He went to the hatch and rang the bell. He saw to his relief that it wasn't the same operator as had fallen asleep that night when he had made his secret visit to the exchange.

"I'd like an address and telephone number in Stockholm, please," he said.

"Do you want to phone them or send a telegram?" asked the woman behind the hatch. She looked stern, and Joel immediately felt nervous.

"Neither just now," he said. "I'm going to make a call later."

"What's the name of the subscriber?"

"Sonja Mattsson."

"And her address?"

"I don't know."

"But you are sure she lives in Stockholm?"

"Yes."

"Just a moment."

She closed the hatch. Joel waited. He read a notice on the wall that explained how much it would cost to send a telegram.

But what would he put in it?

I'm coming on Sunday by train from Norrland. Please meet me. Joel. PS. Samuel will be there as well. My father.

That was too many words. Twenty-three of them. He tried to cut it down.

Meet the train Sunday afternoon. Joel.

That was only six words. But then she wouldn't know which train to meet. And she probably wouldn't remember him anyway.

The hatch shot open again.

"There are seven persons called Sonja Mattsson in Stockholm."

The woman handed him a telephone directory through the hatch.

"You'll have to work out which one it is you want to contact."

She gave him a pencil and a sheet of paper. Joel took the directory over to a table and sat down to make a note of all the addresses and telephone numbers. Five of the seven were listed as "Miss." The other two didn't have a title at all.

Joel wrote them all down. Then he went back to the hatch and rang the bell. He returned the directory and the pencil.

"Do you know which one it is?"

"I think so."

The hatch closed. Joel wondered why he hadn't told the truth. That he hadn't a clue which Sonja Mattsson was the right one.

As he left the telegraph office he also wondered why he didn't go to Ehnström's and ask. But he didn't want to. They'd only start asking questions.

The days were long. But time passed quickly even so. On the Thursday they decided they would in fact take the *Celestine* as a present for Mummy Jenny. Samuel and Joel helped each other to lift the ship carefully out of her case and wrap her up in newspaper. Joel found a suitable cardboard box. So that was the present sorted out. Earlier in the day Samuel had been to buy rail tickets.

"I thought we could sleep on the seats," he said. "It would be unnecessarily expensive to splash out on sleeping car tickets."

Joel had no intention of sleeping at all. No way was he going to sleep throughout this journey.

27

● ● ●

Saturday finally dawned. When Joel went into the kitchen in the morning, Samuel was sitting at the kitchen table cleaning up his old suitcase with a damp cloth. It was brown, and the handle had been repaired with a piece of string.

"I never thought I'd have a use for this old suitcase again," he said.

Joel didn't like the sound of that. Did it mean that Samuel had never seriously considered leaving the place where they lived now, and going back to sea? Joel wanted to ask. But he didn't. When they were standing at the quayside in Stockholm, looking at the vessels moored there, he would ask his dad that question.

No, he wouldn't ask. He would plead. Now that they knew where Mummy Jenny lived, wasn't it time to move away at last from all the cold and snow?

Joel didn't possess a suitcase. He would have to make do with his rucksack. He didn't like that idea. People traveling to Stockholm ought to have a proper suitcase. Even if they were only fifteen years old. Samuel would certainly have been able to afford to buy a new suitcase if he'd been working as a sailor.

They weren't going to be away for long. Four days would soon pass. Joel packed his best clothes. He placed the map of Stockholm on top of everything else. Everything was ready by nine o'clock. That left another eight hours before they needed to go to the railway station. Samuel was shaving. Joel made sure he did a thorough job of it.

"Your chin," he said as Samuel started to dry his face.

"My chin?" Samuel wondered.

"You still have some stubble left under your chin."

Samuel examined his face carefully in the little mirror, then applied the razor once more.

"Is that better?" he asked.

Joel nodded. He was satisfied.

It was a quarter past four when they went to the station. Joel felt indescribably happy deep down inside. It was as if he'd only just grasped what was about to happen.

They were going to make a journey.

And they were going to meet Mummy Jenny.

— THREE —

Joel was on tenterhooks as the engine lurched and started moving. The journey had begun.

He looked out of the window and saw Stationmaster Knif waving his flag. The train gradually gathered speed. Samuel was holding on to his suitcase. They were approaching the railway bridge. There was their house. The engine thundered onto the bridge. The railings hurtled past. Joel could see the water down below, and the logs floating down to the sawmills at the mouth of the river. Samuel had stood up now and joined Joel at the window. They were over the bridge already. Now came the long curve through the part of the town on the other side of the river. And then they would be swallowed up by the vast forests. Joel had never been as far away from his home as this before, and it was still only the beginning of the journey.

Samuel sat down again. They had found a compartment to themselves.

"There's hardly likely to be anybody getting on until we get to Orsa," said Samuel. "That means we can stretch out and sleep here. Just as good as in a sleeping car."

Joel sat down in a window seat. It was light and summery outside. They were already in the forest. They were traveling fast now. Tree trunks flashed past the window. There's no end to the trees, Joel thought. Samuel would never be able to cut them all down. Not even if he kept going for a thousand years.

The door opened and the conductor came in. Samuel handed him the tickets.

"Change at Krylbo," said the conductor.

Samuel put the tickets back in his inside pocket.

"So, we'll change at Krylbo," he said. "But there's a long time to go before that. A whole night. And the next morning."

When Joel grew tired of watching all the trees, he decided to explore the train. Samuel had already stretched himself out on the seat, using his suitcase as a pillow.

Joel went out into the corridor. He saw a carafe on a special shelf, and took a drink of water. Then he looked closely at a map attached to the wall. He traced the journey to Stockholm with his finger. First they would come to Orsa: by then the forests would have finished. Next would come Mora, Borlänge, and then a bit further south was Krylbo. They would change trains there. That would mean they had completed over half the trip. But there was still a long way to go to Stockholm. Joel wandered along the train. It was rather full. Quite a few people were standing in the corridor, smoking. He could hear somebody singing in one of the compartments. But his walk came to an end when he reached the first-class carriages. The door was locked. He retraced his steps. The passengers who could afford to travel first class didn't want to be disturbed. Joel almost bumped into a girl as she came out

31

of a compartment. She was about his own age. Joel could feel to his annoyance that he was blushing. He didn't want to do that. He soon returned to his compartment and found Samuel sitting up and waiting for him. They had packed enough food to last them all the way to Stockholm. Joel felt hungry. He hadn't been able to eat much earlier in the day, as he'd been so nervous. He'd imagined all kinds of things happening that would cause the journey to be canceled. Samuel changing his mind, for instance. The train failing to appear. Him falling ill. He knew that was childish. Not something a fifteen-year-old ought to be imagining. But he couldn't help being childish.

That was the way he was.

"Shouldn't we have something to eat?" he asked.

"Already?"

"I'm hungry."

Samuel opened the bag of food. It contained sandwiches, hard-boiled eggs and boiled potatoes. He also had the thermos flask with coffee and a bottle of milk. Joel ate. But Samuel wasn't hungry. The tree trunks hurtled past outside. The wheels sang over the little gaps in the rails.

Later on, when Samuel had fallen asleep with his head pillowed on his suitcase, it occurred to Joel that a journey can be boring and exciting at the same time. There seemed to be no end to the trees flashing past the window. That was boring. Like a film in which nothing happens. Nevertheless, Joel couldn't tear himself away from the window. Sometimes there was a glittering reflection from a lake. An occasional house. What was really exciting was that for every minute that passed, for every little gap in the rails the train sang over, he was further and further away from the town he'd grown up in. Doing this had always been his dream.

They were only going as far as Stockholm. Even so, that was a bit of the way to the end of the world.

Which existed even if it didn't exist.

The conductor passed by in the corridor. That was a job Joel had on his list, becoming a train conductor. But he'd crossed it out. It could never match up to being a sailor. Railway lines and a sea channel marked out by flashing buoys could never be the same thing.

Joel carefully fished Samuel's watch out of his coat pocket. Midnight already. He put it back and stretched out on the seat. He had his feet towards the window so that he could still see out.

The tree trunks streaked past.

He tried to imagine what would happen when he and Samuel met Mummy Jenny. Would she shake Samuel's hand?

And what would she do to Joel? Give him a hug? Or shake his hand as well?

Joel sat up. It was Elinor who had written the letter to Samuel. Not Mummy Jenny herself. Why hadn't she written? Perhaps she didn't want to meet them at all? Maybe the man she was married to would be angry? Perhaps there was some law or other that said it was forbidden for him and Samuel to visit her without announcing themselves in advance? Joel was sure that Samuel didn't know much about the law. And what did he know himself? Nothing at all.

Joel looked at Samuel. Grown-ups were strange. How could Samuel sleep so peacefully? He must be just as nervous as Joel. But he was asleep. Fast asleep, with his hands clasped on his chest.

Or was he lying there and saying a prayer?

Dear God, please make Jenny glad to see me again. And Joel.
Amen.

Joel sat down by the window once more. The train was

shuddering its way round a long bend. He could just make out a lake behind the trees. His face was reflected in the window. His hair was short. Almost a crew cut. But the quiff immediately above his forehead made that part of his hair stand on end. It always did that. No matter how much water he used in an attempt to make it lie down.

Maybe Mummy Jenny would think he was ugly?

I know nothing, Joel thought. That's the worst thing of all. Not knowing anything.

He lay down on the seat again. The train was shaking and lurching. He tried to count the gaps between the joinings of the rails.

Then he fell asleep.

Joel woke up when the train came to a halt. When he opened his eyes he knew immediately where he was. But when he looked at the seat opposite, he saw that Samuel was no longer there. He sat up. There wasn't a sound. He opened the door and looked out into the corridor. And saw Samuel, who had opened a window. He smiled when he saw Joel.

"Did I wake you up?"

"Why has the train stopped?"

Joel was so sleepy that he could hardly keep his eyes open.

"Maybe we have to wait for an oncoming train to pass. Or there might be a signal at red."

"Where are we? What's the time?"

"We'll be in Orsa an hour or so from now."

"Hasn't the forest finished yet?"

Samuel laughed.

"Nearly," he said. "The forest's about to come to an end. For now."

"Is that why you're standing here? To take a last look at the trees?"

34

"Could be."

Joel had the impression that Samuel wanted to be left alone. Perhaps he was thinking about Jenny?

"I'm off to lie down again," he said.

Joel fell asleep the moment he lay down.

When he woke up it was broad daylight. The sun was shining. Samuel was sitting by the window, drinking coffee. Joel sat up like a shot, as if he had to go to school but had overslept.

"Have we come to Orsa yet?" he asked.

"We've passed there. And Mora as well."

Joel looked out of the window. The countryside was completely different. He could hardly believe his eyes. An enormous lake stretched out in front of him, whichever way he looked.

"Lake Siljan is beautiful," said Samuel. "It almost makes you think you're at sea."

"That's what I keep saying," said Joel. "Why do you hang about in the forest when you really want to be at sea?"

Samuel shook his head slowly, but he didn't say anything. Joel went out into the corridor to pour himself a beaker of water.

Then they had breakfast. The train stopped at Rättvik, and an elderly couple came to sit in their compartment. Samuel moved his suitcase. The man and woman chatted away. They sounded quite different from the people back home in the little town. Joel very nearly burst out laughing. Samuel noticed, and gave him a stern look.

They got off in Krylbo and changed trains. It was a very large station. Samuel was worried about boarding the wrong train. He asked three different porters if they were on the right platform. When the train arrived, it was difficult to find any empty seats. They eventually found two, and Joel sat next to the door. He was annoyed when Samuel tried to talk to him. He didn't like Samuel talking to him when others could hear. He pretended to be asleep, and quickly fell asleep in fact.

Some of the others in the compartment got off in Sala. Samuel and Joel ate the rest of their food.

"Only four more hours to go now," said Samuel. "Then we'll be there."

They were the longest four hours of Joel's life. He tried to will the train to go faster. But at the same time, he tried to make it go slower. He both wanted to get there, and not to get there.

But they eventually arrived in Stockholm. All the other passengers left the train. It was all hustle and bustle and noise on the platform. Samuel and Joel were sitting opposite each other. Each of them was clinging on to his suitcase or rucksack. The cardboard box containing the *Celestine* was on the shelf in front of the window.

Samuel suddenly looked small and unsure of himself.

He's regretting it now, Joel thought angrily. What he really wants to do is to keep sitting where he is and hope that they'll attach a new engine to the other end of the train, so that he can go back home. To his confounded trees.

"We'd better get off now," Joel said. "Otherwise it'll set off again, and goodness only knows where we'll end up."

Samuel nodded.

"I suppose we should," he said. "We'll have to find somewhere to stay."

Samuel had often told Joel about his visits to Stockholm, but now he was acting as if this was the first time he'd ever been there. When they came to the big station concourse, Samuel had no idea which way to go. Joel had become so hot and bothered by the masses of people that he started shouting and tugging at Samuel's overcoat. There was so much to see, so much to hear.

Samuel pointed at a bench.

"Let's sit down," he said. "There are so many people rushing around, you can't see where you're going."

They sat down. Samuel was still holding tightly on to his suitcase.

Joel started to get annoyed. Or was he afraid, perhaps? Because Samuel seemed to have no control over the situation.

"Where are we going to go?" he asked.

Samuel pulled a face.

"There are some cheap hotels near the station."

Joel felt as if he'd been punched in the stomach. It was as if he were seeing Samuel, his father, for the first time. Small and with drooping shoulders. Wearing old, worn-out clothes. Despite the fact that they were the best he had. And then that accursed suitcase. With the broken handle.

He'd never felt like this before. Not even when Samuel had been drunk and Joel had to drag him home.

But now it happened. Joel was ashamed of him.

He was ashamed of having a father like Samuel.

"Where are those bloody hotels, then?" he snarled.

Samuel looked at him in surprise.

"Yes, I swore," said Joel. "I'll swear as much as I like."

Samuel seemed to notice that his son was angry. He seemed to shrink even more.

"Maybe we can help each other to find our way," he said tentatively.

Joel was still upset.

"I've never been to Stockholm before. How should I know where the exit is?"

37

Samuel didn't answer. He looked round hesitantly, and then he suddenly seemed to make up his mind. Joel could see it coming. Samuel straightened his back with a little jerk, as if it was fitted with a clockwork mechanism that somebody had just wound up.

"Anyway, I need a pee," he said, gesturing towards a notice that said *Toilets*. "You can keep an eye on my suitcase while I'm gone."

Samuel stood up and walked away. Joel watched him. Noticed how he kept stopping to let people in a hurry pass by him. Joel pulled the suitcase towards him and put his hand over the broken handle. He was still ashamed. Had anybody seen him? Sitting there covering up the broken suitcase handle with his hand? Joel tried to look relaxed, but it was as if he was surrounded by a halo of light announcing that he didn't belong here.

Samuel seemed to be away for a long time. Joel became more and more irritated. He wondered if he ought to go away and leave the suitcase to look after itself. In order to punish Samuel. But what exactly was it that Joel wanted to punish him for?

Thoughts were buzzing round and round inside his head. At the same time he was trying to take in everything that was happening all around him. A voice blared out from a loudspeaker, and there was a wheezing and screeching from a locomotive somewhere.

Somebody sat down beside him on the bench. It was a boy not much older than Joel. But he was wearing a suit, and a tie, and shiny black shoes. And his hair was not cut short. His hair was combed and gelled to form stiff black waves. The Black Wave, Joel thought. He shuffled slightly away from the boy. I hope he doesn't say anything.

But he did, of course.

"Hi!" said The Black Wave.

"Er, hello," said Joel.

The Black Wave eyed him curiously. Joel glanced towards the toilets. What he wanted least of all just now was for Samuel to come back.

Only a few seconds ago it would have been too late. Now it had suddenly become too soon.

"Are you going off somewhere?" asked The Black Wave, running his hand over his hair.

"I've just arrived," Joel mumbled.

The Black Wave didn't say anything. He just kept on eyeing Joel. Then he produced a packet of cigarettes out of his pocket.

"Do you smoke?" he asked.

"No," said Joel.

And immediately asked himself why. It wouldn't have done any harm to accept a cigarette.

The Black Wave lit one and blew a smoke ring.

"Where have you come from?" he asked.

"From up north," said Joel.

"I can hear that," said The Black Wave. "I can hear that very clearly. 'From up north.'" He imitated Joel's pronunciation, and burst out laughing. Not nastily. It sounded most like a smoker's cough.

"Are you waiting for somebody?" asked The Black Wave.

"I'm waiting for my dad," said Joel.

"Where's he gone?"

"He's in the toilet."

"So your old man's in the john, is he?" said The Black Wave. "Maybe he's nipped in there for a crafty drop of booze."

Joel gave a start. How could this boy know that Joel's father sometimes drank too much? And could it be true? Was Samuel in there drinking?

"I'll go and fetch him now," said Joel. "We're in a bit of a hurry."

"I'll bet you are," said The Black Wave. "Go on, then, I'll look after your things for you."

Joel was just going to let go of the suitcase handle when he remembered that it was broken. He didn't want The Black Wave to see that.

"I expect the old man will want his suitcase," he said. "But you can keep an eye on my rucksack."

The Black Wave smiled. It seemed to Joel that his luck was in—he'd met somebody who'd offered him a cigarette and was prepared to keep an eye on his rucksack for him. Now he only had two things to carry: Samuel's suitcase and the box with the *Celestine*.

"I won't be a minute," said Joel, getting to his feet.

When Joel entered the toilets, he stopped short, looking around in confusion. There were two rows of cubicles. Most of the doors were closed. He had no idea which one Samuel was in. It seemed to him that he might just as well leave, and wait for Samuel to come when he was ready. But there again, he ought to tell Samuel that The Black Wave was sitting out there in the concourse, looking after Joel's rucksack.

Joel waited. Doors opened. He suddenly started to wonder how much crap was flushed down all those lavatories in a single day. The thought made him want to burst out laughing.

An attendant eyed him up and down, suspiciously.

"Are you waiting for somebody?" he asked.

"Yes," said Joel. "My dad."

At that very moment the door of the cubicle furthest away opened, and Samuel emerged. He didn't see Joel standing there. He went to the sink and washed his hands. He looked tired. Then he turned round and caught sight of Joel.

"Where's your rucksack?" he asked.

40

"Out there. Somebody's looking after it."

Samuel frowned.

"Who?"

It occurred to Joel that he didn't know The Black Wave's name.

"You don't always have to know what people are called," he said angrily. "He volunteered to keep an eye on my rucksack while I went to look for you."

"I was a bit constipated," said Samuel. "That happens sometimes."

Then he looked sternly at Joel.

"Are you telling me that you've left your rucksack with somebody you don't know?"

Joel could see that Samuel's worry was genuine. That made him feel a bit worried as well.

They left the toilets.

The bench was empty. There was no sign of The Black Wave or the rucksack.

Samuel looked at Joel.

"Where's your rucksack, then?"

Joel could feel the tears forming in his eyes. He pointed to the bench.

"There," he said. "But he's disappeared. And so has my rucksack."

"That's blown it!" said Samuel. "You can't trust all and sundry. He's obviously nicked your rucksack."

Joel was struggling to hold back the tears. He realized how stupid he'd been. The Black Wave had sat down on the bench next to Joel in order to try and steal the suitcase and the cardboard box and the rucksack. He'd seen immediately that Joel was in town for the first time. And what had he asked about? Are you going off somewhere? And what had Joel told him? I've just arrived. From up north.

How stupid could you get?

"We're in a bit of a mess now," said Samuel. "We'd better find a policeman and report this."

"Maybe he's still around somewhere," said Joel.

"No chance," said Samuel. "You can bet your life there'll be no trace of him."

"But what use would my rucksack be to him?" Joel asked. "There was nothing in it. Only my old clothes."

"A good question," said Samuel. "But we're not going to get an answer."

Samuel walked purposefully towards a police constable who was patrolling the concourse. He explained what had happened. Joel noticed that Samuel was different now. It was as if his back had straightened itself out. The policeman escorted them to the police station. Another officer noted down everything Joel said. What the rucksack looked like. And what had been inside it.

But what the policeman wanted to know most of all was what The Black Wave had looked like.

Joel could remember him well. The shirt and the suit, the tie and the pointed shoes.

When they finished, Samuel signed a document.

"We don't have a local address," said Samuel. "We're only here for a visit."

"Then you'll have to come back here to ask if we've managed to catch the thief," said the police constable.

They went back out into the station concourse. Joel looked round.

"They'll never find him," said Samuel. "He's vanished."

"My toothbrush, though," said Joel. "What does he want my toothbrush for?"

Samuel didn't answer.

"We'd better find ourselves a hotel now," he said. "And then we can try to buy you a few items of clothing."

"I don't need anything," said Joel.

Samuel looked him up and down, worried.

"We mustn't forget why we're here," he said. "And after all, we can be pleased that we still have the *Celestine*."

They left the station and went into the street.

Joel was overwhelmed by all the traffic.

Samuel looked around to establish his bearings.

Then they started walking.

— FOUR —

Samuel spotted a building displaying a hotel sign.

At that very moment it started raining.

The building was old and gloomy. It was squeezed into a block next to the railway station. Samuel stopped several times, hesitated, then started walking again with Joel a couple of paces behind him.

Joel was still fretting about being so stupid as to allow The Black Wave to make a fool of him.

All kinds of thoughts went shooting through his head.

He ought to have stayed at home.

He was too stupid to be let loose in the world.

He ought to forget all about the possibility of becoming a sailor one of these days.

He should do what Samuel had done. Become a lumberjack. Nothing else.

He ought to acquire a stoop, shave carelessly and get drunk whenever things were getting him down.

Joel was so angry and bitter that he sometimes started talking to himself aloud. Samuel turned round.

"What was that you said?" he asked.

"Nothing."

"But I heard you say something."

"You heard wrong."

Samuel eyed him thoughtfully. Then they carried on walking.

They stopped outside the hotel. The building was in a bad state of repair. Patches of plaster had fallen off the facade. An upstairs window was banging in the breeze.

"This place looks good," said Samuel, as if he were trying to cheer himself up.

"It looks awful," muttered Joel; but he was careful not to speak loudly enough for Samuel to hear what he said.

They went into the lobby. There was a strong smell of disinfectant. A bald man with thick-lensed glasses was sitting at a desk, peering at a newspaper.

They took a double room. Samuel paid in advance for two nights.

"Will breakfast be served?" Samuel asked, as he stood with the key in his hand.

"Of course it will," said the bald man. "But not here."

Joel saw that Samuel was blushing. He'd never seen that happen before.

"If I ask a sensible question I expect to get a sensible answer," said Samuel. His voice was shaking. He was angry.

The bald man lowered his newspaper.

"If you're not satisfied you can always go and find another hotel."

"Where can we get breakfast?" Samuel asked. "And where can we get dinner?"

He was still angry.

"There are lots of cafés and restaurants around here."

Joel could feel Samuel's anger brushing off onto him.

Joel took a step forward and stood shoulder to shoulder with Samuel.

"We also need to find a clothes shop," he said. "Somebody's stolen my rucksack."

"First turning on the left," said the bald man.

They went to the lift. The room they had been given was on the third floor. Samuel paused and turned round.

"One other thing," he said. "If we get a telephone call, we're not in."

The bald man bowed and nodded.

They walked up the stairs.

"What was all that about?" asked Joel. "What telephone call? Why aren't we in?"

Samuel chuckled.

"We can't have him thinking that he can treat us however he likes. If you're expecting a telephone call, people think you are on important business. People are stupid."

"I'm stupid," said Joel. "I let somebody nick my rucksack."

"You'll learn," said Samuel. "I've had things stolen, in the past. When I was a sailor. And had gone on shore leave in various places. You do silly things at times. And clever things at other times. That's life. You'll learn."

It was dark in the corridor.

They eventually located room 303.

They unlocked the door and went in. Everything in the room was brown. There was a patch of damp on the wallpaper, which was also brown. Samuel looked round and went over to the window.

"At least we've got a view of the street," he said. "It'll do."

Joel thought the room was fine. It was the first time he'd

ever stayed in a hotel. He couldn't imagine how it could be any better. Two big beds with a table and bedside lamp between them.

"Choose which of the beds you want," said Samuel.

Joel took the one closer to the window. From it he had a view of a rooftop.

Joel carefully unpacked the present they'd brought for Mummy Jenny. He was worried that it might have been damaged. He and Samuel examined it.

"All in one piece," said Samuel.

Joel placed it gently on the chest of drawers.

"*Celestine* has traveled just as far as we have," he said.

They both stretched out on their beds.

"Take your shoes off," said Samuel. "So that you don't dirty the cover."

In his head Joel unpacked his invisible rucksack. No doubt The Black Wave would throw away everything he found in it. Joel's shirts, and his best trousers. Not to mention his trainers. That was the worst thing. Not having those anymore.

"Don't think about the rucksack," Samuel said out of the blue. "That's life. It's gone."

"I wasn't thinking about the rucksack," said Joel. "I was thinking about my trainers."

They lay there in silence. It was pouring with rain now. Drops were hitting hard against the windowpane.

I'm in Stockholm, Joel thought.

I've left school. I've traveled here with Samuel. And somewhere out there in the rain is Mummy Jenny.

He turned his head to look at Samuel. His dad's eyes were closed, but he wasn't asleep.

"What shall we do now?" Joel wondered.

"Wait until it stops raining," said Samuel, without opening his eyes.

"But it might rain for a whole week."

Samuel didn't respond. He smiled. Joel wondered what he was thinking about. Most probably about Jenny. But were his thoughts anxious ones? Or was he angry?

Joel decided it might be easier to ask Samuel questions when they weren't at home. Perhaps it was easier to get answers to your questions when you were in a hotel room?

"What actually happened?" he asked.

Samuel turned his head and opened his eyes.

"Happened?"

"When Mummy Jenny vanished."

"She packed a case and left."

Joel waited for what was coming next, but nothing did.

"Is that all? Just packed a case and left?"

"Yes."

"Surely there must be something else?"

"The suitcase was brown. She was wearing a green coat. And a red hat. I can't remember what color her shoes were."

"And you were in the forest?"

"I was in the forest."

"Where was I?"

"You were downstairs in old Mrs. Westman's flat. She used to take care of you when Jenny was out shopping, or taking an afternoon nap."

"And you knew nothing about it? You hadn't seen her packing her case? Or going to the railway station to buy a ticket?"

"She took a bus."

"Didn't she leave a letter?"

"No, nothing at all. The only thing on the table was the outside door key."

Joel felt as if he were going round in circles. Now it was time to stop and jump into the middle. Where the important questions were.

"Had you been quarreling?"

"No."

One more jump now, Joel. A bit closer to the middle.

"Had you been drinking?"

There was a pause before the answer came. But come it did.

"I hadn't been drinking. I didn't drink in those days. Not when she was around. Never ever. And if she hadn't left me I'd never have started either."

Joel was right in the middle now. He couldn't get any further in.

"Mums don't run away like that. It's dads who vanish. Not mums. Something must have happened."

Samuel sat up on the bed. So violently that it gave Joel a start. He thought he must have said something that had made Samuel angry.

But the eyes that were looking at Joel were not angry. They were Samuel's normal eyes. Tired and perhaps a little sad.

"Do you think I haven't been wondering about that?" said Samuel. "I've been thinking about it for thirteen years. Every single day. Why did she leave me? All I know is that she's the only person who can answer that question. And that's why we're here. I want to know. Once and for all. Why she packed her case and left us."

"Maybe she won't want to tell us," said Joel hesitantly.

Samuel had lain down again.

"At least she ought to explain it to you," he said after a while. "You're her son, after all."

The sound of a vacuum cleaner came from the corridor. Joel looked out of the window. The rain was easing off.

"What shall we do?" he asked.

"First we'll have something to eat," said Samuel. "Then we'll go and buy you some clothes. And then we'll go looking for Mummy Jenny."

"I don't need any clothes," said Joel.

"I've no intention of letting you meet your mum in scruffy old clothes," said Samuel. "But we don't need to buy the most expensive clobber we can find."

The rain died away.

Soon there was just the occasional drop on the window ledge. Samuel disappeared into the corridor, looking for a bathroom where he could get shaved.

Joel was looking at a painting hanging on the wall above the chest of drawers.

It depicted a woman with large breasts sitting down under a tree, leaning against the trunk. Next to her was a man kneeling down and playing the violin.

Joel started to think about Sonja Mattsson. If only he'd known her number, he could have phoned her from reception.

But what would he say to her?

This is that idiot Joel who's come to Stockholm and had his rucksack nicked. Come and rescue me.

He banished the thought. Took another look at the picture. The woman leaning against the tree really did have very big breasts. He went to the mirror next to the door. Examined his face. From the front. Then in profile. When he turned his head he got cramp in his shoulder. He swore and shook his arm until the cramp eased off. Had another look at himself. That quiff over his forehead refused to go away. He tried to imagine himself with hair like The Black Wave. Put on a make-believe tie and black pointed shoes. Then he clenched his fist and gave The Black Wave in the mirror a punch.

Right on the nose. Broke it. Blood came pouring out.

Nobody stole Joel Gustafson's rucksack without being punished.

Joel stared at the mirror. The Black Wave disappeared. The only thing left was himself. Nobody else.

He went back to the picture hanging on the wall. Stroked the woman with his hand.

The door opened. It was Samuel coming back. Joel gave a start and fell over backwards. Samuel gave him a funny look, but didn't say anything.

When they left the hotel it was still drizzling. Samuel looked around, doubtfully.

"It's amazing how little you remember," he said. "I used to visit Stockholm quite a lot. In the old days."

"That way," said Joel, pointing. "That's where most people are heading."

Joel was surprised at how big a hurry everybody seemed to be in. Where on earth were all these people going?

When they had found a department store and Joel had seen an escalator for the first time in his life, he wondered why people were even running on that, when the stairs were moving anyway.

They eventually came to the floor with men's clothing. Both Joel and his father turned pale when they saw the price tags.

"Let's go," said Joel. "There must be cheaper clothes than these in other shops."

By the time they emerged into the street it had started raining again.

Joel had started to dislike Stockholm. This wasn't how he had imagined it. Crowds of people, loud noise everywhere, high prices and rain that never seemed to stop.

And he couldn't stop thinking about his rucksack. Stockholm had sent The Black Wave to welcome him. With a sneer.

"We must have something to eat now," said Samuel. "I noticed a licensed café on the way here."

They hurried through the rain and came to the café entrance. Once they were inside, Joel felt at home. The place smelled the same as the bar back home where he sometimes sold newspapers or went to fetch Samuel when he'd had too much to drink. The waitresses wore the same black and white clothes as Sara, and he recognized the stale smell of rain, wet wool and tobacco. They found an empty table and sat down. Joel was already worried that they wouldn't have enough money. A waitress brought them a menu. Joel leaned over the table to be able to read the menu. Not the choices on offer, but what they cost.

"We can afford this," said Samuel. "Beef stew."

Joel didn't like beef stew. But he didn't say anything.

By the time they finished eating, it had stopped raining again. Whenever the door opened Joel could see the sun shining.

They had eaten in silence. Joel had been thinking about his rucksack. He didn't know what Samuel had been thinking about.

Samuel paid and put his wallet away in the inside pocket of his coat.

"Now we must find a decent map," he said. "Then we can look for the shop where she works."

Joel was surprised.

"Shouldn't we start by looking for where she lives?"

"Lots of people go in and out of a block of flats," said Samuel. "But there won't be nearly as many standing behind the counter in a shop."

Joel could see his point.

"I thought you said you would recognize her?"

"Maybe we shouldn't be overconfident about that," said Samuel hesitantly. "It's best to be on the safe side."

The only way of being on the safe side would have been not to come here in the first place, Joel thought angrily.

It was the rucksack again. And The Black Wave.

They found a bookshop that sold maps. They bought the cheapest one Samuel could find. Then they sat down on a park bench that had had time to dry out, and unfolded the map.

There was Medborgarplatsen. And here was where they were now.

"There must be a tram that goes there," said Samuel.

But Joel had noticed something else. If they walked, they would pass by the quay where boats were moored.

"Let's walk," he said. "It can't be all that far. And it's not very late."

He pointed at a clock outside a watchmaker's shop. It said seven minutes past twelve.

Samuel stood up.

"You'd better take the map," he said. "I don't think I'm as good at finding the way as I thought I'd be."

Now it was Joel taking the lead. He kept checking the map to make sure they were going the right way. They soon came to the water. There was the Royal Palace, and there were bridges, hotels, museums, and most important of all, boats. But Joel was disappointed to find that there weren't any cargo ships. Small white passenger boats, the occasional fishing boat. But no big ships. No ships of the kind that would need a sailor like Samuel, or a young boy like Joel who would be signing on for the first time.

"Where are all the boats?" he wondered. "Like the ones that you used to work on?"

53

"Oh, they'll probably be in the harbor at Värtahamnen,"
said Samuel. "Or in Frihamnen."

Joel stopped dead, unfolded the map and looked up Värtahamnen. But that was miles away from where they were now.

It would have to wait until another day.

They continued on their way.

Samuel had started sweating. He couldn't walk as fast as
Joel, and several times used his handkerchief to mop his brow.

Joel stopped at the corner of a street. A large open square
was spread out in front of them. If the city had been a forest,
they would have come to a large clearing.

"This is it," said Joel, after checking the map. "Medborgarplatsen."

Samuel bit his lip. Joel found himself doing the same thing.
He didn't like copying what Samuel did, but he couldn't help it.

There was a sidewalk café in the square. Samuel pointed at
it and nodded.

"I must have a cup of coffee," he said. "And something cold.
Meanwhile you can scout around and see if you can find the
shop."

"Shouldn't we do that together?"

"We have to find the place before we can do anything," said
Samuel. "You'll be best at doing that on your own."

Joel left Samuel at the sidewalk café.

It felt as if he were setting out on the most important re-
connaissance expedition of his life. He knew that was a childish thought, but he couldn't help thinking the way he did. He
was childish. And he'd decided he was going to stay that way
for as long as he wanted to.

He suddenly stopped dead.

It had dawned on him where the limit was.

There was a river that childishness would never be able to swim over. And he would soon find himself on the bank of that river when he stood in front of Mummy Jenny and said:

Here I am. Joel.

He started walking round the square. Noticed how nervous he was. He could just make out Samuel somewhere in the background.

He was close to Mummy Jenny now. Assuming the letter from Elinor in Gothenburg was right. And it must surely be.

He continued walking round the square, looking for a grocer's shop.

He paused several times, when he thought he had seen The Black Wave.

He found himself back at his starting point, and frowned. There wasn't a grocer's shop here.

He walked all the way round again. Same result. No grocer's shop.

He was quite sure. He hadn't overlooked it.

Samuel was stirring his half-empty cup with a spoon. Joel joined him at the table.

"There is no shop," he said.

Samuel looked at him uncomprehendingly.

"What do you mean, there isn't a shop?"

"You heard what I said. There isn't a grocer's shop in this square. What did it actually say in the letter?"

"That Jenny works in a grocer's shop in this square."

"How could she know that?"

"Elinor would never write anything she wasn't sure about."

"Have you got the letter with you?"

"I left it at home."

"Why?"

"I know exactly what it says. I've read it so many times, I know it more or less off by heart."

55

•••

Joel didn't know where his anxiety came from, but it was suddenly there. It was as if a blast of cold wind had blown past.

He didn't know what was the matter.

But he hadn't made a mistake.

Something was very wrong.

— FIVE —

The cold wind drifted away.

Then they started quarreling. As far as Joel was concerned it was obvious that they should now start looking for the block of flats where Jenny lived, but Samuel thought they ought to wait.

"Wait for what?" Joel wondered. "There is no grocer's shop. Perhaps there isn't a flat either."

"Of course there is."

As Samuel answered he beckoned to a waitress and ordered some more coffee.

"You've just had a cup," said Joel.

"It was very weak coffee."

"It will be getting dark by the time we find the place where she lives."

"I think we can wait for a bit. Besides, we don't have *Celestine* with us."

Joel could feel himself growing really angry. He wasn't sure what was causing it. There was the business of the rucksack and The Black Wave. The harbor with the cargo ships being miles away from where they were. The grocer's shop that didn't exist. Samuel and all his cups of coffee. And finally that cold wind. Anxiety. The feeling that something was wrong.

It was something to do with the letter from Elinor. The letter he hadn't been allowed to see for himself.

"Hurry up and drink your coffee, and let's get away from here."

Samuel didn't respond.

Joel stood up.

"I'll find the place where she lives myself."

"Sit down," said Samuel. "I think we should wait until tomorrow."

"Why do we always have to wait for everything?"

Samuel pointed up at the sky.

"It'll start raining again shortly."

"There are trams. And there are buses."

"Do you know which ones go where?"

"You can find out."

Samuel put his cup down on its saucer. He tried to sound firm and decisive.

"We shall do as I say. We'll wait until tomorrow."

They started walking back to the hotel, the same way as they'd come. Samuel first, Joel following a couple of paces behind. As they approached the Royal Palace it started raining again. There was nowhere to shelter. The rain was bucketing down. By the time they reached the hotel they were soaked through and through. After drying himself down Joel was forced to put on one of Samuel's shirts. He hung his trousers over the radiator.

Joel felt like a prisoner. Without any dry trousers, he was stuck in the hotel room.

He sat on the edge of his bed and carefully unfolded the wet map. There was the street where Mummy Jenny lived— Östgötagatan. They had been quite close by. But Samuel had insisted on waiting.

Joel knew full well it had nothing to do with the rain.

Samuel was lying on his bed. He hadn't said a word since they got back to the hotel room. And now he'd fallen asleep. Joel had his back to him, but could hear the snores.

He didn't know where the determination came from, but before he knew where he was, he had made up his mind. Carefully, so as not to disturb Samuel, he got up from his creaky bed.

Samuel's suitcase was lying open on the floor. Joel searched through it, but the letter from Elinor wasn't there. Joel felt in all the pockets in Samuel's clothes, but it wasn't there either.

So it was true. The letter really was at home.

He looked out of the window. Just for a brief moment he felt ashamed. He hadn't believed that Samuel was telling the truth.

Perhaps the simple fact was that Samuel was nervous. He needed time to steel himself before meeting Jenny again.

But why couldn't he just explain things as they were? Why did he need to hide behind lots of coffee cups all the time?

Joel felt his trousers. They had started to dry. Then he looked at Samuel. He was asleep. His chest was rising and falling. Fast asleep.

Joel couldn't stand being cooped up in the hotel room any longer. He put his trousers on. And his shoes, which were wet as well. He borrowed a dry pair of socks from Samuel's suitcase.

Samuel had a pencil in his jacket pocket. Joel tore off a piece of the margin of the map and wrote a note.

I've gone out. Just for a little walk. I'll find my way back.

He put the note on the table. Then he opened the door quietly and slipped out. When he came to the lobby he found the bald man sitting on his chair, asleep. The street door was open. On the wall next to the desk was a large-scale map of Stockholm. Joel traced the way to Värtahamnen with his finger. It would take ages to walk there. He felt in his trouser pockets. He had nineteen kronor in there. He made up his mind on the spot. While Samuel was asleep, he would make his way to the harbor where the big ships were berthed.

There was a bell on the desk.

I'm staying in this hotel, Joel thought. We're paying to live here.

He smacked the bell with the palm of his hand—far too hard. It made a very loud clanging noise. The bald man gave a start and dropped his newspaper. He gave Joel a very dirty look.

"It's not necessary to break the bell. I'm sitting here after all."

Joel was a bit afraid and could feel himself blushing. That made him angry.

"I want to know how to get to Värtahamnen," he said. "I gave the bell a light tap, but you didn't wake up."

The bald man eyed Joel up and down suspiciously.

He doesn't believe me, Joel thought. He'll throw us both out of his hotel.

But the man behind the desk seemed to have forgotten about the bell already.

"You need to take a tram to Ropsten," he said. "From Stureplan. Go all the way to the terminus."

The telephone rang. The man answered. Joel went to the map and found Stureplan. It wouldn't take long to walk there.

• • •

It was drizzling when Joel left the hotel. But it had stopped by the time he came to Stureplan. He soon found the tram stop. He didn't have long to wait. He bought a ticket and found somewhere to sit. He got off when they came to the terminus. He could see that this was the right place. At the end of a long bridge to the left was a large cargo ship, its hatches open. Big mechanical scoops were digging down into the hold and coming up with something belching black dust. Coal, perhaps. Or possibly iron ore? Joel moved closer to it, so that he could read the name of the ship.

MS *Karmas*.

A gangway led from the ship to the quay. A man was leaning over the rail, smoking. He was wearing a chef's hat. Joel was unable to venture as far as the quayside because it was fenced off.

But the ship was berthed there even so. MS *Karmas*.

Waiting for Samuel and Joel.

He didn't know how long he stood there, but in his mind's eye he could see first Samuel and then himself walking up the gangway.

Then he noticed with a start that somebody was standing beside him. It was an old man with long white hair, smoking a pipe. Joel noticed that the man had an anchor tattooed on his wrist.

"So we're standing here and dreaming, are we?" said the man with a smile.

He had hardly any teeth, but his smile was friendly.

"I'm just looking," said Joel.

"I think you're picturing yourself walking up the gangway," said the man.

Joel stared at him. How come that this man could read Joel's thoughts?

"You can always tell when somebody wants to be a sailor,"

said the man. "There's some kind of magnet that attracts people who long to go to sea. Once upon a time I stood on a quay dreaming, just like you. In my case it was in Norrköping."

He knocked out his pipe and gave Joel a wink.

"I'm right, aren't I?"

"Yes."

"What's your name?"

"Joel."

"I'm known as Geegee. George Edward Edgar Gerald Everton Edwardsson. But that's a bit of a mouthful, so people call me Geegee. Sailors and horses are very similar, really. When it comes to the bottom line."

"Are you a sailor?" asked Joel hesitantly.

"I used to be," said Geegee. "But I went ashore three years ago. After forty-five years. I thought it would be great back on land, but in fact there's always something missing. So I come here to look at the ships. You stand here to dream about what's to come, and I stand here to dream about what used to be. That's life, I suppose."

"My dad's a sailor," said Joel. "Although he's a lumberjack at the moment."

"That's life," said Geegee.

"What do you have to do to become a sailor?" Joel asked.

"Your dad ought to be able to tell you all about that," said Geegee.

"But I don't want to ask him."

Geegee nodded thoughtfully.

"That's life. That's the way it is with dads. You prefer to ask somebody else. But you have to get yourself a seaman's discharge book, and in order to get that you have to undergo a medical examination. Once you've got the necessary document, you have to go to the Seamen's Employment Exchange to find out what jobs are going. I take it you're dreaming about becoming a captain?"

"I don't know. I just want to become a sailor."

A gurgling noise came from Geegee's pipe.

"Start from there, then. And see how things go. That's life. Some young lads want to be in the engine room, others want to be the first mate. And some lads want to be deckhands. And then there are those who can't wait to get ashore . . ."

Joel thought about what Geegee had told him. Now he didn't need to ask Samuel.

"There's the MS *Karmas*," said Geegee. "You can see from the flag that she belongs to the Grängesberg Shipping Company."

"Where has it come from? And where's it going to?"

"Not 'it.' A ship's a 'she.'"

"Where has she come from?"

"England perhaps. Or Narvik. As for where she's going to? Maybe Liberia. Or possibly Belgium."

Joel knew that Narvik was in Norway. And Belgium was in Europe. But Liberia? Where was that? He wanted to ask, but didn't want to seem stupid. So he didn't.

Geegee put his pipe in his pocket, and yawned.

"I'm getting old and tired," he said. "That's life. It's time I took an afternoon nap."

He nodded at Joel, and left, his white hair fluttering in the breeze. There was so much more Joel would have liked to ask him about, but still: he now knew the most important thing—what he needed to do in order to become a sailor.

He stayed for a bit longer, watching the mechanical scoops emptying the holds.

Then he took the tram back to the hotel.

•••

When he got to their room he found Samuel sitting on his bed, waiting for him.

"Where have you been?" he asked. "I was worried."

"I left a note," said Joel. "And now I'm back again."

Joel didn't want to tell Samuel what he'd been up to. He wanted it to be a surprise when Samuel discovered that his son knew all about what to do in order to become a sailor.

"I fell asleep," said Samuel. "And I had a dream, but I can't remember what it was about."

I expect you dreamt about trees, Joel thought. You dreamt about your axes and your saws and all the trees you haven't felled yet. But I bet you didn't dream about walking up the gangway of a ship that was about to sail to Liberia.

"Where's Liberia?" Joel asked.

"Why do you want to know that?"

"There was a man outside the hotel who said he came from Liberia."

Samuel looked doubtfully at him.

"Have you been talking to a black man? Could he speak Swedish?"

As soon as his dad said that, Joel remembered. How could he have forgotten? He'd always been top of the class in geography. How could he have forgotten that Liberia was in Africa?

"Perhaps it was Lebanon," said Joel. "Or even Linköping. He was difficult to understand."

"What did he want?"

"He was trying to sell a magazine. A Christmas magazine."

"In the middle of summer?"

Joel realized that he'd stumbled into a totally unnecessary

maze of lies. He would have to get out of it as quickly as possible.

"It was from last year. And it was cheap. But I didn't buy it." Samuel shook his head.

"Let's go and have dinner," he said, getting to his feet. "And then I thought we could go to the cinema."

Joel was surprised. That was a first. Samuel had never suggested that they should go to the pictures together. Samuel never went to the pictures anyway.

"Why?" asked Joel.

"I thought it might be fun. Seeing as we're in Stockholm."

"I thought we were here to look for Mummy Jenny. And to look at boats."

"I thought that could wait until tomorrow," said Samuel. "If we happened to bump into Jenny, I don't think I could cope. Not until tomorrow."

Joel understood. And he had a guilty conscience. Samuel was afraid. He didn't want to wait because he was lazy, but because he really was scared of meeting Mummy Jenny again.

"OK, we'll wait until tomorrow," said Joel.

They had dinner at the same place they'd been to earlier in the day. Afterwards they wandered down a wide street where there were lots of cinemas. Joel let Samuel choose.

"Kirk Douglas is somebody I've heard of," said Samuel. "That film's bound to be good."

Joel thought it was bad. Nothing happened. The actors just hung around, talking. He found it hard to concentrate. He kept imagining he could see himself on the screen. Walking up and down a gangway.

"That was a good film," said Samuel as they emerged into the street.

Joel said nothing.

65

On the way home they paused and bought a hot dog. Joel started to worry about how long Samuel's money was going to last.

When they got back to the hotel the bald man was no longer there. Instead, a fat woman was sitting behind the desk.

"Would you like a wake-up call?" she asked.

"That won't be necessary," said Samuel. "We'll wake up anyway."

Samuel fell asleep the moment the light was switched off. But Joel lay awake. A streetlamp was shining into the room through a gap in the curtains. And it was so noisy. Very different from home, where everything was so quiet. Where the only sound was the creaking from inside the walls.

The beam of light from outside illuminated the *Celestine*.

What's Mummy Jenny doing just now? Joel asked himself. What's she thinking about? Not about Samuel, that's for sure. Nor about me.

She doesn't know that we are so close by.

Joel pulled the covers up to his chin and tried to sleep. But there was no sleep in him. He tossed and turned. In the end he sat up. There was no point. He got out of bed and looked at Samuel's watch. A quarter past eleven. As he walked to the window he cast a glance at the picture on the wall. The young man was still playing the violin. And the woman was still sitting under the tree. He opened the curtain slightly. No rain.

Then it dawned on him.

The night was waiting for him. He didn't know how many times he'd roamed around the streets at night on his bike, but there was nothing to stop him wandering around the streets of Stockholm on foot tonight, looking for Mummy Jenny.

He got dressed as quietly as he could, then wrote another

note for Samuel. To make sure it wasn't overlooked he put it on Samuel's pillow.

I can't sleep. I'm going out. Back soon.

That was all. No times. Samuel wouldn't be able to work out how long he'd been away.

The corridor was deserted. He closed the door carefully behind him. He didn't dare to take the lift. There were carpets on the stairs, so his footsteps wouldn't be heard.

A radio was playing in reception. He paused on the stairs. Perhaps the woman behind the desk wouldn't allow him to go out? Perhaps the law said you had to be in the hotel after eleven o'clock?

He tried to work out what to do.

But the solution came of its own accord. He could hear somebody snoring. He approached the desk. The snores were louder now. He peeped cautiously over the desk. The woman was asleep on a chair, asleep with her mouth open. He crouched down and hurried to the door. If it squeaked she might wake up. He took hold of the handle and eased the door open. Not a sound.

Now he was outside. He had remembered to take the map with him. It had dried out now, but it was crumpled. Then it occurred to him that perhaps it wasn't a good idea to sneak around Stockholm at night with a map in your hand. He put it in his pocket and started walking. It was a warm summer's night. Even though it was late there were a lot of people out in the streets. A tram clattered past. He could hear music coming from somewhere or other. On the other side of the street, two men were approaching, swaying unsteadily and trying to support each other.

He passed by the Royal Palace and came to the square where he'd failed to find a grocer's shop. The sidewalk café was closed, the chairs and tables covered by a canvas sheet. There were fewer people about now. And not so much traffic. But he noticed a police car. He crouched down, as if trying to make himself invisible. The police car passed by. Joel stood in front of an illuminated shop window and took out the map. He found Östgötagatan. Left, right, then left again. He took a step forward. Then another. How many more meters would he have to go before he found himself standing outside Mummy Jenny's home?

He tried to act like a grown-up. It was childish to wander around in the night, looking for a block of flats where a missing mum lived. But there again, it could be a grown-up thing to do. He remembered how Samuel had gone out roaming the streets when he had been madly in love with Sara.

He turned left, then right. He could hear a man and a woman arguing about money through an open window. He would never be like that. An adult arguing about money. On a warm summer's night.

Then he stopped dead. What would happen if Samuel woke up? He might be so worried, he'd phone the police.

But then he calmed down. Samuel wouldn't do that. In the first place he never woke up during the night. And besides, he knew that Joel could look after himself.

Left again. He'd soon be there. If the map was right. If the letter from Elinor was right. If what Samuel said was in the letter was right. If everything was right.

If in fact he really did have a mother called Jenny.

He looked at the street sign.

Östgötagatan.

It ought to be number 32. He crossed the street so that he was on the side with odd numbers.

First a brown building, then a red one with a furniture shop. Then a brown one, and another, then a gray one.

Then he was there.

He held his breath.

The number 32 was on an oval plate over the front door, lit up by a lamp. He looked up at the facade. Nearly all the windows were dark. People were asleep. Mummy Jenny was asleep. Somewhere up there behind a window.

He put his hand over his mouth to stop himself shouting out her name.

But he would never do that. It happened sometimes that he did things without knowing why, but not anything like that. He would never stand in a street shouting out names.

The light went out in another window.

Joel decided to cross the street. Perhaps the front door wasn't locked? In that case he'd be able to read the names of everybody who lived in the flats.

And then it dawned on him.

He had no idea what Mummy Jenny's surname was. If Samuel had never married her, it couldn't be Gustafson.

But he could check even so. Maybe people's first names would be listed as well.

Jenny Andersen, he thought.

Jenny Svensson.

Jenny Jansson.

Jenny Jesus Mary.

Jenny Joelsson.

Jenny Jennyson.

Jenny the mum who just ran away, damn her.

Enough of that. A car was approaching. When it had gone past he would cross the street and try the door.

The car passed by.

He was just going to start walking when the door on the opposite side of the street opened.

Joel didn't move a muscle.

69

A woman came out.

She glanced at him. Then set off walking along the pavement.

He could see in the light from a streetlamp that she was wearing a green coat.

— SIX —

Something was hurting his arm.

When Joel looked to see what it was, he realized that he was pinching it himself. He watched the woman walking down the street. And told himself that her wearing a green coat meant nothing at all. It was thirteen years since Mummy Jenny left them. This couldn't be the same coat. There was nothing to say that this woman was Mummy Jenny. There were no doubt lots of women living in that building.

Joel was sure he was imagining things. It was always the same. Imagining things that led him to reach false conclusions.

Nevertheless, he crossed the street and started following the woman. Perhaps he would catch a glimpse of her face? Samuel always used to say that he looked so much like his mum.

She turned a corner. Joel increased his pace. He was missing his trainers now. He cursed The Black Wave, who couldn't keep his hands off Joel's rucksack.

He peered cautiously round the corner. She had stopped

and was looking round. Then she crossed the street. Her heels clicked on the paving stones. A nearby clock struck twelve. Midnight. Joel tried to think where she might be going. In the middle of the night. On her own. And she seemed to be in a hurry.

Who needed to hurry when it was turned midnight?

Now she turned another corner. Joel increased his pace again. Perhaps she would disappear through some door or other before he had a chance to see which? He peered round this corner: there she was. Still hurrying along. Heels clicking.

Joel kept on following her. As long as he didn't know for certain, this could be Mummy Jenny.

She suddenly stopped and turned round. Joel just managed to sidle into the shadows. Had she seen him? He held his breath and waited. If she retraced her steps to see who it was following her, he would run off as fast as he could. But perhaps she would scream for help? What would he do then?

He held his breath. Then he heard her start walking again. Her footsteps were getting softer. He counted to five, then peeped out. Waited. Then continued following her.

They came to a square. Some young people were sitting on a bench. One of them looked like The Black Wave. But it wasn't him.

She stopped again. In front of a shop window this time. Then she set off once more. When Joel came to the window he saw it belonged to an ironmonger's.

Why would Mummy Jenny be interested in tools?

It didn't fit in.

But then, nothing fitted in.

"I don't know if it is her," he said aloud to himself. "I just want to see her face, in order to be sure. I just want to see if I recognize myself in her."

He darted into the shadows once more. She had stopped.

This time she went in through a gate. Joel hurried over to the other side of the street. The gate led into a courtyard in front of a large house. It looked like a school. He could see that there was a sign over the imposing entrance, but it was too dark and too far away for him to read it. There were steps leading up to the door. He watched her open it and walk into a brightly lit hall. Then the door closed behind her. She had vanished.

Joel waited. Then he crossed the street and read what it said over the entrance.

The Autumn Light Foundation.

Joel had no idea what a foundation was. And why was it called Autumn Light?

There was a streetlamp close to the gate. He slunk into the shadows.

What on earth was he doing? Somebody comes out of the front door of the building where his mother might possibly live. So he follows her. When he ought really to be asleep in bed in his hotel room.

That almost gave him a guilty conscience. Samuel didn't have much money. But he had paid for a hotel room, and Joel wasn't even using the bed. He made up his mind to spend as much time as possible in it the following day.

He also made up his mind to leave. But he stayed.

He made up his mind not to open the gate.

Then he opened it.

But I'm not going to go as far as the steps, he told himself.

Then he walked up to the steps. But he didn't dare to open the door. He tried to listen. But there wasn't a sound to be heard.

There was a wide gravel path surrounding the house.

I'm not going to walk along that, he told himself.

Then he started walking.

73

The building was very large, with lots of windows. Most of them were dark, but there were lights on here and there. Very bright lights.

Autumn Light, he thought. The light of Autumn. What kind of a building could this be?

There was a large garden at the back. He paused outside a shed. The doors were standing open, and inside were several old wheelchairs.

Curiouser and curiouser. No doubt he would have been scared stiff some years ago. But not now.

It was just odd.

He continued walking and came to a side door. He noticed immediately that it was ajar.

I'm not going to go in, no matter what, he told himself.

Then he found himself taking hold of the door handle. The door creaked. But only a little. It was light inside. He let go of the handle and the door closed.

Then he opened it again.

I can always say I'm lost, he thought. They'll hear that from the way I speak. Here's a young man who's very lost indeed. He's come all the way from the north of Sweden.

I can also say that I've been sleepwalking. And that I'm staying at a hotel, but can't find my way back.

He listened. There was a single ceiling light. Not a sound. He slipped in through the door and made sure it didn't close of its own accord. For safety's sake he placed a small twig between the door and the jamb.

There was a strange smell. Musty. Old. But something else as well. Then it dawned on him what it was. Hospital.

He remembered the smell from the time when he'd been almost killed by a bus and had to spend some time in hospital.

But how could a hospital be called anything but a hospital? Autumn Light? It seemed strange. He tiptoed along the

74

corridor and came to a wide double door. He opened it carefully and peeped inside. There was a gurney along one of the walls, and next to it a wheelchair.

Now he knew it was a hospital. He listened. Somewhere in the distance he could hear a door being opened and then closed again. Then all was quiet once more. He stepped cautiously back into the corridor. How would he be able to find the woman in the green coat among all these doors? He crept along the corridor, expecting somebody to appear at any moment. He was rehearsing his excuses all the time. That he was lost, had come all the way from Norrland. Or that he was a sleepwalker who had gone astray while taking a nocturnal stroll.

All the doors looked the same. He decided to open one at random. He peeped in and could see that it was almost completely dark. Just a faint light from a lamp in one corner. He went in. His eyes got used to the darkness, and he saw that he was in a room with a lot of beds.

The room was filled with snores. There was a squeaking and sighing and grinding and singing. He took another couple of paces forward, and saw that there were very old people in each of the beds.

A hospital, he thought. Or an old people's home. Or a mixture of the two.

There was a strong, pungent smell. In one of the beds was an old man who wasn't snoring. Joel suddenly had the feeling that the man was watching him through half-closed eyes.

And then he thought the man was dead.

The panic came from nowhere. Joel raced out of the room and paid no attention to the fact that the door creaked.

As he hurtled into the corridor he heard voices. A door opened and closed. The voices were getting louder. Joel turned round and ran back along the corridor. But he no longer knew which door he'd just come out of. There were lots of double doors. The voices were very close now. Joel ducked in through the nearest door. He heard footsteps going past in the corridor. Two women talking. And then all was quiet again.

The room was suddenly lit up. Joel whipped round, but there was nobody there. Then he realized that he must have brushed against the light switch with his shoulder. He was about to switch off it again when he saw that he was in some kind of changing room. There were rows of lockers and benches. And there was a name on every locker door.

Mummy Jenny, he thought. If it really was you coming here tonight, your name will be on one of these lockers.

Doctor Jenny, or Nurse Jenny. Or Manager Jenny.

He started to work his way along the rows of lockers. Nearly all of them had women's names on the door. There was an Arne Bergström and somebody called Hagge K, but all the rest were women.

There was a Judith and a Johanna in the first row. Joel started to work his way through those opposite.

He'd come more or less to the middle of the row.

And then he saw the name.

Jenny Rydén.

He held his breath.

Was this his mum? Jenny Rydén?

He just knew it was. But there again . . .

The locker door wasn't locked. If he opened it and found the green coat hanging there, he would be sure.

He decided to leave the door closed.

Then he opened it.

The coat hanging inside the locker was even greener than he'd thought. It was the same color as a lawn.

Jenny Rydén's coat. His mother's coat.

There was a handbag hanging from a hook next to the coat.

76

I could open it, he thought. There might be a wallet inside it. With an address. Saying "Östgötagatan." There might even be something else. Making it clear if she's my mother or not.

Ever so carefully, he unhooked the handbag. It was fastened with a strap and a little silver stud.

He had the feeling that he was about to open a treasure chest that he'd been looking for as long as he could remember.

But maybe he should resist the temptation to open the bag. Samuel ought to have been there as well. Jenny was just as much his as Joel's.

But he couldn't resist it. He opened the handbag. It contained a pair of gloves. And a powder compact.

And a wallet.

He put the handbag down on the floor and opened the wallet.

As he did so the door burst open, and a man in a white coat was staring at Joel.

He had no way of knowing if it was Arne Bergström or Hagge K.

Joel tried to say something by way of explanation, and he even bowed to the man in the doorway.

But that was as far as he was allowed to go. The man strode towards him. Joel tried to duck, but two powerful hands grabbed hold of his arms.

"A thief," he yelled. "You're a thief. What are you doing in here? How did you get in? What have you pinched? How did you break into that locker? What's your name?"

The questions came tumbling out of the man's mouth. He was shouting, and red in the face.

He'll hit me, Joel thought. He's going to hit me.

When the man paused to breathe, Joel tried to say something. But the man started shouting and yelling again. The door to the corridor was flung open. An old man wearing shabby pajamas and carrying a walking stick was peering short-sightedly at them.

"What's going on?" he asked.

"Go back to bed, Erik."

The man holding Joel still sounded angry. The old man looked scared, turned and left.

"I'm not a thief," Joel said. "I'm lost."

"A thief," said the man again. "You're a thief."

"I'm just looking for my mum."

Joel heard the words coming out of his mouth, but he had no idea where they originated. Nevertheless, the man holding him seemed to hesitate.

"Your mum?"

"Yes."

"What's her name?"

"Jenny."

"There are two women working here called Jenny. What's your surname?"

"Gustafson."

Joel realized that was the wrong answer. But it was too late. The man's grip on him tightened even more.

"There's nobody here called Jenny Gustafson. You're not only a thief, you're a liar as well."

Joel thought he had nothing to lose. If there were two women called Jenny working here, only one of them could have the surname Rydén. If he was lucky, he would have guessed right. But even if he had guessed right, he could still be wrong. He didn't know if the woman he'd seen entering the building really was his mother.

"Rydén," he said. "My mum's called Rydén."

The man let go, but only with one hand. He was still glaring suspiciously at Joel.

"What do you want her for in the middle of the night?"

78

Joel was thinking desperately how he could get out of this awkward situation. He was usually good at getting out of awkward situations. But on this occasion, his mind seemed to have come to a complete standstill.

"We'd better go and fetch her."

The man started to drag Joel to the door.

That was the moment when his brain started functioning again.

"It would be better if I didn't actually see her."

The man stopped and stared at Joel.

"I thought you just said that was why you'd come here?"

"I can explain."

The man let go of him. But he stood guard in front of the door in case Joel tried to run away.

"I went out after she'd left for work," said Joel. "And then the door slammed shut behind me. I didn't have a key and didn't know how I was going to get back in. She gets angry if I'm out late at night. I thought I'd come and collect her key. Then go home and unlock the door. And then I thought I'd leave the key lying on the floor. That would make her think she'd dropped it."

The words simply tumbled out. One after the other. Joel was amazed by the way in which he'd managed to patch together a story that sounded almost like the truth.

"You expect me to believe that?"

Yes, thought Joel. Or at least, I hope you will. So that I can get out of here.

The door opened again. It was the same old man as before.

"What's going on?" he asked.

"Go back to bed, Erik. You shouldn't be up and wandering around in the night. You'll only get lost and end up in the wrong bed."

The old man went away.

Joel thought he'd better improve his story.

"My mum would be very angry," he said.

The answer he received surprised him.

"You can bet your life she would," said the man, shaking his head.

Then he turned serious again. His suspicions had returned.

"How come you speak with a northern accent? Your mum speaks with a Stockholm accent."

Joel had no idea how to answer that one.

"It's a sort of illness," he said, and recognized at the same time that he had just come out with the daftest thing imaginable.

"What kind of an illness?"

"It's the same as with eyes," he said. "You can inherit your grandmother's dialect. Or your grandfather's."

"That's the first I've heard of it."

"I didn't know either," said Joel innocently. "Not until a doctor explained it to us. Only a few weeks ago."

The man shook his head.

"I think we'd better fetch your mum even so," he said. "This business seems so peculiar. What are you doing out on the streets at this time of night?"

"It's the summer holidays. And I've left school."

The man seemed to be thinking. He was still on his guard. And very suspicious.

"I was under the impression that Jenny only had two daughters."

Joel felt as if he'd been punched in the stomach. So it was wrong after all.

The wrong mother.

Then the man shook his head.

"I suppose I'd better believe you. Take the key. I won't say anything."

Joel walked shakily back to the handbag and felt around in it. But he could find no trace of a key.

Even so he pretended to put something into his pocket. Then he put the handbag back in the locker and closed the door.

"How did you get in?"

"There was an unlocked door at the back."

The man sighed.

"The caretakers are careless," he said. "It's always the same."

"A thief could get in," said Joel.

The man nodded.

"You can leave through the front entrance," he said. "Jenny's drinking coffee at the moment. Upstairs."

The man escorted him to the door.

"I hope you're not having me on," he said.

Joel could feel pangs of his guilty conscience.

"No," he said. "I'm not having you on. It happened once before. I was forced to take a room at the Raven Hotel."

Then he went out into the courtyard.

He could have bitten his tongue off. Why did he have to mention the name of the hotel where he and Samuel were staying? He felt like kicking himself.

But there was nothing he could do about it now. He stood in front of the gate with the make-believe key in his pocket. The key to the building his mother didn't live in. But where two daughters of a woman called Jenny Rydén were presumably lying asleep.

He felt relieved. But also dejected. Relieved at having got away. Dejected because things weren't as he'd thought after all.

Or as he'd hoped.

He knew the facts now. He really had hoped that the green coat would be the same one. The one Mummy Jenny had been wearing when she went away. But now when he thought he'd found her again, he'd only found somebody called Jenny Rydén.

He started walking back to the hotel. He felt really tired now. The clock on a church tower said turned one.

The streets were deserted. Hardly any traffic.

If I wait a bit longer I'll be completely alone, he thought. Just as alone as I've always been when I wandered around the streets at home during the night. On my bike. Looking for a dog that had gone off, heading for a distant star.

The last thing he felt like was somebody who was now fifteen years old.

He glanced up at the sky.

A drop of rain hit him in the face.

It's that dog, he thought. Sitting up there somewhere, spitting at me.

Before long it started raining properly. Joel speeded up. Then it started bucketing down. He couldn't run that fast. So he slowed down again. It made no difference. He'd be soaked through by the time he got to the hotel, no matter how fast he walked.

And needless to say, he took a wrong turn. He soon hadn't the slightest idea where he was. He didn't recognize any of the streets. It took him ages to find the right way again. He was so wet by then that his shoes were full of water.

And needless to say, it stopped raining the moment he reached the hotel entrance. He opened the door slowly. The woman was still asleep behind the desk. He walked up the stairs. When he reached the door of his room, he paused to listen. All quiet.

He opened the door carefully.

But things weren't as he'd expected. Samuel wasn't asleep.

He was sitting on the edge of the bed, holding his stomach.

His face was ashen.

And he didn't ask where Joel had been.

"I have a terrible stomachache" was all he said. "I think I'm going to die."

Nothing else.

I have a terrible stomachache. I think I'm going to die.

— SEVEN —

Joel would look back on that night as the moment when he grew up once and for all. When he slowly opened the door of his hotel room, it was as if he were really opening the door to his future.

He left his childhood behind him in the corridor.

He would never forget it. Never ever.

Samuel sitting on the edge of the bed holding a hand over his stomach. His pajama jacket unbuttoned. His face ashen.

And the words:

I have a terrible stomachache. I think I'm going to die.

It was several seconds before it sank in. Before he grasped properly that nothing was as he'd thought it would be. A dark room and Samuel snoring in his bed.

Instead Samuel was sitting on the edge of the bed and was in pain.

He had so much pain that it hurt Joel as well.

And then Joel felt scared.

What he had felt when he'd been caught red-handed with

Jenny Rydén's handbag was nothing compared to this. Now he was seriously scared. His heart started pounding, like a fist beating at a door.

"What's the matter?" he asked, and could hear his voice trembling.

Samuel shook his head.

He really was in agony. Joel could see the pain oozing out from his father's eyes, from his nose, from his tousled hair and his worn-out pajamas.

"I woke up," said Samuel. "I'd been dreaming that I had a stomachache. But when I woke up I found it wasn't just a dream."

Joel had sat down beside Samuel. He'd started to feel cold now. He didn't know if it was due to his wet clothes or because he was scared. But it didn't matter either way. The important thing was that Samuel was in pain.

Samuel was rocking back and forth. The pain came and went.

"Perhaps you ought to go to the lavatory?" said Joel.

Samuel shook his head again. Joel could see that he was in so much pain that he was sweating.

"It'll pass," said Samuel. "But it hurts something awful."

They sat for a while in silence. The pain wandered back and forth between them. Joel tried to think. What could he do? What did Samuel generally do when Joel had a stomachache? Give him something to drink. Or say he should try to be sick.

"Perhaps you ought to be sick?" he said.

Samuel shook his head for the third time.

"It's not that. This is different."

Then he lay down gingerly, holding on tight to the bed frame with one hand. Joel stayed sitting where he was. He was now so cold that he started shivering.

More than ten minutes passed. Joel counted the minutes by Samuel's watch, which was lying on the bedside table.

"It feels as if it's easing off a bit," said Samuel.

Joel's pain immediately started to ease as well.

Samuel closed his eyes. Joel stood up carefully and took off his wet clothes. When he looked at Samuel again he saw that his dad had opened his eyes.

"Is it any better?"

Samuel nodded.

"Where have you been?" he asked. "In the middle of the night?"

Joel realized that Samuel hadn't seen his note.

"I just nipped down into the street. I couldn't sleep."

Samuel turned his head slowly and looked at his watch. It was past two.

"I've never understood why you always go wandering around at night," he said. "You've done it ever since you were a little lad. You go riding round on your bike. Or you lie down and go to sleep in a bed outside in the garden. In the middle of winter."

Joel looked at him in astonishment.

So Samuel knew all about what Joel had always thought was a secret: that Joel went out on his bike at night and rode around the streets of the little town where they lived. He'd known about it, but never said anything.

It seemed that Samuel understood Joel's astonishment.

He smiled.

"You didn't think I knew about it," he said.

"No."

"You didn't think I'd woken up when you crept out as quietly as you could?"

"No."

"But I did. I wondered what you were up to, of course. But I thought it better not to ask."

"Why not?"

"Because you always came back. I suppose I thought you must be going on one of your adventures."

Joel wanted to ask more questions, but Samuel raised a hand to indicate that he shouldn't. The pain was coming back.

It immediately came back to Joel as well.

They carried on like this until morning. But without Joel being able to remember how it happened, he had evidently gone to bed and fallen asleep.

And he had dreamt. It seemed as if he were running around inside himself. As if it were raining inside his head. Samuel had been trying to open an umbrella, but the umbrella turned into a bird that suddenly flapped away.

Joel woke up with a start. At first he didn't know where he was. Then it all came back to him. When he turned his head he saw that Samuel's bed was empty. He jumped out of bed in panic. As he did so the door opened and Samuel walked in. He had started getting dressed. But his braces were hanging down, which must mean he had been to the lavatory. Joel could see that he was still in pain.

Samuel sat down on the edge of his bed. He looked even more ashen now, as the morning light shone in through the gap in the curtains.

"It's only five o'clock," he said, "but I think I'd better go to the hospital."

It was immediately clear to Joel that his dad must be in far more pain than he could comprehend. Samuel would never normally even consider the possibility of going to a doctor. Never mind a hospital.

"I'll come with you," said Joel, starting to pick up his clothes, which were still wet.

"No," said Samuel. "It'll be better if you stay here at the hotel. You never know how long it's going to take at a hospital. I'll give you some money for food. I've spoken to the woman down in reception."

"But what can I do here?" Joel complained, realizing that he sounded like a whining child.

"You'll manage," said Samuel. "I'll phone from the hospital if it's going to take a really long time."

His tone of voice was very firm, and Joel could see there would be no point in protesting. He sat down on his bed and watched Samuel getting dressed. He was obviously in great pain. Every movement hurt.

"A taxi is coming to pick me up," he said, taking out his wallet.

"I've got some money," said Joel.

Samuel seemed surprised.

"You mean you've got some money of your own?"

"I've got fifteen kronor. That'll be enough."

Samuel took out three ten-kronor notes and put them on the bed.

"It's better to have too much than too little," he said. "But you don't need to spend it all. Unless it's necessary."

Joel helped Samuel on with his jacket.

"Is it serious?"

Samuel pulled a face.

"No," he said. "I'll be OK as long as I can get to a doctor."

That told Joel that it really was serious.

Samuel was afraid. And he was a bad liar. Much worse than Joel.

Joel wanted to go down to the lobby with him, but Samuel pointed at the bed.

"You've got to get some sleep," he said. "I won't be away for long. And then we can go and look for Mummy Jenny."

In fact, he's only too pleased to be able to put that off, Joel thought. But he didn't say anything.

Samuel nodded and patted him on the shoulder.

"Everything will be OK as soon as I see a doctor," he said.

Samuel left. Joel looked at the picture hanging on the wall. The young man was playing the violin. The woman with the big breasts seemed to be looking straight at him. Her mouth was half open, as if she were saying something.

It won't be OK at all, said the woman in the picture.

The violin screeched away in the background.

"Oh yes it will," said Joel.

Then he carefully took down the picture and leaned it against the wall. With its back to the room.

There was a lump of old chewing gum stuck to it.

Right in the middle of her backside, Joel thought angrily. Why does she have to say that things won't be OK?

Joel hung up his clothes to dry.

Then he snuggled down between the sheets again.

After a while he moved over to Samuel's bed. He tried to picture Samuel in his mind's eye. Getting out of the taxi and entering the hospital.

But he was far too tired. His thoughts ran away from him. He was soon fast asleep.

He was woken up by somebody tapping on his head. He tried to duck down under the covers, but the tapping continued. As he became increasingly wide awake, he realized that it was in fact somebody belting hard on the door. He wound a blanket round his naked body and went to open it. There was a chambermaid standing outside. She looked angry.

"It's nearly midday," she said. "If this room is going to get cleaned today, I need to do it now."

Midday, Joel wondered, somewhat confused. Had he really slept for as long as that?

"I'll be back in ten minutes," said the chambermaid.

Joel closed the door. Samuel had taken his watch with him. He started to get dressed as quickly as he could. His clothes were dry, so he must have been asleep for a long time.

When the chambermaid knocked on the door again, Joel was just hanging the picture back up on the wall. He wondered if the chambermaid would need paying. And where was Samuel? Why hadn't he come back?

The chambermaid came in and gave him a dirty look.

"How on earth can anybody stay in bed until twelve o'clock?" she said. "But it's none of my business, I suppose."

Exactly, Joel thought.

"There's a lump of chewing gum stuck on the back of the picture," he said. "But it wasn't me who put it there."

Then he left. Before she had time to say anything.

On the way down to reception he tried to make up his mind what he was going to do. He was hungry. But where was Samuel? He could feel his fear beginning to return.

The bald man was back on duty. He nodded to Joel, and gave him a friendly smile.

"I'm sorry to hear that your dad has been taken ill."

"He'll soon be OK again," said Joel. "Hasn't he rung?"

"Not yet. But it usually takes a long time at hospital."

Joel looked at the wall clock. Ten minutes past twelve. He'd slept half the day away. But at least he'd made good use of the bed Samuel had paid for. That was some consolation. Not much, though.

"It's stopped raining," said the man, pointing towards the window. "I think it would do you good to get some fresh air."

"But what if Samuel rings while I'm out?"

"I'll make a note of what he says for you."

Joel nodded. He really did need to go out. Not least in order to get something to eat.

When he came out into the street he could feel the heat. People were dressed for summer. Many of them looked cheerful.

They haven't got a father who's ill, Joel thought glumly. And they don't have a mother who ran away either.

He went to the café where they'd eaten the previous day. Joel was pleased to see that one of the waitresses recognized him and gave him a smile. He sat down at the same table as last time. First in Samuel's seat. Then he moved to the other side.

"Where's your friend?" asked the waitress as she placed a menu on the table. It occurred to Joel that she looked like the woman in the picture. The one with a lump of chewing gum stuck to her bottom.

"He's my dad," he said. "He's eaten already."

"Mashed turnips with pork," said the waitress. "Or herring."

"Herring, please. And a glass of milk."

The waitress wiped down the table and left. Joel watched her go, to make sure there was no chewing gum stuck to her black skirt.

Then he wondered why he could never bring himself to tell the truth. That Samuel had stomach pains and was at the hospital. Why had he claimed that his dad had already eaten?

He couldn't think of a suitable answer.

His head was completely empty.

When he'd finished eating and left the café, he didn't know what to do. He ought to go back to the hotel and ask if Samuel had phoned. But something told him it was too soon yet.

He started walking down the street. The night in the old people's home, the woman in the green coat, the man who had discovered him, it all felt as if it had never happened.

We should never have come to Stockholm, he thought. If that confounded Elinor hadn't written that letter, Jenny would still have been missing. Which would have been just as well.

We should never have come here. Samuel would never have had stomach pains if we'd stayed at home. Maybe all that shaking on the train ruined his stomach?

A shop window attracted his attention. There was a large map of the world hanging in it. He pressed his nose against the glass and tried to find Pitcairn Island. He found it eventually. A tiny little dot in the middle of the Pacific Ocean.

He stood for ages gazing at the map. Thinking about the MS *Karmas* being unloaded. Perhaps it had already left the dock and was heading out to sea again? Once again he could picture himself and Samuel walking up the gangway.

He dragged himself away from the shop window. It was half past one now. He'd go back to the hotel in an hour's time. Samuel might have returned by then? Or telephoned, at least?

He came to a square with stalls selling fruit and vegetables. He hesitated for a moment, then bought an apple. He sat down on a bench to eat it. There were people everywhere. And all of them were in a hurry. He wondered where they were going to. To help pass the time he tried to count the number of passersby wearing sandals, but he soon got tired of that. Two girls sat down on the bench. They were about his own age. They were talking loudly about somebody called Knut who had done something silly. One of them looked at Joel, who felt embarrassed.

"Have you got a fag?" the girl asked.

Her voice was shrill and she spoke fast. As if it wasn't just people's legs that were in a hurry, but their voices as well.

"I've run out," said Joel.

"Why don't you buy some more, then?"

"I shall," said Joel, standing up.

"Hurry up, then," screeched the girl. "What's your name?"

"Rickard," said Joel.

Then he walked away. And didn't go back.

He tried to walk as fast as everybody else was doing, and to barge his way forward.

But he didn't know how to do it. No matter what he did, somebody always got in front of him. Beat him to the next paving stone, the next street corner, the next shop window. He was always last.

I've had enough of this, he thought. When Samuel gets back from the hospital we're either going to go back home, or to the Seamen's Employment Exchange.

The hour was up at last. Joel went to the hotel reception and looked expectantly at the bald man, who shook his head ruefully. Samuel hadn't rung.

"It always takes time at hospital," he said. "You have to be patient."

Joel decided to walk up the stairs, and did so slowly. It was like climbing up an incredibly high mountain. Every step needed all his strength. When he came to the room, the door was locked. The chambermaid had obviously left the key at reception. But why hadn't the bald man said anything?

Joel hurtled down the stairs. Just as he reached the desk, the man behind it remembered.

"You forgot the key," he said.

Who forgot it? Joel wondered. You or me?

He trudged up the stairs again. To make it easier he imagined that he was really clambering up some steep cliffs.

He unlocked the door. Remembered what had happened during the night. Pictured Samuel sitting on the bed, clutching his stomach.

He lay down on his bed and stared up at the ceiling.

Then he checked to see if the chambermaid had removed the chewing gum.

She hadn't.

Then he pulled down the blind.

Stood in front of the mirror and thought he looked like the very devil.

Back to his bed again. Now the girl with the shrill voice was sitting on the edge of the bed. Wondering if he had any fags.

He tried to imitate her voice.

Then she lay down next to him. For the first time since he'd woken up, several minutes passed without him thinking about Samuel.

There was a knock on the door.

Joel leapt out of bed.

Samuel, he thought.

But when he opened the door, it was the chambermaid.

"You're wanted on the telephone," she said.

Joel flew downstairs. But he had no control over the propellers or the wings, and just as he was about to land in reception he tripped over the edge of a carpet and flew headlong over the floor. He knocked over a pile of suitcases belonging to a newly arrived traveler. The bald man burst out laughing and pointed to a little booth with a telephone. Joel closed the door behind him, took a deep breath and picked up the receiver.

"Joel here," he said. "Where are you? How are you? When are you coming? I'm here at the hotel, waiting for you."

There was no answer. All he heard was a little click. The line went dead. He shouted in vain at the receiver. But Samuel wasn't there. Nobody was there. He replaced the receiver and went back to the desk.

"There was nobody there," he said.

"Really?"

"What did he say?"

"Who?"

"Samuel. My father."

"It was a woman asking for you. Presumably a nurse."

"But why was I cut off?"

"It happens. No doubt they'll ring again."

Joel sat down to wait. After half an hour he gave up and went back up the stairs.

They weren't a mountain any longer.

They were an abyss.

He lay down on the bed to wait. Then he got up, took Samuel's penknife and scraped the chewing gum off the back of the picture.

"Don't say anything," he said to the woman in the painting.

Then he hung it up again.

He went down the corridor to the toilet.

When he came back he couldn't be bothered to lie down again.

He tried to improve the repair to the broken handle on Samuel's suitcase.

In the end it came off altogether.

Just then there was another knock on the door.

Joel leapt to his feet.

Opened the door.

There was a woman standing outside. Wearing a blue jacket.

But Joel recognized her immediately.

Despite the fact that the night before, she had been wearing a green coat when she emerged from the front door of Östgötagatan 32.

— EIGHT —

Joel searched.

He searched frantically. He eventually thought he'd found what he was looking for. Around her eyes. They were similar to his.

But he was staring at her in horror. When he looked back later, he could distinctly remember thinking that this wasn't how he'd imagined it was going to happen. Meeting Mummy Jenny.

How many times had he experienced this meeting in his imagination? Conjured up the circumstances? He didn't know. He had pictured them meeting in a street. Or on a beach. Or in the depths of a forest.

But never like this, in a hotel called the Raven, opening a door and expecting to see Samuel standing there.

She had walked into the room and closed the door behind her. Joel was still staring at her.

"Where is he?" she asked.

Her voice was dry and tense.

That was also something Joel had wondered about many times. What was his mum's voice like?

Now he knew. Dry and tense.

"Samuel isn't here," Joel said.

"Where is he? When will he be coming?"

Joel decided on the spur of the moment not to tell her the truth. Not to say that Samuel had stomach pains and had gone to the hospital.

"He's gone out. I don't know when he'll be back."

Then there was a question he wanted answered right away.

"Was it you who phoned?"

"Yes. But I wanted to meet you in person rather than on the telephone."

Well, that's one way in which we are similar, at least, Joel thought. I don't like speaking on the phone either.

She was in the middle of the room now. Joel had backed away towards the window. He was still staring at her all the time. Even so, he wasn't at all sure that he could really see her. She was a sort of mirage. Something that existed and yet didn't exist.

She sat down on the very edge of the chair. It struck Joel that she might be just as scared as he was.

"I don't know what to say," she said, studying her hands.

Joel immediately looked at his.

Silence.

What can I say if she doesn't know what to say? Joel thought. He'd stopped staring at her now. He was embarrassed instead. He glanced surreptitiously at her as she studied her hands.

He'd always imagined that this occasion would be full of joy. When he met his mum at long last. Not a time for stares and embarrassment.

All the pictures he'd imagined had been a waste of time. Nothing had turned out as he'd expected.

He kept on looking surreptitiously at her. All the time looking for similarities. Her hair was soft and curly. Not tufty like his. Her eyes were blue, the same as his. But she was small in stature. And thin. In a way, she was like Samuel.

Then it occurred to Joel that she was also pretty. If Jenny Rydén really was his mum, he'd been lucky. He had a good-looking mother. The question now was whether she wanted a son looking like Joel.

At that moment she looked up from her hands.

"I don't know what I should say. But I suppose I ought to say I'm sorry."

Her eyes were moist. Joel got a lump in his throat immediately.

She stood up and turned her back on him. She took a handkerchief out of her handbag. Joel recognized it from the previous night.

She turned round again. Now she was smiling. Joel could see that her teeth where white and regular. Not like his own, that seemed to point in various directions.

"I wish Samuel was here," she said. "But at the same time, I'm glad he's not."

She sat down on the chair again. And looked at him. All the time she was slowly shaking her head.

Joel broke into a sweat. She doesn't like me, he thought. She'd expected something completely different.

That made him feel angry. He didn't know where the anger came from, but he had no say in the matter. He suddenly wanted to tell her about how it had been. All those years. All those thoughts, dreams, fantasies.

She interrupted his train of thought.

"You are so big," she said. "But you were so little then."

"It was Elinor who sent Samuel a letter," said Joel. "But we couldn't find a grocer's shop."

"I stopped working there when it closed down," she said. "But how did you manage to find me at Autumn Light?"

Joel shrugged. But he said nothing.

"When Arne came and told me you'd been there, I couldn't understand what he was talking about. I thought he was making it up. But when he said that you spoke with a northern accent, I realized it must be you. No matter how unlikely it seemed. And he remembered the name of the hotel. The Raven. So I rang. And now I'm here."

"I've just left school," said Joel. "It was that letter from Elinor. Samuel thought we ought to come here. So that I could find out what you looked like."

He regretted that last sentence the moment he'd said it. But she wasn't annoyed. Instead, she stood up.

"Can't we go out? It's so hot in here. And I want to talk to you on your own, before Samuel comes back. I don't even know if I want to see him."

"Why not?"

"I don't know. So much of this is hard to cope with."

"I think he wants to see you."

"Really?"

"Yes."

She shook her head again.

"Let's go out," she said.

Joel looked at the *Celestine*.

"This is for you," he said. "From Samuel as well."

He pointed.

"I remember that," she said slowly. "It was in the kitchen."

"Yes," said Joel. "It's always been on the kitchen wall. And it's for you."

He produced the cardboard box they'd kept it in, that had been stashed away under the bed.

"It's for you," he said again.

"Why should it be for me?"

"We couldn't think of a better present for you," said Joel. "Samuel thought you should have an elk steak. But I didn't agree. And so this is what we agreed on."

"An elk steak?"

"Yes—but to get one at this time of year Samuel would have had to go poaching."

She burst out laughing.

"Nobody but Samuel would ever have thought of an elk steak," she said. "Nobody but him."

Joel wasn't sure how he ought to interpret what she had said. Was it positive or negative? He didn't know.

She suddenly took hold of his arm. It was the first time she'd touched him. The first time he'd felt her hand. He'd been so little all that time ago that he had no memories of it at all.

It also made him feel a bit scared. Was this really his mother, standing there in front of him? This Jenny Rydén? Or could it be somebody just pretending to be his mum?

"There's such a lot I'd like to explain," she said. "I don't know where to start. And I don't even know if I can."

"It doesn't matter," said Joel. "That's life."

"That's what Samuel used to say: 'That's life.'"

Joel seemed to recall that it was really Geegee who'd said that. But perhaps it was something everybody said when they were grown up.

That's life.

She was still holding on to his arm, and more or less whisked him to the door. She was holding the cardboard box in her other hand.

"I can carry that for you," said Joel.

She gave him the box.

Joel locked the door. Jenny Rydén pressed the button for the lift.

I'm about to travel in a lift with my mum, Joel thought. If the lift crashes and we're killed, at least I'll have met her. Assuming she really is my mum.

"Why are you called Rydén?" he asked.

The words just came tumbling out of his mouth. He ought to have bars there, just in front of his teeth, to prevent words from jumping out whenever they felt like it.

"My maiden name was Nilsson. Then I married a man whose surname was Rydén. I'm divorced now. But I've hung on to the name."

It seemed to Joel that it was a good thing she was divorced. That meant there wasn't a man waiting for her to come home to the flat she lived in.

But it also struck him that he had just acquired two sisters. Always assuming that what the agitated man in the changing room had told him was true.

"Arne said that you had two daughters."

"Maria and Eva. Maria's ten, and Eva's nine."

"Was Rydén their father?"

"Yes."

They stepped into the lift. Joel could see in the mirror that his hair was all over the place.

They found themselves looking at each other in the same mirror.

The eyes, Joel thought. That's where we're similar. We have the same eyes. And we don't like talking on the phone.

He tried to work out what it meant, having just acquired two sisters. Two younger sisters. He'd suddenly become a big brother.

Everything was happening too quickly. He didn't think he could keep up.

The lift stopped.

Joel handed in his key at reception.

"We won't be away long," said Jenny Rydén. "In case his dad rings."

"We still haven't heard anything from the hospital," said the bald man.

They stepped out into the street.

Jenny Rydén was serious now.

"Is Samuel ill?"

"He had a stomachache."

"Is that why you came to Stockholm?"

"No. But he started having stomach pains last night."

"I hope it's nothing serious."

So do I, Joel thought. But he didn't say anything.

They went to a park with lots of lawns, lots of gravel paths, and lots of benches. Jenny asked if he wanted anything to eat or drink. But he said no.

It was clear to Joel that he wasn't the only one having trouble thinking of what to say. She was in the same boat.

It's not simply a case of me finding my mum. She's just found her son as well.

They eventually selected a bench to sit on. They put the box containing *Celestine* between them.

She gave the impression of bracing herself before making a big effort.

"It was so cold," she said. "The winters were so cold, and the nights so long, and there was so much darkness and so much forest. There was so much ice, and so many people who never said anything. And nothing to do. I thought I was going mad. In the end, I couldn't take any more. I just packed a suitcase and left."

"You had a green coat," said Joel.

"Yes. I had a green coat. And all the time I kept thinking that what I was doing was absolutely wrong. That I ought to have taken you with me, at least. But I couldn't. I couldn't take you away from Samuel."

That was something that had never occurred to Joel. The possibility of her taking him with her. If she had, he'd have grown up in Stockholm. With a stepfather called Rydén. And two younger sisters.

Was that what he would have wanted?

He knew the answer to that. Nothing would have been able to make him want to do without Samuel. Despite the fact that he'd always been forced to be his own mum.

"I've always been meaning to get in touch with you," said Jenny. "Write you a letter. Pay you a visit. But I've never managed it. Because I didn't dare."

Joel couldn't understand why anybody wouldn't dare to send a letter. He had posted lots of letters, with stamps on the envelopes that he'd drawn himself. And he'd made up the addresses.

But he didn't say anything. Just now it seemed to make more sense for him to listen.

"But now you've come," she said, taking hold of his arm again.

It seemed to Joel that this Jenny Rydén was extremely nervous.

He wondered if he would ever be able to bring himself to call her "mum."

But maybe that wasn't necessary. He could call her Jenny.

"I have to get back to Autumn Light," she said. "I only have a couple of hours off."

That was a relief as far as Joel was concerned.

They went back to the hotel and said goodbye in the street outside. She held on to both his arms. Joel found that a bit embarrassing. He thought that people passing by were staring at him.

103

"Say hello to Samuel," she said. "I want to meet him as well now. Seeing as I've discovered that you are not dangerous."

She let go of his arms and took a step backwards.

"It's amazing, how big you are."

"What was wrong with Samuel?"

She didn't hear his question. He'd mumbled it. And he didn't repeat it.

She took a pen and a piece of paper from her handbag. She noted down her telephone number.

"Ring me this evening. Then we can meet tomorrow. I have the whole day off."

"I don't know how long we'll be staying here," said Joel.

But he'd still been mumbling. Or she hadn't heard what he said again. And she didn't ask.

Then she left.

Joel watched her go.

Jenny Rydén.

When he came to reception, he was told that there was still no message from Samuel. Joel was starting to get seriously worried now. But the bald man urged him to be patient. Joel was given his key. He was hungry. But he had no desire to eat on his own yet again. When he came to his room he lay down on Samuel's bed and learned Jenny Rydén's telephone number off by heart. Then he tore the bit of paper into little pieces and threw them into the wastepaper basket.

He looked at the table. Where the *Celestine* had been standing.

Jenny Rydén, he thought. Joel Rydén. But he backed away from that thought double-quick. His name was Gustafson. Nothing else. Thoughts were racing around inside his head. What was it she'd said when they'd been sitting on the park bench? That there'd been too much forest?

He took a deep breath, and sighed. How could you abandon your son simply because there'd been too much forest?

There was so much he didn't understand, it wasn't even worth trying to do so.

He closed his eyes.

Now he could see the MS *Karmas* again. Out at sea somewhere. Captain Joel Gustafson is on the bridge. They're sailing in tropical waters. Dolphins are jumping alongside the ship. Another ship is approaching. He adjusts his telescope and sees that it is a Swedish cargo boat. He zooms in on the bows and sees that the ship's name is the MS *Jenny*.

He sat up. Why had there been no word from Samuel? Why was it taking so long?

He went down to reception. The bald man shook his head. Joel asked to borrow the telephone directory. There were two of them for Stockholm. After a lot of effort he succeeded in finding the Seamen's Employment Exchange, and noted down the address. He found it on the map. It was quite close by. He checked the time. If he got a move on, he might be able to get there before they closed.

When he emerged into the street, he was like everybody else.

He was in a hurry.

They were still open. He opened the door of the Seamen's Employment Exchange and went inside. The walls were covered in notices advertising various vacant jobs. A woman was sitting at a desk, filling in a football pools coupon.

"I'd like a seaman's discharge book, please."

"Are you fifteen?" the woman asked.

"Yes."

She passed him some papers for him to fill in.

"Two photographs," she said.

Then she gave him yet another sheet of paper.

"The address of your doctor, please."

"Is there no charge for this?"

"There's no such thing as a free lunch," she said, continuing to fill in her football coupon. Joel hoped she wouldn't win anything.

Then he sat down at a table and filled in all the papers. The next day he would go to a photographer's studio. And to a doctor. Then he would be able to collect his seaman's discharge book.

As he made his way back to the hotel, he found himself unable to hold back his hunger any longer. He stopped at the café he'd eaten at previously. This time he didn't recognize the waitress who tossed a menu in his direction. He chose the casserole known as Sailor's Beef.

When he got back to the hotel, the bald man nodded in greeting.

"Has Samuel rung?"

"He's in your room."

Joel raced up the stairs. He was forced to pause outside the door and get his breath back. Then he opened it.

Samuel was sitting on the chair by the window. Just like Jenny Rydén, he was studying his hands. He was still very pale.

"Where's *Celestine?*" he asked tentatively.

"I'll tell you later," said Joel. "What did they have to say at the hospital? Are you still in pain?"

"It's all over now. I've got medicine."

"You must be feeling pleased, then?"

"Of course I am."

Joel looked doubtfully at Samuel. He didn't seem the slightest bit pleased.

"What did they do?"

"What do you mean, do?"

"At the hospital. The doctors."

"There was only one. And it took a damned long time before he turned up."

"What did he say?"

"That I have to go back again tomorrow morning."

"Eh? Are you supposed to report back to the hospital tomorrow morning? But you're not in pain anymore."

"They want to take some more tests."

"Blood tests?"

"Yes."

"Why?"

"To be on the safe side."

"But you're not in pain any longer?"

Samuel sighed.

"They want to find out for certain what's wrong with me. So as to make sure that it doesn't come back again."

A particular thought had gradually started belting on all the doors inside Joel's head. But he didn't want to let it out. He was resisting for as long as he could. But in the end, he couldn't keep it out any longer. The thought forced itself out of Joel's head.

Samuel is very ill. He might be going to die.

Joel took a deep breath. Samuel looked at him.

"I'm not allowed to eat anything today. They want to make their tests on an empty stomach."

"I've already eaten."

"What else have you been up to today?"

"Nothing."

"The bloke downstairs in reception says that you've had a lady visitor."

"You must have misheard him."

"He said you went out with a female person who came to visit you."

Joel wondered where to start.

But he didn't need to wonder for long. Samuel came to his rescue.

"The *Celestine* has vanished," he said slowly. "And I can't imagine you giving her to anybody but your mum."

Joel waited anxiously for what was coming next.

"I'm right, aren't I?"

Joel nodded.

Then he started to tell Samuel what had happened.

— NINE —

Just for once, Joel told the full story, exactly as it had happened.

He left nothing out. Samuel was able to relive the whole thing, from the moment when Joel slipped out of the hotel door. He told his dad how he'd stood in the shadows outside the building where she lived, how the door had opened and a woman wearing a green coat had come out.

Samuel listened in astonishment. When Joel got to the point where he'd been standing in the changing room holding the open handbag and the door suddenly opened, Samuel seemed to give a start.

He's with me, Joel thought. He understands exactly what it felt like.

But Joel didn't say anything about his visit to the Seamen's Employment Exchange. He thought that might be too much for Samuel to take—he still looked very pale.

As Joel told his story, he kept thinking over and over again that Samuel really was very ill. But he brushed the thought aside. Stowed it away in a corner of his mind.

"This is an amazing story you're telling me," said Samuel when Joel had run out of steam. "But how could Jenny know that you were staying at this particular hotel?"

"I suppose I must have mentioned the name of it. The Raven. And the man who caught me in the act must have remembered it."

"And so she phoned here?"

"Yes. I thought it must be a nurse. Because she didn't ask for you; she wanted to talk to me."

"All these things you are recounting are making me tired. I think I'd better lie down."

Samuel lay on his bed. Joel sat down beside him.

It used to be the other way round, he thought. Samuel used to sit on the edge of my bed: now it's me sitting on his.

"What did she think of *Celestine?*" Samuel asked after a while.

"She remembered it. From the kitchen."

Samuel frowned.

"Could she really remember that? It's not just something you're making up?"

"No, it's really true. She remembered it."

"And she wanted us to ring?"

"Yes."

Samuel shook his head.

"Funny, how things turn out," he said. "We were going to track her down together, and knock on her door. But nothing happens the way you'd expected. Never ever."

"I have two sisters," said Joel. "Maria and Eva."

"Two half sisters," said Samuel.

Joel said nothing. But he didn't like the idea of having half people as sisters.

"Their father's called Rydén. But he's not there."

Samuel pricked his ears up.

"Where is he, then?"

"He's gone. I don't know where."

Samuel sat up.

"Tell me what she looked like."

Joel did his best, but he didn't think he was very successful.

"How was she?"

"What do you mean?"

"Was she cheerful? Or nervous? Or what?"

"She was nervous."

Samuel pulled a face.

"I should think so too."

There was a hard edge to his voice now. Something that surprised Joel. Something hard and firm.

"The bottom line is that she abandoned you and me."

Joel felt the need to defend her.

"She said she left because it was too cold."

"Eh? She left because it was too cold?"

"And too much forest. And too few people."

"That's rubbish," said Samuel. "Nobody abandons their child because it's cold."

"I'm only telling you what she said. Ask her yourself."

"I shall do, don't worry."

Joel thought Samuel was whinging. Why couldn't he just be pleased that Joel had found her?

"There's a lot I ought to talk to her about," said Samuel. "Lots and lots of things."

"If you're going to start causing trouble, I'm not going with you."

"I shan't cause trouble. But there are some things that need saying."

"Such as?"

"You simply don't do what she did. And then, afterwards, not even get in touch. All those years."

"She didn't dare."

Samuel looked angry.

"How do you know that?"

Joel was trying to defend Jenny Rydén.

"She said so."

"That she didn't dare to get in touch?"

"Yes."

Samuel muttered something that Joel didn't catch.

Then there was silence.

He can't be all that ill, Joel thought. If he was, he wouldn't have the strength to get so upset.

Samuel poured out some water from a carafe and took a pill.

"How can we go and visit her tomorrow if you have to go back to the hospital?"

"That's exactly what I was thinking," said Samuel. "I suppose it'll be best if you phone her and have a chat."

"You mean you want me to ring her?"

"I have no desire to talk to her on the phone."

"Why not?"

"The way she behaved."

"But that was over ten years ago."

Samuel had stood up and walked over to the window. There was a pause before he answered.

"I've never liked a woman as much as I did her," he said, with his back turned towards Joel. "Not Sara, not anybody. And she just ran off. When we were going to spend the rest of our lives together. One day she simply vanished. And left me to look after you on my own."

Samuel turned round. His eyes looked moist.

"I think it's best if you phone her," he said. "Meanwhile, I'll think about whether I really do want to meet her again."

Joel stood up to leave for reception.

"Didn't she ask anything about me?" Samuel asked.

"Not much."

Samuel nodded.

"Off you go," he said.

Joel stood in the telephone booth and dialed the number. As he listened to it ringing at the other end, he noticed that he was sweating. It was due not only to the heat inside the cramped booth, but at least as much to his nervousness.

What should he say to Jenny Rydén? And what should he call her?

But she wasn't the one who answered.

Joel had forgotten that he'd acquired two sisters.

"Maria," he heard a girl's voice say.

Joel slammed down the receiver. It was as if he'd been bitten. If he didn't even know what to call Jenny Rydén, what on earth should he call his sisters? He'd only discovered their existence a few hours ago.

Then there was another question that had flashed in horror through his mind.

Did they know that he existed? That they had acquired a brother? Perhaps Jenny Rydén had never told them that there was a boy miles away in the far north of the country called Joel Gustafson?

What was it the man in the changing room had said? That Jenny Rydén had two daughters, but he'd never heard any mention of a son.

Joel left the telephone booth.

He suddenly felt devastated.

So she had never even mentioned that he existed.

Not only had she run away and abandoned them, and never bothered to get in touch.

113

She hadn't even mentioned that he existed.

Joel Gustafson was a secret. He was hidden away right at the back of a wardrobe.

His devastation turned into anger.

I've got by without Jenny Rydén for many years, he thought. I'll continue to get by in the future as well.

When I've become a sailor I shall send her a banana spider. A big, hairy spider.

With greetings. From the boy at the back of the wardrobe.

Joel sat down on a sofa in the lobby. What should he do? Perhaps it would be as well if he and Samuel forgot all about that letter from Elinor in Gothenburg?

But that wasn't a good idea either.

Joel got up wearily from the sofa and went back to the telephone booth. He counted up to ten, gave the receiver a good shaking, as if it had been an enemy of his, and dialed the number once more.

The same girl's voice answered.

"I'd like to speak to Jenny Rydén."

"Are you Joel?"

Joel gave a start. So she did know that he existed. But how long had she known? He realized also that it was his northern accent that had given the game away.

"I'm your sister," said Maria. "When are we going to meet?"

"That's what I want to talk to Jenny about."

"You do talk funny!"

You stupid little brat, Joel thought.

"Can I speak to Jenny?"

"I'll go and get her."

Joel forced himself not to slam down the receiver again. Jenny answered. Joel explained the situation. How Samuel had to go back to the hospital the next day.

"Is it serious?"

"No. He's just going to have some blood tests. But he wonders if we can meet this evening instead."

She thought for a moment before answering. Joel could hear Maria saying something in the background. And there was another voice as well: that must be Eva.

Good Lord, what a row they're making! Joel thought. I want peace and quiet when I'm there. I'll teach them how to behave.

"Yes," said Jenny. "That'll be all right. But I'd like to meet Samuel on his own first. It was such a long time ago. And I'm so nervous."

"Where do you want to meet?" Joel asked.

"In the square," she said. "Where you thought the grocer's shop was. At quarter past six."

When Joel left the telephone booth he saw that it was five o'clock already. It took at least half an hour to walk to the square. He ran up the stairs.

Samuel didn't want to go. He complained that there wasn't enough time. He needed to get ready.

"All you need to do is have a shave and change your shirt," said Joel.

But Samuel carried on protesting. He didn't want to.

In the end he didn't have time to get shaved, only to change his shirt. Then Joel almost frog-marched him out of the room.

"I don't want to go," said Samuel.

"Too bad. It's decided now," said Joel.

They arrived at the square at dead on a quarter past six. There were a lot of people milling around, but Joel spotted her immediately. She was standing beside a shop window on the other side of the square. He pointed her out.

"There," he said.

Samuel couldn't see her.

"She's wearing a blue jacket."

Then Samuel spotted her as well.

"I'm not going over there," he said. "I don't know what to say."

"She's the one who wanted to see you," said Joel. "You don't need to say anything at all. All you need do is listen."

"I don't want to anyway."

Joel thought Samuel was acting like a little kid.

"Get going," he said. "But don't start causing trouble. I'll wait here."

Samuel reluctantly shuffled off. Joel ran after him.

"Put your shoulders back," he said.

Samuel tried to straighten up.

Joel stood and watched him go. It struck him that everything had been so different once upon a time. Then Jenny and Samuel would no doubt have run towards each other.

If they hadn't done that, Joel wouldn't be standing where he was now.

Samuel was almost there. Jenny had seen him. But she didn't go to meet him; she stayed by the shop window.

Then he saw them shaking hands. He wished he'd been much closer to them. So that he could hear what they said.

He saw they were standing about a meter apart. But what were they saying? He tried to imagine, but his mind was a complete blank.

But then something happened. Samuel took a step towards her. He raised an arm. Joel's heart missed a beat. Was Samuel going to hit her?

Then he lowered his arm again. Jenny Rydén walked past

him. She was walking fast. Samuel followed her. He was waving his arms about. Joel still couldn't hear what they were saying.

Then Samuel stopped. Jenny continued walking. She was almost running. Joel was bewildered. What had happened?

That stupid idiot Samuel, he thought. He started arguing. And now she's going away again.

He didn't know who to run after. In the end, it was Samuel despite everything.

"What did you do?" Joel shouted. "What did you say? Why did she leave? Were you going to hit her?"

"I just told her a few home truths," said Samuel. "I said what I've been wanting to say to her every day since she left us."

"What?"

"It doesn't matter. Let's go back to the hotel."

"You can go yourself."

Samuel stopped dead.

"What did you say?"

"I said you can go back to the hotel on your own. I want to know what you said."

"I told her I thought she was a bloody hateful witch."

Joel gaped at him.

"Why did you say that?"

"Because that's what I think. You don't abandon your son like that. You don't run away simply because you think the winters are too long. That's what I told her. But she didn't like it."

Samuel was so upset that he was shaking.

"I said what I'd made up my mind I was going to say. Now I've finished with her. I'm not going to give her another thought. Not a single one for the rest of my life."

"But what about me?"

Joel thought his voice had turned into a squeak.

"But what about me?" he said again. His voice was back to normal now.

"That's up to you," said Samuel. "She's your mother. If you want to meet her, do."

Samuel set off walking. Joel ran after him and raised an arm. Just like Samuel had done to Jenny. Samuel noticed and ducked away. Then they stood facing each other in the middle of the square, staring.

"Were you going to hit me?"

"Yes," said Joel. "Just like you were going to hit Jenny."

Samuel grabbed hold of Joel's arm.

"We're going back to the hotel now!" he roared. "And when I've been to the hospital we'll take the next train home."

Joel was completely calm.

"I'm not going with you."

"You mean you're going to stay here in Stockholm?"

"I've been to the Seamen's Employment Exchange. I'm going to sign on with a ship. I can't wait for you any longer."

Samuel was silent for a while.

"Hmm," he said eventually. "Hmm, so that's what you've done, is it?"

"It's not too late for you to do the same."

Samuel looked thoughtfully at him.

"Maybe not. Maybe not."

They started walking back to the hotel.

Samuel suddenly stopped dead.

"I don't regret it," he said. "I don't regret saying what I did to Jenny. You have to understand that. What she did to us is something I can't forgive her for. You don't necessarily have to see it the same way. Do you see what I mean?"

"No," said Joel. "But just now I couldn't give a toss."

118

As they approached the hotel, Samuel stopped outside a bar.

"A pilsner would be just the thing right now," he said.

"No," said Joel. "It wouldn't be just the thing at all. Besides, you have to go to the hospital tomorrow without having had anything to eat or drink."

"I don't think a pilsner would do any harm."

"We're going back to the hotel," said Joel. "No pilsner."

They got up early next day. Joel went to the café for breakfast and Samuel took a bus to the hospital. Joel had money from Samuel to pay the photographer, but it would be several hours before the studio opened. Meanwhile he wandered around the streets, wondering if he dared to phone Jenny. Or should he simply write her a letter?

Samuel is an idiot. Greetings, Joel.

He found it hard to make up his mind.

He suddenly noticed the girl who had asked him for a cigarette the previous day. She was sitting on a bench, by herself, reading a magazine. Joel went to a kiosk and bought four loose cigarettes. Then he approached the bench.

"It took a little while," he said, "so you can have four to make up for the delay."

The girl didn't recognize him at first. Then she burst out laughing.

"You're mad!" she said.

She put the cigarettes in her pocket.

Then she stood up and walked away. Without even saying thank you.

Joel was disappointed. Despite the fact that he didn't really know what he'd expected, or hoped for.

He thought of Sonja Mattsson, who had been naked underneath a transparent net curtain.

119

Things will be better once I go to sea, he thought. Then there'll be no stopping me.

He went to the photography studio and had his pictures taken. Then he looked up the address of the sailors' doctor.

The waiting room was packed.

It occurred to Joel that in a way, both he and Samuel were in their respective hospitals.

And Jenny was working in a third.

He eventually got to see the doctor, who instructed Joel to take down his trousers. He then felt around Joel's groin and pronounced him fit. He was issued with a certificate, which he took to the Seamen's Employment Exchange.

They told him he should call back after a couple of days and collect his seaman's discharge book.

He was just about to leave when he heard a voice behind him say:

"*Karmas* requires a steward and an engine room assistant."

Two men stood up and went to a hatch in the wall.

It's my turn next, Joel thought.

The problem was what Samuel intended to do. Had he been serious? Was he really considering going to sea again? You never knew with Samuel. He could change his mind whenever it suited him.

But it was possible. Maybe he really had decided he'd had enough of wandering through the forests with an ax and a saw in his hand.

In that case, what would they do with the house by the river? And all the furniture? Joel decided he couldn't face waiting any longer. Samuel would have to follow on later.

• • •

Joel wandered around town for a few more hours. He paused twice to buy and eat a hot dog.

Then he went back to the hotel.

No sign of Samuel yet.

But when he collected his key, the bald man gave him an envelope.

It was a letter. From Jenny Rydén.

— TEN —

The letter was short and handwritten.

Joel sat on the steps outside the hotel and read what she had written.

> My dear son,
>   When Samuel started shouting and yelling at me in the square, it dawned on me why I'd really left all those years ago. Without saying anything.
>   I couldn't say anything to you. You were too small. You wouldn't have understood.
>   I don't want to see Samuel ever again. But you have to understand that it wasn't easy, living with him.
>   I just hop you and me can continue to see each other.
>   I'd like that.
>
>   Jenny

Joel read the letter again.

Jenny had spelt a word wrongly. "Hop." She really meant "hope."

Then he realized that there was something in the letter he could understand fully. That it wasn't easy to live with Samuel. He'd discovered that for himself.

And how had it been for Sara? The waitress in the bar back home who hadn't been able to put up with him either?

I expect it's all to do with the fact that he shaves so carelessly, Joel thought. If you're slapdash with that, you're slapdash with other things as well.

He felt his cheeks. Only down so far. But he was quite certain that he would never shave carelessly. He'd prefer to grow a beard.

Joel wondered what to do. Should he show Samuel the letter? Or should he do what Samuel had done with the letter from Elinor? Show that it existed, but not say what was in it?

He went back into the hotel. He'd noticed that there was headed paper in one of the desk drawers. And Samuel had a pen. He'd be able to write a reply to Jenny on the spot.

"I hope it was good news," said the bald man behind the desk. Every time he saw Joel he became more friendly.

"It couldn't have been better," Joel said.

He sat down at the desk with the paper in front of him, pen in hand. He didn't really want to use Samuel's pen when he wrote to Jenny, but he didn't have any other.

What should he write?

He read Jenny's letter once again. He could hear her voice. What had Samuel shouted at her? That she was a hateful witch.

Was that something you could really say to a woman? Samuel must be a boor. Had he really been planning that for over ten years? To tell Mummy Jenny that she was a hateful witch?

Joel decided once and for all that Samuel was incompre-

123

hensible. He had an incomprehensible dad. A person nobody could understand. A boor.

He was worried that he might have inherited that boorish character. That there might be aspects of it inside himself. Only seeds so far, but seeds that might sprout and grow as he grew older. Might he one day go around calling women things he shouldn't?

He knew now what he was going to write. And he would be very careful to avoid any spelling mistakes.

When he'd finished writing, he read it through.

To Jenny Rydén,

I'd like you to know that I'm not as boorish as my father, Samuel Gustafson. I never bellow. I'd love to see you again.

Greetings from Joel Gustafson

That would have to do. He hadn't made any spelling mistakes. He folded the sheet of paper and put it in an envelope, which he sealed.

He was able to buy a stamp in reception. He'd noticed a postbox in the street not far from the hotel. He went there and posted the letter.

So that was that done.

When Samuel came back from the hospital, Joel had just been out for a meal. He'd gone to a different café, but the food tasted exactly the same. He was looking at the picture of the woman leaning against a tree, and thinking about Sonja Mattsson, when the door opened.

Samuel was wearing a hat.

A gray hat with a light blue band.

Joel stared at him. The hat was drooping down a long way below Samuel's ears.

"Wherever did you find that?" he asked.

"Find?" said Samuel. "I bought it. And it was far too dear. But I thought I had a right to treat myself to something for once."

"And so you bought a hat?"

Samuel examined himself in the mirror.

"Isn't it elegant?"

"It's elegant. But what are you going to do with it?"

"I'm going to wear it."

"Out in the forest?"

"When I'm in my best clothes. On Sundays."

Joel sighed. It was just as both Jenny Rydén and he himself had established: Samuel was a totally incomprehensible person. He never got dressed up on Sundays. He never went for walks. The hat would end up on a shelf in the wardrobe. And it would stay there.

Joel changed the subject.

"What did they have to say, at the hospital?"

"They'll be getting in touch. By letter. So we can go home now."

Samuel walked past Joel and sat down on the chair.

Joel noticed immediately that Samuel smelled of pilsner. That meant that he hadn't been at the hospital all day. But his eyes were not shiny. So he wasn't drunk.

"Have you eaten?" Samuel asked.

"Yes. Have you?"

"No. But I'm not hungry."

That's not true, Joel thought. Samuel tells lies just as badly as he shaves himself. He's eaten already, and he's been drinking beer. And no doubt bought rounds for lots of old men he's never seen before. I expect he also told them he was a sailor. On shore leave.

"Have you any money left?" Joel asked.

He was starting to wonder if they'd be able to pay for the hotel room if they stayed for two more nights.

"I have enough for us to get by on," said Samuel. "And we'll be going home tomorrow anyway."

Joel could see that there was no point in waiting any longer. He'd have to speak to Samuel. It was a case of now or never.

"When are we going to look at the boats?"

"We can do that tomorrow. Before we set off home."

He doesn't want to, Joel thought. All that talk about me having to finish school first, and then we could move and Samuel could become a sailor again.

All talk. Nothing but talk.

Joel took a deep breath and braced himself.

"I'm not going with you," he said. "I'll be collecting my seaman's discharge book a couple of days from now. Then I'm off to sea. I can't wait for you any longer."

Samuel stared long and hard at him. It slowly dawned on him that Joel was serious.

He said nothing. He seemed to be retreating into himself.

"That's a bit of a shock," he said eventually.

"Why? It's what I've been dreaming about for ages. And I thought we were going to go to sea together."

"I have to wait for the letter from the hospital."

Lucky for him that there's something he has to wait for, Joel thought. But even if there hadn't been, he'd have thought up something. Any excuse at all to delay matters.

Then Samuel seemed to get a second wind.

"This is what we'll do," he said. "We'll go back home tomorrow, and then we can plan everything calmly and carefully. I'll resign from the logging company. And then we'll go to Gothenburg. There's more boats to choose from there.

126

Stockholm's nothing. It's not a good idea to sign up for the first boat you clap eyes on. Then we'll start our travels. Best would be a boat heading for South America. They are good boats. Good boats and good ports. And you have to be careful which shipping line you choose. That's the way it is. There are good boats and there are bad boats. I think that's what we'll do."

Joel listened. He'd sat down on his bed.

He felt sorry for Samuel. Because all he said was just words. Words that would never lead to anywhere, least of all up a gangway.

Samuel didn't want to go back to sea. Or didn't dare. Or didn't have the strength. Or perhaps it was a combination of all three.

But he couldn't change his mind now. If he did, he'd become like Samuel. He'd stay up north in that house by the river. At first he'd get a job as an errand boy for the ironmonger's shop. And then? Whatever happened next, he'd stay up there. And if he eventually had any children of his own, he wouldn't even have a sea chart on which he could show them the places he'd been to when he was a sailor.

"What do you think?" asked Samuel.

"I'm not going with you. I can't wait any longer."

Silence again. Joel waited.

"Where will you live? While you're waiting for a ship?"

The answer was obvious.

"Maybe I can stay with my mum."

Now he's said it. For the first time. Not Jenny. Not Jenny Rydén. But my mum.

Samuel said nothing for a long time.

"That means that I'll be on my own," he said. "I've looked after you for all these years, and now you're leaving me. And moving in with your mum."

127

"I'm going to sea. With luck I might get a job on a boat without having to wait."

"I'll be on my own," said Samuel.

Joel could feel that it was getting difficult now. Whenever Samuel started to feel sorry for himself he could carry on moaning and complaining forever.

"You're the one who doesn't want to become a sailor again. That's not my fault."

"I'll be on my own," said Samuel again.

Joel would have liked to hit him. Shout at him. But first of all Samuel would have to stop feeling sorry for himself.

Anything was better than that.

"Let's go out," he said. "And you can have a beer. But only one. If you drink more than one, I'll leave you to it."

Samuel stood up.

"That sounds like a good idea," he said. "When you're in Stockholm, you shouldn't just sit around in a hotel room."

They went to the usual bar.

Samuel had a pilsner. Joel had lemonade.

There wasn't anything much to say now. The decision had been made. Both Samuel and Joel were well aware of that.

But Joel couldn't help thinking that he might just as well go back home with Samuel. How would Samuel be able to manage on his own? How would he get enough to eat? Who would do the shopping? Who would drag him home when he'd been out drinking?

Joel tried to think of a solution. But there wasn't one.

He wasn't the only one who was beginning to grow up. Samuel would have to learn how to look after himself as well.

• • •

Joel allowed Samuel to have two beers. But no more.

Then they went back to the hotel.

They lay awake for a long time.

The light was turned off. And neither of them spoke.

Samuel's train left at 3:22 p.m.

By then Joel knew that he could stay with Jenny. He'd phoned her in the morning. It was Eva who answered this time, and she fetched Jenny.

She hadn't received Joel's letter, but she said yes as soon as he asked her if he could stay there for a couple of nights while he waited for his seaman's discharge book and a position on a cargo ship.

Samuel was sitting waiting on a sofa in the lobby. He had paid for the room. He'd placed his suitcase in a storage room, having first mended the handle again.

"I tried to repair it," said Joel. "But I made a mess of it."

"It doesn't matter," said Samuel. "It's an old case. Besides, I don't do much traveling."

Samuel didn't have a lot to say that morning. Even less than usual. But he shook his head when Joel asked if he had stomach pains.

When they'd finished breakfast they took a tram to Värtahamnen. The MS *Karmas* had already sailed. Another ship was just berthing. It was flying a flag that Joel knew was Belgian. The MS *Gent*. Joel glanced surreptitiously at Samuel. Didn't he feel the urge now? To walk up the gangway that was slowly being lowered? But Samuel displayed no emotions. It was as if his eyes were asleep.

Afterwards, in the tram, Samuel asked Joel what kind of work he wanted to do. Did he want to be on deck, or in the engine room? Or would he become a steward?

"I'll take whatever's on offer," Joel said. "You've got to start somewhere."

"I always used to work on deck," said Samuel. "It was too hot and noisy in the engine room. I always worked on deck."

"I'll take whatever's on offer," said Joel again.

They got off at Stureplan, and realized they had no idea what to do next. It was a matter of waiting for several hours until the train left.

Joel was both worried and excited. All the time he was afraid that he'd suddenly change his mind.

They strolled around along the quays where the smaller boats were moored. Joel kept thinking he ought to say something. But what? And didn't Samuel have any good advice to give him?

They wandered about, dragging behind them a heavy cargo of silence.

Eventually it was time to collect Samuel's suitcase and head for the station.

When they got there Joel went to the police office and asked about his rucksack. But it was still missing. As was The Black Wave.

Samuel took out his wallet and gave Joel ninety kronor.

"That's all I've got," he said.

Joel didn't want to accept the money. There was nothing he needed.

"You must have a change of clothes or two," said Samuel. "You should really have a kit bag, but you can buy one of those after you've started to get paid."

Then they found the right platform. The train hadn't come in yet.

"You're doing the right thing," said Samuel. "It's right for you to go to sea. But I don't have the strength. Not at the moment."

"I hope you can find somebody to cook for you."

"That will sort itself out, no doubt."

"Don't forget to add salt to the potatoes when you boil them. And don't turn the heat too high."

Samuel nodded.

"I'll remember that."

"When I boil your eggs I usually count up to two hundred. Then they turn out exactly as you like them."

"Do you count slowly or fast?"

Joel started counting, to demonstrate. Samuel nodded. He'd bear that in mind.

"You must remember to pour some cold water into the saucepan after you've made porridge. Otherwise it will be impossible to wash it up properly."

Samuel promised to do as Joel said. And then the train clattered in.

They shook hands. They both had lumps in their throats.

"I'll write," said Joel. "As soon as I know which boat I'll be sailing on."

"I'll remember what you said about the porridge pan," said Samuel. "Cold water. Otherwise it'll be difficult to wash it up."

That was all they had time for.

Samuel boarded the train. The doors were closed. Samuel had opened a window.

"Did you say it was two hundred you counted up to?"

"Yes."

The train shuddered and started to move.

Samuel nodded and raised his hand.

"I hope you aren't seasick," he shouted.

Joel watched the train pulling out of the station.

For a moment he felt the urge to run after it and jump aboard the last carriage.

But it was too late now.

The train had already left.

Joel arrived at Östgötagatan 32 shortly after five o'clock. He'd bought some underclothes and a shirt. But no trainers. He still had forty kronor left. In his pocket was the toothbrush he'd bought that first day.

But that was all he had.

He'd dragged it out for as long as possible before coming here. He'd even wondered if he had enough money to stay at the hotel for another night.

Everything was happening so quickly. He had difficulty in keeping up with himself. It was as if his head was in one place and his body in another.

He'd also considered phoning Sonja Mattsson. But he decided not to. He didn't dare. Everything was difficult enough without that.

All the time, he was thinking of Samuel. With each second that passed, they drifted further and further apart.

He'll forget to add salt to the potatoes, Joel thought. He'll never learn how to count so that the eggs are done as he likes them.

What I really ought to do is write it all down.

A cookery book from Joel to Samuel.

For dishes that won't be all that good, but won't get burnt and stick to the pan.

But there came a point when he couldn't delay things any longer. Jenny Rydén and her daughters were no doubt wondering what had happened to him.

He entered through the front door. The Rydéns lived on the fourth floor. There was a lift, but Joel walked up the stairs. He wanted time to prepare himself.

Now he was going to meet his sisters.

Perhaps he ought to have brought presents for them as well.

He paused when he came to the last landing before the fourth floor. He sat down.

He wished he had a hiding place. A small scarf that could be folded up and stuffed into his pocket. And taken out again whenever necessary.

Just now was such a moment.

He needed a hiding place here on the staircase. Somewhere to which he could withdraw, suspend time, and think through all the things that had happened these last few days.

It still wasn't too late for him to change his mind. The last thing Samuel had given him at the railway station was the return half of his ticket. If he didn't use it, he could send it back to Samuel in an envelope. Then Samuel would be able to take it to the station and get a refund.

Joel would have preferred not to have it. But Samuel insisted. Something could happen. He might change his mind.

Joel felt in his pocket. The ticket was still there.

He could take the train leaving the next day. And when Samuel got back home from work, the potatoes would be ready for him.

It was tempting.

But he forced himself: there would be no going back. In a few days' time he would be issued with his discharge book.

Until then he'd stay with Jenny Rydén. And his sisters.

Somebody came in through the front door down below.

Joel stood up. He couldn't delay things any longer.

He walked up the last few stairs and rang the bell on the door where it said *J. Rydén*.

— ELEVEN —

It was Jenny Rydén who opened the door.

On each side of her was a little girl, peering out at him. One of them, the elder girl called Maria, had blond hair and a round face. But Joel gave a start when he set eyes on the other girl.

There was no doubt about it: Joel and Eva were very similar. He couldn't put his finger on exactly what it was, but looking at her was like seeing his own face in a mirror.

"We'd started to wonder," said Jenny Rydén with a smile.

She seemed less nervous now. Her voice wasn't as tense as it had been that first time.

Joel hung up his jacket and put down the bags containing his new clothes. They went into the living room. The sun shone in through the windows.

"So, these are your sisters," said Jenny. "Maria and Eva."

The girls were shy, and tried to hide behind each other. Joel felt embarrassed. Should he shake hands with them? Or what?

"They've been going on and on," said Jenny. "Wondering when they were going to get to see their brother."

So I haven't been a ghost hidden away in a wardrobe, Joel thought. That was a relief, despite everything. The man who caught Joel in the changing room hadn't known anything about him, but he'd been real enough for the two girls.

"There's something I want to show you," said Jenny.

She led Joel to where several framed photographs were hanging on a wall. A man with close-cropped hair and glasses caught Joel's attention.

"Is that Rydén?"

"It's our dad," said Maria.

"That's not the one I wanted to show you," said Jenny.

She pointed at a photograph of a little boy lying naked on a blanket. It was black and white, and rather dark. Joel leaned forward.

"Who is it?"

"It's you. Can you see where it was taken?"

Joel looked hard at the picture. He had some difficulty in making out the background. But there was something about it he felt he recognized.

Then the penny dropped.

The picture had been taken in the kitchen at home. He could even see the *Celestine* in its case on the wall.

So it's true, he thought. Jenny Rydén really is my mum.

Once upon a time, a long time ago, she and Samuel had lived together. And I lay on the kitchen table and had my photograph taken.

"Who took the picture?" he asked.

"Samuel."

"But surely he can't take photos? He's never even owned a camera."

"He borrowed one. I can't remember who from."

Joel studied the picture of himself. He was looking straight at the camera, laughing.

Joel didn't recognize himself.

The picture was from a long time ago, when he still hadn't started to accumulate any memories.

Joel examined the other photographs. There was something missing. In one place there was a faint mark on the wall, showing that there had been a picture hanging there as well.

Samuel, Joel thought. After he'd shouted and yelled at her in the square, she went home and took down the picture. But Rydén was still there.

"Now you know," she said. "That it really is true."

"Yes," said Joel.

But he didn't like that mark on the wallpaper. Just because Samuel had boiled over and shouted at her, she didn't need to take down his picture.

She showed him where he could sleep: in a little room behind the kitchen.

Then they made a tour of the flat. Joel had never seen so many toys as there were in the girls' room. As soon as he'd entered the flat he'd started to wonder how somebody who worked in an old people's home could afford to buy such elegant furniture. Perhaps Jenny Rydén was rich? But where had she got her money from? He decided it was probably the man with the close-cropped hair who'd had the money to buy all the furniture and all the toys.

He took an immediate dislike to Rydén. He thought about Samuel, who'd never had any money all his life.

He would tell Jenny to hang up the photograph of Samuel again. Not just now. But before he left them and went to sea.

Instead of mentioning the photograph, he said something that wasn't true.

"Samuel sends his greetings. He didn't mean to hurt you. He sometimes says things he regrets afterwards."

"Oh, I know all about that! But it suddenly became too much for me."

Perhaps it became too much for Samuel as well, Joel thought. After all, more than ten years had passed without him even knowing where you lived.

They'd returned to the living room. The girls were with them all the time, but said nothing. They never took their eyes off Joel.

"I hope you're hungry," said Jenny. "We'll be eating shortly."

Joel said he was looking forward to that.

"There's one thing I've often wondered about," she said. "Who did the cooking for you and Samuel? I ask because I know Samuel is hopeless when it comes to preparing food. At least, he was in those days."

"Oh, it varied," said Joel tentatively.

"Maybe Samuel has a girlfriend?"

"Occasionally."

Joel had no desire to go any deeper into that question. Least of all did he want to tell her that he'd been his own mum all those years since she'd left them. And how angry he'd sometimes been at the mother who'd run away.

They had dinner in the kitchen. Joel sat at one short end of the table, opposite Jenny. The two sisters were still shy. Joel tried to think of something to say. But most of the time he was thinking about Samuel, who was by now lying on a bench in a train compartment, resting his head on his suitcase.

He hadn't packed any food to take with him for the journey. He'd be hungry all the time until he got home. Even if there was a restaurant car on the train, it was bound to be far too expensive.

Joel had to acknowledge that he had a guilty conscience. He shouldn't have accepted the money. At the very least he ought to have thought of buying something for Samuel to eat on the train.

Jenny had lots of questions to ask. And Joel answered them all. About how things had gone at school. And why he wanted to become a sailor like Samuel. Joel answered very tersely. He felt under pressure. Already he was thinking about finding a job on a ship as soon as possible.

It was beginning to get late.

The girls started getting ready for bed. Joel thought they were making a terrible din in the bathroom. But Jenny didn't seem to hear anything. Joel sat in the living room while they prepared for the coming night. Then Jenny came to ask him if he would like to accompany her to the girls' room and say good night.

He didn't want to; but he did even so.

"I expect you're probably tired," said Jenny when all was quiet in the sisters' room.

Joel wasn't the least bit sleepy, but he wanted to be left in peace. After all those years without a mum, it was a bit much to suddenly find her hanging around all the time.

"Yes," he said. "I think I'll go to bed."

"When you wake up tomorrow I'll probably have left already."

She gave him a front door key.

"The girls are with a neighbor when I'm at work. So you don't need to worry about them."

That was a big relief. The mere thought of having to be with them for a whole day was enough to make him want to run away.

"What are you going to do tomorrow? Will you be able to find your way round Stockholm?"

"I have a map. I'll manage OK."

He had snuggled down into bed and was just about to switch off the light when she knocked on the door and came in.

"There's so much I want to know," she said. "And no doubt there's lots you want to know about me. We'll have to give it time."

Joel mumbled something inaudible. He wanted her to leave. He couldn't cope with any more now.

She said good night and left the room.

The whole flat was soon silent.

Joel lay thinking about Samuel.

He missed the snoring that had always come rumbling into his bedroom through the walls.

Joel was on his own now. Although he had Jenny Rydén and two little sisters not far away.

But it was Samuel who wasn't there. That was what really mattered.

When he woke up next morning, the flat was quiet and empty. Outside, it was overcast but not raining. Joel had breakfast and changed into some clean underwear.

Then he went out.

When he came to the Seamen's Employment Exchange, the waiting room was full of people. All of them were seamen. They included a few boys who couldn't have been any older than he was himself. That worried him a bit. Perhaps all the boats were fully manned by now? Perhaps there wouldn't be a job for him?

When it was his turn he went to the desk and asked if his seaman's discharge book was ready yet.

It was!

It was dark blue. And had his name printed on the front. He felt as if he were already standing on deck. He could feel the floor swaying under his feet. He felt so happy.

He was forced to sit down so as not to lose his balance.

"Your first time?" somebody asked.

"Yes," said Joel.

The one who asked had a freckled face and bright ginger hair.

"They'll be calling up soon now," he said.

Joel didn't understand what he meant. Who would be calling up? Calling up what? But he didn't ask.

The explanation came almost immediately.

A hatch in the wall opened. A man with a sweaty face waved a few sheets of paper in the air.

"Electricians for *Neptun*. A bosun, an engineer. The engineer must be experienced. A steward for *Lindfjord*. And a deckhand. That's all for today. We'll be calling up again at ten tomorrow morning."

Some of those waiting stood up and went to the desk. Others muttered in disgust and headed for the door. Joel understood what happened now. He would be back the next day at ten o'clock.

He could be a deckhand. Or a steward.

His excitement was tangible.

The man with the sweaty face was holding the whole world in his hands.

The waiting room slowly emptied. Joel stayed behind. He leafed through some of the magazines lying on a table. There were adverts for various shipping lines. What a lot of ships! Carrying cargoes of coal and iron ore, bananas and oil.

He was just about to leave when the hatch opened again. The man with the sweaty face stuck his head out and looked round. He was just about to close it again when he caught sight of Joel.

"What job are you looking for?" he shouted.

"I want to be a sailor," said Joel.

"That's the daftest thing I've ever heard. Why else would you be sitting here?"

The man waved a sheet of paper at Joel.

"There was one more job going," he said. "The paper had fallen on the floor. The MS *Alta* is looking for a mess steward."

Joel held his breath. Thoughts were racing through his head. A mess steward only went on deck in order to empty rubbish bins. He served meals in the mess, did the washing up, made beds and cleaned out cabins. Like a chambermaid in a hotel.

"I assume you're not interested," said the man, and started to close the hatch.

"I'll take it," Joel shouted.

The next moment he was standing by the hatch and produced his discharge book.

"She'll be docking at Värtahamnen tonight. Be there tomorrow morning at eight o'clock. Ask for the chief steward."

"Who?"

The man behind the hatch opened Joel's discharge book and nodded.

"Your first voyage, I see. Go on board and ask for the chief steward. His name's Pirinen. He's a Finn. But he speaks Swedish. Go and see him. If he likes the look of you, you come back here and sign on. Is that clear?"

Joel nodded.

He was handed the sheet of paper, and the hatch closed.

Everything had happened so quickly that he'd hardly been able to keep up.

First he'd been given his seaman's discharge book. And then he'd got a posting the very first day.

What kind of a ship was it, this MS *Alta*?

Joel hesitated. Then he knocked on the hatch. It opened immediately.

The man was wiping the sweat from his face with a piece of newspaper.

"Are you still here?"

"I just wanted to know what kind of a boat it was."

"Grängesberg line."

"Where's it sailing to?"

The man behind the hatch sighed deeply.

"How the hell do I know? But it's an iron ore freighter. So it'll be going to a port where it can load up with iron ore. And then it will sail to another one where it can unload."

Liberia, Joel thought. Africa.

He remembered what Geegee had said.

So it was the same shipping line as the MS *Karmas*.

"Anything more you want to know? We're about to close now."

"No," said Joel. "Nothing else."

The hatch closed once more.

Joel went out into the street.

His first thought was to tell Samuel about it. But that was impossible. He was still on a train somewhere on his way north.

Joel felt extremely excited.

All the ships he'd ever dreamt about had faded away.

Now there was a real one. A ship called the MS *Alta*, at this very moment heading for Stockholm.

Joel set off walking. Slowly at first, then faster and faster.

On the way to Östgötagatan he bought a picture postcard

and a stamp. When he came to Jenny's flat he found a pen and sat down at the kitchen table.

He wrote to Samuel.

I got my seaman's discharge book today. And I've got a job. On a ship called the MS Alta. I'm off to sea now. See you on Pitcairn Island.

Greetings, Joel

He wasn't sure about the last sentence.
See you on Pitcairn Island.
Maybe Samuel would think he was being provoked? But he left it anyway. They'd talked about that so many times, after all. Sat poring over sea charts and looking for the little dot in the middle of the Pacific Ocean. Where Fletcher and his men had gone into hiding after their mutiny against that cruel Captain Bligh.

That was what he'd written. It could stay as it was.

He ran down the stairs and into the street, and soon found a postbox. He read through what he'd written one more time. Then he popped the card into the box.

Jenny and his little sisters came back together. Joel was lying on his bed in the little room behind the kitchen, and heard their voices. He went to the living room and greeted them. Then he told them what had happened.

"I'll be signing on tomorrow. I'm afraid I won't be able to stay any longer."

Jenny sat down on a chair. She seemed disappointed.

"So you're leaving already?"

143

"Yes."

"Where are you sailing to?"

"Africa. Liberia."

"As far away as Africa?"

"Or Oxelösund. Nothing is certain. It depends where the cargoes are. And where they have to be taken to."

"You must know if you're going to Africa or Oxelösund, surely?"

"I'll probably be going to both places. And Belgium as well."

Jenny shook her head. Then she burst out laughing.

"You're just like Samuel. He was always going to either Rio de Janeiro or London. And I never knew where he'd come from."

"You know how it is, then," said Joel.

The two sisters stood and listened but said nothing. They gaped wide-eyed at their big brother.

"If it is Africa, I'll bring a present back for you," said Joel. "A monkey skin or something like that."

"Good Lord, no!" said Jenny. "I wouldn't want that. Not a monkey skin. Anything at all but that."

That evening Jenny and Joel sat up for ages, talking. Time had turned out to be so short. But when Joel finally went to bed and switched off the light, he could hardly remember anything they'd said.

All he could think about was the next day.

I'll have time to think about Jenny later, he told himself.

I've found her now. That's the main thing. And I've got two little sisters—who kick up a hell of a row in the bathroom.

But what all that means is something I can think about later.

The first thing I have to do is to walk up the gangway onto the ship that at this very moment is on its way to Stockholm to pick me up.

And the next day, shortly before eight o'clock, Joel got off the tram and saw the ship that had berthed during the night. The MS *Alta* was bigger than the MS *Karmas*. The hatches were just being opened. Joel could feel his heart pounding. Then he went through the dock gates and approached the gangway. The side of the ship towered above him like a mountain. He went on board.

A sailor wearing overalls came towards him. He gave Joel a friendly smile.

"Are you going to sign on?"

"Yes."

"Deck or mess?"

"I'm going to be a mess steward."

"Our new Kalle, then. He was good, the one we had before you. Apart from the washing up—he wasn't much good at that."

The man looked Joel in the eye.

"Can you wash up?" he asked.

"Yes," said Joel. "That's about all I can do."

The man pointed towards the stern of the ship.

"Pirinen will no doubt be back there, drinking coffee with the cook. I assume he's the one you have to see."

Joel walked slowly in the direction the man had indicated. He was so high up above the water.

He took a deep breath. As if to convince himself that what he was doing was true.

Then he went to meet Pirinen. And was duly approved and signed on. That very same day he moved into his cabin.

Jenny wanted to take the girls with her and have a look at the ship. But Joel said no.

If it had been Samuel, that would have been different.

He started work the following day. He was disappointed to discover that the ship would be staying in Stockholm for a whole week. Nobody knew which would be their next port. Somebody said Narvik. Somebody else said England. But nobody knew. It would be some days before they found out.

And Joel worked. He laid tables and washed up, cleaned and made beds. He got to know the ship and the people working on it. And every night he collapsed into bed exhausted.

They eventually discovered where they would be sailing to. Joel was disappointed. Their destination would be Luleå.

The far north of Sweden, he thought. Even further north than the place where Samuel and I have been living all those years.

Nevertheless, he was on his way at last.

He was woken up at four in the morning by the vibrations from the engines. He could hear the mooring ropes being cast off. Then the propeller rumbled into action.

The journey had begun.

— TWELVE —

In Luleå Joel bought a notebook with a black cover.

That same day he started his logbook. His first entry was dated June 17.

> *Arrived Luleå.*
> *Perhaps it was good that my first voyage brought me here.*
> > *You can't get any further north.*
> > *Now I have to sail south.*
> *Luleå. June 17, 1959. 8:35 p.m.*

He'd made up his mind to write something every day. It didn't need to be much. But there would have to be at least one word, a date and a time.

He also posted two letters in Luleå.

The first was to Samuel. He explained how he'd collected his discharge book and the very same day signed on with his first ship. He described the vessel, how it was 20,000 tons, and that he was currently in Luleå.

He hoped that Samuel's journey home had gone well.

He promised to write from his next port of call, and included the unused half of his train ticket in the envelope.

If Samuel wanted to write back, he knew what he needed to do. The letter should be addressed to the shipping line.

The other letter was to Jenny Rydén.

That was more difficult to write. He tore up several attempts. In the end he didn't have the strength to write any more, and so his latest effort would just have to do.

He asked her to hang the photograph of Samuel up again. Assuming he was right in thinking she'd taken it down. If she didn't do that, he would never visit her again.

But he gave her an alternative. If she didn't want to have Samuel on her wall, instead she could remove the picture of the man with the close-cropped hair. Then there would be two marks on the wallpaper.

He wondered how she would react. She might be angry? Perhaps she wouldn't want to see him ever again? Well, he'd just have to take that risk.

And so Joel's life at sea got under way.

The ship sailed from Luleå to Middlesbrough. They docked at first light. Joel was standing on deck, gazing at this foreign country swathed in mist. It was the first time he'd ever been outside Swedish territory. They'd had fine weather all the way. The North Sea had been dead calm.

That evening, Joel went ashore with a deckhand by the name of Frans, who was from Gotland. Frans had been a sailor for two years already, and had been to Middlesbrough before. He knew the dockland district. Joel drank two pints of beer in a pub, and got a splitting headache. By the time they had to go back to their ship, Joel had fallen asleep over the table. The following day, when he was woken up at six o'clock, he was sick.

He'd got used to the work by now. The days were humdrum. First of all he had his own breakfast. Then he set the tables and served twenty-four meals in the mess where the ordinary sailors ate. There were two other messes. But the one where the captain, the mate and the chief engineer ate was called the wardroom, and the steward there was called a wardroom steward. After breakfast, Joel's work was to wash up and then clean out the cabins. He had a few hours' free time in the afternoons, and then worked again until eight in the evening.

He had a cabin of his own. That had surprised him. In the days when he'd dreamt about becoming a sailor, he thought everybody slept together in a big dormitory. He realized that a lot of what Samuel used to talk about no longer applied in modern times.

His cabin wasn't very big. It had a bunk fixed to the wall, a washbasin, a wardrobe and a chair. And a porthole.

It seemed to him that he'd never had better living quarters in the whole of his life. The engines throbbing away deep down inside the ship rocked him to sleep.

They stayed in Middlesbrough for a whole week. On Saturday Joel accompanied several of the other crew members to a nearby city called Sunderland, where they watched a football match.

Every day was different.

Something new was happening all the time.

They left Middlesbrough and headed for Narvik. Northwards again. But Joel had decided to be patient. This was his first ship after all. An iron ore trader. He would begin by getting used to life at sea. Then he would apply for work on other types of boats. He had plenty of time.

The second night on the North Sea, Joel was woken up by being tossed around in his bunk. A wind had blown up. He could feel his stomach reacting already. But he forced himself to go back to sleep. It would have blown over by morning.

But in fact it was gale-force winds when he woke up. When he staggered out of bed, he had to cling on to the wardrobe door so as not to fall over.

The rest of the day was a nightmare. Joel alternated work with throwing up, had to watch plates of food falling onto the floor and sliding around, and he began to wonder why on earth he'd ever wanted to go to sea. Samuel had talked about being seasick. But this was something far worse than he'd ever imagined. He spoke to the cook, whose name was Axelsson and who was holding on to the stove to remain upright while he was frying the potatoes, and asked how long it was going to go on like this.

"Oh, it'll last all the way to Narvik. But it'll blow over eventually."

Joel stared at the potatoes sizzling away in the fat—and only just managed to get to the nearest toilet before throwing up again.

That evening he was so tired that he collapsed into bed without even bothering to get undressed. He was dreading the next morning.

Joel was seasick until they were well into the fjord at Narvik. Then, at long last, he could feel it ebbing away.

He was never seasick again.

He was one of the lucky ones who had the ability to get used to it. But Frans had stories about a bosun he knew who'd suffered from seasickness for over forty years.

• • •

The weeks passed by.

Joel found himself in Narvik four times. And then Bristol, Middlesbrough again, Ghent, and eventually Holland. A port close to Amsterdam.

Frans had been to Amsterdam before. One evening he told Joel a series of stories that Joel suspected were made up. About women sitting in windows and offering themselves for sale. A whole district full of women sitting in windows. Joel refused to believe that it was true.

"You go there and see for yourself," Frans said.

Joel made up his mind to do just that. When they came to Holland, Pirinen gave Joel a day off. So he went to the telegraphist's office and cashed in two hundred kronor of his wages. This was the first time he'd taken out money. He'd never had so much money in his hand before.

The intention had been that Frans would go with him to Amsterdam. But Frans wasn't allowed shore leave as there was some essential work to be done that needed his presence. So Joel had to travel alone.

He'd decided that now was when it was going to happen.

He'd written in his logbook:

We're sailing through the Kiel Canal. It's high time I took the step from Sonja Mattsson to something more. August 22, 1959. 7:44 p.m.

Joel took the train.

Frans had told him that the women who sat in the windows were in a district close to the Amsterdam central railway station.

When he got there, he consulted a timetable in order to establish when the last train left for the harbor where his ship was berthed.

Then he stepped out into Amsterdam. He was nervous. He didn't know what was in store. Frans had tried to explain it to him. He ought to walk around, have a good look at all the windows, and choose a woman he fancied. Then they'd let him into a room at the back of the house. He'd have to pay first. Frans had kept stressing how important that was, over and over again. First the money. Otherwise he might find himself confronted by some frightening character who'd been sitting in another back room, listening to the radio.

First the money, Joel thought. He had it in his pocket. The telegraphist had paid him in Dutch guilders.

Joel hadn't a clue about what would happen next. He was worried that he wouldn't be able to cope. And he wasn't at all sure what it was that he'd be expected to cope with. She might throw him out if he did it wrong.

But obviously, he hadn't mentioned to Frans that this would be his first time. Or that he was worried.

He had a suspicion that it would be easier if he'd had something to drink. Not too much. Just enough to banish his nerves. So he went to a bar next to the station. He had a beer. Only one. His body felt warmer already. When he left the bar, he found his way to the red light district. There were a lot of people in the streets. Lots of sailors, just like him.

And then there were all the women.

Frans hadn't exaggerated.

They were sitting on chairs in brightly lit windows, with fixed expressions on their faces. Just like tailors' dummies.

Joel felt both nervous and sexually excited. He hardly dared look at the women. Most of them were half naked and heavily made up. Some were smoking. Joel paused at a window where lots of other men were already standing, and took a good look. He could hide in the background there.

Then he went to a bar and ordered a whiskey. Frans drank whiskey. Nothing else. Joel forced it down.

Samuel would have swallowed it in a single gulp, Joel thought. No doubt Samuel has also been to this very same place.

Who would he have chosen?

Joel decided to drink another whiskey. That would have to be enough.

He paid and left. Now he felt bold enough to stand in front of a window all by himself.

But how would he be able to choose?

He wished there had been a girl who looked like Sonja Mattsson. But he couldn't see one. He moved on. The lit-up windows came to an end. He was just going to retrace his steps when somebody spoke to him from out of the shadows. He couldn't see who it was at first. Then a woman appeared in front of him. She hadn't come from one of the brightly lit windows, but Joel had no doubt she was one of the same type. For sale. She spoke English. Said how much it cost, and pointed into the shadows. Joel could just make out the outline of a door.

She couldn't have been more than twenty-five. Like Sonja Mattsson. She had brown hair and wasn't as heavily made up as the women Joel had seen in the windows.

She took hold of his arm.

Joel thought he ought to make a run for it.

But instead he accompanied her into the shadows.

There was a steep staircase behind the door. She ushered him up it, in front of her.

What the hell am I doing in here? Joel thought.

They came to a room where there was a bed with a red cover. A radio could be heard in a neighboring room.

She sat down on the bed and stretched out her hand.

He gave her the money she'd asked for.

Then she started to unzip his trousers.

Then she took off her own green trousers. Joel just had time to see that she was wearing nothing underneath before she pulled him down on top of her on the bed. She hadn't removed the cover.

He wasn't at all sure what happened next. He was aroused. Then it was all over almost before it had started.

It all happened so quickly, he was rather confused. She pulled him up off the bed, gave him a tissue to wipe himself with, and urged him to take care when he went down the stairs.

"Be careful," she said. "Be careful."

Then she vanished into the room where the radio was on.

Joel pulled up his trousers and stumbled out onto the staircase.

Once he was out in the street again, he asked himself what had happened. It was nothing like he'd imagined it would be.

Even so, he knew exactly what he was going to write in his logbook.

Amsterdam.
Done it at last.
August 24, 1959. 10:10 p.m.

He went back to the railway station and found the right platform. Shortly before midnight he found himself walking up the gangway again.

Frans was standing by the rail, smoking.

"Well," he said. "How did it go?"

"Good," said Joel. "Bloody good."

Then he went to his cabin before Frans had time to ask any more questions. But he could hear Frans chuckling to himself by the ship's rail.

The days passed. Joel was still waiting for a message: next destination, Liberia. But it was still Narvik and Bristol and Ghent. In the middle of September they also undertook a voyage from Narvik to Luleå. It took fourteen days. Joel began to lose faith. By the end of November he began to wonder if he ought to sign off this ship and try one from another shipping line. One that didn't only fill its holds with iron ore.

All this time Joel had only received one letter from Samuel. It had arrived at the end of October. Samuel wrote that all was well, but not much more than that. Joel had a suspicion that things weren't as good as Samuel claimed. How was he managing on his own? Who was cooking for him? Had he remembered to put cold water in the dirty porridge pan?

What worried Joel most of all was if Samuel was drinking heavily. Who was keeping an eye on him when Joel wasn't around?

Joel had almost made up his mind to sign off. But then came the message he'd been waiting for: the next voyage would be to Liberia. They would be there for Christmas. Joel didn't hesitate for a moment. This was what he'd been waiting for. Once he'd been to Africa, he would sign off and pay a visit to Samuel.

He wrote to both Samuel and Jenny. She had written him several letters, but she'd never referred to Joel's request that the photograph of Samuel should go back up on the wall. Or that the man with the close-cropped hair should be taken down.

Joel had never referred to that again. Soon enough he would be able to see with his own eyes what had happened, if anything.

He wrote about the forthcoming voyage.

The journey to Liberia.

The journey to the end of the world.

Joel arrived in Africa the day before Christmas Eve, 1959. The African coast could be seen like an enticing mirage on the port side of the ship. Every morning when Joel woke up, it was warmer than the day before. And the sea changed color. It became lighter. The blue gradually turned into green. He saw dolphins and flying fish. Every evening he stood at the stern of the ship and looked up at the starry sky.

On December 20 he wrote in his logbook:

I sometimes think about that dog. The one I thought I saw that time. On its way to a star. But I was only a child then. I didn't know any better. Here everything is just as bright and sparkling as it is at home in midwinter. December 20. Just south of the Cape Verde Islands. 10:22 p.m.

They stayed in Liberia for four days.

Joel went ashore whenever he was free. He wandered around in the teeming mass of people, breathed in all the unusual smells, and was fascinated by the beautiful women carrying extremely heavy burdens on their heads. He bought some shells for his little sisters, a colorful loincloth for Jenny and a drum for Samuel. On Christmas Eve he wrote in his logbook:

Liberia.
I know now that I've done the right thing. A sailor is what I'm going to be. On my next ship I'll be a deckhand. One day

I might start to study in order to become a bosun. After Christmas, I'll go home and collect Samuel. He's forgotten what it was like. I shall remind him. December 24, 1959.

While they were berthed in Liberia, Joel also fell in love.

Every time he went ashore, a young girl came up to him and asked if he needed anybody to wash his clothes. He said no. But she was persistent and came back every day. Her name was Milena. And she was sixteen years old.

They used to speak on the quay. Always the same thing. But Joel thought she reminded him of Sonja Mattsson, despite the fact that she was very black.

The day before New Year's Eve they weighed anchor and headed north. Milena stood on the quay, waving. Joel had given her some money as he'd realized she was very poor.

Pirinen was standing beside him at the rail, smoking.

"When will we be coming back here?" Joel asked.

Pirinen grinned. He'd seen Joel waving, and Milena waving back.

"Never," said Pirinen. "Forget her."

But Joel had no intention of forgetting Milena. And he knew that what Pirinen had said wasn't true. Pirinen could be annoying at times. But Joel had learnt how to deal with that.

Their next port of call after Liberia was Narvik. Joel had decided to sign off at the end of January. By then he would have saved nearly a thousand kronor. It was time to pay Samuel a visit.

But when they got to Narvik, and the heat of Africa had become a distant memory, he found a letter waiting for him. The telegraphist gave it to Joel just after he'd finished washing up after breakfast. It was from Samuel. Joel recognized the spidery handwriting.

He went to his cabin, lay down on his bed and opened the letter.

It was very short. Not many words. But Joel would never forget them.

Joel,

I hope all is going well for you on the Alta. I hope the trip to Africa was a great experience. I think it would be best if you came home now. You'll remember that I had stomach pains last summer. They've become worse now. It's not possible to say what will happen. So perhaps it would be best if you came home.

Samuel

Joel felt as if he'd been punched in the stomach.

So Samuel was ill.

He recalled what he'd thought at the hotel, when Samuel came back from the hospital.

Samuel might die.

He started to panic. He would have to go to Samuel straightaway. He couldn't put it off. But he couldn't just abandon ship and leave his work just like that. There were rules about how much notice you had to give before handing in your discharge book and asking to sign off.

I need to speak to somebody, he thought. Pirinen? He wouldn't understand. The telegraphist? He wouldn't be able to do anything.

Joel got up from his bunk. He would speak to the captain. Captain Håkansson.

He was often gruff and angry, but that couldn't be helped. Joel left his bunk and walked up the stairs to the bridge. If the captain wasn't ashore, he'd be bound to be in his cabin.

Joel knocked on the door.

"Come in."

Joel opened the door. Captain Håkansson was sitting at a desk, writing. He frowned.

"I'm busy," he said.

Joel could feel that he was in danger of bursting into tears.

"It's my father," he said. "He's very ill."

Joel held out the letter. Captain Håkansson beckoned to him.

Then he stared hard at Joel, who could feel the tears in his eyes.

"I don't want to read a private letter you have received," said the captain, "but I can see from your face that it's true."

"I have to go home," said Joel.

The captain nodded.

"I'll fix it," he said curtly.

He stood up.

"I'll have a word with the chief steward and the tele-graphist. Prepare to leave by this evening."

"Thank you," said Joel.

"I've had good reports about you," said the captain. "You do your job well. Never any problems."

He nodded towards the door. The conversation was over.

That same evening Joel boarded the night train to Sweden.

— THIRTEEN —

It was late when Joel got off the train that winter evening.

And it was very cold. The thermometer hanging on the station wall showed minus 31 degrees Celsius. Joel pulled his scarf over his mouth and nose. He was the only one to leave the train. The stationmaster waved his flag and withdrew to the warmth of the staff rooms.

Joel was all alone. He had bought a sailor's kit bag in Narvik. Inside it were his clothes and the presents he'd bought in Liberia.

He set off walking. He took the old road by the river.

He didn't know how many times he'd walked or cycled along that road. But now it felt like the first time ever.

He was in a hurry. During the long journey from Narvik he had felt his unease growing all the way. He must have read the letter from Samuel at least a hundred times. In order to grasp what it meant. He'd tried to convince himself that Samuel was drunk when he wrote the letter. Drunk and lonely, in a kitchen full of burnt saucepans. Joel had to go home now in order to clean up and wash the dishes.

But Samuel would never write a letter after being out drinking. So Joel tried to convince himself his father was exaggerating. That might be a possibility. Samuel sometimes imagined that he was more ill than he really was.

But deep down, Joel knew. He'd known even in the hotel in Stockholm, the moment Samuel came in through the door.

Samuel was so ill that he might die.

Joel walked as fast as he could. The cold air was scratching at his lungs.

He suddenly stopped in his tracks.

What if Samuel was dead already? Or was in hospital?

He set off again even more quickly. He was on the hill now. He'd soon be able to see the house. See if there was a light on in the kitchen.

The road was deserted. Snow was piled high on both sides.

There was nobody else about.

Another twenty meters and he'd be able to see the house. He increased speed even more, despite the fact that he really wanted to stop.

But now he could see the house. And there was a light on in the kitchen.

So Samuel wasn't dead. And he wasn't in hospital.

He was at home.

Joel slowed down. He needed to prepare himself now. What was in store for him? What would Samuel say when Joel suddenly appeared in the doorway, stamping the snow off his boots? Joel hadn't been able to inform Samuel that he'd be arriving that very evening.

He went through the gate and into the garden. Past where he'd slept in an old bed one night a year ago. When he'd resolved to live to be a hundred, and had started to toughen himself up. He shook his head. He'd never do anything like that again. He opened the door and listened. As he did so it occurred to him that he ought to have knocked. Samuel wasn't expecting visitors. He might think it was a burglar.

He went into the kitchen. The door of Samuel's room was half open. The radio was silent. But the light was on.

He put his kit bag on the floor. The sink was empty, he noticed. No sign of any burnt saucepans. Or empty bottles.

He took off his woolly hat and mittens, and approached the door.

Samuel was in bed.

He was awake, and looked at Joel.

He smiled.

"So you've come?" he said. "I thought you would. But I didn't know when."

"I came as soon as I got your letter," said Joel.

There were bottles of medicine on the bedside table. And Samuel was pale. Unshaven and pale. Although he was under the bedclothes, Joel could see that his dad had lost weight. He hasn't been eating enough, Joel thought. Perhaps he hasn't been eating properly since he got back home.

Pools of water started to form round Joel's boots.

"I'll just take my boots off," he said, and went to the kitchen. He pulled out his usual chair. It scraped against the floor. He recognized the sound.

When he'd taken off his boots and jacket he went back to Samuel's room. He sat down on the edge of the bed.

"You're growing bigger and bigger," said Samuel.

"I'm five foot eleven now," said Joel.

"That's taller than I am."

Silence.

"I got your letter," said Joel.

Samuel pulled a face.

"I had to write it," he said. "But we don't need to discuss that now. How long do you intend staying?"

"I don't know."

"We can talk about that tomorrow."

He always wants to put everything off, Joel thought. Samuel Gustafson has never come straight to the point. The whole of his life has been an elaborate detour.

"I'm not really sure if there's any food in," said Samuel apologetically. "In case you're hungry."

"I'm not hungry."

"You can take a look in the pantry."

"I'm not hungry."

"But I've made your bed. As I knew you'd come to see me."

That was an important piece of information, Joel thought.

It means he's not so ill that he can't stand on his own two legs.

"I got your letter," he said again.

"I had to write it."

We can sit here like this all night, Joel thought, saying the same things over and over again. I ask and he answers, and we get nowhere.

"We can wait until tomorrow," said Samuel. "You must be tired."

"We can't wait until tomorrow at all. I want to know how you are."

Samuel nodded.

Joel waited.

"You remember last summer," Samuel began.

"I remember."

"At the hotel. How I had stomach pains. And then all that hospital business."

"They were going to send you a letter."

163

Samuel paused again.

Joel was so frightened that he was trembling.

They were nearly there now. The reason why Samuel had written that letter.

"They sent me a letter," he said slowly, as if every word was the result of a big effort.

"What did it say?"

"That things weren't all that good. The tests they'd done. They said I should go to the hospital here and show them the letter. So I did. I showed it to one of the top doctors. He said I had cancer. In my liver. And that it was incurable."

There was a thudding in Joel's head. Samuel was dying.

He wasn't trembling anymore. He was completely calm.

"It was incurable," Samuel said again. "So now I'm here in bed. I can't go to work. I just lie here."

Joel didn't know what to say.

"Who does your food shopping for you?" he asked in the end.

"Sara's arranged for somebody to buy me the basic necessities. And a nurse comes to see me every other day. But I'll probably have to go into hospital soon."

"Are you in pain?"

"Not much. Not like it was in Stockholm."

He produced one of his skinny hands from under the covers and pointed at all the tubes and bottles.

"They've given me some excellent medicine. That sorts everything out."

"But you said it was incurable?"

"I mean it deals with the pain."

"What else did they say?"

"There wasn't much more they could say. If it's incurable, that's that."

"Are you going to die?"

Joel wished he could have eaten his words.

But strangely enough, Samuel only laughed.

"I'm not going to die," he said. "Not while you're here at home, at least. You can still go on living even if you've got something incurable. I actually think I've been feeling better these last few days. It might go away, even if it is incurable."

"Yes," said Joel.

"For God's sake," said Samuel. "People go on living even if they have no arms or legs. It would be a poor show if I couldn't go on living without a liver. Don't you think?"

Was that a real question? Or was Samuel convinced that he was right? Joel didn't know.

And so he merely nodded.

He agreed. With whatever it was that Samuel thought.

Samuel was trying to raise himself into a sitting position.

"There must be something to eat," he said.

"I'm not hungry."

"But you must want a cup of coffee, eh? And then I want to hear all about what you've been doing."

"That can wait until tomorrow."

Samuel sank back into the pillows.

"You're right," he said. "That can wait. I'm a bit tired."

"Can I get you anything?"

Samuel looked at his glass.

"A drop of water. That's all."

Joel took the glass to the kitchen. Perhaps it's possible to live without a liver. Joel didn't understand why you needed a liver. And where was it? In the stomach somewhere?

When he'd given Samuel his glass of water, he went back to the kitchen and unpacked the drum. It was quite small. The skin was brown, and the drum was a hollowed-out piece of tree trunk.

Samuel put on his glasses and examined it carefully.

"It's terrific," he said.

He tentatively tapped his fingers on the skin.

"Sounds good," he said. "A real drum."

Joel wondered why he'd bought it. Why on earth had he bought Samuel a drum? Couldn't he have thought of something better?

"Perhaps I can learn to play it," said Samuel. "Become a drummer in my old age."

"I'd thought of buying you a monkey skin," said Joel. "But I didn't get much time on shore leave."

"A drum's fine," said Samuel. "I've always wanted a real African drum."

Joel knew that wasn't true. It was just Samuel's way of saying thank you.

Joel put the drum on the floor.

"I want to know everything tomorrow," said Samuel. "But I think I'd better go to sleep now. All this medicine makes me sleepy."

"We'll talk tomorrow," said Joel.

"I lie here thinking," said Samuel. "When I can't sleep, it's as if the house were a ship. And I can hear the anchor being lifted, and the house sails out of the harbor."

He shook his head.

"Funny how childish you can get sometimes."

Joel stood up.

"I hope you can get some sleep."

"I'm glad you've come. We can talk more tomorrow."

"Yes, we can talk tomorrow."

Joel went to his room.

Everything was still there. The bed, the table, the chair, the alarm clock, the roller blind. Just the same as when he'd left it. It felt as if that was a long time ago. He lay down on top of the bed. There was a creaking and knocking in the wall beside his head. The cold was singing in the wooden beams behind the wallpaper.

Joel tried to understand the situation. Samuel was incurably ill. But he thought he might be able to go on living even so. He didn't seem to be afraid. If you're going to die, surely that must instill fear? Joel couldn't imagine any other possibility.

He listened for Samuel's snores. But everything was totally silent.

So Samuel has had the same dream as I had, Joel thought. He's dreamt that the house was a ship. That casts off and floats down the river towards the sea. This flat is the bridge. Captain Samuel Gustafson. First Mate Joel Gustafson. A father and son who can steer the ship through the worst hurricanes imaginable.

That was a remarkable thought for Joel. That he and Samuel had experienced the same dreams. They'd both transformed this ramshackle, rickety old house into a ship.

Joel got up and tiptoed into the kitchen. Samuel had switched off the light. The door was ajar, just as Joel had left it. Samuel still hadn't started snoring. But Joel could hear that he was asleep. His breathing in the darkness of his room was deep and heavy.

Joel crept up onto the window seat. It was barely big enough to hold him now. A streetlight illuminated the deserted road. It was minus 32 degrees now. Midwinter. Joel shuddered. And thought about Liberia. And the girl who had waved to him.

Before he knew where he was, he had fallen asleep. When he was woken up by cramp in his leg, he had no idea where he was. Then the penny dropped. And he could hear Samuel snoring.

I must find out if you can go on living with a liver that's

incurably damaged, Joel thought. That's the very first thing I need to do.

Joel woke up the next morning and heard Samuel clattering away in the kitchen. He investigated and found Samuel making porridge. But he hadn't got dressed. He was wearing his old dressing gown over his pajamas.

"Cold water in the pan," he said with a smile.

Joel couldn't believe that Samuel had a life-threatening illness. Perhaps it was incurable. But was it life-threatening?

When they'd finished breakfast Samuel wanted to talk about what Joel had experienced during his first months as a sailor.

"I'll tell you all about that later," said Joel. "I have a few things I must see to first."

It was still very cold when he left the house. He set off up the hill to the hospital. There were several people about now. But he didn't see them. He burrowed his chin down into his jacket, and walked as fast as he could. But after a while, he paused. Why was he going to the hospital? There were easier ways of finding out what a liver was. He turned round and started retracing his steps.

He didn't stop until he'd come to the slaughterhouse, on the very edge of the town. He'd worked there as an errand boy a couple of summers ago. He knew the boss and several of the slaughtermen. He stamped his feet to shake off the snow and went into the office. The boss was called Herbert Lundgren, and had a freckled face despite the fact that he was nearly sixty. He was wearing a white coat and a peaked cap.

"Joel?" he said. "I heard you'd gone to sea?"

"So I have. I'm just visiting."

Lundgren frowned.

"I heard that Samuel was ill. How is he?"

"He's fine. But that's why I've come. I want to know what a liver is."

"A liver?"

"Yes. Where it is, and what it does."

"Why do you want to know that?"

"Samuel's liver is damaged beyond repair."

Lundgren said nothing.

"But Samuel thinks he can carry on living even so."

"Maybe he can," said Lundgren slowly. "I'm not a doctor. I don't really know about such things."

"Where is your liver?"

Lundgren pointed to the side of his stomach.

"That's all I wanted to know."

Joel put his woolly hat back on, and started wrapping his scarf round his face.

"There's one thing you ought to be clear about," said Lundgren.

Joel looked at him.

"What's that?"

"Oh, nothing. Nothing at all."

Joel left the slaughterhouse. It was getting light now. The sun was just beginning to rise above the fir-covered hills that surrounded the little town. He wondered what Herbert Lundgren had been going to say. But Samuel will no doubt pull through, he thought. It takes more than this to knock out an old sailor like Samuel Gustafson.

He went to Ehnström's grocery store and bought a few things. It was Mrs. Ehnström who served him.

"Joel," she said. "I thought you were at sea?"

"I'm just visiting. Samuel is ill."

"So we heard. Poor man."

"He'll be all right. It's just something about his liver that's not as it should be."

"No doubt he's drunk too much over the years. That's how it goes."

Joel could feel himself getting angry. Samuel's drinking habits had nothing to do with Mrs. Ehnström.

"It affects the liver."

"Samuel feels better now," said Joel angrily. "Potatoes, please. And jam."

His anger lasted all the way home. But when he got as far as the kitchen door, he heard some mysterious noises coming from inside. At first he couldn't understand what it was.

Then he realized.

Samuel was playing the drum. He was tapping his fingertips on the brown skin.

He's not going to die, Joel thought. A man who gets out of bed in the middle of winter in order to play an African drum can't possibly be so ill that he's going to die.

Joel coughed and stamped his feet to dislodge the snow. The noises from the kitchen ceased abruptly. Joel waited for a few seconds before opening the door.

Samuel was sitting in his usual place at the table.

He'd shaved. And he was smiling.

"I'm so glad you've come home," he said. "We've a lot to talk about. I feel much better already."

That evening they took out the old sea charts again.

Joel had made the dinner and then done the washing up. Samuel didn't eat much. But he said he thought the food was very good.

They finished off the meal with a cup of coffee. And Joel talked about his travels. He said nothing about that evening in Amsterdam. But he did tell his dad about the girl who wanted to wash his clothes in Liberia.

At no time during the evening did Samuel ask about Jenny. Nor did Joel mention her. If Samuel didn't want to know, that was up to him.

It started to get late.

"I've been thinking," said Samuel. "I think it's time now. For me as well."

Joel couldn't believe his ears. Had Samuel really made up his mind? Did he really have to be struck down by an incurable illness before realizing that it was high time he put away his saws and axes?

"Are you serious?"

"I've never been more serious in all my life. As soon as I feel a bit better, I'll sign on again."

"Maybe we can both work on the same ship?"

"Then it won't be long before we go ashore on Pitcairn Island."

"How long will it take? Before you're better?"

"Not very long."

"A month?"

"At most."

"What about the incurable illness?"

"It doesn't show."

Joel could still scarcely believe that it was true. It was as if he could hear a distant foghorn sounding inside his head. A foghorn warning all ships enveloped by the mist.

That feeling he'd had at the Raven Hotel. And the letter.

Samuel is so ill that he's going to die.

But Joel banished the thought.

Samuel really did seem to be better now than he'd been the night before.

It was turned midnight when Samuel went to bed. Joel stayed up a bit longer at the kitchen table, poring over the sea charts.

Then he went to bed as well.

The next day he'd start writing to other shipping lines.

A few hours later he was dragged out of his slumbers by an unfamiliar noise. He opened his eyes in the darkness and wondered what it was.

Then he froze stiff.

It was Samuel.

He was sitting in the kitchen, crying.

— FOURTEEN —

That night Samuel told Joel the full facts.

He would never be able to sign up on a ship again. The illness he was suffering from would never go away. Nor could he count on it getting any better. When Joel appeared in the doorway with his sailor's kit bag, Samuel had felt that despite everything, things could go back to normal. But when he woke up in the night, he couldn't indulge in make-believe any longer. He would never sail to Pitcairn Island. The only journey he would make in the rest of his life would be to the hospital.

Joel didn't feel afraid. He had gone along with Samuel's dream of everything turning out all right because that was easier than facing the difficult realities. Now he felt relieved. Knowing the facts.

Samuel was going to die. No matter how odd that seemed.

Joel felt helpless. And angry. It was unfair that Samuel had fallen ill. Why couldn't it have been somebody else instead? Everybody had a liver. Why should it be Samuel's that had gone wrong?

There was an invisible word that was never mentioned that night. Death. Neither of them wanted to say it. But they both knew what they were talking about even so.

"I try not to think about it," said Samuel. "So as not to be frightened. It's true that I always make a mess of shaving, and I've done some silly things in my life. But nobody will be able to say that I'm afraid."

During the night they also spoke about Jenny.

It happened out of the blue.

"I don't regret what I said to her. But there again, I'd like you to know that I can understand her. She was never suited to life up here in the forests. She was never suited to life with me. She thought I was different from the way I am. And the same applied to the person I thought she was. I know I'm not easy to live with. What with all my peculiar habits."

Joel had made some more coffee. He gave Samuel a refill.

"But you know all about that, of course," said Samuel. "That I'm not so easy to live with."

Joel said nothing. He had nothing to say.

"I think that you and Jenny can be good friends," said Samuel. "And nothing makes me more pleased than that."

Samuel lifted his cup of coffee, but as he did so the pain came back. He grimaced with pain.

"I think I'd better go and lie down," he said. "You don't need to help me. I'll manage. And you need to get some sleep as well."

Joel remained in the kitchen. He didn't even go to sit on the window seat. His head was empty. Various images were hopping around. Totally without context.

After a while he got up and trudged back to bed.

I'll never be able to sleep again for the rest of my life, he thought.

Then he fell asleep. With the covers over his head.

174

．．．

When he came to look back, Joel would recall Samuel's last days as the most remarkable he had ever spent with him.

Samuel was cheerful, even exhilarated. He talked about his life in a way he'd never done before.

Joel knew that adults were often odd, but it had never occurred to him that they could also be odd when they were going to die.

Samuel practiced playing the drum every day. Morning and evening. And they spent hours poring over sea charts. Samuel told stories about all the ships he'd sailed in. And about all the ports he'd visited.

Joel did the shopping and the cooking. And the cleaning. He went to see Sara at the bar where she worked, and told her that nobody needed to go to help Samuel now that he was at home. She had tears in her eyes, but Joel hurried away before she started crying.

The only person he wanted to speak to was Gertrud.

But he didn't even go to visit her. It was as if he wanted to be in peace with Samuel.

After a few weeks Samuel became so ill that he had to go into hospital. Neither he nor Joel had expected it to go as quickly as this. Now Samuel was in a room with four beds. His pains came and went like breakers on a beach. They had taken the sea charts with them to the hospital, and continued their make-believe voyages.

They laughed often and a lot, sometimes so loudly that a nurse came to see what was going on.

But sometimes they were serious as well.

"You can ask Göransson to help you," Samuel kept saying. "When it comes to sorting out the flat and its contents."

Göransson worked for the logging company. He was Samuel's boss. He sometimes came to visit Samuel in hospital. And Sara visited him as well. Even Ehnström came. Ehnström and his wife. But Joel always left the room when they were there. He hadn't forgotten what she'd said that time in the shop.

It was forbidden to consume strong drink in hospital, but Göransson had brought Samuel a bottle of cognac that he took a sip from now and then. It didn't worry Joel. He thought he would almost miss never again having to drag Samuel home when he was drunk.

Joel was alone in the house by the river. Every evening he left the hospital once Samuel had fallen asleep. It was still very cold. It sometimes seemed to Joel that the house was like a sailing ship with all its sails in tatters. Now it was going to be chopped up. Nothing would be left of it.

When he wasn't visiting Samuel, Joel wrote letters to various shipping lines. And all the time he tried to avoid thinking about what was going to happen.

One morning, while he was having breakfast, there was a knock on the door. It was Göransson. Joel offered him coffee. Göransson was a man who didn't beat about the bush.

"I'm sure you know your dad's going downhill. He's not got much longer to live. You're a sensible lad, and I've no doubt you are aware of the situation."

Joel nodded. There was nothing he could say.

"I've promised Samuel that I'll help you. But first I have to know if you want to carry on living in this flat. I've spoken to the owner of the house, and you can stay on if you want to. For the same rent."

Joel didn't answer.

But he had a question:

"Was Samuel a good lumberjack?"

Göransson looked at him in surprise.

"Yes," he said. "Of course he was. One of the very best."

"That's all I wanted to know. And I'm not intending to stay on here."

"What have you thought of doing with the furniture?"

"I don't want it."

"You ought to think about if there's anything you'd like to keep. Then I'll help you to sell what's sellable: we'll have to throw away the rest."

Göransson stayed for nearly an hour. Joel didn't really want to talk about all the things that were going to happen. But at the same time, he was grateful to Göransson for helping him.

When Göransson had left, Joel worked his way through the flat, picking out what he wanted to save.

The sea charts. The photographs of Samuel. And some old letters.

Samuel's discharge book. And the old alarm clock that had always stood by his bed.

But nothing else.

A few days later a letter arrived.

Joel was informed that he could sign on for a ship called the *Rio de Janeiro*. It was on its way from Argentina and was going to a shipyard in Gothenburg where it would undergo repairs. If Joel was interested, they wanted him to sign on at the beginning of March.

Joel was pleased. But he didn't know if he'd be able to.

Nevertheless, he wrote a reply. He spelled out the truth. He wanted to, but he didn't know if he'd be able to.

That same afternoon he told Samuel about the letter.

"That's a good shipping line," Samuel said. "And it sounds like a good boat. Good boats must have a good name. *Rio de Janeiro*. Names don't come any better than that. When do they want you to sign on?"

Joel tried to avoid answering. But Samuel persisted. He wanted to know.

"Of course they told you that. You can't fool me."

"The beginning of March," Joel mumbled.

Samuel lay for a while without speaking.

"The beginning of March," he said eventually. "And it's the beginning of February already."

The last evening of Samuel's life, he'd got it into his head that he wanted to play cards. Joel had brought him a pack of cards. Samuel was in an unusually good mood, and wasn't in pain.

They played poker. For fantasy money.

Samuel bet a million. And Joel bet a million as well. But neither of them could work out who'd won.

In the end, a nurse came and told Joel it was time for him to go home.

"We'll continue tomorrow," said Samuel. "Then I'll win back all the money I've lost."

"But you were the winner!"

"Well, we'll see if you can beat me next time, then."

Joel was still sitting on the chair at the side of the bed.

"I used to play cards with Jenny," Samuel said. "And we used to have lots of fun. Believe you me. When things were good, they were very, very good. I've never regretted that she was the person who was your mother. It's important for you to know that."

Joel stood up and put on his jacket.

"The cold isn't going to go away," said Samuel. "But it's

warm in Brazil. There's no such place as the end of the world. But there is a place called Brazil."

Samuel died during the night. After Joel had left he fell asleep and never woke up.

Joel was told when he arrived at the hospital the next day. He started crying. But he didn't cry for long.

Instead he thought about the last words Samuel had spoken to him.

There's no such place as the end of the world. But there is a place called Brazil.

It seemed that there might be a secret message hidden in those words. That the end of the world is only a dream. A place that doesn't have a name. That doesn't exist on any map. But Brazil does. You can go there.

They asked Joel if he wanted to see his father.

But Joel said no.

He knew what Samuel looked like. He didn't need to see somebody who no longer existed.

Joel went home. Despite the cold he walked slowly. The first thing he did was to write a letter to the shipping line.

I'm coming.
Greetings, Joel Gustafson

Then Sara turned up. And Göransson. And Ehnström. And some of Samuel's old workmates. Some old men that Samuel used to go out drinking with also came, but Sara threw them out without more ado.

Both Göransson and Sara suggested that Joel should go and stay with them. But Joel said no. He didn't want to.

●●●

That evening Joel crossed over the bridge on his way to Gertrud's house. She must have seen him coming. Or possibly heard him. As he went through the gate she came out to meet him.

"Samuel's dead," said Joel.

"I know."

Joel ought to have known that it wouldn't be news to her. Although Gertrud seldom went out, she knew about everything that happened.

They sat in her kitchen.

He found it difficult to look at her. If he did, he'd start crying. And he didn't want to do that.

They sat in silence. Joel knew nobody as easy to be silent with as Gertrud.

After a while Gertrud asked him to tell her what it was like, being a sailor. Joel told her.

She asked about Jenny.

He had no idea how Gertrud could have known that he'd found his long-lost mother.

Last of all she asked what he was going to do now.

"I've got a ship waiting for me in Gothenburg," he said. "Then I don't know."

"You'll come back here, surely?"

"Why should I do that? When Samuel no longer exists?"

"I exist."

Joel didn't answer. She was right. She was still there. And there were other people he knew and liked.

"You grew up here," she said. "All your memories are here. I'm sure you'll come back."

It was long past midnight when Joel went home.

The house felt empty and spooky. Joel had closed the door of Samuel's room. What he'd have really liked to do was to lock it and throw away the key.

He went to bed. Thought about what Göransson had said regarding the funeral. He wondered if he ought to phone or write to Jenny. But he didn't want to talk to her. So it would be a letter.

Joel sat up in bed.

He'd have to put a death notice in the local newspaper. He'd almost forgotten that.

But what should it say?

Samuel Gustafson
Much loved and missed

Those were not appropriate words. Not for Samuel.

Joel got up and went to sit at the kitchen table. He took out a piece of paper and a pencil. Thought about various possibilities. Then eventually made up his mind.

But when he went to the newspaper office the following day Mr. Horn, the editor, frowned when he saw the text Joel wanted to insert.

Samuel Gustafson
Who has journeyed to the end of the world

"I don't know if we can print that," he said.

"Why not? It's my dad who's dead."

"The text isn't really appropriate."

"Why not?"

Mr. Horn shook his head.

"I don't know if it's suitable."

"But that's what Samuel thought death was. A journey to the end of the world."

Mr. Horn continued to shake his head.

"Have you spoken to the others about this?"

"What others?"

"The other mourners? The rest of the family?"

"There is nobody else. Only me."

Mr. Horn was starting to melt.

"I've never published anything like this before in the deaths column. That's for sure."

"But this is precisely what I want it to say."

Mr Horn looked hard at Joel. Eyed him seriously for a long time. Then he nodded.

"I'll get a lot of flack," he said. "But if that's what you want, that's what you'll get."

When Joel left, he thought that Samuel would have been pleased. He'd never had much time for God. But the end of the world was something else again.

Something that existed, and yet didn't exist.

That was the journey Samuel had undertaken.

The funeral took place a week later.

Joel was dreading it. But Sara and Göransson had been on hand for him all the time.

A few days before the funeral the local vicar, Boman, had asked Joel to come and see him.

Joel put on his best clothes and went to the vicarage. He'd never met Rev. Boman before. He was a new, young clergyman who'd only arrived in his new parish a couple of months ago.

Boman asked Joel to sit down, and expressed his condolences. Joel mumbled something inaudible in response.

"I saw the death notice in the newspaper," Boman said.

"And I understand that you were the one who wrote it. I must say the text was most unusual. *He's journeyed to the end of the world.*"

"Samuel was unusual," said Joel. "That's the way he wanted it."

"How was he unusual?"

"He thought the house we lived in was a ship. And that our flat was the bridge. And he was a good lumberjack. Göransson says so."

"An unusual man," said Boman. "Is that how you'd like me to describe him at the funeral?"

Joel could feel a lump in his throat. He was close to tears, but braced himself.

"Yes," he said. "Samuel was unusual."

And that is what Boman said at the funeral.

There weren't many people in the church. Joel was in the front row, between Sara and Göransson. The coffin was brown. Joel avoided looking at it. He still couldn't grasp that Samuel was lying in there.

Samuel had gone away.
He'd gone on a journey.
He'd signed on for an invisible ship and was on his way to a port that didn't exist on any map.
But perhaps the name of the ship was Celestine?

Samuel's grave was by the west wall of the churchyard.

As the coffin was lowered into it, Joel couldn't stop himself bursting into tears. All the time he tried to cling fast to the idea that Samuel was on a ship on the way to somewhere. On the way to a warmer climate. But despite all his efforts, he couldn't help himself. Not at that moment.

Afterwards they had coffee at the Tourist Hotel.

183

Göransson told Joel that they would have to go through the contents of the flat the very next day. Now that Joel had decided not to stay there, other tenants would be moving in.

It took a week.

The furniture vanished. Joel packed his belongings in his sailor's kit bag and a suitcase.

In the end the only thing left was a mattress. A sheet, a pillow and a blanket. Joel would sleep in the house one final night. Then he would leave.

He said goodbye to Göransson and Sara.

And that last evening, he took a walk round the town.

It was still cold.

He wandered along the familiar streets. Paused outside the Community Center and studied the film posters. Walked round the deserted schoolyard. Round and round until he ran out of strength.

He was in a hurry now. In a hurry to get away.

He went back to the empty flat and fell asleep almost immediately on the mattress.

The night outside was full of moonlight, the sky full of stars.

— FIFTEEN —

Joel woke up with a start.

When he opened his eyes it was completely dark. He felt freezing. It was as if the cold from the floor had forced its way through the mattress and all his clothes. He lay still in the darkness and listened. There was a creaking and tapping from the walls and the roof beams. He thought about all the times he'd woken up and heard those very same noises. They had always been there, ever since he'd been very young. So young that he had virtually no other memories.

He pulled the covers up to his chin and curled up. The alarm clock was standing on the floor next to him. The hands were lit up. A quarter to five. Half an hour from now the clock would ring.

He could feel a pain in his stomach. Something was stabbing at him. It was his very last night in the house by the river. His last night and his last morning. He was about to leave. New people would move in that very same day. They would bring with them different furniture, and hang different pictures on the walls. Then there would be no trace left of Samuel or Joel. Time would pass. Other voices would be heard in the two bedrooms and the kitchen. Other fingers would make marks on the wallpaper. Other ears would be woken up during the cold winter nights by the beams groaning and creaking inside the walls. Soon nobody would remember that a lumberjack and his son had once lived in this house.

That hurt. The idea was massive and scary. Joel curled up as tightly as he could.

He wished everything had been as before. That Samuel's snores would come rolling through the half-open door. But everything was silent. Apart from the walls groaning and creaking in the cold.

When he was little, he'd sometimes thought that it was possible to bring time to a standstill. To cling on to a moment he'd enjoyed. But that wasn't possible any longer. Joel wondered what exactly it meant, being grown up. Before, he'd have asked Samuel. But that wasn't possible anymore.

Nothing would be like it used to be. Nothing at all.

I'm so lonely now, Joel thought.

Samuel is dead. And Jenny Rydén can never be my mum. She can only be a friend. In the same way that Eva and Maria can only be my friends.

In a few hours' time I shall leave this place.

Nobody will come to the station to wave me off. Nobody will notice that I vanish.

Joel could feel that he was starting to cry. He didn't want to do that. He was fifteen years old, and a sailor. Somebody like that doesn't cry. Children can cry. And adults. But not somebody who's fifteen years old. That's an age when it's forbidden to give in to anything. Especially tears.

Joel listened. The walls creaked. He allowed the thoughts and memories to wander through his mind. He'd always lived in this house. Once upon a time Mummy Jenny had lived here as well. But one morning she packed a suitcase and went away. He'd been so little at the time that he didn't remember it happening. The only person around for the whole of Joel's life had been Samuel. Nobody else. Samuel with his drooping shoulders and badly shaved cheeks, his tired eyes and his longing for the sea.

Celestine had always been there as well, in her case. And the sea charts over which they had made their fantasy voyages together.

Joel wondered if Samuel had ever really believed that he would go to sea again. Or had it only been an impossible dream? From the very start? Joel didn't know. And now it was too late to find an answer.

Everything that had existed before was now too late. Samuel was lying in the churchyard. He would never speak to anybody again. His voice was dead. Samuel with his badly shaved cheeks. And his drooping shoulders.

Joel made another attempt to understand. What exactly did it mean, being dead? How long would anybody have to be dead? A thousand years? Or longer? He thought the worst thing about it was having to be dead for such a long time. What existed before you were born didn't count. But afterwards, when your life was over, what existed then? Samuel hadn't merely gone out for a short walk. He was lying under the ground, and would be dead so long that nobody knew how long that would be. Or perhaps there was no end?

He noticed that the pain in his stomach was getting worse now. He got up and folded up the blanket. He felt very uneasy, but there was nothing he could do about that. It was a bit easier if he moved about. He wrapped the blanket round his shoulders. He went to the kitchen, then clambered up into the window seat. It was a cold night. The single streetlight lit up the snow-covered road. Everything was motionless. The only thing moving was invisible time passing. Somewhere out there in the darkness and the cold, a new morning was waiting.

Joel suddenly recalled that night when he'd been sitting on the window seat and seen a solitary dog walking away down the street. That was a lot of years ago. But he'd never managed to forget that dog. He started to think about it yet again. Where had it been heading for? For a whole year Joel had run a secret society whose only task was to look for that secretive dog. Then he hadn't thought about it for quite a long time.

But now it was as if the dog had returned.

He strained his eyes. He felt certain that the dog would come running out of the darkness on silent paws. From the opposite direction. To say goodbye. He could feel his heart starting to beat faster. But the road was deserted.

Joel stood up. The light from the streetlamp shone into the kitchen. He shuddered. Now all he wanted was to get away as quickly as possible. The empty flat scared him. The walls were no longer creaking. It seemed as if they were howling.

Perhaps a house was capable of grieving as well? Perhaps the walls were howling over the loss of Samuel? Samuel who was now lying under the ground and would never come trudging up those stairs again. Joel folded the blanket and quickly fastened his boots. He'd put the alarm clock on the kitchen table. He thought he could see the marks made on the wall by the case containing *Celestine*.

Then he found himself in two minds.

It was still far too soon to go to the station. But he didn't want to stay in the flat. He picked up his suitcase and his sailor's kit bag and walked down the stairs for the last time. He hesitated on the last step. How many times had he walked up and down these stairs? How many times had he run? He

188

didn't know. But he could still remember how proud he'd been when he cleared the whole staircase in three enormous leaps.

Then he raised his foot. The last step. For the last time. There was no going back now. It was as if he were opening a new door, at the same time as the door to his childhood slowly closed, creaking all the way.

When he'd locked the front door he removed his mitten and pushed the key under the door.

It was cold. He pulled up his scarf to cover his mouth and nose. What should he do? Wander round the old streets one last time before heading for the station? He didn't know.

But as he passed through the gate and entered the street, he made up his mind.

He would go to the railway bridge. If there was one place he ought to say farewell to, it was the bridge and the river.

He hurried down the street and turned off down the hill leading to the bridge. He was walking alongside the railway lines. There was an old, rickety platform where the milk churns used to stand. He hid his suitcase and kit bag behind it. Then he started running so as to keep warm.

He had the feeling that there were several boys running alongside him. A full gang, in fact. It was really himself at different ages. He felt that he was surrounded by what he used to be.

He paused when he came to the abutment. He was alone again now. His ghostly companions had left. The arch of the bridge loomed high over his head. He couldn't resist the temptation to place one hand on the freezing cold iron. The chill penetrated him immediately. He shuddered.

At that very moment it occurred to him that there was one person he ought to say goodbye to. Gertrud. Noseless Gertrud who lived in her strange house on the other side of the river. But something held him back. No doubt she was asleep in bed. Besides, he didn't want to say goodbye to her. It was as if he wanted to cling on to something. Something that linked him with this little town. Something that would give him an obligation to come back. Not just to plant a palm tree on Samuel's grave, but also to meet Gertrud and say goodbye properly.

To prevent his feet from getting too cold, he sprinted over the bridge. He didn't stop until he came to Gertrud's house.

The light was on in her kitchen. He stopped outside her gate. Remembered the time when he and Ture had hacked open a frozen anthill and then thrown the bits into her kitchen through the window. He slowly opened the gate and crept up to the window. The snow creaked under his boots. He raised himself on tiptoe.

The kitchen was empty. Gertrud sometimes left a light on when she went to bed. She was bound to be fast asleep now. He tiptoed further along the wall until he came to her bed-room window. When he pressed his cheek against the windowpane he could hear her snoring. But how could some-body without a nose snore? He regretted the thought.

He ought not to think like that about Gertrud.

Despite everything, she was one of the few friends he had.

He didn't know where the feeling came from.

But all of a sudden he had been transformed into the loneli-est person in existence. He thought he could step outside himself and observe himself from a distance. In the middle of the night, in the freezing cold. A boy aged fifteen standing next to a window and listening to somebody snoring. He felt the urge to cry. He left the scene. Ran up the hill, over the bridge, and didn't stop until he got back to his case and his kit bag.

He was bending down to pick them up when he noticed tracks in the snow. They weren't his own. Something else had been there.

A dog.

He straightened up and looked round.

He tried to spot it in the cold moonlight. But there was no dog to be seen. He started to follow the tracks. They led down to the river. The snow was deep. He had to plow his way through it. But he knew now that the dog had returned. The dog that had once been heading for a distant star.

It had returned in order to say farewell.

He forced his way through the thick bushes on the bank of the river. The tracks led straight out onto the frozen river. He tried to spot the dog in the moonlight. He carefully made his way onto the snow-covered ice. The effort had made him sweaty. But there was no way he could turn back. Not now when he was so close.

The paw marks in the snow were very clear. Before long he was a long way out onto the ice. The arch of the bridge loomed up like an enormous animal crouching by his side.

And then the tracks came to an end.

Joel looked round. He didn't understand what he could see. Absolutely clear pawmarks that suddenly petered out. There was no hole in the ice. Nothing but an expanse of white, virgin snow.

He looked up at the night sky and turned his back on the moon. There was only one possible explanation, he thought. An explanation that somebody who has reached the age of fifteen shouldn't really believe in. That the dog had taken off and flown away on invisible wings. Heading for the star he'd selected to be his goal.

I must be childish to believe that such a scenario is possible,

Joel thought. Now, when my father's dead and I'm a sailor, I can't be childish any longer. Even if I am.

Joel turned and went back to the riverbank. He paused once, turned round and gazed up at the sky.

The dog was somewhere up there, flapping its invisible wings.

Joel retrieved his suitcase and his kit bag and walked through the deserted little town. When he came to the station, he found that the waiting room was still locked. He put his bags behind a dustbin and walked out onto the tracks. Stood between the rails and gazed southwards. He was in a hurry now. Not long ago he'd have liked to put time on hold. Now it was passing far too slowly. He was in a hurry to get away.

Somebody eventually came and unlocked the waiting room. Joel went in and sat down. He could feel the warmth returning to his body. He checked his inside pocket, to make sure he had his rail ticket and his discharge book. And in his pocket was his money. Eighty kronor.

An old man with a rucksack came into the waiting room and sat down. He nodded a greeting to Joel.

"Off on a trip, are you?" he said.

Joel mumbled something inaudible in reply. He had no desire to talk to anybody just at the moment.

"I'm going to Orsa," said the old man.

"I'm going further than that," said Joel.

"Are you going to Mora?"

"I'm going to the end of the world," said Joel.

The old man looked thoughtfully at him.

Joel stood up and examined the map hanging on the wall. He found Gothenburg. And the harbor. And the shipyard. And the ship that was waiting for him.

The train arrived. The engine snorted and sighed. Joel scanned the platform before boarding the train, but needless to say, there was nobody there to wave goodbye to him.

Only Samuel's ghost. Standing there nodding to him, and whispering:

"Off you go."

As the train passed over the railway bridge Joel contemplated his reflection in the frozen windowpane.

He was on his way now. On his way at last. Away from the little town he'd grown up in. On his way to Pitcairn Island. To the end of the world.

That existed and yet didn't exist.

Three days later, shortly before dawn, the cargo ship *Rio de Janeiro* left Gothenburg. Joel woke up in his cabin when the engines started to throb.

It was late winter, 1960.

During the next few years Joel signed on with several different ships. At the beginning of 1963, a few days before his eighteenth birthday, he worked on a little cargo boat that docked at Pitcairn Island.

While on shore leave, he collected a coconut from a coconut palm.

At the beginning of December that same year, he returned to Sweden and made the long trip back to the little town where he was born.

In the evening of December 4 he got off the train and made his way straight to the churchyard. He dug away the snow and planted the coconut in the frozen soil on Samuel's grave. He knew it wouldn't survive, so he also spread out a few palm leaves he'd brought with him from Pitcairn Island.

•••

The following day Joel left the little town.

He'd spent the night in a boardinghouse.

He didn't pay a visit to Gertrud in her house on the other side of the river.

When his train left the station, there was nobody there to wave goodbye to him this time either.

His childhood was over.

Joel had begun his long journey out into the world.

And somewhere up there, over his head, there would always be an invisible dog flapping its invisible wings.

TOWARDS A NEW AMERICAN POETICS:
ESSAYS & INTERVIEWS

Charles Olson

Robert Duncan

Gary Snyder

Robert Creeley

Robert Bly

Allen Ginsberg

Edited *by* Ekbert Faas

Black Sparrow Press : Santa Barbara : 1978

LIBRARY OF CONGRESS CATALOGING IN PUBLICATION DATA

Faas, Ekbert.
     Towards a new American poetics.

     Bibliography: p.
     1. American poetry—20th century—History and criticism. 2. Poets, American—20th century—Interviews. 3. Poetics. I. Title.
PS325.F3   811'.5'409   78-1559
ISBN 0-87685-389-0
ISBN 0-87685-388-2 pbk.

For my wife Barbara

Prefatory Note

As a general rule, the following essays were completed before the interviews and, to allow for a double perspective, left unchanged even where my findings seemed to be at variance with the poets' responses. At the same time I am deeply aware of the debt I owe Robert Duncan, Gary Snyder, Robert Creeley, Robert Bly and Allen Ginsberg for the many new insights which have given final shape to this study. The Preamble, in particular, tentative as it may be in trying to map the groundwork for the following sections, could hardly have been written without the liberal education I have continued to enjoy since my first talks with Duncan and Snyder in the summer of 1973.

I should also like to express my gratitude to the *American Council of Learned Societies* for supporting my 1972-4 research period in New York City, to the *Canada Council* for generous financial support, to Diana Gay of the Poetry Collection at SUNY, Buffalo, for helping me with the bibliographical work, to Seamus Cooney for his fine editorial advice and, finally, to Barbara Lecker for her help and encouragement all along the way.

E.F

Contents

Preamble   9

Charles Olson
   Essay   39

Robert Duncan
   Interview   55

Gary Snyder
   Essay   91
   Interview   105

Robert Creeley
   Essay   147
   Interview   165

Robert Bly
   Essay   203
   Interview   223

Allen Ginsberg
   Essay   249
   Interview   269

Bibliography & Abbreviated References   289

PREAMBLE

Poetic inspiration, as Lu Chi recognized ca. 300 A.D., must take its own course:

> When it comes, it cannot be checked;
> When it goes, it cannot be stopped.

(Li,T,73)*

Far from being an imitation of nature, art embodies the "resonance or vibration of the vitalizing spirit and movement of life" (*ch'i-yün shêng-tung,* Si,A,21-2), and by its spontaneous self-realization comes as a surprise even to those who are creating it. According to one Chinese painter-critic, "there is no knowing how it will take shape . . . it always goes when it should go and stops when it has to stop" (Bu,L,35). "When I begin to paint," comments another, ". . . I entirely forget that it is myself who holds the brush" (Ch,C,204). "How is the impersonality of the [cosmic] Creator any different from this?" asks a third (Bu,L,39).

Of course, the artist uses craft. But only in order to turn himself into a perfect medium for the self-expression of the life-force (*ch'i*) which breathes in him as in nature. Thus it may take a painter years to learn how to trust his hand (*hsin-shou*) before his brush-strokes turn into "obedient servants to the spirit of his object" so that the latter "makes its own picture" (Su,M,32). Yet the aim of this disciplined spontaneity is the very transcendence of craft. "[H]e who, when writing a poem, insists on its form, is surely far from being a poet," wrote Su Tung-p'o (Ch,C,210). And whatever forms the poem will assume organically as an extension of its contents, must, as Tung Yu wrote, emerge "like the unfolding and blooming of leaves and flowers" (Bu,L,56).

The final aim of such art is an approximation of *śūnyatā*, the ultimate "void of inexhaustible contents" (Su,M,28), and a reenactment of its cyclic emanations. A literary composition, writes Lu Chi,

---

* For an alphabetical list of the bibliographical abbreviations used in the Preamble and in the following essays, see BIBLIOGRAPHY & AB-BREVIATED REFERENCES at the end of this study.

is "created by tasking the Great Void, / . . . 'tis sound rung out of Profound Silence," while at the same time being "the embodiment of endless change" (Bi,A,207,209). Yet there are few artists like Ni Tsan (1301-1374) or Wang Wei (699-761?) who have left unquestionable evidence of such enlightenment. For most, the pursuit of literature and art is simply "a vehicle of the Way" *(wen yi tsai Tao)* which, besides the notion that poetry expresses "the intent of the heart [or mind]" *(shih yen chih)*, is the most widely quoted principle of Chinese poetics (Li,T,69,114). And the Way is as long as the mind is deep, comprising, as Buddhist philosophers knew long before Carl Jung, not only the personal "mind-system," but the huge memory storehouse of the "Universal Mind" in which "discriminations, desires, attachments and deeds" have been collecting "since beginningless time" and which "like a magician . . . causes phantom things and people to appear and move about" *(Laṅkāvatāra-sūtra,* Go,B,300). Lieh Tzu has given striking testimony to what may happen to the quester-artist somewhere along the middle of the Way. After nine years of study, he writes, his self

> both within and without, has been transformed . . . My eye becomes my ear, my ear becomes my nose, my nose my mouth. (Ch,C,87)

No wonder that Chinese poetry, long before our own, managed to cover the full spectrum of human consciousness from the rational mind through the subconscious towards mystical illumination. The following lines by Li Ho (791-817) give an example of the middle realm with its wondrous phantasmagoria:

> When the wind brushes the cassia leaves and a cassia seed
>   drops
> The blue racoon weeps blood and the cold fox dies.
> Dragons painted on the ancient wall with tails of inlaid gold
> The God of Rain rides into the autumn pool;
> And the owl a hundred years old, which changed to a goblin of
>   the trees,
> Hears the sound of laughter as green flames start up inside its
>   nest.[1]*

All this may strike a familiar chord to the unprejudiced observer of twentieth century art and help rectify the distorting perspective of those who continue to define art as *"form created by a human, intellectual act"* (E. Kahler) or criticism as a concern "with the problem of

*Notes for this section on p. 33.

unity—the kind of whole which the literary work forms or fails to form" (Cleanth Brooks).[2] Yet even though we may ignore a non-Western body of æsthetics like the Chinese, there is no reason why modern poetry, for instance, should continue to suffer Procrustean mutilations at the hand of critics who, in slavish adherence to such obsolete Aristotelian concepts, simply reduce their study objects, say, to the first 84 of Pound's *Cantos* or to the first four books of Williams' *Paterson*.[3] Pound's life-long quarrel with critics clamoring for symmetry, plot and form, or Williams' comment "that there can be no end to such a story as I have envisioned" in *Paterson* (W,P,7) ought to be sufficient caveats against such critical malfeasance. Pound and Williams may have failed to provide traditional Western æsthetics with a full-fledged alternative for the interpretation of their own works. But something close to it seems to emerge when their workshop poetics are placed within the wider context of similar theories by other poets, artists and composers or when they are viewed through the perspective of Olson, who as Pound's and Williams' disciple brought this evolving new æsthetics in progress to its most comprehensive synthesis to date.

These developments which, in Olson's phrase, point towards an open form art no longer of "mimesis but [of] kinesis" (O,W,148) are the subject of a previous study[4] to which the present volume is a sequel. As open-ended as its predecessor, it attempts to graph several further evolutions of the new art by focusing on some of its major practitioners amongst American poets. The opening essay on Olson, an adapted version of the previous volume's concluding chapter, should map some of the groundwork supporting the subsequent interviews and monographs. This additional preamble may help clarify several further premises, trace connections to recent American poetry in general, survey the individual sections on Duncan, Creeley, Snyder, Bly and Ginsberg, and hint at some possible future developments.

In terms of obvious simplification, the new art and æsthetics may be said to reflect a non-anthropocentric, a-teleological and frequently monistic understanding of life. As such it in many ways seems closer to notions like the classical Chinese ones referred to above than to the orthodox thought patterns of our post-Aristotelian and Judæo-Christian heritage. This is not to invoke the mouldy cliché of a marriage between East and West but rather the concept, held by Robert Duncan, of multiphasic modern man as he emerges into a global culture for the first time in history. Present-day æsthetics is an eclectic hybrid of the primitive and civilized, the old and new—a constantly widening conglomerate made up of scrappy bits of information ranging from quantum mechanics to Shamanism or biology. And the forces behind its ever changing patterns, which have caused the most drastic reorientation of Western art since its beginnings, are all the more elusive as they are unprecedented. Any attempt to locate them—like the effort to describe the house in which we live—will therefore have to proceed not only from within but from without. Primitive culture can throw light on obvious neo-Primitive symptoms in our own, as it tries to reclaim some of the vital primordial powers suppressed by our hyper-rationalist tradition. Yet now that the new art, after its iconoclastic *Sturm und Drang* phase, is apparently coming to rest in a period of self-consolidation, its central notions seem to find more and more analogues amongst the high cultures of the East. The few examples chosen here will also try to indicate the scope of the new æsthetics and some of its immediate origins in our own tradition.

§   §   §

The latter, of course, lie in the Romantic period when the arts, to use Shelley's phrase, arose "as it were from a new birth" (Ab,S,11). Shelley himself unwittingly echoes Lu Chi where, in opposition to a rationalist understanding of the poetic imagination, he likens "the mind in creation" to "a fading coal, which some invisible influence, like an inconstant wind, awakens to transitory brightness." As far as inspiration is concerned, in other words,

> the conscious portions of our natures are unprophetic either of its approach or its departure. (Ab,M,192)

This anti-mimetic, neo-Heraclitean understanding of art as an enactment of *panta rhei,* in which modern æsthetics again resembles the Chinese, has found a succinct formula in D. H. Lawrence's description of poetry as "life surging itself into utterance at its very well-head" (L,C,87). Even this concept, according to which nature finally comes to realize itself to the creator's bewildered surprise (e.g. Jackson Pollock's "When I am *in* my painting, I'm not aware of what I'm doing. It is only after a sort of 'get acquainted' period that I see what I have been about," O'C,P,40), can be traced back to the Romantics. Theoretically speaking, it is implicit in Coleridge's definition of the imagination as "a repetition in the finite mind of the eternal act of creation in the infinite I AM" (Ce,B,167), and at least two English poets, less obsessed with their egos than Coleridge, also bear witness to the total self-abandonment which according to various Chinese literati should accompany this reenactment of cosmic

creativity. Blake wrote his poem *Milton* "from immediate Dictation
. . . without Premeditation and even against [his] Will" while Keats'
own creations often "struck him with astonishment and seemed
rather the production of another person than his own"
(Ab,M,214,215). Keats, whom Olson considered as his most important Romantic predecessor, describes this egolessness of the "came-
leon Poet" as the *"Negative Capability"* by which "he is continually . . .
filling some other Body" (K,L,71,226-7). And anticipating Olson's
"form is never more than an extension of content" (O,W,16), he
finds an image directly reminiscent of Tung Yu's. If poetry, he wrote,
"comes not as naturally as the Leaves to a tree it had better not come
at all" (K,L,107).

Before we reach contemporaries like Snyder or Creeley, painter
Mark Tobey or composer John Cage, we find little genuine mysticism in post-Romantic Western art that could compare with Wang
Wei's or Ni Tsan's translucid approximations of *śūnyatā*. Like
Gottfried Benn, Piet Mondrian or today's minimal artists, Mallarmé,
following his sudden discovery of "Nothingness, which [he] found
without any prior knowledge of Buddhism" (M,E,88), went astray in
a mysticism *à rebours*. For in his coercive attempt to make the ultimate
void of inexhaustible contents reveal itself in his "Sumptuous Allegories of Nothingness" (M,E,92) or "silent poem[s], all white"
(M,Œ,367), Mallarmé only displayed his one-sided and hence erroneous apprehension of the ultimate paradox. Yet long before the
Surrealists, in their *Second Manifesto* of 1930, came to surmise that
beyond their subconscious phantasmagoria there may be a point
from which "the real and the imaginary, the past and the future . . .
cease to be perceived as contradictions" (Br,M,76-7), there was a
"terrible worker" who tried to hew his Way through these subliminal
jungles towards the light beyond. Like today's psychedelic artists,
Rimbaud proceeded by "a long, gigantic and deliberate *derangement
of all the senses*," which resulted in a total transformation of his ego
reminiscent of the surreal experiences recorded by Lieh Tzu:

> It is wrong to say: I think. One ought to say: people think me.
> . . . For *I* is someone else ("Car *JE* est un autre."). If brass wakes
> up a trumpet, it is not its fault.

Rimbaud's new understanding of form as retrieved from the depths
of the "universal soul" ("l'âme universelle") in which he immersed
himself, again anticipates 20th century art theories even as it harks
back to comparable notions which the East has held for centuries: "if
what he brings back from *down there* has form, he gives form; if it is
formless, he gives formlessness" (R,W,303-9). Rimbaud, like his
Chinese peer Li Ho, excelled in both—in the conscious and formally

artistic portrayal of everyday reality as much as in the turbulent poetic enactments of his subconscious fantasies.

§   §   §

Rimbaud along with Keats and many other artists, scientists and thinkers provided some of the mainstays for Olson's theory of projective verse. This major effort of polyhistoric syncretism, as we shall see, draws upon a phenomenal range of information from nuclear physics to anthropology or recently unearthed non-Western sources and combines the practical know-how poetics of Pound and Williams with the visionary insights of D. H. Lawrence. The appearance of Olson's famous essay in 1950 paved the way for the eventual ascendance of the new art and æsthetics over the Eliot-dominated New Critical literary hierarchy which still controls most universities. When Donald Allen, in 1960, assembled the then active practitioners of open form poetry in his influential anthology *The New American Poetry,* Kenneth Rexroth was about the only well-known critic to come to its support, while James Dickey denounced it as presaging "the death of all authentic expression in this generation" (Di,B,6). It was quite another matter, when, nine years later, S. Berg and R. Mezey brought out their *Naked Poetry: Recent American Poetry in Open Forms,* which quietly took its place beside the major anthologies of our time. Excluding Olson and Duncan, the editors were right in feeling "like intruders," and it is easy to guess why they quickly abandoned their "original plan to discuss the theory and practise" of open form. Yet despite such shortcomings, now partly amended by the inclusion of Duncan in the second edition (1975), they were far from wrong in gathering Rexroth, Ginsberg and Creeley under one cover with such poets as Lowell, Wright or Kinnell. In fact, it comes as a surprise that the unofficial poet laureate of the Carter administration is missing from the volume.

For although Dickey has continued to denounce Olson, Duncan and other open form poets and theoreticians, he by 1964 "discovered" the "open," "conclusionless," "ungeneralizing" poem for himself—

> a poem which would have none of the neatness of most of
> those poems we call "works of art" but would have the capacity
> to involve the reader in it, in all its imperfections and im-
> purities, rather than offering him a (supposedly) perfected
> and perfect work for contemplation, judgment, and evalua-
> tion. (Di,B,290)

And when all is said, one has to grant that some of Dickey's poems since *Buckdancer's Choice* (1965) belong to the major achievements of open form poetry in America. Paralleling his recent development Dickey also turned into an ever more active and articulate apologist of the new æsthetics, now denouncing "all marmoreal, closed to-be-contemplated kinds of poems" and instead speaking of poetry as

> a minute part of the Heraclitean flux, and of the object of the poem as not to slow or fix or limit the flux at all but to try as it can to preserve and implement the "fluxness," the flow, and show this moving through the poem, coming in at the beginning and going back out, after the end, into the larger, nonverbal universe whence it came. (Di,S,173-4)

A no less dramatic change marks the career of Robert Lowell, who to many, and in particular to academic critics, has inherited the mantle of T. S. Eliot. What seems like a *volte face* in Dickey's case, however, corresponds to a much earlier and more deep-rooted change of artistic sensibility in Lowell's. Curiously enough, Lowell was one of the first to acknowledge the importance of *Paterson* and in fact, as he tells us, wrote his earliest, unpublished poetry in Williams' manner (Sc,P,258). Influenced by the New Critics, however, he subsequently joined the "university poets" in their long feud with the followers of the older master:

> My own group, that of Tate and Ransom, was all for the high discipline, for putting on the full armor of the past (L,W,535) . . . both Tate and I felt that we wanted our formal patterns to seem a hardship. (Sc,P,244)

His religious conversion at age twenty-three reinforced these formalistic tendencies. "Catholicism," as he said in 1961, "gave me some kind of form, and I could begin a poem and build it to a climax" (Sc,P,260). Thus, "The Quaker Graveyard in Nantucket," the most celebrated of his early poems collected in *Land of Unlikeness* (1944) and *Lord Weary's Castle* (1946), follows a traditional genre, the funeral elegy, with its sequence from exclamations of grief to the *consolatio*, and is formally modelled on Milton's "Lycidas."[5] Yet the final lines with their dogged affirmation of suffering, death and destruction sound like a cry of despair rather than of consolation:

> When the Lord God formed man from the sea's slime
> And breathed into his face the breath of life,

And blue-lung'd combers lumbered to the kill.
The Lord survives the rainbow of His will.

Here as elsewhere, Lowell's early poetry seems to portray the
world of a Christian living in fear of eternal damnation, yet bereft of
all hopes of salvation. The later poetry reads like a secularized
psychograph of this Kafkaesque nightmare or, in Ted Hughes's
words, evokes "a torture cell walled with family portraits, with the
daily newspaper coming under the door."[6] The first hints of such
change are to be found in the "strange autobiographical phantasmagoria" (David Daiches)[7] of *The Mills of the Kavanaughs* (1951). As
the largely confessional content hides under fictitious characters and
localities, so a new creative impulse seems to writhe in the fetters of
the tortuous narratives and monologues. Yet Lowell still clings to
traditional concepts. While acknowledging the existence of these
"amazing new poems" which can absorb everything—"quotations
from John of the Cross, usury, statistics, conversations and newspaper clippings"—he criticizes *The Waste Land* and the *Cantos* for
their lack of "plot and character, just those things long poems have
usually relied upon" (L,B,620).

The mid-fifties, a time crucial for the final emergence of open
form poetry in the wake of Olson's projective verse poetry and
theorizing, was a period of religious and creative crisis for Lowell—
"six or seven years ineptitude—a slack of eternity" (L,IR,12). The
religious outcome is announced on the very first page of *Life Studies*
(1959) which like a sudden windfall put an end to that sterility:

Much against my will,
I left the City of God where it belongs.

The outburst of creativity unleashed by these changes came as a total
surprise to the poet himself. Soon, however, Lowell began to recognize that his own development was part of a much larger one, and
that young poets had grown "more conscious of the burden and the
hardening of this old formalism . . . And once more, Dr. Williams
[became] a model and a liberator" (L,W,535-6). This modest bow
before the older poet, however, should not blind us to the independence of Lowell's own achievement. What the poet tells us about the
actual genesis of *Life Studies* testifies to a period of solitary experiment, trial and error rather than of apprenticeship. Some of the
poems published in the collection were first written in the rhymes
and prosodies of the early style, until Lowell realized that this "regu-
larity just seemed to ruin the honesty of sentiment" (Sc,P,246-7).
And it was not until he temporarily abandoned the writing of verse
in favor of prose that he finally found his new poetic voice. Working

on his autobiography (partly published in *Life Studies*, New York, 1960) and having to write within the crippling limitations of discursive continuity, he was driven back to poetry.

> I found it got awfully tedious working out transitions and putting in things that didn't seem very important but were necessary to the prose continuity. Also I found it hard to revise. Cutting it down into small bits, I could work on it much more carefully and make fast transitions. (Sc,P,247)

The impulse of ruthless self-scrutiny which thus broke the fetters of both traditional prosody and prose also accounts for the influx of a new subject matter into modern poetry.

It is misunderstanding "confessional" poetry to claim that the better poems written in that genre achieve a "fusion of the private and the culturally symbolic" (M. L. Rosenthal).[8] Although such may be the case at times, it is more appropriate to say that confessional poetry is a new phenomenon in Western literary history for the very reason that it allows the privately autobiographical to become the central subject matter of poetry. In contrast to recent confessionalism, Romantic subjectivity was only a springboard towards the absolute, and the demand for sincerity had a claim on those emotions alone which would lead the way to that goal. When private confessionalism began to invade poetry with the breakdown of the Romantic ideal, the poets themselves were the first to denounce it as a degeneration of the earlier mode. This was the case with Browning, who after *Pauline: A Fragment of a Confession* (1833) escaped into more objective genres and, most notably, into the dramatic monologue, which the author could claim contained "so many utterances of so many imaginary persons, not mine."[9] Due to the influence of T. S. Eliot, to whom poetry was "an escape from personality" rather than an expression of it (E,W,58), such prudishness continued to dominate Anglo-American poetry in our century, and it is only since *Life Studies* that the portrayal of one's private agonies and neuroses has ceased to be considered a breach of poetic decorum. Lowell's "Skunk Hour," the celebrated masterpiece of the volume, for instance, gives us the poet's self-portrait as a mentally unbalanced voyeur. Yet out of the "Existentialist night" of his despair the speaker seems to be reaching out for a new religious awareness rooted in life itself. "Somewhere in my mind," the poet recalled later,

> was a passage from Sartre or Camus about reaching some point of final darkness where the one free act is suicide. Out of this comes the march and affirmation, an ambiguous one, of my skunks in the last two stanzas.[10]

Lowell himself has commented on the influence his action painter friends exerted on the writing of *Life Studies*.[11] Yet the full efflorescence of the new impulse they encouraged was yet to come. In *Life Studies* Lowell still hoped "that each poem might seem as . . . single-surfaced as a photograph," and the following collections, *For the Union Dead* (1964) and *Near the Ocean* (1967), only modified and expanded upon the earlier style. The *Notebook* poems, however, mark a new breakthrough:

> Words came rapidly, almost four hundred sonnets in four years—a calendar of workdays. I did nothing but write; I was thinking lines even when teaching or playing tennis . . . Ideas sprang from the bushes, my head . . . As I have said, I wished to describe the immediate instant. (L,IR,14)

It is no wonder then that the publishing history of the book came to resemble that of *Paterson*, which, as Williams recognized after the completion of the four books he had planned, was a "story" he would never finish. In the 1969 edition Lowell still seems to cling to an overall closed conception of the sequence. Yet the inadvertent self-contradictions contained in the "Afterthought" already seem to indicate what was to follow:

> as my title intends, the poems in this book are written as one poem, jagged in pattern, but not a conglomeration or sequence of related material . . . The separate poems and sections are opportunist and inspired by impulse. Accident threw up subjects, and the plot swallowed them—famished for human chances.

What happened during 1969 must have come as a surprise to Lowell just as the writing of *Paterson*, Book V did to Williams. In a "Note to the New Edition," dated January, 1970, the poet admits that his "one poem" had undergone severe changes and expansions. "About a hundred of the old poems have been changed . . . More than ninety new poems have been added . . . I couldn't stop writing, and have handled my published book as if it were manuscript."

Lowell's development, although more dramatic than that of most of his peers, is no less than typical for the majority of contemporary American poets. It would be easy to document similar changes in the work of James Wright, W. S. Merwin, or Sylvia Plath, to name only some of the more important ones. The most obvious indication of the general revolution they bear witness to is the fact that the writing of verse in regular rhyme, meter and stanza has by now almost become an anachronism. Yet however interesting such individual changes may be in signaling the final ascendance of open form poetry, they are less significant than the contributions of poets like those discussed in this volume who in one way or another have devoted their lifework to the pursuit of the new art.

§ § §

Ironically, the artistic conversions of poets like Dickey and Lowell find a diagonal counterpart in an evolving new attitude amongst their previous opponents, many of whom seem increasingly inclined towards a reassimilation of more traditional modes of expression. As Duncan said in a 1969 interview, "I'm not going to take the closed form versus the open form because I want both, and I'll make open forms that have closed forms in them and closed forms that are open" (D,I). Of course, Duncan has always held on to tradition far more than his friend Olson, for instance, or most other Black Mountain poets. But this conservational attitude ("I'm always immensely conservative of everything," as he says, D,I) seems to find numerous analogues in recent statements made by his contemporaries. Denise Levertov's "Some Notes on Organic Form" (1965), for instance, refers back to Hopkins' "inscape," which itself derives from Duns Scotus' *hæcceïtas* principle of individuation as well as from Plato's idealistic philosophy. Both these elements are clearly evident in Levertov's own use of the æsthetic vocabulary provided by her Victorian predecessor:

> Gerard Manley Hopkins invented the word "inscape" to denote intrinsic form, the pattern of essential characteristics both in single objects and (what is more interesting) in objects in a state of relation to each other, and the word "instress" to denote . . . the apperception of inscape. (Lv,P,7)

Equally mimetic rather than projective in its basic metaphysical assumptions is Levertov's concept of "organic form" proper which, as she claims, arises "out of fidelity to instress"—

> a design that is the form of the poem—both its total form, its length and pace and tone, and the form of its parts (e.g., the rhythmic relationships of syllables within the line, and of line to line; the sonic relationships of vowels and consonants; the recurrence of images, the play of associations, etc.). (Lv,P,10)

Less traditional in their philosophical assumptions but equally tradition-*oriented* are recent experiments, or at least speculations about a possible reintegration of rhyme, meter and stanza into open form poetry. Led by Pound's "paradigm tracing the degeneration of Poesy from Greek dance-foot chorus thru minstrel song thru 1900 abstract voiceless page," Allen Ginsberg, as early as 1966, proclaimed a new era of poetry "returned to song and song forms" (B-M,P,221) and recently contributed a whole volume of his own songs entitled *First Blues, Rags, Ballads & Harmonium Songs 1971-74* (1975) to the new development. Similarly, Bly raised the question of how the "sound sensuality" lost by discarding rhyme and meter can be brought back into the open form poem,[12] while Snyder suggested that "using ballad meter and using any of a number of easily available forms surely has its value, just as it's very difficult to sing songs that don't have these forms." Generally speaking, Snyder, like Duncan, has

> no antipathy as such to closed form. Like, anything that works, I'll use. I'm impressed by the fact that almost all the poems that I can remember by heart are poems with regular meters that rhyme.[13]

In their search for the appropriate formal models, poets today, of course, no longer confine themselves to Eliot's claustrophobic concept of a tradition which will only survive by a "continued veneration of our ancestors . . . in the literatures of Greece, Rome and Israel" (E,P,211). No matter where they place their individual emphases, they instead draw on the heritage of world culture comprising Western, Eastern and Primitive. As Duncan puts it, "we are coming from what were once national traditions . . . into . . . a community of meanings . . . A psyche will be formed having roots in all the old cultures" (D,C,17).

It is true that the diverse cultural orientations of poets frequently result in what may appear to be radical disagreement rather than common pursuit. Duncan, for instance, has criticized Snyder for his single-minded exclusion of most of Western culture, or Pound and Olson for ignoring Christianity;[14] Snyder in his turn has called Charles Olson "an apologist for Western culture" (S,IA,111), while Robert Bly, advocating a poetry inspired by Spanish and South American Surrealism, criticized American poets generally for their "elegant isolationism" (B,S,6,22) and the "Black Mountaineers" for continuing to foster the American "formalist obsession":

> The Olsonite poets are always approaching poetry through technique; Creeley is a perfect example. All their talk about technique is academic, and a repetition, in a different decade and different terms, of the Tate-Ransom nostalgia for jails. (B-M,P,163)

Yet more important than such disagreement is the intellectual fervor which inspires it, and which, if viewed without the understandable party prejudice, seems to contribute to a common goal.

For by relating the new art and æsthetics to ever new strands of world culture, each individual poet helps transform the once iconoclastic movement into an unprecedented world poetry deriving its roots from all the various layers of man's consciousness. A major landmark in this direction was *Technicians of the Sacred* (1968) in which Jerome Rothenberg relates, as his subtitle puts it, *A Range of Poetries from Africa, America, Asia & Oceania* to modern poetry, trying to show "some of the ways in which primitive poetry & thought are close to an impulse toward unity in our time." Such ways are the " 'pre'-literate" as compared to the "post-literate" (McLuhan) situation of poetry; "a highly developed process of image-thinking"; an " 'intermedia' situation" whereby poetry operates "through song, non-verbal sound, visual signs, & the varied activities of the ritual event"; the "recognition of a 'physical' basis for the poem within a man's body"; or, most importantly, the notion of the poet as shaman (Rg,T,xxiii-xxiv). Considering the early discovery of Primitive sculpture, this integration of Primitive poetry into the mainstream of Modernism had long been overdue, and as a consequence its impact on American and British poets came to be felt all the more strongly. Many poems from Gary Snyder's more recent work, for instance, would hardly exist without this model, which Rothenberg was quick to reinforce by subsequent publications such as *Shaking the Pumpkin* (1972), containing traditional poetry of the North American Indians, and the anthology *America a Prophecy* (1974), edited in collaboration with George Quasha and subtitled *A New Reading of American Poetry from Pre-Columbian Times to the Present*. Although the first of its kind, this anthology, as the editors themselves seem to realize, is itself only one more step towards the goal which it sets itself in the introduction:

> When we understand . . . tradition as an active force, we are able to make genuine use of the discoveries of archæologists, linguists, anthropologists, historians, and translators . . . The spread of information about the past and the culturally remote has made the present generation, in Gary Snyder's words, "the first human beings in history to have all of man's culture available to our study" and to be "free enough of the weight of traditional cultures to seek out a larger identity." (Rg,A,xxx)

A major contribution to this larger identity was, of course, made by Gary Snyder himself, who in his essays and poems expanded the range of modern poetry to receive the impulse not only of "the most archaic values on earth" but more specifically of Far Eastern art and philosophy. If Eliot called Pound "the inventor of Chinese poetry" for his time (P,P,14), there is reason to pay similar tribute to Snyder in our own. Probably no Western poet before him spent equal time in study and meditation in order to penetrate the secrets of Buddhist mysticism, and certainly no one emerged with similar results. The most obvious sign of this lies in the very fact that Snyder's poems have little in common with most of what is known to us of Far Eastern poetry in translation or imitation. The elliptic terseness of his lines never yields to facile mellifluousness or grace, and especially where Snyder equals the transparent luminosity of a Han-shan or Wang Wei—"going out into emptiness and into the formless" while resting on "an absolute foundation of human experience and insight" (S,IR, 64, 68)—the achievement is the obvious result of an arduous struggle with the insufficiencies of our language:

> The corrugated roof
> Booms and fades night-long to
>
>   million-darted rain
>   squalls   and
>
>   outside
>
>   lightning
>
> Photographs in the brain
> Wind-bent bamboo.
>   through
>
>   the plank shutter
>   set
>
> Half-open   on eternity.
>   (S,W,28)

Robert Creeley, albeit as the result of a totally different development, has achieved a similar fusion of almost pre-conceptual concreteness and mystical luminosity in more recent poems such as "The Moon"—

>   a lovely
>
> bright clarity and perfect

> roundness, isolate,
> riding as they say the
> black sky.
>
>   (C,F,59)

While Snyder's career has been one of single-minded study and
growth within non-Western culture, Creeley's parallels and, in a
sudden transformation during the early sixties, transcends the work
of others such as Mallarmé, Robbe-Grillet, or the minimal artists. A
prose work like "3 Fate Tales" seems to take place in an "eternal *now*"
(Robbe-Grillet, R-G,R,134) or repeatable arbitrariness; the early
poetry—the "poem supreme, addressed to / emptiness" (C,P,29)—
seems to follow a poetics of *"abolition"* and *"élimination"* like that of
Mallarmé who after his sudden 1866 revelation of Nothingness tried
to write the "silent poem, all white." Similarly, Creeley for several
years seemed to work "toward a final obliteration of himself"
(C,G,39), mainly by such means as abstract vocabulary, simple word
repetition, repetitive relocation of phrasing and the faltering staccato movement of his speaking voice, which "despairs of its own /
statement, wants to / turn away, endlessly / to turn away" (C,P,159).

What for Mallarmé remained an aim in itself, however, only
served as a starting point for Creeley. Although

> All [he] knew or know[s]
> began with this—
> emptiness
>
>   (C,F,95)

he gradually came to realize that the latter is ultimately a void of
inexhaustible contents, or, speaking in his own words, that "There
is / a silence / to fill" and that "It is possible, in words, to speak / of
what has happened—a sense / of there and here, now / and then"
(C,W,106,122). "Before a man studies Zen," wrote Seigen Ishin,

> to him mountains are mountains and waters are waters; after
> he gets an insight into the truth of Zen . . . mountains to him
> are not mountains and waters are not waters; but after this
> when he really attains to the abode of rest, mountains are once
> more mountains and waters are waters. (Su,Z,24)

During the sixties Creeley seemed like a man about to enter the third
stage, trying to recapture the 'Small facts / of eyes, hair / blonde,
face" or tentatively positing his own identity: "Here I / am. There /
you are" (C,F,43,53). And before long, figures and objects of an
often unearthly concreteness which now are recorded as a continuous "day book or journal . . . to deal with reality over a man's
life" (C,C,17) began to emerge from the maze of disembodied

abstractions so typical of the poet's earlier mode.

While Creeley gradually came to locate himself, although half unawares, within a specific strand of Western spiritual history, Robert Bly, from his very beginnings, made himself the forceful apologist of another. Surrealism, despite the isolated efforts of a David Gascoyne or a Philip Lamantia, had never been able to hold its own against the overwhelmingly Objectivist orientation of poetry in England and America. This is why Bly, in the late fifties, came to announce that American poetry was cut off from "the greatest tradition of all modern poetry, and the *avant-garde* for a century" which is characterized by "the heavy use of images" (B,F,2,14). Because the "other poetries have passed through surrealism; we have not" (B,F,3,7).

Yet Bly is no follower of Breton and *écriture automatique* and in his own poetry tries to transcend the psychographic one-sidedness of his French predecessors by following the model of such Spanish and South American Surrealists as Lorca and Neruda. Analogously, Bly evolved his Surrealistic mode by writing, not so much about himself, but about the life of his country, which according to his programmatic essay "On Political Poetry" (*The Nation,* April 24, 1967) "can be imagined as a psyche larger than the psyche of anyone living." As in the powerful "Counting Small-Boned Bodies" whose Surrealistic imagery is contained within an obvious rhetorical framework, Bly usually refuses to yield his imaginative control to the autonomous flow of subconscious imagery:

> Let's count the bodies over again.
>
> If we could only make the bodies smaller,
> The size of skulls,
> We could make a whole plain white with skulls in the moon-
>   light!
>
> If we could only make the bodies smaller,
> Maybe we could get
> A whole year's kill in front of us on a desk!
>
> If we could only make the bodies smaller,
> We could fit
> A body into a finger-ring, for a keepsake forever.
>
>   (B,L,32)

Bly's single-minded belligerence in defense of Surrealism and against the "formalist obsession" of American poetry has performed a salutary function, and as his influence increased he started to mellow in his attitude towards others and to adopt elements from poetries he had initially opposed. A recent poem such as "The Teeth Mother Naked at Last" (1973) combines the earlier Surrealism with Pound's fragmentation techniques and Ginsberg's Whitmanesque rhetoric. In 1974 Bly suddenly spoke of Olson as the man who "wonderfully understood . . . that the roots of form go back to the body and its breath" (B,R,33) and in 1972 he hailed Ginsberg whom he had earlier criticized for his "unkindness" or "fear of the unconscious" (B,S,5,70) as "the rebirth of a very powerful spiritual man" and as a fellow traveller in a common pursuit who, unlike Gary Snyder or himself, had gained his access to a new consciousness "not through the Tibetans and Japanese—but through the Hindus" (B,IL,54). Buddhism, from which, as Bly himself said in 1972, he had "learned most" during the previous decade (B,IL,50), played an important role in this development.

In the light of its philosophy, Bly would probably agree that Surrealism and Objectism are complementary rather than opposed to each other, and hence share the attitude which arose from Creeley's earlier "battle against objectivism." As Creeley had explained in a marginal comment to his "Note on the Objective" (1951), sent to Olson shortly before its publication, "to be *objective* . . . MEANS to be so *subjective* that the possession of content . . . is complete enough for the poet to hand over." But he soon realized that his notion of the "*subjective* in a more basic character" was merely, as it were, the photographic negative of Olson's Objectism; or in other words that "subjective" and "objective" are both misleading and obsolete concepts in a description of the new consciousness. As Creeley concluded in the final paragraph of his "Note," it therefore is "perhaps best to junk both terms" and to replace them with a more neutral and monistic vocabulary as in "a man and his objects must both be presences in this field of force we call a poem" (C,G,18-19).

It may well be that Ginsberg and Duncan are the two poets to most reorient open form poetry since Olson. Their joint contribution lies in a new emphasis on those underground Western traditions which are only now, with the help of scholars such as Frances Yates, beginning to assume their rightful place in our spiritual and artistic consciousness. Following their lead it may become possible to relocate within our own heritage what in the iconoclastic theorizing of a Pound, Lawrence or Olson was largely derived from non-Western sources. For "underneath the academic and public traditions of the West," as Ginsberg points out,

> there's always been the esoteric private hermetic stream. Go
> back through the great Western poets—Whitman, Emerson,

Shelley, Coleridge, Blake—back through Boehme, all the way back to Pythagoras who said, "Everything we see when awake is death; and when asleep, dream." This Gnostic transmission ... proceeds originally out of the same middle Eastern consciousness that also travelled into the Orient ... So the whole argument about the Orient being alien to us is in essence silly—and not interesting—because it assumes that Western thought is all hard Jehovah Christ the Church liberal humanism but forgets the more interesting thought. Shakespeare's "our little life is rounded by a sleep" and "we are such things as dreams are made of" is, precisely, the same statement about the nature of suchness, the nature of existence, as the Prajna-paramita Sutra, the "highest perfect wisdom" Buddhist sutra. (G,IO,16-7)

Ginsberg himself admits to having borrowed most of these ideas from a friend who may well be the most erudite among the major poets in present-day North America, Robert Duncan. Duncan is frequently misnamed a follower of Olson despite the fact that even during the latter's most influential period he frequently dissociated himself from the older poet, who himself had expressed suspicion of Duncan's particular areas of interest. In "Against Wisdom as Such," for instance, a reply to Duncan's 1953 self-description as "a poet, self-declared, manqué," Olson referred to Duncan's San Francisco as "an école des Sages ou Mages as ominous as Ojai, L.A." (O,U,67). In his turn, Duncan published a programmatic statement concerning his "radical disagreement" with Olson in *The Black Mountain Review* of summer 1955 (pp. 209-12), acknowledging Olson's criticism ("He suspects, and rightly, that I indulge myself in pretentious fictions") and declaring his own allegiance to the Romantics, particularly concerning the belief "that form is Form, a spirit in itself."

Duncan's concept of his "Romanticism" was well established by the time he first met Olson in 1947. The foster-child in a household of middle-class occultists, he could often, after having been put to bed, hear his parents and their associates from the *Hermetic Brotherhood* in an adjacent room—"speaking in hushed or deepened voices, or speaking in voices that were not their own" (D,T,14). Contemporaneous with Yeats' *Order of the Golden Dawn*, the *Brotherhood* drew its inspiration from a multiplicity of sources: "The theosophy of Plutarch, Plotinus and Pseudo-Dionysius the Areopagite, the hermeticism of Pico della Mirandola, or *The Light of Asia* and the *Bhagavad-Gita*, joined in the confusion of texts and testimonies of libraries that could include accounts written by trance-mediums of travel past time or far planets, manuals of practical astrology and numerology." Thus Duncan "heard of guardian angels and of genii, of vision in dreams and truth in fairy tales, long before Jung expounded the gnosis or Henri Corbin revived and translated the Recitals of Avicenna" (D,S,6). From such childhood impressions Duncan evolved his idiosyncratic sense of a new poetic tradition—an oddly erudite conglomerate of all that was half or totally heretical in the course of Western cultural history.

> From Alexandria of the Roman era, where the master of Yoga and the Zoroastrian mage met with the professor of a god-magicking neo-Platonism; from Spain and the Provence, where, in the eleventh and twelfth centuries, Arab, Jew, and Cathar, mixed a rich culture, producing in the dialectic of its psychology . . . the inspiration of mystics, gothic masons, and two schools of a poetic mystery—the *trobar clus* and the Grail romance; from the Academy of Cosimo de' Medici in the fifteenth century where, following the teaching of Gemistos Pletho, Ficino and Pico della Mirandola mixed the Emperor Julian's orations and the conversations of Moses of Leon's *Zohar* to set into motion the ideas of a Christian Kabbalism and the practises of a demonic and spiritual magic; from the speculative symbolism and legendary history of fifteenth century alchemy and astrology; from the brotherhoods of the seventeenth century—the Freemasons, the Rosicrucians, or such religious sects as the Brothers and Sisters of the Free Spirit, that Adamite mystery in which as Fränger argues, Bosch was initiate, or the "Hidden Seed" of the Moravian Brethren after the Thirty Years War; from such sources the Romantic Movement in the eighteenth and nineteenth centuries inherited and made up its "tradition."   (D,A,50-1)

Such thinking opened the way to a new understanding of Whitman and Blake, whose integration into the mainstream of modernist poetry may well turn out to be the major development in American literary history since mid-century.

In 1954, the year preceding his declaration of independence from Olson, Robert Duncan, who was "already a convert to the Romantic spirit," suddenly, during a reading given by poetess Helen Adam, discovered the possibility of a new poetry in the "sublime and visionary manner [of Blake]." This experience finally broke, as he puts it, "the husk of [his] modernist pride" or previous "conviction that what mattered was the literary or artistic achievement" instead of the "wonder of the world of the poem itself" (D,T, 41-2). But before his final evolution into a major poet as apparent in *The Opening of the Field* (1960), Duncan absorbed the even more crucial influence of Whitman, who quickly gained a dimension capable of subsuming the previous impact of more recent poets under his all encompassing poetics of "the grand ensemble." As Duncan relates himself, "*Leaves of Grass* was kept as a bedside book" in the course of writing *The Opening of the Field* while "Williams' language of objects and Pound's ideogrammatic method were transformed in the light of Whitman's hieroglyphic of the ensemble." To a mind familiar with the Hindu *ātman* concept, even the Coleridgean notion of the self as the "only entrance to all facts" (Whitman, Wn,L,487) now appears in a positive light. "In Whitman," Duncan writes, "there is no ambiguity about the source of *meaning*. It flows from a 'Me myself' that exists in the authenticity of the universe." The very notion which, in the wake of Romantic philosophy, had proved so fatal a legacy to writers from Coleridge to Pater, now turns Whitman into a guide to the poets of the future:

> Back of our own contemporary arts of the collagist, the assembler of forms, is the ancestral, protean concept, wider and deeper, of the poet as devotee of the ensemble. Back of the field as it appears in Olson's proposition of composition by field is the concept of the cosmos as a field of fields. Our field in which we see the form of the poem happening belongs ultimately to . . . the grand ensemble Whitman evokes. (D,W,78,100)

A fusion of influences similar to that which informed *The Opening of the Field* marks the genesis of a poem whose general influence seems to emulate the previous impact of *The Waste Land*. Ginsberg's *Howl*, whose reading at the San Francisco *Six Gallery* in 1956 virtually launched the Beat movement, was written in a rapid outburst of creativity—but after a long period of gestation. The earliest impulse derived from his 1948 Blake vision which had left Ginsberg with the conviction that he "was born to realize . . . the spirit of the universe" (Pl,W,304). Reading one of Blake's poems,

> he heard a deep ancient voice, which he identified as Blake's, as the Creator's, pronouncing the poem, bringing him into a deepening understanding of the poem and the universe. (G,A,15)

Almost a decade of experimenting had to elapse before Ginsberg found the poetic means to turn such visions into poetry. Unaware of Olson's "Projective Verse" essay at the time, he relied on

Kerouac's similar "theory of breath as measure" (Ke, IR, 83) and on the "eccentric modulations of long-line composition displayed" by Blake, Whitman and others (B-M,P,221). *Howl* was to convert this theory into practise. "Ideally each line" in that poem, as the poet pointed out, is "a single breath unit." But there were other more general influences. As Ginsberg remembered in 1959,

> I realized at the time that Whitman's form had rarely been further explored (improved on even) in the U.S. Whitman always a mountain too vast to be seen. Everybody assumes (with Pound?) (except Jeffers) that his line is a big freakish uncontrollable necessary prosaic goof. No attempt's been made to use it in the light of early XX Century organization of new speech-rhythm prosody to *build up* large organic structures. (A,P,416)

Since then, Ginsberg's major formal concern has been exploring the relations "between poetry and mantra chanting by means of the yoga of breath" (G,IS,12), and trying to evolve a language whose psycho-physiological impact would even affect today's political arena or, in Ginsberg's own words, would "make every hard hat vibrate with delight." Blake, who more than two decades earlier had sent Ginsberg on his poetic quest, again became the major influence at this stage. It was "The Sick Rose"—"with the voice of Blake reading it" to him in his Harlem flat—which had brought about Ginsberg's first cosmic vision. Because Blake's poem, as Ginsberg now came to realize, was an example of "pure Mantra" within English poetry— "as penetrant & capable of causing Transcendental Knowledge as any Hindu Hare Krishna or Hari Om Namo Shivaye." So, Ginsberg finally set about to reinvent Blake's unrecorded melodies to the *Songs of Innocence & Experience*, in the belief that "only the prophetic priestly consciousness of the Bard—Blake, Whitman or our own new selves—can Steady our gaze into the Fiery eyes of the Tygers of the Wrath to Come" (G,B).

As Ginsberg would be the first to admit, the genealogy table of Western poets with "the prophetic priestly consciousness of the Bard," of course, goes back much further than to Blake. Within the Hermetic tradition, for instance, Orphic incantations formed a common practise of the Magus, and where Ginsberg uses his Indian harmonium, Ficino, who around 1463 translated the Greek *Corpus Hermeticum* into Latin, is said to have accompanied his singing of the *Orphica* on a *lira da braccio* decorated with the figure of Orpheus taming the animals (Y,B,78,80). For as Pico della Mirandola pointed out in his *Conclusiones Orphicæ,*

> nothing is more efficacious than the Hymns of Orpheus, if
> there be applied to them suitable music, and disposition of
> soul, and the other circumstances known to the wise. (Y,B,79)

By the time Pico declared Cabalistic magic as an indispensable part
of such chanting, its ultimate orientation became even clearer. It was
geared towards the Absolute which Ficino had described as "God
[who] is nothing, and yet . . . is all" or which in Pico's Cabalistic
conviction was the Ensoph with its ten Sephiroth emanations but
which in itself "is the Nothing, the unnameable, unknown *Deus
Absconditus*." As Pico added elsewhere: "Idem est nox apud Or-
pheum, & Ensoph in Cabala" ("The night in Orphism is the same as
the Ensoph in Cabala," Y,B,125,126). Through Giordano Bruno or
Philippe Du Plessis Mornay, friend and favorite theologian to Sir
Philip Sidney, who translated the French philosopher's *De la vérité de
la religion chrétienne* (1581) into English, such knowledge must also
have reached William Shakespeare (Y,B,177-8).

It is easy to see how much these notions resemble the Eastern
concept of the ultimate void of inexhaustible contents and its
analogues in contemporary open art theories. And as *śūnyatā* finds
its psycho-physiological counterpart in "extinction" (*nirvāṇa*), so did
the "Orphic night" correspond to what Pico, in his *Conclusiones
Cabalistæ*, and, even more significantly, in his commentary on Beni-
vieni's *Canzona de Amore,* calls "mors osculi": "In a supreme trance,"
as Frances Yates paraphrases,

> in which the soul is separated from the body, the Cabalist can
> communicate with God . . . in an ecstacy so intense that it
> sometimes results, accidentally, in the death of the body, a way
> of dying called the Death of the Kiss. (Y,B,99)

Equally striking are the resemblances which emerge when we compare Eastern and Modernist notions of both cosmic and artistic
creativity with those of the neo-Platonists and Hermeticists. According to Proclus, an influential systematizer of Plotinus' philosophy,
"all things proceed in a ciriuit . . . originating from the unmoved and
to the unmoved again returning" (Ab, S, 149). Or as the *Corpus
Hermeticum* proclaims in talking about "the nurse of all beings . . .
who gives birth to all things":

> Whether you speak of matter or bodies or substance, know
> that these things are energies of God, of God who is the All.
> (Y,B,34)

Man, the *magnum miraculum* "brother" to the creative World-

Demiurge, is capable of recreating these cosmic processes in his imagination. As Pico states in his *Oration on the Dignity of Man*,

> he passes into the nature of a god as though he were himself a god; he has familiarity with the race of demons, knowing that he is issued from the same origin. (Y,B,28)

To Bruno this imagination, as the most powerful inner sense, becomes "the sole gate to all internal affections and the link of links." As he came to believe, following the neo-Platonist poet Synesius' study *De somniis*, much of its power is derived from dreams through which the divinities communicate with man (Y,B,266,335).

By the time Bruno enunciated these ideas in England and on the Continent, the Inquisition, which was to send him to the stake in 1600, had already started to win its battle against the new philosophers. Their final efforts to join forces on a European level, in which Shakespeare and his friends seem to have taken an active part, were crushed by the defeat of the Winter King and Queen of Bohemia at the Battle of the White Mountain (1620) and ultimately drowned in the spiritual devastations of the Thirty Years' War. This, Frances Yates suggests (Y,S,21), may have been the tempest dreaded by Shakespeare, who would have been equally aghast at the subsequent era of "Enlightenment." As Robert Duncan writes,

> The neo-Platonism and Hermeticism or Rosicrucianism of the early 16th century that carried men's religious thought across barriers of church and Bible into realms of imaginative synthesis were put into the quarantine of irrational contagions. Only the ideal of rationalism, projecting its shame-taboo against what reasonable men did not conclude upon, held off the knowledge that the revelation of the soul was written in many religions and the traces of many experiences. Churchgoer or atheist, the rational man was immune to psychic information. A ghost or two, perhaps, but not the gods. (D,F,68-9)

So persistent was rationalist supremacy that even during the Romantic period when William Blake, inspired by Thomas Taylor's various translations of Orphic and Hermetic writings, revived the ancient wisdom in his poetry and art, such efforts were either ignored or attacked as "a farrago of nonsense" or "the wild effusions of a distempered brain." Similar conflict surrounds Coleridge's definition of the imagination "or esemplastic power" from the famous fragmentary 13th chapter of the *Biographia Literaria*. Auspiciously introduced by a motto culled from Synesius' Hymns and indirectly characterized as "An orphic tale indeed, / . . . / To a *strange* music chaunted!," this crucial landmark in the evolution of the new arts reads like Hermetic theorizing on the imagination put in a nutshell:

> The primary imagination I hold to be the living power and prime agent of all human perception, and as a repetition in the finite mind of the eternal act of creation in the infinite I AM. The secondary I consider as an echo of the former . . . It dissolves, diffuses, dissipates, in order to re-create. (Ce,B,162,165,167)

Yet even Coleridge remained a slave to the Zeitgeist of his era, joined his rationalist contemporaries in their attacks on Taylor's neo-Platonism,[15] and finally, as he grew older and more orthodox, crossed out the crucial "a repetition in the finite mind of the eternal act of creation in the infinite I AM" in a copy of the *Biographia Literaria* annotated in his own hand.[16]

Such rationalism also dominated Victorian Europe. And even Yeats who, unlike Coleridge, intensified his youthful studies of Hermetic philosophy as he grew older, did not develop a following to hold its own against the renewed onslaught of critical orthodoxy led by T. S. Eliot and his New Critical followers in our century. But by now their often fatal influence on poets and artists has been broken by a new understanding of art as a reenactment of nature in process, achieved by projective empathy and psycho-physiological spontaneity, rather than as an imitation of reality in stasis, perpe-trated by imposing upon its subject a unity or *"form created by a human, intellectual act"* (E. Kahler).

In understandable reaction against the orthodox critical estab-lishment, these insights often tended to evolve by a radical rejection of our cultural heritage and a wholesale adoption of related notions from non-Western cultures. Yet in the light of the recently un-earthed treasures of unorthodox Western thought, such iconoclasm now often tends to assume a pose of empty gesturing. And it may well turn out to be one of the major tasks for present-day artist æstheticians and scholars to follow pioneers such as Duncan or Ginsberg in the attempt to reformulate the new æsthetics in terms of this heritage and to rewrite literary history surrounding such major figures as Dante, Shakespeare, Goethe, or Yeats, whose works played a crucial role in rescuing the heretical wisdom from total suppres-sion and in preparing the ground for a total redefinition of art in our century.

[1]*Poems of the Late T'ang,* ed. A. C. Graham (Harmondsworth: Penguin Books, 1970), p. 95.

[2]E. Kahler, *The Disintegration of Form in the Arts* (New York: Braziller, 1968), p. 3; C. Brooks, "My Credo," *Kenyon Review* 13 (1951), 72.

[3]See for instance D. D. Pearlman, *The Barb of Time: On the Unity of Ezra Pound's Cantos* (New York: Oxford University Press, 1969), p. 13 or B. Sankey, *A Companion to William Carlos Williams's Paterson* (Berkeley: University of California Press, 1971), p. 213.

[4]E. Faas, *Offene Formen in der modernen Kunst und Literatur* (Munich: Goldmann Verlag, 1975).

[5]Cf. H. B. Staples, *Robert Lowell: The First Twenty Years* (London: Faber and Faber, 1962), p. 45.

[6]*Tri-Quarterly* 7 (Fall, 1966), 81.

[7]*Yale Review* 41 (Autumn, 1951), 157.

[8]*The Art of Sylvia Plath,* ed. Charles Newman (Bloomington, Ind.: Indiana University Press, 1971), p. 69.

[9]R. Browning, *The Poetical Works* (London: Oxford University Press, 1962), ix. There is a more extensive discussion of these matters in my *Poesie als Psychogramm* (Munich: Fink Verlag, 1974), pp. 18f.

[10]*The Contemporary Poet as Artist and Critic: Eight Symposia,* ed. A. Ostroff (Boston: Little, Brown, 1964), p. 108.

[11]See *Athanor* 4 (Spring, 1973), 20.

[12]See below p. 239.

[13]See below pp. 125, 126.

[14]In conversation.

[15]See *Thomas Taylor, the Platonist. Selected Writings,* ed. K. Raine and G. M. Harper, Bollingen Series LXXXVIII (Princeton, N.J.: Princeton University Press, 1969), p. 35.

[16]See J. Benziger, "Organic Unity: Leibniz to Coleridge," *PMLA*, 66 (March, 1951), 24-48, 42.

Charles Olson
Robert Duncan

Photo: Gerard Malanga

CHARLES OLSON (1910 - 1970)

"I am an archeologist of morning. And the writing and arts which I find bear on the present job are (I) from Homer back, not forward; and (II) from Melville on, particularly himself, Dostoyevѕky, Rimbaud, and Lawrence. These were the modern men who projected what we are and what we are in, who broke the spell. They put men forward into the post-modern, the post-humanist, the post-historic, the going live present, the 'Beautiful Thing.' "

Born in Worcester, Mass., the son of a Swedish father and Catholic Irish-American mother, Olson was "uneducated" at Wesleyan, Yale and Harvard (B.A., 1932; M.A., 1933). He taught at Clark University in Worcester and, from 1936-39, at Harvard. His first book *Call Me Ishmael* (1947) appeared two years after the publication of his first poem at age thirty-five. From 1939-48 he worked in various jobs, from fishing-boat hand to government official in the Office of War Information. "I have had to learn the simplest things / last."In 1948, he took the place of his friend and mentor, novelist Edward Dahlberg, at Black Mountain College and as its rector (1951-56) began his influential career as teacher, æsthetician and leader of the Black Mountain movement (Creeley, Levertov, Duncan, etc.). His epoch-making essay on "Projective Verse" was published in 1950, its propositions enlarged and developed in further essays (*Human Universe*, 1965; *Selected Writings*, 1966; *Additional Prose*, 1974), letters and reading lists to friends (*Mayan Letters*, 1953; *Letters for Origin 1950-1956*, 1969; *A Bibliography on America for Ed Dorn*, 1964) and lecture series (*The Special View of History*, 1970; *Poetry and Truth*, 1971). Of his poetry (*In Cold Hell, In Thicket*, 1953; *The Distances*, 1960), *The Maximus Poems* (1-10, 1953; 11-22, 1956; combined in 1960; *Maximus IV, V, VI*, 1968; *Maximus Poems*, vol. 3, 1975) in the tradition of Pound's *Cantos* and Williams' *Paterson* are his most important legacy.

Charles Olson

When I first entered the American literary world in 1972, I was amazed to find that Olson, a man of firmly established international reputation abroad, was at best considered a figure of ridicule in New York literary circles. Here, James Dickey's derisive comments from the early sixties still seemed to be the stock-in-trade for polite cut-throat party chatter: that Olson's poetics were largely derivative (Dickey quotes René Nelli's *Poésie ouverte, poésie fermée*) and that his "trump card" was to have discovered the influence of the typewriter on modern poetry (Di,B,136-7). Since then we have witnessed a veritable explosion of Olson research: there is an Olson journal, an Olson archive, a 367 page *boundary 2* (1973/74) Olson issue and above all an ever increasing number of Olson Ph.Ds. Another lit. crit. "industry" has started, and only eight years after his death in 1970, the poet seems to be well assured of his niche in the mausoleum of academic scholarship.

As pointed out, Olson's poetics may be considered as part of a general new æsthetics in progress in which the modern tradition seems to be gradually coming to a full understanding of itself. The ideas of the composer John Cage and the painter Jackson Pollock, for instance, were well known to Olson. Others like the novelist Robbe-Grillet or the composer Karlheinz Stockhausen have formulated comparable theories in which the American poet would have found welcome confirmation for parts of his own. Yet it may well be that no other poet or artist before him has discussed the evolving new æsthetics in more far-ranging and comprehensive terms than Olson himself.

In our world of specialized knowledge any such polyhistoric attempt is, of course, bound to fail in a strictly scholarly sense, and it would be easy to point out the errors, misconceptions and above all the eclecticism to be found in Olson's writings. But the same applies to a comparable figure such as Coleridge, whose ideas had an unceasing influence on generations of later poets. And as the desire to understand poetry in its widest implications persists, there will be people grateful for the insights these men have afforded us. They will share some of the excitement with which William Carlos Williams greeted the publication of Olson's essay on "Projective Verse." "[It] is as if the whole area lifted," he wrote Robert Creeley (O,W,6). By printing part of the essay in his autobiography Williams conceded how to him as to many others Olson's insights brought a fulfillment and clarification which their own efforts had denied them.

It has by now become a commonplace of literary history to see Olson in a continuing line of poets which includes Pound, Crane, Zukofsky and Williams; it is thus easy to forget that it was Olson himself who as early as 1953, at the height of Eliot's fame and influence, described these poets as the great and future tradition of American poetry, and the school of Eliot as a dead end in the development of modern literature. And though there is disagreement as to the "great tradition of American poetry," Eliot's reputation among poets of the 60's and 70's seems now to be more or less what Olson predicted two decades ago. On the other hand even Olson himself had reservations about the "advance in discourse which Pound & Williams, and Crane, after his lights, led the rest of us on to" (O,U,63).

Although he acknowledged Pound as the founding father of this development, he considered the philosophical understanding shown by his predecessor both wrong-headed and limited. It was Fenollosa's rather than Pound's ideas which, according to Olson, could have helped Hart Crane to a full unfolding of his poetic temperament, crippled under the dictates of the New Criticism (O,W,21). Pound's thinking was almost violently anthropocentric, whereas Olson, following philosophers such as Whorf and Whitehead, was searching for an "ALTERNATIVE TO THE EGO-POSITION" (O,W,83). Pound's major importance lay in his "methodology" ("the necessities that the execution of form involves," O,L,105), Williams' in his emphasis on the particular and concrete, his "no ideas but in things." Neither of them offered a model for what Olson called his "stance toward reality": "if i think EP gave any of us the methodological clue: the RAG-BAG; bill gave us the lead on the LOCAL . . . Neither of them: WHAT" (O,L,129).

Olson's "stance toward reality" was based on extensive studies ranging from nuclear physics, non-Euclidean geometry and modern philosophy to Primitive culture, Eastern religion and metalinguistics. There was one poet, however, whom he acknowledged to have anticipated the general drift of his theorizing: D. H. Lawrence, whom Olson considered the only "prospective" poet of that generation (O,U,102). It was one of Pound's worst mistakes to ignore Lawrence, who could have provided him with intuitive insights denied to his more strictly critical genius. Yet the American poet had an ineradicable aversion to the British novelist. "Detestable person but needs watching," he remarked in 1913 (P,L,17). As it happened, Pound didn't follow his own advice, and it was left to a later writer to combine the achievements of these two most important and influential pioneers of modern Anglo-American literature. "Pound and Lawrence more and more stand up," Olson wrote in 1951, "as the huge two of the 1st half of the 20th century" (O,L,63).

As Olson recognized, D. H. Lawrence deserves a far more eminent place in the history of the modern movement than he is granted this side of the Atlantic. A pioneer of a new kind of open form novel,[1]* he visualized, as early as 1920, an open form "poetry of this immediate present" in the tradition of Whitman; a poetry with no beginning or end, whose essence lay in "the sheer appreciation of the instant moment, life surging itself into utterance at its very well-head" (La,C,86,87). In his painting he anticipated the impulse of abstract expressionism[2] and his descriptions of the dances of the North American Indians seem to foretell the most recent developments in music, choreography and multi-media art forms.[3]

More specifically, it was Lawrence's criticism of Western civilization which exerted a direct influence on Olson. In reversal of the Christian doctrine Lawrence had described the fall of man as a fall into teleological, future oriented thinking about the beyond: "[B]y the time of Christ all religion . . . instead of being religion of *life,* here and now, became religion of postponed destiny, death, and reward *afterwards,* 'if you are good.' " For Lawrence there was no beyond and no eternity, only the timeless here and now—"there is no goal. Consciousness is an end in itself. We torture ourselves getting somewhere, and when we get there it is nowhere, for there is nowhere to get to" (La,A,32,43). As the herald of abstract thought, of the "disease of idealism" (La,F,85), Socrates, besides Christ, was the second most pernicious influence on the evolution of Western civilization. "With the coming of Socrates and the 'spirit,' the cosmos died. For two thousand years man has been living in a dead and dying cosmos, hoping for a heaven hereafter. And all the religions have been religions of the dead body and the postponed reward" (La,A,46). Lawrence spent his life in search of this living cosmos. And like Olson after him he believed he had found it among the North American Indians, the Mexicans, among the earliest, pre-Socratic cultures of the world, or even among the debris of our own civilization.

*Notes for this section on p. 51

Part of this search was for man's original language, uncorrupted by our Judæo-Christian and Greek ways of thinking. Like Fenollosa in his analysis of the "Chinese written character" (F,C,22f.), but independently, Lawrence describes it as a language of "rotary image-thought" instead of our "modern process of progressive thought"; of concrete symbols and "picturegraphs" instead of allegorical equations or abstract concepts; as a language of autonomous and open semantic entities instead of our "monolinear . . . sentence structure" (E. Pound, P,B,475), our "logical chain[s] . . . [where] every full-stop is a mile-stone that marks our 'progress' and our arrival somewhere." The *Apocalypse,* especially in its early parts, "before the birth of the Child," served him as a document for this language of the "old pagan civilisation":

> in it we have, not the modern process of progressive thought, but the old pagan process of rotary image-thought. Every image fulfils its own little circle of action and meaning, then is superseded by another image . . . Every image is a picturegraph, and the connection between the images will be made more or less differently by every reader.(La,A,43,45)

According to Lawrence there were no abstractions in this primordial language. And the concrete had a numinous and dynamic quality equal to the mutual interrelatedness of all being, or what Lawrence describes as "the rapid momentaneous association of things which meet and pass on the for ever incalculable journey of creation: everything left in its own rapid, fluid relationship with the rest of things" (La,C,86). Even to the early scientists and philosophers words like "cold" did not denote a quality, but embodied an "existing entity." The "cold," the "moist," the "hot," the "dry" "were things in themselves, realities, gods, *theoi.* And they *did things*" (La,A,46).

If Olson differed from these theories it was mainly in his definitions of the terms "symbol" and "allegory." Lawrence praised the symbol as a "complex of emotional experience" (La,C,158) and as a primary constituent of myth, whereas Olson attacked symbolism for the very qualities which Lawrence would have criticized as allegorical—that denotative character, which, ever since Plato discovered his realm of ideas, has made all signs, images and words stand for abstract ideas rather than concrete and numinous entities—"the suck of symbol which has increased and increased since the great Greeks first promoted the idea of a transcendent world of forms" (O,W,61). It was in this sense that Olson tried to refute the Eliot critic Grover Smith who had criticized Williams' poetry for its lack of symbolism. "It doesn't take much thought over Bill's proposition—'Not in ideas but in things'—to be sure that any of us intend an image as a 'thing,' never, so far as we know, such a non-animal as symbol"(O,U,65). But even Olson was aware of the fact that this use of the word was due to a corruption of its original meaning. Taken back to its radical, he wrote, it "will reveal its proper meaning: fr. Greek *symbolon*, 'a sign by which one knows or infers a thing'" (O,M,11)—a meaning even Lawrence would probably have agreed with.

Not only the symbol, our whole language, "as it [has] been since Socrates" (O,U,117), was corrupted by this process of allegorization. Our words have "suffered from the tendency . . . to acquire abstract meanings" (O,M,10,11), the syntax, originally characterized by a cumulative addition of autonomous entities, was subjected to a system of predicative logic and its *"rational patterns of discourse"* (O,U,63). Olson pointed to Havelock's *Preface to Plato* (1963) as proof of these Lawrentian speculations on a pre-Socratic language. For according to Havelock, poets such as Homer and Hesiod had used "a wholly different syntax . . . [or] *parataxis* in which the words and actions reported are set down side by side in the order of their occurrence in nature, instead of by an order of discourse, or 'grammar' " (O,R,41).

The alienation of language from nature is a result of what Olson, again echoing Lawrence, described as the "fall of man" into our scientific and teleological ways of thought. In what looks like a deliberate *mise au point* of Lawrence's notion, Socrates and Christ play the devil's role in this pseudo-Christian mystery play (O,W,146-47; O,L,33). Olson enlarged upon this notion in his critique of our Western concept of history. Originally, history was neither a search for objective facts and their causal interconnectedness, as initiated by Thucydides, nor the attempt of Christian writers to justify the ways of God amidst the suffering and meaninglessness of man's historical destiny. As shown by Herodotus, the first, greatest and last of Western historiographers, it was a "finding out for oneself " (O,V,20), an attempt to relate to the world in its here and now, where time "was not a line drawn straight ahead toward future, a logic of good and evil" (O,I,97-98), but a returning on itself. It was a pursuit circumscribed by an idea of life with no beyond, fulfilled in the "preoccupation with itself " (O,W,152). With such writers as Captain John Smith, the poet John Keats, or the early Melville, this original understanding had been preserved at isolated points in Western thought. On the whole, however, our concept of history had been a self-contradictory compound of scientific claims

and providential speculation. As Olson came to recognize in anticipation of recent scholarly investigation, even Hegel's dialectic (like
Marx's materialism) was but a secularized variant of this principle.
When Hegel interpreted history as a gradual unfolding of the spirit,
he merely made it fit a preconceived notion of what history ought to
be. "He takes what is condition as result, instead of leaving it, as
Keats does, *penetralium*" (O,V,43).

Olson found a similar variant of Judæo-Christian providential
thinking in what Robbe-Grillet, after the American poet, has described as the "tragic humanism" (R-G,R,71) of Existentialist
philosophy and its notion of the absurdity and meaninglessness of
life. As Olson wrote in *The Special View of History*, his most brilliant
piece of general criticism,

> a teleology of form as progressive was the hidden assumption
> of the old cosmology, and Void is what's left when the kosmos
> breaks down as the interesting evidence of order, Man falls
> when that purpose falls, and so Void is the only assumption
> left.(O,V,47-48)

To Olson, as to Robbe-Grillet, history and reality are "neither meaningful nor absurd" (R-G,R,21). There is neither progress nor tradition. "NATURE TAKES NOTHING BUT LEAPS" (O,L,11). "The
motive, then, of reality, is process not goal . . . the chance success of
the play of creative accident" (O,V,49). This is a concept of reality
reminiscent of Zen Buddhism and, like this Eastern religion, it is
contrary to what Olson describes as the "peculiar presumption by
which Western man has interposed himself between what he is as a
creature of nature . . . and those other creations of nature which we
. . . call objects," a presumption that finally resulted in suppressing
nature within and outside ourselves. To Olson "man is himself an
object" (O,W,24), his true function not a controlling of nature, but
the attempt to be one with her. And again D. H. Lawrence had been
the first to point the way out of this dilemma—through those
"primordial & phallic energies & methodologies which . . . make it
possible for man, that participant thing, to take up, straight, nature's, live nature's force" (O,U,23).

If Lawrence had upheld pre-Socratic and non-Western cultures
as models for these new concepts of man and the world, the results of
modern science, as interpreted by Olson, seem to point in the same
direction. Describing reality as "continuous" instead of "discrete"
("the old system . . . [including] discourse, language as it had been
since Socrates"), the non-Euclidean geometer Riemann, according
to one of Olson's typical sweeps of eclectic syncretism, reverted to the

Heraclitean idea of a "flow of creation" (O,U,117,119), first re-
envisioned through Keats' *"Negative Capability"* and finally reclaimed
for our modern world picture by Heisenberg's quantum theory:

> Our advantage is that a century and a half after Keats, the
> universe as seen by Heraclitus' naked eye and mind has been
> restored . . . One cannot abstract from it. One has to get it in its
> place or occurrences. And study it in place and in motion
> (what Heisenberg gave us the wonderful words for to go with
> Keats' ambiguity: The Uncertainty Principle. Right out of the
> mouth of physics one can seize the condition Keats insisted a
> man must stay in the midst of: . . . "a man is capable of being in
> uncertainties, mysteries, doubts . . ." Only thus do you have
> *both* mass and momentum, or substance & motion. (O,V,33,39)

Morever, Olson believed himself in the advantageous position
of finding the intuitive insights of a Keats, Melville or Lawrence
confirmed by recent linguistic and anthropological research. There
were Fenollosa and Whorf, guides "fr the Old Discourse to the New"
(O,P,7), there was Eric A. Havelock on pre-Socratic syntax, as well as
a host of other scholars such as Michael Ventris, C. H. Gordon, Hans
Güterbock and S. N. Kramer in the fields of Cretan, Ugaritic, Hittite
and Sumerian studies. "A tremendous moment" in the history of
Western thought, as Olson thought:

> We live in an age in which inherited literature is being hit from
> two sides, from contemporary writers who are laying bases of
> new discourse at the same time that such scholars as the above
> are making available pre-Homeric and pre-Mosaic texts which
> are themselves eye-openers. (O,U,150)

As is well known, Olson had himself carried out extensive
studies of Mayan culture and language, and it was in a similar spirit
of learning and research that he pursued his vocation as poet and
creator of a new language. He believed that this "new discourse"
could be gained by restructuring the old and that the English language, following the model of non-Western languages, could ultimately return to its pre-Socratic origins. As Fenollosa taught him,
the general changes concerning syntax and grammar would have to
be based on the potential vitality of the spoken word, the "language
as the act of the instant . . . [not] the act of thought about the instant"
(O,W,54). And it was probably Hopi language, as analyzed by
Whorf, that inspired his attempts to reorganize the tenses, to "drive
all nouns, the abstract most of all, back to process—to act" (O,U,70)
and to regain "the kinetics of words" (O,M,10) in

general. For under a thin semantic layer of abstraction there was the old dynamic potential, and the syllable, that "least logical" part of the language, offered a direct access to this latent etymological force. Our abstract "is," for example, "comes from the Aryan root, *as*, to breathe. The English 'not' equals the Sanscrit *na*, which may come from the root *na*, to be lost, to perish. 'Be' is from *bhu*, to grow" (O,W,18; also see F,C,15). In this way "both the phonetic and ideographic" elements are "still present and available for use as impetus and explosion in our alphabetic speech" (O,U,18). And for Olson it was the poet's task to reclaim them.

Naturally, the syllable and its prelogical elements, as divined by the poet's ear, become the prime element of poetry: the "king and pin of versification." It is by their syllables, not by any preconceived patterns of discourse, that words are "juxtapose[d] in beauty," by a process of physio-linguistic empathy rather than of intellectual organization. "In any given instance, because there is a choice of words, the choice, if man is in there, will be, spontaneously, the obedience of his ear to the syllables" (O,W,17,18). As hearing recovers the old vitality of human language, the poet's creativity springs from a fusion with the "flow of creation," for which man's original language had been the direct medium. Poetic creation becomes a simple release of these natural forces, in which the poet feels himself to be a part of the cosmos. Poetry is not made but happens, is not an abstraction that tries to transcend nature but a natural event that embodies it—what Lawrence describes as "life surging itself into utterance at its very well-head," and Olson as the poet's "projective act":

> if he is contained within his nature as he is participant in the larger force, he will be able to listen, and his hearing through himself will give him secrets objects share . . . It is in this sense that . . . the artist's act in the larger field of objects, leads to dimensions larger than the man. For a man's problem, the moment he takes speech up in all its fullness, is to . . . cause the thing he makes to try to take its place alongside the things of nature. (O,W,25)

The poet's "projective act" resembles the gestural autodynamics of action painting or the meditative sound releases in recent Stockhausen compositions[4]—a common impulse, perhaps antithetical to our Western concept of art, but with precedents in cultures that are equal, if not superior to our own; as in Sino-Japanese calligraphy and *Sumi-e* painting which flow from the autonomous spontaneity of the artist's bodily movements (Wa,W,174), or in Zen Buddhist flute music, in which the breath rhythm, expressing man's vital harmony with the universe, determines the sequence of sounds (G-R,W,610).

Similarly Olson declares breath—"the breathing of the man who writes, at the moment that he writes"—to be the second most important factor in poetic creativity besides our hearing. The "projective poet," he writes at the end of his famous essay,

> [goes] down through the workings of his own throat to that place where breath comes from, where breath has its beginnings . . . where . . . all act springs. (O,W,19,26)

It is here that we come to what Dickey has derided as the "trump card" (Di,B,137) of Olson's theorizing: that the poet, thanks to the typewriter, can "indicate exactly the breath, the pauses, the suspensions even of syllables, the juxtapositions even of parts of phrases" and thus mirror in print the "presentational immediacy" (Whitehead, Wh,S,21ff.) which is the poem's essence. In this way the reader will be able to "voice [the poet's] work" (O,W,22), and, given that it is successful, will be drawn into the poem rather than analyze or judge it. He will relive the process of creation and share the dance of cosmic forces that has found a voice in the poem's words and rhythms. Being a direct release of the unceasing "flow of creation," there can be neither "prior concepts of COHERENCE" (O,L,105) nor any preconceived limitations to the "projective act." The poem, like a painting by Pollock, has "a life of its own," its creator simply trying to "let it come through" (Rn,P,194). Rather than the poet writing the poem, the poem writes the poet.[5] From the moment he ventures into "FIELD COMPOSITION," as Olson calls it, "he can go by no track other than the one the poem under hand declares, for itself " (O,W,16).

Like Robbe-Grillet, Olson could have spoken of the poet's "total subjectivity" (R-G,R,148), and it is not surprising to find that Olson, several years before the French novelist, expanded upon this notion in his introduction to Robert Creeley's short stories. Olson and Robbe-Grillet share a concept of reality as "neither meaningful nor absurd." And they both know about the difficulty of describing it. Our language, or rather what Robbe-Grillet (after Roland Barthes) defines as its socio-political component ("l'écriture"), represents a dense semantic network that tends to subject reality to the "tyranny" of its cultural, religious or ideological "significations." This, however, is the very language of our traditional novels, which therefore fail to render reality in its phenomenological existence of "being there" (R-G,R,24,25). A normal description, as Olson puts it, does not come to grips with what really matters: that a thing, any thing, impinges on us by a more important fact, its self-existence, without reference to any other thing, in short, the very character of it which calls our attention to it, which wants us to know more about it, its particularity. This is what we are confronted by, not the thing's 'class,' any hierarchy, of quality or quantity, but the thing itself, and its *relevance* to ourselves who are the experience of it. (O,W,56)

Reality has to speak for itself, through a medium that is an inextricable part of its flux and change—not through the omniscient author of traditional novels, but through "a man placed in space and time, conditioned by his passions . . . [and] involved . . . in an adventure so passionate and all-engrossing that it will tend to deform his vision" (R-G,R,149). In other words, reality, as Lawrence had been one of the first to realize, must be reenacted instead of being described. And according to Olson there were two narrative techniques or "methodologies" to achieve this. One was Joyce's "exit author," "what I call DOCUMENT simply to emphasize that the events alone do the work, that the narrator stays OUT, functions as pressure not as interpreting person." The other technique, which Olson found in Creeley's stories, equals Robbe-Grillet's "total subjectivity" of the narrator: "the total IN . . . total speculation . . . the narrator taking on himself the job of making clear by way of his own person that life *is* preoccupation with itself." Although the exact opposite of the former, it "drive[s] for the same end": to let reality speak for itself, "so to re-enact experience that a story has what an object or person has: energy and instant." For the narrator may be present at every moment of his narrative, but his "total subjectivity" renders him a mere object among other objects. "And the writer, though he is the control (or art is nothing) is, still, no more than—but just as much as—another 'thing,' and as such, is in, inside or out" (O,U,127-8).

To be sure, Olson does not share the almost schizophrenic combination of hyper-empirical phenomenalism and analytical intellectuality that tends to reduce Robbe-Grillet's world to a labyrinth of geometric abstractions. For to Olson, as to Lawrence before him, the essence of reality is its life-force, and poetry as well as the other arts has to partake of this vitality in order to reenact it. Far from being intellectual, this is a concept of art reminiscent of what W. Schmalenbach defines as the foremost principle of Primitive art: the embodiment of nature's animistic forces, which turns art into an "expression of intrinsic vitality" ("Ausdruck . . . von Kraft an sich,"

(G-R,W,431). And, indeed, Olson demanded "the replacement of the Classical-representational by the *primitive abstract*," a form of art, that, within the framework of an animistic universe, becomes the only valid form of religion. "There is only one thing you can do about kinetic, reenact it. Which is why the man said, he who possesses rhythm, possesses the universe. And why art is the only twin life has—its only valid metaphysic" (O,W,61).

Olson was a professionally trained dancer, and as any reader of his criticism realizes, dance and rhythm are his most frequent and central metaphors to describe poetry and art in general. More explicitly he called "dance the base of his discipline" (i.e., of the "recognition of the kinetic as the act of life") "and its syllabary the source of any other" (O,M,12). What he meant by dance, however, was radically different from the programmed choreography of traditional dance, which he found "altogether too descriptive and so . . . of all things for dance to be!—non-active." To Olson dance is "not mimesis but kinesis." But at the time he formulated this principle in his *Apollonius of Tyana: A Dance, with Some Words, for Two Actors* (1951), he could only think of "one or two" people who were trying to recover this original form of dance. In a letter of the same year he identified Merce Cunningham as one of these (O,L,53). And indeed Cunningham (by 1951 still an unknown or at best ridiculed artist) has since fulfilled Olson's promise by becoming one of the foremost innovators of choreography in America. Olson and Cunningham collaborated at Black Mountain where they performed what is regarded as the first happening in the history of modern art. In their ideas about dance they were both inspired by Primitive culture, a model Olson's Apollonius finds among a fictive tribe of the Upper Nile. These GUMNOI or "NAKEDS" "have taken up direct from energy . . .[from] the dæmonial nature in anything, including ourselves," so that their dances are a spontaneous reenactment of cosmic forces, uncontrolled by any mental principles or preconceived patterns; where each dancer is "allowed to be himself alone in the midst of the phenomenal world raging and yet apart" (O,W,152).

Again, Olson seems to draw upon the prophetic insights of his greatest and most important predecessor. In 1922 D. H. Lawrence visited the North American Indians, and although at first repelled by the tourist industry surrounding them, he finally seems to have found in their dances an embodiment of the original and future ideal of art as he conceived it. What he describes is a kind of Primitive happening in which dance is a spontaneous release of cosmic energy, a segment of the "untellable flood of creation," with "no beginning and no end," with "no division between actor and audience" and consequently "no judgement: absolutely no judgement . . . because there is nothing outside it, to judge it" (La,M,62-3).

"Lawrence . . . alone," Olson writes, "had the true mask, he lacked the critical intelligence, and was prospective" (O,U,102). This equally paradoxical and insightful remark could stand as an appropriate epitaph for Olson's own achievement. More than any American poet of his generation he gave his successors a goal towards which to direct their own endeavors. But his message is destined to remain a goal rather than become accepted doctrine. Like Lawrence before him, Olson lacked the "critical intelligence" and erudition to relate his insights to the mainstream of Western thought of which they remain a product, however much they tend to reverse it. And there are more than half a dozen figures besides Melville, Rimbaud or Keats who are part of this mainstream. But one should not forget the debt modern poetry owes to Olson as to Lawrence, even for their very lack of "critical intelligence" which gave them part of the courage needed to discard the dead weight of a tradition that frequently stifled the insights of men more learned and prudent than themselves. And there have been poets younger than Olson, both amongst his followers and enemies, who, as we shall see, have since tried to remedy these deficiencies.

[1]See Alan Friedman, *The Turn of the Novel: The Transition to Modern Fiction* (London: Oxford University Press, 1970), pp. 130ff.

[2]Compare Pollock's statement quoted above, p. 12, with Lawrence's "Making Pictures" (La,E,301): "It is to me the most exciting moment—when you have a blank canvas and a big brush full of wet colour, and you plunge. It is just like diving into a pond—then you start frantically to swim. So far as I am concerned, it is like swimming in a baffling current and being rather frightened and very thrilled, gasping and striking out for all you're worth. The knowing eye watches sharp as a needle; but the picture comes clean out of instinct, intuition and sheer physical action. Once the instinct and intuition gets into the brush-tip, the picture *happens*, if it is to be a picture at all."

[3]See pp. 49f.

[4]See *Texte*, 3 vol. (Cologne: Verlag DuMont Schauberg, 1963-71), III, 108 f., 313 f.

[5]Alain Bosquet's phrase; in his *Verbe et Vertige: Situations de la poésie* (Paris: Hachette, 1961), pp. 89f., he describes a similar phenomenon in modern French poetry.

Robert Duncan (1919-   )

"What released my sense of a new generation in poetry was first a poem ("The Shifting" by Denise Levertov) in *Origin* VI, 1952; then in 1954 thru *The Gold Diggers* a grasp of the art of Robert Creeley, where such minute attentions and cares moved in the line; and third, but from the first, the break-thru to a meaningful reading of Olson's *Maximus*, from which his *Projective Verse* and *In Cold Hell, In Thicket* took on new meaning: that, for one thing, the task in poetry can be promethean. In Whitman's words: 'The theme is creative and has vista.' "

Born in Oakland, California, Robert Duncan never knew his mother, who died shortly after his birth, or his father, who gave him up for adoption at the age of six months. His foster parents' association with the local Hermetic Brotherhood prompted the poet's life-long, but not uncritical, fascination with the occult, Hermeticism, Gnosticism, neo-Platonism and Christian religion. Such interests fused with others in psychiatry, field psychology and modern art during his post-1938 period of travel between West and East coast as a 20th century vagantes scholar poet: first in close proximity with Anaïs Nin and her New York circle, then as a pivotal figure in various groups (around Robin Blaser, Jack Spicer, Philip Lamantia, Kenneth Rexroth, Helen Adam, James Broughton and others) that led to the San Francisco Renaissance of the 50's. After a first meeting with Olson in 1947, he became an important member of the movement associated with Black Mountain College where he taught in 1956. Though recognized by Anaïs Nin and others as a poetic genius in his late teens, Duncan was a late developer like his friend Olson. Aside from *The Venice Poem* (1948), which marked his transition "from the concept of a dramatic form to a concept of musical form," most of his major poetry is contained in three collections: *The Opening of the Field* (1960), *Roots and Branches* (1964) and *Bending the Bow* (1968). He has vowed not to publish another volume before 1983. A one-time disciple of Ernst Kantorowicz at Berkeley as well as a scholar of life-long dedication, Duncan never took an academic degree. For all that, his critical prose (including his semi-autobiographical H. D. book in progress) published in avant-garde journals and booklets (*The Sweetness and Greatness of Dante's "Divine Comedy," 1265-1965*, 1965; *The Truth and Life of Myth: An Essay in Essential Autobiography*, 1968) represents a unique achievement, both for its theoretical originality and erudite comprehensiveness. It badly needs collecting.

Robert Duncan

I

Faas: On January 1, 1972 you flew from San Francisco to New York to pay a last visit to Olson shortly before he died. What did you talk about while you were with him?

DUNCAN: Charles was trying to work something out around the notion of liver. Being a devout Jungian, he was trying to figure out what the meaning of that cancer taking place in his body was. And an analyst had told him that liver was feminine. last session So one of the things he was writing on a piece of paper with Olson while I was with him was "live-her," as a kind of formula of liv-er. So off and on we were talking about that "her." You have seen the letter I wrote Jess the following day. It was published in the first Olson journal. That gives my own account right on top of that session.

Charles opened our conversation by saying: It's been twenty-five years of adventure. And my first flash was, of course: Oh, no. But then I realized that, indeed, I had first met him in 1947. I have always had a feeling of panic that those people I knew before I knew Jess would feel some prior claim. And it was as if Charles at that point was making that prior claim. Of course, he was like this with everyone. He had the special message for everyone that was with him. But certainly, I had been on an adventure with him. Although my age of Olson was really between 1950 and 1972.

Faas: You first read Olson's essay on "Projective Verse" in 1950, I remember.

DUNCAN: Yes, it was by 1950 that I was beginning to read it. From 1950 onwards I began to answer Olson's call and to step into that arena and to take my place there. But not before 1952 did I really absorb his essay.

Faas: Obviously, Olson knew that he was dying.

DUNCAN: Oh, yes. He had terminal cancer. We couldn't have any doubt about his dying. As a matter of fact, at that point, he only had about three weeks left to live. The cancer was in his liver so they really couldn't give him pain killers and he was just out of his mind by that afternoon. But during our morning session, he was talking all the time, and I felt: Gee, he's going to exhaust himself. But he wanted to go on. It's only when he lapsed into sleep that we finished talking.

Faas: Was he in pain all the time while he was talking?

DUNCAN: No. I think he was so keyed up in talking and working that he didn't feel it. So he worked on that "live-her" thing. And the one thing I wanted to say to him right away was: Isn't it remarkable, Charles, maybe you and I are the only ones, as it looks like, who are concerned about composition by field. Of course, Creeley's *Pieces* is composed by field. But only Charles and I seem to have had field theory. And we are the only ones after all from the thirties when Koehler's field theory was very exciting. Koehler's field theory of the æsthetics of painting and his attempt to read music that way. That was the important thing before Freud completely took over riding high in certain American circles.

composition by field

Faas: What was Olson's reaction?

DUNCAN: Well, he grinned, and I added: To think that at the end of it we each just have our own actual duties to do and that we aren't leaders, and that it wasn't part of history. And he entirely concurred with that. But he said: Well, we've been on a great twenty-five year long adventure together.

Faas: What was his sense of his own life at that time?

DUNCAN: He told me that he had completed *Maximus* which shocked me. Although I had already seen that *Maximus* was a poem which wasn't open. I mean, in my sense of open. Because Olson had never observed that open would mean that you wouldn't begin or end. He always remained a good Roman Catholic who does begin and end.

Faas: Was Olson afraid of death?

DUNCAN: Well, the second thing I said was: I came to see you die. You've always been an older poet adventuring ahead of me, and I have come to see you die in order to practise, in order to see how appropriately a man would die. And he said: Well, no it's that "live-her" thing, I am not doing that. And by the time he died he was completely out of it. Although I saw him die almost as if he was going to unlock "live-her." And he had quite a number of jokes about "her" and "she," meaning the *anima*.

unlocking "live-her"

He had no clothes on and he was naked entirely except for a sort of sheet which he wore a little as if he were some huge Socrates. And he had lost all his flesh, so that he seemed like a truly magnificent and very Nordic looking creature. He really looked like some kind of Wotan. And his skeleton was much more appropriate to his size than his flesh had ever been. He really looked like his Oceanus. And he said to me: Come and hold me. And I went to the bed and held him. At that point the nurse came in and was very upset. And Charles said: I asked this man to hold me in his arms. Do you want to do something about it? And the nurse let out a scream and ran out of the room.

And yes, he did talk about dying. They had taken him to a special cancer hospital and at that point he was unwilling to admit that he was in terminal cancer. But after a couple of days they took the liver puncture and found that they couldn't operate because the cancer had reached the liver and he would never have been able to survive the anæsthetics. So then they threw him away. I mean, they were just a repair factory.

At one point he said: I want some doctor and you know what I mean, Duncan, your dream. He meant the dream that I brought into print in Charles's lifetime, the dream in which Charles and I are at the springs and we are releasing the springs. As a matter of fact, Robin Blaser is on the horizon in the far West in that dream. So while I had come to get my instructions on how to die he was concerned with the fact that he didn't have a doctor to attend him. Meanwhile, I was shocked that he didn't have a priest and that he didn't receive the Extreme Unction which he didn't.

Faas: A priest for Olson?

DUNCAN: Well, you see, my idea of death is ritualistic. And Charles himself insisted upon the Catholicism throughout. When Betty, his common-law wife, died, he wanted to put Charles Peter into a very strict convent school. Only his friends prevented that. But his first impulse was to do that. And he had a Catholic funeral service read over Betty and was very upset because they now read it in English. He said: I didn't know that they would read it in English.

Faas: Betty was the woman who died in the car accident?

DUNCAN: Yes. So Charles wanted to keep the Catholic origins somewhat in the same way that I kept my Hermeticism. Although Charles didn't go to Church. So finally he didn't ask for a priest either, but he asked for a doctor. So he is Jungian and that was a better place for him. He didn't have an analyst, of course, any more than, I mean, who? And at death he wanted a doctor, a kind of mystery doctor to take him through the mystery of death, preparing him for that mystery. But as a poet, of course, he had to do it all on his own. I am sure I will have to do it on my own, too. Since we have hugged all those moments ourselves and had only language to do it, we have to do it in language. And he must have been doing it with "live-her." You know, "live-her," once it was divided and he was staring at it, he

[margin note] Olson's Catholicism

may have been staring not at the *anima,* but at Persephone herself in her awful character as Queen of the Dead. So "live-her" may be "life-death." He was unable to unlock it and he kept on looking at it and trying to see what it was that was happening there, and that went back and forth on his mind.

Letters for Origin had just arrived and he inscribed a copy for me and that is the last piece of his writing. And there he

last inscription addresses the fact that I was the poet that had been writing before his age began. Of course, at the same time he was very questioning of the fact that I might not be the person properly active in the new poetry and that I might be the person rather to disgrace it. But still, from his whole sense of continuity and tradition, he needed a key that before he started to write there had been a poet preceding him. And that identity I came in some way to occupy. It was a little like Anaïs Nin trying to find a poet when I hadn't written any poems yet. So he was excited about my poetry, but it was not the new poetry. The new poetry of that age was to be worked out entirely between Creeley and Olson. I was always then an intermediate between that and the poetry of the generation of the masters.

Faas: Could I see that last inscription?

DUNCAN: Of course. Let's go up to the attic and have a look at it. [After walking up to the attic.] This is it. [Handing me the book.]

Faas: It's quite illegible.

DUNCAN: [reads]: "To Duncan who taught me first the way," signed "from Charles, New York Hospital."

Faas: What does the rest say?

DUNCAN: [reads]: "To Duncan who taught me first the way and thought which I now" . . . The rest I can't decipher . . . "carry"? And then: "I am told"? No, I think, it's "I am tired."

Faas: And it's in *Letters for Origin* that Olson expressed the suspicion that you may not be quite reliable after all!

II

DUNCAN: Even Creeley, I think, at first thought I was going to be a little bit like the characters he had known at Harvard. Something like *The Venice Poem* must have spoken to him of some precious scenes at Harvard that none of us would exactly want to resurrect.

the Black   Remember that I was quite an old person in relation
Mountain poets to the Black Mountain generation. Although Olson was ten years older than I was, I had already begun to write

long before him and all the others, of course. So in a way it is an odd
thing that I ended up with that group of writers. Yet not before they
appeared on the scene did I find home ground. And home ground is
very hard to find. Even if we had thrown in a university education, I
would have found it very difficult to find a home ground with the
poets of my own generation. I mean, the generation of Lowell,
Jarrell or Berryman in which I would have just been the youngest.
All these were published in the magazines at the time when I was. In
View, for instance, there was Jarrell's poem along with a poem of
mine. All of them, as we know, were very sick boys who drank
themselves to death or committed suicide except for Lowell, who, if
it's a death, is one that has taken the longest time going around. But
that was not the kind of person I was. So I was really incommunicado
with whatever they were.

Faas: Your discovery of Denise Levertov's poem "The Shifting"
seems to have been the decisive turning point in your relation to the
Black Mountain poets.

DUNCAN: Yes, I was reading *Origin*, trying to figure out what was
going on. And I had been seeing poems that had been doing things.
But that poem I understood completely. I mean, how and
why the lines were moving in such and such a way. What   Levertov's
puzzled me at first was the typography. So I concluded   "The Shifting"
that this was a notation and that the lines stood for possibilities of feeling that would have no fillers. And more than that,
there was not just an absence of fillers, but she seemed to recognize
that there were breaks and junctures that are part of the utterance.
Of course, I wouldn't have analyzed it like that at that time. And the
poem I wrote right afterwards was for an amusement and I sent it off
to Corman. He did not accept the poem but sent it to Olson instead,
asking why I was making fun of Olson. And he sent it to Denise
asking why I was making fun of her. And the lead to Denise may
have come from the fact that I had written to Corman saying her
poem, "The Shifting," was terrific and here was a poem of mine. So
she wrote to me saying in great distress: Can you write this about me
and so forth if you are the same Duncan who has written *Heavenly
City, Earthly City*. Because Rexroth had sent her *Heavenly City, Earthly
City* which wasn't too far from her first books of poetry.

Faas: You mean the poetry written in England?

DUNCAN: Right. So I got into a correspondence with her and it was a
very intensive correspondence.

Faas: How did you react to her letter?

DUNCAN: Well, I wrote back that I hadn't intended a satire. But otherwise
I don't remember, because I don't keep copies of letters and this

is a long time ago. But then we were corresponding very heavily. So she was one of the first people I wanted to meet when I was on my way to Europe in 1955. We left for Europe from New York so I did meet Denise finally. And I absolutely loved her. And then for a matter of almost ten years, we had a very constant correspondence. Now often that correspondence was on poetry. And she found it intolerable when I would get over into the Sitwell area and would reprove me right away. So it was really Denise who determined my returning to a rhetoric of Stevens and Sitwell as I do in the poem at that point. She was very worried about my retrograding in that direction.

Faas: You mean in reaction to her.

DUNCAN: Yes, in answer to her. Remember that I was determined to go back to that rhetoric.

Faas: So it would be like your reaction to Williams when *he* told you off.

DUNCAN: Yes, if he scolds me, then I'll go and do medieval things. As a matter of general principle I don't understand that anything in writing is prohibited. Like what if it *were* sloppy! Meanwhile, I would be very disturbed by certain things in Denise's poetry and it would go back and forth.

Faas: You once told me how you had interpreted one of her poems by drawing attention to sexual puns which she hadn't been aware of.

DUNCAN: She was always infuriated by my tendency to read things first in a Freudian systematic way. Also, when the interview with Hogg and Bowering came out, I realized that it wasn't that recent that I had been disturbed with Denise's poetry.

Faas: The interview was in 1969.

DUNCAN: Yes, already at that time I was very vocal about my troubles and disappointments and mistrusts about what was going on in her poetry.

It had been awfully important to me to feel that
break with   Denise Levertov and Robert Creeley and Charles Olson
Levertov   and myself were a kind of movement and that they took
              care of a lot of areas that I even by temperament wouldn't
be likely to cover. One important aspect of my work is the difficulty of getting a picture of experience. And in a group, of course, you can assume that your reader is also going to read Olson. So you can save a lot of time, because all you have to do is take a potshot that hits off against a facet of Charles Olson and he covers miles of territory of what you are. Of course, you don't do it by agreement. But you only have to make the slightest distinctions and your reader will realize how a lot of things are disposed. And then in the composition of a

poem you don't have to do lots of explication. There is a difficulty about truth in relation to the fact that it is always being created and hence cannot be located. This was evident to Charles Olson who immediately grabbed the whole of Heisenberg's Uncertainty Principle. The other thing is : if I have an anxiety it is not because I am afraid I might die tomorrow, or some work won't be completed. It is rather my concern with fitting in the mosaic of the accounts so that there are enough hints that it might be an adjusted picture. This is the only way in which I can understand what it means to do justice to an event as being. I keep worrying about the fact that I have not yet given account of something or that I have not yet given another account of it. And in that respect, I felt that I had lost an ally in Denise. And yet I knew that sooner or later Denise was going to be a lost ally in some very important areas.

Faas: At various points you have emphasized your "entirely differentness" from Olson, once stating that to you poetry was a revelation of language, not of personality.

DUNCAN: Where was that?

Faas: That was in an open letter published in *Origin*. And then there is a statement concerning your "radical disagreement" with Olson published in the *Black Mountain Review* in 1955.

DUNCAN: These were very much directed at "Against Wisdom as Such." You remember we were just beginning writing and we had to sort out all sorts of things, to make these opposites, pose them as possibly being there. So I wouldn't put that forward at this point.

Faas: And yet in your 1969 interview with George Bowering you stated that what you had made of composition by field was very different from Olson's practice, adding that you didn't want any dichotomy of closed versus open. Instead you would make poems which are open, but which also contain closed elements.

DUNCAN: Of course. If we have a field, how can we throw out closed forms? They are only forms within a field. In the early *Passages* there is a proposition that the universe has only the boundaries we imagine. Every step in science is the imagination of a new boundary and every boundary gives us a new figure of the universe. And all of them are imagined. Of course, there are boundaries that don't fit any more, and they are let go. And that's all right. Some boundaries prove to be fitting but then a new factor enters and the boundary proves not to be a boundary any more. This would suggest exactly what an open field or an open mind is. And it may actually be an intuition about the nature of the universe. On the other hand, I find myself in great emotional conflict when I read that there is no reason to believe that the universe is integral. That there is no rationale to the universe being integral. Well, I find myself emotionally incapable of entertaining the notion of a non-integral universe. You see, there are no trivial events for me. This is really the question raised by Williams' famous "so much depends / upon / a red wheel / barrow." The real point of that question is: Are there any trivial events, are there any trivial people or trivial anythings, trivial beings or propositions? And for me, everything happening in the poem is properly apprehended and therefore not trivial.

Faas: You mean this is an emotional need.

DUNCAN: No, it is really that I can't feel it any other way. So I have a closed form at this point.

Fass: When you talked about changing models for the universe right now, you almost sounded like a Buddhist.

DUNCAN: No, I think what I meant was something really more scientific. Where boundaries are replaced by new scientific facts found in actual scientific discovery. That is something different isn't it, from ever-changing models of the universe. On the other hand, of course, I do agree that Gary's poetry and mine, for instance, look remarkably similar except for the fact that Snyder's poetry my verbal events are primary events and none of his are. His verbal events all convey an idea which stands at the back of them. My ideas are thematic and they operate like themes in music. That is to say, they are like themes in music and the music themes are just one thing and we know that everything else also counts. For Creeley, too, everything is in the verbal event. So in that sense, Gary to Robert seems to be very much out of order. I tend not to read Gary, like I don't read Rexroth. Because their sense of language is not what I use and yet when I read Gary and hear his poetry, I find that his actual picture of the universe is very much like mine. There is one big exception, of course, which is that his picture of the universe excludes Christ. Rexroth, for instance, who is also a kind of Western Buddhist, has Christ in his poetry. For there is nothing in the Buddhist universe which disallows the presence of any divinity, and you can also have an order of creation going on.

Faas: In this specific sense of language you are talking about, Creeley seems to be very close to people like Robbe-Grillet.

DUNCAN: He sees that himself, by the way. When we went to Majorca in 1955 he was excited by Beckett, and he gave me *Waiting for Godot* in French. So he must have read it in French. He French influences also gave me Cocteau's *La difficulté d'être* and then I remember having discussions with him about these books.

Faas: Does he know Roland Barthes' *Le degré zéro de l'écriture?*

DUNCAN: No, he has never mentioned that book to me. The people in the next generation who stem from Creeley are very close to Barthes. But I have never heard Creeley himself talk about it, whereas I myself have taken a whole bunch of things from Barthes. I get the impression that Creeley deliberately avoids him. It's too close for comfort, as it were. But he definitely stems from Existentialism and then seems to keep his distance from allying himself with those things which like him have developed away from Existentialism. The same thing happened to me when one of the first people to write a Ph.D. on my work started sending Merleau-Ponty and Barthes to me. I had previously consumed Piaget and I had read everything of Gestalt psychology which I was able to put my hands on. So Merleau-Ponty sounded to me like some sections of my journals. So I wrote back to that Ph.D. student saying all this makes me a little ill. I do enjoy Merleau-Ponty, but I find him almost impossible to read. He seems too redundant and robbing of my own thoughts. This may be the reason why I became acquainted with his work relatively late. Younger people had been reading him, but I didn't. So Creeley may have had a similar intuition. Like this is too close for me, I've got to look at something that will challenge that.

Faas: Yes, he never mentioned either Robbe-Grillet or Barthes in his writing.

How did you get to teach at Black Mountain?

DUNCAN: When we were in Majorca early in 1956, Ruth Witt had a grant for The Poetry Center in San Francisco. So there would be a salary for me to come home to if I would be Assistant Director to The Poetry Center. And I accepted, saying I would come back the following September. So, when teaching at Black Mountain Charles heard that, he wrote: If you are going to come back anyway, will you come in April and take two terms at Black Mountain before you return to San Francisco? So I went there.

Faas: What did you teach at Black Mountain?

DUNCAN: I taught basic techniques.

Faas: Of writing?

DUNCAN: Of poetry. A three hour course every day which was vowels and consonants and syllables and stress, interestingly enough. And we were getting somewhat sketchy although we were meeting three hours a day. It wasn't lecture courses, we were practising. We would sit at a long table and do exercises like write thirteen syllable lines as fast as you can and then see how many syllables come out, when you think you are going to do thirteen. And also exercises of line to stanza, not much more.

Faas: And the other courses?

DUNCAN: Then there was a lecture course I gave in the evenings three times a week. The first time a student gave a talk on what was then going to be my lecture the following Wednesday. Then on Friday, we would meet and talk about the whole thing. In that, the question of the law came up. The first one was genesis, the second one was law, and then tragedy and comedy. It was still revolving around the proposition that one could take approaches to the meaning of form. The kind of questions like what is the meaning of law.

Faas: What do you mean by law?

DUNCAN: Well, that was exactly the question they were to address. And that poem, *The Law I Love Is Major Mover*, came because Joe Dunn who had that project felt that the law was just the law, you know, cops and robbers. I remember one day going into the library at the school there and he was pouring over everything trying to get it into his head. And nothing could have been more garbled than the account he finally gave. And when he finished I said to him: Well, Joe, when you write a sentence beginning with the word "the," aren't you already under the law of "the"? No matter what you do from here on, you are under its law. And I think that's part of what a law is. In other words, lawful action to me is total responsibility to what is present. So I began to realize that at the time.

Faas: And during the summer you produced your *Medea*?

DUNCAN: Yes, and besides the *Medea* I gave a course on the *Illuminations* by Rimbaud.

teaching
Rimbaud

Faas: Rimbaud is an interest of yours which had begun much earlier. You did "A Derivation from Rimbaud" in '48.

DUNCAN: Right. Also, my quarrel with Verlaine starts fairly early. I know, Verlaine shot Rimbaud, but I would have shot *him* first. [Laughing] I can never translate a Verlaine poem without correcting it. Which is the most atrocious thing you can do to a poet—change the ending or something.

By contrast, Rimbaud is a real challenge. Two of the students in my group really knew some French, so they were way ahead of me. But we proceeded as if we didn't know a thing, no matter what. We had all the translations and all the dictionaries and all the guesses and we filled the board with them. So there were huge maps of what was going on in any sentence. It got to be a demonstration. I had started writing *The Structures of Rime* at Black Mountain and I knew about the Rimbaud prose poem. That's why I took the *Illuminations* that summer. I wanted to find out to what extent Rimbaud was a part of this, and I was sure that he was.

Faas: And then Olson came to San Francisco to give his Whitehead lectures at your house.

DUNCAN: Yes, and Whitehead comes immediately into action while I am working on *The Opening of the Field.* Charles is there giving his lectures and I am scribbling poems while he is lecturing.

Whitehead's "presentational immediacy"

Faas: Really.

DUNCAN: Yes, the minute he started, I also started reading *Process and Reality.* But of course, I was reading the book with an entirely different mind. So his Whitehead was turning into mine before I could turn around. I saw all sorts of things in Whitehead that would probably never have dawned on him. I remember the moment in Whitehead where he talks about "presentational immediacy" as being analogous to being cross-eyed. Wow! These are times when I identify as being the very center of the kind of consciousness that's talked about. Because being cross-eyed, I have been subject all my life, except for the first three years, to one of the states of presentational immediacy. While all the kiddies were going out taking drugs and getting hallucinations, I was subject to one which was much more mysterious. When I look at something, I see it double and I can never tell which one is the real one—the one which I see with my left eye or the one that I see with my right eye. As a child I used to go forward and touch it. But even then I was still the victim of the reduplication. So ever since my third year, I have been steadily in a quandary of presentational immediacy.

III

Faas: You first met Ginsberg around '54. What was your reaction when *Howl* came out?

DUNCAN: Well, I started to write a poem like it the day it arrived.

Faas: When it arrived?

Ginsberg's *Howl*

DUNCAN: Yes, I sat down and read it aloud to myself.

Faas: Was that in Europe?

DUNCAN: No, at Black Mountain. Allen himself had sent it to me. Then when I stared at what I wrote, I noticed that it was simply inappropriate. I couldn't do it. Because I was going in a completely different direction.

At that time whenever I was invited to give readings, people used to ask me what I thought of *Howl.* And I had no proper thoughts on *Howl.* My thoughts on *Howl* were very much colored by

my wanting it out of my way. And I think that was true of people
from Daddy Rexroth to anybody that had to ride that same period.
Though I wanted to do something like it the day or night that it
arrived. The other thing about it was that the pan-sexuality directly
came in conflict with my very strong Apollonian dedications. I mean,
strong enough for a householder. Allen himself, of
course, wants to be a householder, so it goes in other
directions. What I did not at all like was its wanting to
break down the high demands for mutuality. And I also
mean mutuality in relation to the poem. As you know, it became an
enormously popular poem. And that's a phenomenon, because it's
not like Ferlinghetti. It is not an easy poem. It is filled with trouble,
and it is a poem that daringly brings together the Orient and the
Occident which is an enormously productive and always fecund level
for the poem. But in Ginsberg you have the Oriental or rather
Hindu promise that the poetic furor would be sustained which in
fact is sustained remarkably throughout *Howl*. And in the sexual
sense there is the promise that if we would just respond immediately
everything would be all right. But that to me is kind of a fantasy from
high school. I can only see it as a kind of agony which in fact it has
been for me. And it has been agony for Ginsberg as a matter of fact.
But whatever it was to him personally, I found it very threatening.

My own poetry was going so much for a higher and higher
demand for a kind of *areté*. And while I may be multiphasic there *will*
be phases. That is to say, there will be boundaries. And I am very
much concerned with the boundaries and various centers. The
whole thing has to have an architecture. It's got a character armor, to
use the Reichian term, and in that I am identifiably Protestant.
Ginsberg's melting down, or breaking down, and wanting to disappear, or Burroughs' tendency to the same effect, was very disturbing
to me. Are we really going to dissolve all the boundaries? So I was in
direct conflict. When we came to our poetry conference at Vancouver in 1963, I was frequently on the floor challenging Ginsberg's
position. And a lot of it was concerning his position on the poem.
Mine would be the Constructivist poem, the poem as a work of art,
and I very well understood where Ginsberg was in
that. I knew about the prohibition that you shouldn't *make*
a poem from the *Zohar*. You should pour forth God's
voices, and that I went exactly against. Fine, go ahead and
pour forth that God voice, but let's distinguish that
from the poem. A poem, to me, is a mystery in making. Always, of
course, with tutelary address. Often with the address of a lure.
Faas: Of another poet?

disagreements with
Ginsberg

poetry a mystery
in making

DUNCAN: Yes, a presence of a poet which would be comparable to falling in love. And frequently the presence of a God, Helios or Apollo. *The Venice Poem* is the first model of those presences. Although "Toward the Shaman" is already an exercise in presences.

Faas: Your own rediscovery of Whitman seems to coincide with the point at which Whitman was finally integrated into the mainstream of American poetry through the influence of *Howl*.   Whitman

DUNCAN: Well, I started going to Whitman a little earlier than that.

Faas: You mentioned that *Leaves of Grass* became a kind of bedside book for you around 1956 when you were writing *The Opening of the Field*.

DUNCAN: Of course, I had read Whitman in high school. I was reading Whitman and Crane in order to assert the nature of homosexuality. And at that time everybody in college considered Whitman's poetry as very poor stuff. People would be embarrassed about it all. Of course, it was poor poetry to them mainly because they were embarrassed by the content.

So I did have some returns to Whitman before the '56 point. I think, I even took Whitman with me to Majorca. Anyway, when I started *The Opening of the Field*, I knew very well that *Leaves of Grass* were the field. That's why I am reading it from there on. And I still read it.

Faas: Did you discuss Whitman with Olson?

DUNCAN: Not very far. One wouldn't have gotten very far in trying to explain to Olson what was going on in a Whitman line. As a matter of fact, it is not that easy to explain. I have   Whitman and Olson done some analyses of sections of the *Cantos*. But I haven't analyzed the kind of lines in which I find Whitman astounding, I mean literally within single lines.

Faas: Did Olson ever see your essay on Whitman?

DUNCAN: He may have, but it sure didn't strike him.

Faas: At first it puzzled me that you place Whitman above and beyond Olson, Pound and Williams. But literary history seems to prove you right.

DUNCAN: Well, if you think about how large Whitman's vision is: he completely expands his concept of man so it goes far beyond questions of European man, or modern man, or man of some period. And that I do think of as largeness. Shakespeare does the same thing, although even more amazingly. Because he is able to invent personality.

But that largeness also seems to me to have an immediate hinge in the understanding of how a cadence is built in a line. In other words, I think of Whitman as having melodic intelligence the way Beethoven has. And we know now that Whitman's lines derive from the fact that he was listening to arias in which melody opens up so it can pour forth while still remaining melody. I mean, it can still have all its elements properly intoned, so to speak, so they remain significant.

Of course, the lines in *Howl* are not at all Whitmanic lines. In fact, Ginsberg himself never lost track of the fact that it was Christopher Smart who gave him one of the hints as to what that line was going to be. And the lines in *Howl* are very much Christopher Smart lines.

Whitman and Howl

Faas: Ginsberg actually denies the direct influence of Whitman on *Howl*. He told me that Whitman's influence on his poetry came much later.

DUNCAN: Ginsberg's long lines tend to sprawl, something I don't find at all in *Leaves*. You remember when Whitman talks about line or rhyme, he talks about a tree or vine growing, or simply about an organism. And Whitman had the true feeling of organisms where every part is actually growing out of another and having a role throughout. No wonder his world doesn't look too different from Whitehead's who is talking about a philosophy of organism. Of course, Whitman is no philosopher, so he doesn't develop a philosophy of organism but simply rides the wave of philosophies that feed his feeling of organism in the poem. Organism also means that any part can function in coordination with any other part, so you aren't building perfect bodies, for instance. Whitman doesn't have the superstition of perfection which life itself doesn't have, of course. My Whitman is a Random House Whitman which I acquired when I was a freshman in college. And that edition has Whitman's little essay on Darwin, and he right away sees that Darwin is his man. And he doesn't have Darwin wrong. He doesn't believe that evolution produced the marvellous thing called man. He takes Darwin right straight and sees that the local, immediate event is evolving and that that doesn't mean the event perfecting itself and climbing up a ladder.

Faas: It seems to me that your own and Ginsberg's return to Whitman represents a major reorientation of the Pound-Williams-Olson tradition.

a major poetic reorientation

DUNCAN: Well, the æsthetics of Pound and Williams in their negative response to Whitman seem to me a regression in poetics. Especially for me because it puts me in a threatened position. It was a regression from the kind of confidence that Whitman had. *Personæ*

by Pound still had that kind of confidence and freedom. And so did
Spring and All by Williams. Lawrence has it all the way through, of
course,—the freedom which is essentially the freedom of a created
"I" that can do anything in a poem. In that way, I thought Whitman
and Lawrence remarkably resembled my own poetry.

Faas: O'Hara seems to have been another major force behind the
recent Whitman renaissance.

DUNCAN: What was so striking about O'Hara was the tremendous
emotional power of the early poems. He must have felt that he was
on an entirely different level than anyone around him.
It's amazing how O'Hara has widened the common lan-
guage of Whitman. And that is something that I do be-   Frank O'Hara
lieve in myself. I am not interested, and increasingly not
interested, in my poetry, in any uncommon language, any specifically poetic language. I think that when mastery increases poetry
gets much much simpler word-wise.

Faas: To me it has never made sense to lump Ashbery and O'Hara
together.

DUNCAN: But you see they grew up together. Temperamentally they
are quite different. John never had to make any step of this kind of
democratization of the poem. But Frank did it because I think he is
Whitmanesque. In many ways Frank is more Whitman than Allen is.
Allen's stepping in front of these huge audiences and commanding
them is very non-Whitmanic. So they are like a funny split of the
Whitman tradition really, aren't they? But my critique of O'Hara
would be that in his democratization the poem becomes almost
simple-minded. I can see no difference between our admiration and
thrill when an athlete clears the eight foot bar when we couldn't even
jump over a table, and our thrill at an intellectual performance. So
what I admire in Shakespeare is simply what I could never do, not
what is "simple."

Faas: So many parallels have been drawn between O'Hara's work
and action painting.

DUNCAN: But the painters he was interested in really were not action
painters. I mean, he wrote about Pollock, but his actual contemporaries among painters were an entirely different group.

Faas: Exactly. In fact, his kind of poetry strikes me as a kind of
equivalent of pop art.

DUNCAN: Quite. And Rivers becomes a really trivial painter under
the O'Hara course. The trivialisation of the painters that he was close
to is very obvious.

IV

Faas: Robert Bly claims that American poetry has missed out on Surrealism. I am sure you wouldn't agree with that.

DUNCAN: Those remarks of his I simply find humorous. Or his remark that I stem from French Surrealism and not from Spanish. I mean, he just doesn't know. We read our Lorca over and over again. The impact of Lorca and Rilke was what made the big jolt from Pound, and that was in the late thirties.

Lorca and Rilke, the big jolt from Pound

Faas: So you feel that you have absorbed the influence of Surrealism.

DUNCAN: Yes, although not of South American Surrealism. Neruda was translated but somehow we didn't read him. Maybe because as Anarchists we were anti-Neruda. Because he was Stalinist and we were violently anti-Stalinist, Neruda was reactionary to us as kids when we were in our teens. At that time, Neruda was for the Moscow trials. So while I could stand Pound's Fascism because I didn't even have such a tendency, I felt that people like Zukofsky and Neruda had betrayed the Socialist Communist Revolution.

Faas: You once stated that an image could be close to the psychological archetype of Jungian analysis, or that images should be an evocation of depth. One could compare these definitions with similar ones by Robert Bly and other poets of the deep image school of poetry.

the "deep image"

DUNCAN: What interested me more at the time was Robert Kelly's remark about a melody of images, and that formula remains interesting to me. It is a more suggestive possibility than my sense of themes. A melody is a little different from a theme, a much freer invention. Concerning deep image our critique and my witticism right away was: one inch deep, two feet deep, how deep? It's like, what is important and what trivial? In my sense of things, there is nothing trivial, so that everything has to have depth since it relates throughout. And what we can do is recognize the depth which is going on.

Bly's attack

Then when Bly started out with his magazine *The Fifties*, there was not only an open attack on us as a group, but an attack on the techniques of the poem. He is all in favor of primary intuition, but I don't think that there is any division between techniques of the poem and primary intuition. Olson's great contribution which Bly overlooks is that he relates technique to the body. The most important contribution Olson made is that he studies poetry almost at the medical level, at the morphological level.

His understanding of poetry along those lines is much vaster than mine today. I had studied the ear and the development of the eye whereas Olson was really studying embryonic development. When I first met him, he hadn't related that to the poem yet. But he said that the understanding of man had to proceed from that.

I have to add that my discussion of Bly is rather uninformed because I have hardly read him.

Faas: Didn't you have direct contact with Bly at an early point?

DUNCAN: Yes, I had a little correspondence with him after he had announced that his magazine was going to be Surrealist. So I wanted to find out whether that meant Breton and Romantic Surrealism. And I also wanted to find out if he knew that Surrealism involved magic. What I got back was a somewhat angry letter in which he stated that he didn't believe that Surrealism involved magic, but that instead it involved depth-psychology. And that depth-psychology was an antithesis to magic. From then on, I had not much interest in him, finding that Bly had no concept of magic at all.

Surrealism and magic

Faas: What would be the difference between depth-psychology and magic?

DUNCAN: Well, magic would mean that you are not only dealing with some archetypes in your psyche but with some real entities like angels. I mean, angels in a poem are real and literal and not fancy.

Faas: That, I guess, would also account for your dissent from Jung.

DUNCAN: Well, I must have been extremely attracted to the archetype initially. But then I took Mescalin and I burst into tears when I realized I was seeing something I hadn't made, that I hadn't drawn. And that somebody else hadn't made. So the presence of an image in my mind put me into a total quandary. Because it was difficult for me to accept that there was such an image in my mind. So a poem must be very reassuring to me. You see, in a dream there is a process in which things are put together. So it is a kind of creative process in the mind. I am not so angry with Jungianism because of the fact that it refuses to recognize that there are externals but because it insists that they are internals. During the period that I took the Mescalin, my sense of the external was so acute that I raised the question, as I still often do, whether there is any possible being in me which can be called my ego. Because I recompose what I call myself from a world. So for me there is a question: Is there a me? I? What I do is that I pose a creative process in which I assemble me from surrounding facts including the body and so forth.

dissent from Jung

Faas: Are you referring to any specific drug experiment?

DUNCAN: Yes, the only time that I ever took a hallucinogenic drug was in 1952 in an experiment run by Stanford University. It was Mescalin. What I saw was the world tree. It was also, however, a tree realized in jewels as well as being cosmic with lights. It was like a huge mosaic and I felt it as the existence of an archetype, like what Plato is talking about. It was then that I also had my first experience of dissent from the archetype. I burst into tears, and I also did not accept seeing what I had not made. Later in 1963, at the University of British Columbia, I gave a lecture which was about my refusal to have any mystical experiences because I wanted to be made out of thousands of threads that I myself have tied. My figure is the Muslim rug which one spends a whole lifetime in tying, simply thread by thread. Of course, you know the figure. Everybody knows the figure. So I do not disavow the knowledge of the figure. But I will not let that figure in any way substitute for the work. There we are back with the concept of the poet as maker.

Faas: So a symbol or poetic image would hardly be an archetype.

DUNCAN: Well, I wonder how any poet could be attracted to Jungianism. To me poets use symbols to be initial and in the universe. Jung uses them to be in a psyche and around a center. When we, from my generation, were looking into the universe, there wasn't that apparent a center in time or in space. Charles had the same observation. But the distinction between a centered universe and a non-centered one never bothered him. He took the center to be wherever you are. Anyway, I am not a creature of the center. I am a creature of outside.

Faas: You have often criticized Jung's *maṇḍala* concept.

DUNCAN: Exactly. That's the area I am critical of. I don't disbelieve in the existence of archetypes, but I wouldn't posit their importance in the way Jung does. Where I don't join Eastern philosophy at all, is that I think that everything we see is posited in the material world. So that an archetype doesn't get to be very arche. Instead of looking at an archetype, we'd better look at a tree or a particular individual.

Faas: You have compared the poem with dream-work. On the other hand, you say that the poet in the act of creation must wrestle against sleep, using all his watchful craft and learned art. You also said that the entire area of poetry is consciousness.

DUNCAN: Yes, but what dream do we know that is not consciousness? And now that we have got the map of it, it seems evident that we have not yet gotten to sleep when we are dreaming. By the way, that thing about wrestling with sleep is an instruction that came to me in a poem. So I wouldn't say that I am voluntary in that, although I will

(marginal note: taking Mescalin)

take it once I am given the instructions. When I was in my early twenties we read Kafka and we thought he was an expert reporter of dreams. And I kept extensive notebooks which are now at the University of California and they contain descriptions of dreams. I even recorded conversations and verbal happenings in dreams. So, dream was evidence that you had a primary conscious activity of composition that was tremendous, absolutely tremendous. But I would still call that consciousness, bringing consciousness together. My objection to the Jungian concept, that the unconscious has anything in it, is that I take the unconscious to be *un*conscious. What Jung is talking about is the subconscious, not the unconscious. James already makes such a distinction. And while Yoga observes that there is very little in the body that our consciousness can not inhabit, I personally would allow that there is an unconscious and that it actually is an enormous area. But if it is truly *un*conscious, then there are no images. Because the minute there is an image, it is consciousness. By the time a dream is in our mind, its entire event is in consciousness. And when I am talking about the unconscious, then I am not talking about the dream we don't remember. As Freud found out, there is a sub-conscious which is a kind of reservoir held by consciousness. But that is not the unconscious. The unconscious must mean a sense of void or blankness or unavailable information or otherness. And this the consciousness doesn't dream about. But the conscious mind im-agines what is in it, and fills it with imaginings and in that, it is creating. In my picture then, of God, He is imagining Himself. And the world is the current image of that Self. So we do have an Otherness that is imagining.

poetry and dream

Faas: Would you approve of automatic writing as a viable mode of composition?

DUNCAN: I don't understand what automatic writing is. A require-ment for automatic writing or any autistic activity to take place, is a split personality where there is no connection between the two. Now in a multiphasic personality, we don't have such a split. Because if your personality is a field, then the co-existence of multiple personalities is not carried on as a split. The minute you have a split, then you have another kind of Other, so to speak. And speaking for myself, I call the unconscious the Other. All the other others are integrated. They form some kind of texture and that we can't pose in automatic writing. So that is what is puzzling to me in automatic writing. By the way, the thing that Breton and Éluard are doing is imitating automatic writing. They simulate states of madness. They simulate automatic writing.

automatic versus autistic writing

But a good deal of *The Structures of Rime,* of course, is presumed to be autistic. And *Passages* when it arrives, arrives. So I've got autistic elements that are felt to come from outside, or that I go into. So at that psychological level, much of *Passages* I can't view as anything other than being received. So it obviously has a good area of Other.

V

Faas: To James Dickey the subject matter of poetry seems to be a kind of given which he then proceeds to write poems
the subject matter   about. I guess you wouldn't share this approach.
of poetry   DUNCAN: Of course, he is a narrative poet and then psychologically he is upset.
Faas: Creeley takes the exactly opposite approach.
DUNCAN: Yes, because he is working with the same material over and over again. And I would also take the Creeley position. A subject doesn't give me a poem. The beginning of a line does. But, of course, Creeley has demonstrable subjects.
Faas: But then he always stresses that his poems don't have any referential meaning.
DUNCAN: Well, but then that's balderdash. His subject seems to be a very special kind of Creeley predicament. So that when that predicament rises in his mind, he produces certain poems. One of its features, of course, is stumbling and proceeding in some fashion in which clumsiness is imperative. It's a mysteri-
Creeley   ous predicament to me since I still read the poems. But some of its solutions have been very, very simple. I mean, he proposes subjects I would never dream of being subjects. At some point, he proposed minimal subjects. But that still is a subject proposition, not one that arises from a line.
Faas: None of all that would apply to Dickey, of course.
DUNCAN: No, with Dickey the case is entirely different. Dickey's weakness shows up in the fact that he is quite dependent upon an adequate relation to his *one* subject which is recharging his sense of being alive by the panic of something he is killing and which is suffering pain. And since he can't revivify that by actually shooting and chopping and burning people all the time, his poems often become fantasies of doing this. And they are considerably weakened on account of it. At first I was misled, although not entirely misled. I found the first poems by Dickey
Dickey   which I saw very curious, especially the one about the battlefield with the dead stirring underground. Having

grown up in a family that was also Southern and that also had a cult of spiritualism of the dead, I was intrigued. I thought: Gee, there is somebody from the South with a cult of the dead who is involved in spiritualism again. That seemed to me significant. After all, they had lost the Civil War and they had all these ancestors killed in it. So I wrote to him and corresponded with him briefly and asked him to come and visit. And one couldn't imagine a less fortunate meeting, of course. But "Drinking from a Helmet" is a remarkable poem. And the poem of the shooting of the deer and beginning to feast is also remarkable. But by the time he begins to feast on the panic in the deer, I began to see some of the tangles of what it was. Then I felt: My God, this is really a very strange, murderous cult. And I asked for a book of Dickey's to review and they gave me the volume which has "The Firebombing" in it. Now, that poem already has the deterioration which marks his later work. He, of course, had been in actual missions of firebombing, but that was "The Firebombing" some time ago. So he was now trying to find expression for this terrible nostalgia. He was trying to charge the poem by gloating back to the feeling of the murder. And the poem has some remarkable clues. It seems to expand around a remarkable hostility against everything around the poet. So finally, he firebombs the world which he is actually in, the American suburbs. So in "Up Rising," I took some parts out of that poem, and more than that, I located it in myself in the period when we did our little crayon drawings and burned our whole families. Of course, by locating it back in myself, I wasn't talking about Dickey.

But, gee, by the time you come to Dickey's poem "Falling" about the stewardess falling out of a plane, you have something he read in the newspapers and cannot resurrect in his imagination. Because it still won't be something which he can actually see. So the whole thing becomes ludicrous. He can't connect with her panic. Psychologically, of course, he has to connect with panic in order to write his poems. You've got the same thing in *Deliverance*. The end of the thing is absolutely phoney. Because he has to invent all sorts of pains. And then suddenly on walks James Dickey acting as a sheriff, and it is a better sheriff than you ever saw in a million movies. Dickey also has a split personality, quite apart from the artistic problem. He was once an advertising agent, and when he writes criticism you wouldn't dream he was a poet. He is a Madison Avenue career-maker. And very successful at it. We have had a lot of Madison Avenue career-makers. Yet this is the first one who is actually a poet at times. But he is not a poet who makes me feel happy. I realize there is no conversation I could have with Dickey. Not only did I not have one, but I couldn't even have one in my imagination. But still, his work is very significant. I think it is more significant than he realizes.

Faas: It is interesting how the Black Mountain ideas which he fought more than anybody else have recently caught on with him.

Dickey and
open form

DUNCAN: My God, yes. Just look at the structure of his line. I mean, do you think he can rip off those lines and not get into trouble? [Laughing]

Faas: At some point Dickey wrote an essay where all of a sudden he discovered his predilection for open form poetry and "presentational immediacy."

DUNCAN: But then, I guess, that was a little bit like *Naked Poetry* who also thought that they were open form and presentational immediacy. But, gee, did he get that term "presentational immediacy" from Whitehead?

Faas: Yes.

DUNCAN: Oh, great. I, of course, fell in love with that term "presentational immediacy."

Faas: Would you share Dickey's prognostication that open form poetry is going to be the predominant mode in America?

DUNCAN: Yes, just remember how suggestive open form is to us in America. I mean, there are our open spaces, our open minds, our everything. And Dickey is very much of that era. His opposition to Black Mountain, in fact, was that he felt we were closing down the open possibilities in the poem. He saw us as quite the contrary to what we were proposing.

Faas: Do you think that open form is an American phenomenon?

DUNCAN: Oh, no. It's only of special significance in America. It's the whole modern thing.

Faas: So it would be something common to the whole Western world.

DUNCAN: Yes, and then you have Japan, for instance, opening itself up to the West. In a way, there are no more crucial openings. Everything has been opened up. Nobody is hiding away in a closet today—some poor Eskimos or something.

Faas: You just suggested that the beginning of a line may give you a poem. Do you have a definite feeling about when and how a poem begins?

beginning
of a poem

DUNCAN: Yes.

Faas: What does it feel like?

DUNCAN: It is like a musical feeling. Yes, you do have a primary feeling about fittingness. Naturally it seems to me the criterion of truth in a poem. Its fittingness is pre-Gestalt. That is the notion which interested James.

Faas: William James?

DUNCAN: Right. William James. So when I find that certain parts are not fitting or true, they are never not fitting or true in themselves, but in the way that they are assembled. I was annoyed when Rosenthal said that I was an æsthete or something, because largely I feel that a thing is beautiful when it is fitting. That's not a purely æsthetic intuition.

Faas: Do you have any other criteria for evaluating poetry? The critics writing about *Paterson*, for instance, still remain largely concerned with the question of whether or not the poem has a unity.

DUNCAN: Well, I'm not worried about unity. But let's ask: Where do I have my troubles? Well, *Paterson* was one of the places where we really took hold and where we saw something to be done in the poem. But I'm still wondering: How come he lifted it out of *Finnegans Wake* that it was going to go in a circle and that the man was going to be the city and the woman the river. All that I think of as the superstition of the poem.

evaluating poetry

All right, I think there are superstitions in my poems. There are configurations that are entirely idiosyncratic. That is, they are not pertinent to the immediate poem. They are not structurally important at all in any conceivable community of meaning. I mean, that whole thing about the man, the city, the woman and the river is essential to *Finnegans Wake* because it was so conceived. And that they get confused, is also part of the process of the poem. But in the case of Williams it was simply borrowed as a superstition. So I am criticizing *Paterson* for introducing ideas as if they were as incidental as rhyme at the end of a line. However, there was no harm done. Because when he finished book IV, he had this marvellous example of a coda. Williams realized that after his conclusion he had another book. And his initial real daring is way back in the early twenties in *Spring and All*. When I first began to read those poems, I couldn't even grasp them. *Spring and All* is far beyond all the stuff we are talking about. So I do have some evaluations when I find those superstitions. And I find *Spring and All* to be a poem totally written without any superstitions.

Faas: You rarely comment on your practises as a poet. Do you revise a lot?

DUNCAN: Well, when I was 19 or 20, I was absolutely bowled over by Rilke's *Duino Elegies*. And then in Rilke's letters about the elegies I came across a doctrine that the poet should not rewrite and correct. So I sort of came to feel guilty about any kind of rewriting and correcting. If the poem was received, how could you rewrite it? But then, of course, there is the evidence of *Medieval Scenes*. I considered those poems as absolutely received. But then I wrote revising another version of them which was the one that got printed. And I wrote that second version for public delivery. I introduced a series of thematic bridges exactly in the way the Middle Ages proposes: themes which are absolutely separate and which don't even form a sequence except that they are together, 12 in number. That's the version which appeared in the *Selected Poems* that City Lights put out. In the other version, of course, there were no bridges at all. So there is an example of rewriting.

Faas: But more in the sense that Lawrence proposes, that is to say, of giving your creative impulse another chance to realize itself.

DUNCAN: Yes, and I have become more and more aware of this phenomenon of different versions. *Passages* I write in notebooks which I can show you. [Fetches notebook from the shelf] When they did the N.E.T. film on me, I was photographed writing this poem.

Faas: This is the first draft?

DUNCAN: Yes. I think of this as of a cartoon as you have a cartoon for a painting. Then on the typewriter, this has to be reinterpreted. So these people doing the film asked me to show them how I would write the poem at the typewriter and I realized something I would not have imagined. I was certain that I would not mouth a poem while I was writing it. When I write by hand, I can feel the poem in my hand. Yes, I know what that means. The typewriter doesn't give me this kinæsthetic feeling of the line: the kind of disequilibrium which you feel in the hand—the disequilibrium which produces the new line. So what I mean is that there is a sound which you don't consciously hear, a pitch which is not in the range of hearing and which yet enters the range of equilibrations, like somebody adjusting a horizontal. So no wonder I feel the line in this way. I am a writer in the original sense of writing with my hand.

Faas: When do you end a poem? Stafford once said that he usually concludes a poem when his powers to homogenize an experience come to an end.

DUNCAN: Well, we are not homogenizing. So that can't be poetic closure it. Very frequently, the end of a poem is a close. Analogous to Stravinsky's invention of closes for series. It's sort of very simplistic. Just making a coda. You find that in *The Venice Poem* I do such a coda. And in *Passages* I very often do that. But by no means is that a form of homogenizing.

Faas: So you don't just leave off when your creative impulse has exhausted itself.

DUNCAN: Oh yes, I do that all the time.

Faas: No, I mean in a printed poem.

DUNCAN: Oh, no, in print the end of the poem is when the content of the poem is completely present. And that content of the poem is demonstrably the working out of certain rhymes. The sound level and the significant thing about the sound level I got from Pound who once wrote me about the tone leading of the vowels. That expands the elements of the poem with which you are composing. And I, of course, wanted an expansive content for the poem. If you just take a rhyme, it would give us time and dime and mime and so forth. And that is a very limited series. But if we take the vowel and take the tone lead from that, we expand the vocabulary and thus expand the possible content. So I am working with sound all the time.

If you consider the poem as an object, you can think of it as completed in the area that it is in. But, of course, that doesn't mean that it is really completed. There are several bold decisions one could make at any time, by which one could give an entirely different significance to everything that is going on in there. And there are millions of decisions one could make. I am considerably less skilled as a visual artist than as a poet. So almost any interior form in my drawings, for instance, is schematic.

Faas: So when you finish a poem, you really feel that that's the end of it?

DUNCAN: Oh, sure.

Faas: And it is not open in the sense that it could go on indefinitely?

DUNCAN: But remember that the form is always local. So when we talk about finishing we talk about finishing the poem and not finishing the form. The poem is as specific as when you know how to write a play. You know when you are in act one. So the end is a kind of decision. It is an absolute decision and if I would add two more words, then it would be an entirely different poem. It is not a homogenization. It's like a decision. That's it. In this way, I absolutely feel the end of a poem.

VI

Faas: Often when you talk about the universe as a meaningful creation you almost seem to strike a neo-Platonic or teleological note.

DUNCAN: Well, no. Meaningfulness is intent. But let's look at it from a different angle. I am a Darwinian, not a Lamarckian. Unlike John Cage, I don't believe there is any chance at all. Intent and creation is fundamentally mysterious. It is actually going on. I don't think of creation as something redundant, as God making up something.

It delighted me to come across the Greek criticism of Heraclitus.
They couldn't take it that Heraclitus believed that the
a "meaningful" universe created itself and that the process of creation
universe was actually going on. That scandalized the neo-
Platonists, and it scandalizes the Buddhists. In neo-
Platonism, the universe emanates. There is a source that's more
intent than the actual process of creation. In Olson, the universe has
a beginning and it has declined. It has had a Golden Age and it has
declined. And it is in a state of recovery. So, of course, there you can
have a cycle. For me, what is is what is. And it's creating itself. No
wonder I have the work to do.

Faas: And there is no chance in that creative process?

DUNCAN: Well, no. I mean, we have got testimony about chance,
don't we? But personally I find myself deficient in any sense of
chance.

Faas: You once stated: I do not believe in creation by chance or by
predestined form.

DUNCAN: Yes, right. Like in Darwin, there is no predestination.
Everything is so much cooperation. Creation is everywhere intending, but only in a cooperation you have
chance particulars emerging. So there is no paradigm. What was
interesting to me as it was to Charles, is that Whitehead
pointed out that the primordial is ahead of us. That the past is
actually the thing we keep posing as if it came after the primordial
which it can't possibly have done. So we are always emerging in the
primordial. And resurrection for me really would be a figure of any
definition of the present.

Where I saw all that first was in the post-Martha Graham development in dance. We had a high Fascism of the dance
which dominated the thirties. I mean, Martha Graham
modern music didn't have ovens, but she did resemble Hitler remarka-
and dance bly as a kind of female version. There was an absolute
tyranny in the dance. And some of the people moving away from her
introduced chance operations. But then, chance operations seem to
me more and more the very opposite of chance. I mean, they show a
higher order, not a lesser order. So what was interesting to me was
that a dance was beginning to emerge in which all the dancers
cooperate. That is to say, they had to be attentive to where they were.
Similarly, in Cage's music, you cannot presume a melody. So if you
aren't hearing it, then you simply aren't. If you miss something in
Cage, you really miss it because you missed what's going on, whereas
if you miss something in Mozart you can kind of fill it in in your
mind. So we have come to a completely different kind of music. Of

course, I am referring to Cage's early aleatoric music. Now Cage, of course, claims that he is not in music any longer. But what attracted me to this aleatoric music was a potential recognition that there was something else than the neo-Platonic scale out of which we get all our sense of harmony that has dominated music for so long. Instead of that, we get a larger picture in which every conceivable sound is present. And now we find that our original harmonies don't disappear as being present, but they are co-present with all the other elements, and we have to be attentive throughout. We have to recognize that they are there. But that is only coincident to our recognizing the actual sounds that are there.

Faas: You have often stated that the language of poetry should be an echo of the greater language in which the universe is written.

DUNCAN: Yes, right. I think in human language we turn the sounds of our mouths into a language of things in order to imitate the way we experience. I think there is a primal intuition in our expression: The mountain speaks to me. So we try to speak back. What Piaget says makes sense to me. We speak back to something that speaks to us. So in speaking, there is a cooperation going on between world and person. Our engagement in language is active only as long as we are finding the universe. When we cease to find the universe, then actually we cease to have the occasion of language. That great proportion of modern poets who have suffered shipwreck in language are really no longer engaged in finding the universe. Language has in a way grown sufficient to them. But we have to have a searching psyche, a searching mind or simply a longing or a need for language to continue in the universe. Language for me is an engagement in which we are finding the universe. So, seeing is very closely related to language in a way. We imitate seeing in language. But reading of course far precedes language. For instance, we can read the tracks of the dinosaurs and we can understand them. That is their language. So, we read the universe as long as we are interested in it.

concept of language

Faas: Wendy MacIntyre has called an Orphic concept of language the "quintessence of your poetics." How does Wittgenstein relate to that?

DUNCAN: As compared with Zukofsky's romance with Wittgenstein, my reading of him has been rather peripheral. I find him fascinating, of course. Because like Whitehead he is a poet. But he is never keyed in directly into my work. I have read some of his works here and there, but not extensively. Whitehead, I think, is the most recent philosopher which gave me the illusion that I was reading real news from the

Wittgenstein

real universe. Games, I mean, yes. I played my own games even in language when I was little. It turned me on quite a bit. I mean, I am and was a very bad tempered boy. [Laughing]

Faas: You seem to be equally distanced from Fenollosa's, Pound's and Williams' experiments in fragmentation. I mean their endeavors to break up Aristotelian grammar and logic.

fragmentation

DUNCAN: But I ain't got any Aristotelian grammar or logic. I mean, they had to break up a very strong, presiding, simple construct. And Gary, in a way, still stems from that development. Although he organizes or reorganizes the fragments into intelligible, simple constructs again. But I have got to have a rhetoric because I have got to have something for the flow of the poem. I am not bothered about interrupting things. I mean, I can hardly start something without interrupting right away. And yet, I am still fascinated by melody. Cage once told me: As long as you are concerned with melody you are just not going to get there. But I am concerned with melody and I am just not going to worry about it. I mean, I don't need melody when I am listening to something. Although, on the other hand, my 19th century collection of music seems to be growing, growing and growing.

Faas: A poet like Antin traces post-Modernism to the *Cantos* and *The Waste Land.*

DUNCAN: Well, I'm not a Modernist. He can do that. I read Modernism as Romanticism; and I finally begin to feel myself pretty much a 19th century mind.

"I'm not a Modernist"

Faas: Really!

DUNCAN: I don't feel out of my century, I like this century immensely. But my ties to Pound, Stein, Surrealism and so forth all seem to me entirely consequent to their unbroken continuity from the Romantic period.

Faas: Antin talks of the poetry of collage.

DUNCAN: Well, I use collage and I fragment things.

Faas: But you also use the rhetoric.

DUNCAN: Oh, sure. And I would even refuse to interrupt it.

Faas: It seems to be one of the most important characteristics of your open form poetry and poetics that you try to integrate everything. You integrate rhetoric and you integrate closed form.

DUNCAN: Right. You see, if open form were a correction of closed form, okay. And in Olson's proposition it sounds like that. But I find that superfluous. Would you want to go back and correct, let's say, Housman? What do you think you would arrive at? Actually the open thing is really to contain any closed form. Any passage or anything else can be contained as part of a large open form. The

essential recognition in open form is that every event in poetry has its
form in reference to the total feeling of the formality of
the language. That's the way I put it. Once you recognize   open form
that the language is through and through as formal as it   and integration
is, you realize that every poem is participating in a form.
For one thing, it's our experience of the universe really which makes
open form seem appropriate. If we only take the local fact of our life.
We don't really have much of a memory of being born. We come out
of a darkness and we cannot account for the first years of our life.
And one thing we really don't get to catch up with is how we die. But
if we have even a rudimentary imagination and if we then write a
poem, it has more meanings, more lives than we ourselves in any way
posited by way of actual experience. Even if we posit a closed form its
readings aren't closed, and never have been. And when we have an
open form we let the poem ride the vitality that language always has,
and we ourselves adventure into that.

Faas: What exact role does language play in that?

DUNCAN: Language, first just at the level of names, is our agency
whereby things come close to us and enter our psychic
world. I mean, without any name for table, I have a   language a
suspicion that we don't really know what happens. I think   reification of
the name comes along with the focus, it's a reification of   the universe
the universe. Each name is a reification of things. As long as a person
is in love with and curious about and searching for the universe, he is
engaged in language. And language has to increase for him to get
anywhere in the universe. The symptom of ceasing to be in language, of ceasing to read a poem, of ceasing to be active in your
science, of ceasing to read and of ceasing to wander and talk is a
de-reification of the universe and a letting go of everything around
you. Now that's what I think is the significance of the openness. All
real instincts in language go toward an openness. This is why Eliot
would be closed and why his religion is closed. When you want to be
conclusive about that universe you do not want a new fact to come
into reification. You do not want to realize some new thing.

Faas: There seems to be no language crisis in your poetry. By
contrast, many European poets have given up writing poetry completely when they lost their belief in the Orphic powers of language.
And some of them through reading Wittgenstein.

DUNCAN: And yet, as Zukofsky shows, there is no reason why
Wittgenstein would lead to a poverty of the poem. And personally
I'm not drawn to the different forms of Positivism. Wittgenstein I
read with a great deal of pleasure because he seems to me like poetry.
Like Barthes does. I mean the language itself is like a whole

series of poetic events. And it does not engage my speculations about the universe, it doesn't even pose that. You see, in order to pose Wittgensteinian positive language formulas one has to have a very heavy exclusion of any possibility that language has mysterious presences. When I say, a woman comes into the room, I see one come into the room. He poses that as a game, but I don't experience it as a game. I don't play that I see a woman come into the room, although one of its analogies is that when as a child you played, the things were immediately present. The place where I go entirely with Lawrence is that they are immediately present and I'm not going to pretend they are not. I wouldn't have Christ present in a poem if he weren't really present. It's not a proposition of mine. And that's what makes it true or false. I don't mean that the truth means I've got the true Christ. But it's truly present.

Faas: In the poem.

DUNCAN: Right. And then I'm not bothered at all that I've got absolutely no system of logic. I'm not bothered that the truly present at one time will be entirely different from the truly present at another time. If at one time Christ is a woman, I don't turn that into a dogma so that at another time Christ won't be a man. I'm intrigued by the fact: Do I make it up? Those are not levels that I answer, can answer, so I turn them over and over. When I find that a figure like Christ or the figure of boundaries, that we were talking about, is unsettled in my poetry, then it makes sense to me that it comes again and again in the poem. And I think of it as being turned and turned and turned. And I'm really seeing and feeling myself turning a stone. And clearly my deepest feeling is that I've not come to know this enough yet. Because I'm not going to put a logic on any thing, I'm seeking to come to such a thorough knowledge that I suddenly realize—again in the process of turning into a thing—that it's all together. So I'm seeking altogetherness and not that it checks out in dictions and contradictions. I see it's there and that it often comes to live with you forever. It's the same thing in my relation to Jess. Our emotions developed over 20 years of living together. And I don't mean to say that it's a virtue to live a long time. But in my temperament there is a lot of that slow development. People often don't realize that. Because I talk so fast and grab things in a million different ways within five minutes. But what one might observe is that while I grab things in twenty different ways or go into a great manic spiel in which it is reposed and reformulated twenty different ways in five minutes, I've been doing it for nearly fifty years. I've been doing it since I was a child in

[margin: language not a game]

[margin: a great manic spiel]

stockings at the age of about four or five. And I haven't arrived in all that at greater certainty. It's simply a continuous process of reification.

Gary Snyder

Photo: Layle Silbert

GARY SNYDER (1930 -   )

> "As a poet, I hold the most archaic values on earth. They go back to the late Paleolithic; the fertility of the soil, the magic of animals, the power-vision in solitude, the terrifying initiation and rebirth, the love and ecstasy of the dance, the common work of the tribe . . . Whatever is or ever was in any other culture can be reconstructed from the unconscious through meditation . . . the coming revolution will close the circle and link us in many ways with the most creative aspects of our archaic past."

Born in San Francisco, Gary Snyder was "raised up on a feeble sort of farm just north of Seattle," received his B.A. in anthropology from Reed College in 1951, "studied linguistics one term at Indiana University, & after that sort of bummed around working at logging & forestry work alternate with classical Chinese study at Berkeley." Here he met Allen Ginsberg and Jack Kerouac (who made him the protagonist of his *Dharma Bums,* 1958) and became associated with the Beat movement. *Riprap* (1959), his first collection of poems, and one of the movement's key works besides Ginsberg's *Howl* (1956), Kerouac's *On The Road* (1957) and Burroughs' *The Naked Lunch* (1959), already bears the mark of his formal Zen training in Japan, embarked on in May, 1956. Besides offering "Technical Notes & Queries to Fellow Dharma Revolutionaries," as its subtitle indicates, *Earth House Hold* (1969) contains a poetic travel journal of Snyder's life in Japan and of intermittent journeys through India or "visiting Mediterranean & Pacific oil ports" as a hand on a tanker. In recent years, Snyder, his Japanese wife, and their two children, have lived in a self-made block house on the edge of a gold diggers desert in Nevada County, California. Snyder's major collections of poetry to date *(Myths and Texts,* 1960; *The Back Country,* 1968; *Regarding Wave,* 1971; *Turtle Island,* 1974)* as well as *Mountains and Rivers without End (Six Sections,* 1965), his *No* play-inspired long poem in progress, give a firm sense of his life, personality and numerous commitments.

Gary Snyder

As T. S. Eliot, one time student of Sanskrit and Patanjali Yoga, declared after his self-proclaimed 1927 conversion to classicism, royalism and Anglo-Catholicism: "It is because of our common background in the literatures of Greece, Rome and Israel, that we can speak of 'European literature' at all: and the survival of European literature . . . depends on our continued veneration of our ancestors" (E,P,211). Charles Olson, following Pound and Lawrence, had tried to extend this restricting concept by drawing on non-Western, Primitive and pre-Judæo-Christian civilizations like the Sumerian. Yet for Gary Snyder, who claims "the most archaic values on earth," even Olson's far-ranging cultural internationalism fails to provide us with a satisfactory alternative to the accepted norm of a living tradition. Olson, he feels, was ultimately "an apologist for Western culture; the trip from Sumeria to Gloucester a sort of justification for White-America" (S,IA,111).[1]* What Snyder proposes instead is a complete break with civilization in its present form. To him, civilization is "ultimately the enemy. The very order of the society that we have lived in for the last 4000 years has outlived its usefulness"(S,IG,22). "Judæo-Capitalist-Christian-Marxist" civilization in particular, our "whole Western Tradition, of which Marxism is but a (Millennial Protestant) part, is off the track"(S,E,92,114).

Paradoxically, Snyder believes that it is neither the East nor the underdeveloped nations, but his own country which offers the only prospect for a future society. For America, as Snyder observed in 1967, "is the only culture in which a number of people" have recognized the life-destroying potential of Western civilization "and are able to go beyond it"(Ko,N,167). It is here that in literature, music and art, as well as in countless neo-tribal communities, we witness the surfacing of "the Great Subculture which goes back as far perhaps as the late Paleolithic" and which, although suppressed and persecuted by ruling establishments and institutionalized religions all over the world, has formed a powerful and ineradicable "undercurrent in all higher civilizations":

*Notes to this section on p. 104.

91

In China it is manifested as Taoism, not only Lao-tzu but the later Yellow Turban revolt and medieval Taoist secret societies; and the Zen Buddhists up till early Sung. Within Islam the Sufis; in India the various threads converged to produce Tantrism. In the West it has been represented largely by a string of heresies starting with the Gnostics, and on the folk level by "witchcraft" . . . astronomers, ritualists, alchemists . . . Albigensians . . . and vagantes, right down to the Golden Gate Park.   (S,E,104-5,115)

In this way America may harbor the only hope for mankind. "If we change America we are changing the planet," and that in dimensions far larger than Olson's or Lawrence's return to a pre-Christian or pre-Socratic consciousness and world picture. "We've turned a corner . . . on the order of the change between Paleolithic and Neolithic. It's like one of the three or four major turns in the history of man—not just culture—but man" (Ko,N,168,170).

How is this transformation to come about? Though he repudiates the "Judæo-Capitalist-Christian-Marxist" view of history in favor of Buddhism, Snyder remains deeply committed to Western pragmatism, humanitarian optimism, and belief in progress. Granted, life is "a great mutual sacrifice where we have to eat one another" (S,IG,24), yet man, through meditation, art and ritual, is capable of "intuitive knowledge of the mind of love and clarity that lies beneath one's ego-driven anxieties and aggressions." In this way even the horrific "Universal Form of the Lord" as depicted in the *Bhagavad Gita*—"all created things rushing into Krishna's devouring mouth"—ultimately points to a "loving, simple awareness of the absolute beauty and preciousness of mice and weeds." Snyder acknowledges "the negative and demonic potentials of the Unconsciousness" and in fact feels that art (like the "archaic and primitive ritual dramas") should symbolically act them out and thereby free us from their power. But, generally speaking, "man's natural being is to be trusted and followed . . . and . . . in following the grain, one is being truly 'moral'" (S,E,92,115,122,128).

Yet Snyder is no mere Romantic, unaware of the influence which sociological and historical factors have on human morality. Thus he takes a distinctly hostile view of the political apathy and conformism of most Eastern religions. "Institutional Buddhism," for instance, has in his opinion "been conspicuously ready to accept or ignore the inequalities and tyrannies of whatever political system it found itself under." By contrast, his own conviction that no one today "can afford to be innocent, or indulge himself in ignorance of the nature of contemporary governments, politics and social orders" (S,E,90), would do honor to any hard-core Marxist revolutionary in the severity of its phrasing. Snyder's formula for the future destiny of mankind—

> a totally integrated world culture with matrilineal descent, free-form marriage, natural-credit communist economy, less industry, far less population and lots more national parks—

may differ in aim, but not in spirit from any of the pre- or post-Marxist versions of a secularized theodicy. "The mercy of the West," he sums up in "Buddhism and the Coming Revolution," "has been social revolution; the mercy of the East has been individual insight into the basic self/void. We need both" (S,E,92-3).

While the Beat movement was at its height, this goal seemed almost to be in sight. Within about three generations, Snyder speculated, "automation . . . plus psychedelics, plus . . . a whole catalytic, spiritual change or bend of mind that seems to be taking place in the West" would produce "a vast leisure society . . . [with] a very complex and sophisticated cybernetic technology surrounded by thick hedges of trees" (Ko,N,139-40). More recently, these Fullerian dreams of a paradisaic utopia have been replaced by a nightmare vision of civilization engulfed by an apocalyptic collapse before nature has a chance to restore its ecological balance. "At the moment," Snyder said in 1970, "a breakdown would be better than over-organization . . . There will probably be a transitional period in which there will be predatory tribes living off the remnants of civilization" (S,IG,22-3). Snyder, by now, is as well aware as others of how the pristine impulse of the Beat movement has to a large extent been absorbed by the very mainstream society it opposed ("Japanese-American animal nutrition experts/from Kansas,/with Buddhist beads," S,T,10) or been miscast into yet another variant of life-negating puritanism:

> The ex acid-heads from the cities
> Converted to Guru or Swami,
> Do penance with shiny
> Dopey eyes, and quit eating meat.
> In the forests of North America,
> The land of Coyote and Eagle,
> They dream of India, of
>   forever blissful sexless highs.
>
> .   .   .   .
>
> And the Coyote singing

is shut away
for they fear
the call
of the wild.

                                                      (S,T,21-2)

Despite all this, Snyder seems as determined as ever to practise
the ideas he believes in. The "true heir of Thoreau," as Richard
Howard calls him, he has withdrawn from civilization into a blockhouse he built himself in the foothills of the sierra in Nevada County,
California, though as a "modern Tribesman" (S,E,116) he repudiates the isolationist individualism of his 19th century forerun-
ner, and shares his life with his Japanese wife Masa and their children as well as with sympathetic neighbors, visitors and friends such
as Allen Ginsberg and Michael McClure. His childhood on a "feeble
sort of farm just north of Seattle" (A,P,444) had prepared him well
for such an existence. As Kerouac wrote of Snyder (alias Japhy
Rider), the protagonist of *The Dharma Bums* (1958), he was, from his
beginnings, a "woods boy, an axman, farmer, interested in animals
and Indian lore so that when he finally got to college . . . he was
already well equipped for his early studies in anthropology and later
in Indian myth" (Ke,B,9). After graduating in 1951, with an impressive thesis on a specific North American Indian myth, he at first
planned a career in the University. But faced with the stultifying
ordeal of having to write a Ph.D., he finally decided to set himself
"loose in the world to sink or swim as a poet" (Kh,S,9).

What put an end to his formal academic curriculum marked the
beginning not only of his life as a poet but of his amazing career as
autodidact scholar and oriental sage. From 1953 onwards, he began
to teach himself Chinese and Japanese, and in the fall of that year
decided to go to Japan. In preparation, he temporarily resumed his
studies, this time at the graduate school of Oriental languages in
Berkeley. Then, in May 1956, a grant from the newly founded Zen
Institute of America in San Francisco enabled him to set sail for
Japan where he remained till August 1957, studying and meditating
in a Zen temple. After an 8 months voyage, "working on a tanker . . .
visiting Mediterranean & Pacific oil ports" (A,P,444), followed by an
extended stay in San Francisco, he in January 1959 returned to
Japan, and with the exception of a journey through India in the
company of Allen Ginsberg, spent the following 6 years in Kyoto,
studying under Oda Sessō Rōshi (1901-1966), Zen Master and Head
Abbot of Daitoku-Ji.

This self-education within a non-Western framework provided

Snyder with an æsthetics that matches the radicalism of his sociological convictions. There are few Westerners the poet could claim as predecessors in this quest. Rousseau and Blake, Whitman and Thoreau, Lawrence and Jeffers, Pound and Rexroth are the names Snyder most frequently mentions in this context. Otherwise, he finds it difficult to relate to past America or Europe "because it's Christian. I find it easier to go to the Greek Anthology, the Romans, the medieval Chinese" (S,IA,112). In this way, a new understanding of poetry and art, like a new society, can only be reached by a radical break with our past. "It is a mistake to think," Snyder wrote in 1969, "that we are searching, now, for 'new forms.' What is needed is a totally new approach to the very idea of form . . . The future can't be seen on the basis of the present; and I believe mankind is headed someplace else" (B-M,P,358). A whole-hearted Primitivist at first, Snyder came to recognize through his Far Eastern studies that "traditional Hinduism and Buddhism have added a great deal onto basic Shamanistic and primitive ritualistic, ceremonial practises and life styles" (S,IR,59), and it is through a fusion of both that he evolved this new approach to the idea of form.

Not unlike Olson, who demanded the "replacement of the Classical-representational by the *primitive-abstract*" (O,W,28) and redefined form in terms of body-creativity (the poet's breath rhythm in relation to the cosmic life rhythm), Snyder, by 1959, came to realize that "the rhythms of my poems follow the rhythm of the physical work I'm doing and life I'm leading at any given time" (A,P,420). More recent statements come even closer to Olson's (and Far Eastern) breath-rhythm theory. According to one school of Mahāyāna Buddhism, as Snyder points out, the whole universe is often thought of as "a vast breathing body," while poetry is "the vehicle of the mystery of voice" (S,E,118), a notion which is close to what is meant by *Fushi*, the Japanese word for song, which literally signifies a knot, or whorl in the grain of wood (S,T,114). "The bass tone of the universe," Snyder explains, "stops for a few moments and does some complex things, and then it goes on again" (S,IQ,49).

Unlike Olson, however, Snyder tends to equate this concept of form with the void:

> form—leaving things out at the right spot
> ellipse, is emptiness.
>
> (S,E,5)

What at first may appear to be in contradiction with the breath-rhythm theory turns out to be its natural counterpart when considered in the light of Eastern philosophy from which it is derived. As an analogue of cosmic creation which emanates from the void and in endless cycles returns to it, the work of art must necessarily partake of the ultimate emptiness or *śūnyatā*. For as the Chinese philosopher Chang Tsai (1020-1077) puts it, the "Great Vacuity" is nothing but "material-force." "Things of necessity disintegrate and return to the Great Vacuity," which is omnipresent in all creation, both cosmic and artistic: in its "integration and disintegration, appearance and disappearance, form and absence of form" (Ba,C,460-1). Thus Chinese painters, for instance, follow the principle of *hsü shih*, or vacant space versus solid. For in the composition of a picture, as Hsun Tsu-yung writes in his *Ferry Boat for Painting* "there must be spiritual breath coming and leaving without hindrance" (Ch,C,212). Or as the æsthetician Lu Chi exclaims in his *Essay on Literature*: "A composition . . . is (like the act of Tao) the embodiment of endless change/ . . . it is Being, created by tasking the Great Void,/ And 'tis sound rung out of Profound Silence" (Bi,A,207,209).

Similarly, "true insight" to Snyder is "a love-making hovering between the void & the immense worlds of creation" (S,E,22), and poetry, as its subtlest medium of expression, walks "that edge between what can be said and that which cannot be said . . . [I]t's going out into emptiness and into the formless" while at the same time resting on "an absolute foundation of human experience and insight" (S,IR,64,67-8). The "pure inspiration flow" bringing it forth is "not intellect and not—(as romantics and after have confusingly thought) fantasy-dream world or unconsciousness." On the contrary, true poetry "reflects all things and feeds all things but is of itself transparent" (S,E,56-7).

True to this theory, Snyder's poetry, like that of his Eastern peers, often radiates with an almost unearthly clarity and precision, whereby the sensual concreteness of every detail seems as if suffused with this transparence or awareness of the void. What seems so deceptively simple, is, in fact, a unique, by now widely imitated, yet probably inimitable achievement within Western poetry. Little gaps of silence frequently seem to separate one utterance from the next, and, like the brush strokes of calligraphic paintings, each phrase or remark, like the phenomenon or event it embodies, seems to rest within the energy of its own tension, autonomous, and yet related to all others in the hidden field of force, creating its "complexity far beneath the surface texture" (A,P,421).

> What my hand follows on your body
> Is the line. A stream of love
>   of heat, of light,   what my

eye   lascivious
      licks
over, watching
far snow-dappled Uintah mountains
Is that stream.
Of power.   what my
      hand curves over, following the line.
      "hip" and "groin"
Where "I"
      follow by hand and eye
      the swimming limit of your body.
> ("Beneath My Hand and Eye the Distant Hills,
> Your Body," S,C,108-9)

In the words of one of his earlier poems, there is a "leap of words to things and there it stops" (S,R,22), and, reminiscent of Olson's principle of "FIELD COMPOSITION," the poem, as the reduplication or reenactment of a natural process, seems to follow its own dynamics. In this way, the end of the poem often states the end of an activity ("we sleep in the sand/ and our salt"), the beginning of something new ("& got back in our wagon,/ drove away"), an activity that finds its only purpose in itself ("and made love on the sand") or, by way of a cyclical repetition, restates the beginning ("Three a.m.—a far bell/ coming closer") enhancing and deepening its effect ("A far bell coming closer," S,C,59-63,112). The lyrical "I" or speaker, as the inverted commas in "Beneath My Hand and Eye . . ." suggest, is generally represented as just another of the objects or events enacted and, in Olson's words, "can go by no track other than the one the poem under hand declares, for itself" (O,W,16).

A 1972 "British Assessment" tries to associate Snyder with the decadent Nineties poets in England, "who dissipated their technical expertise on an extraordinarily narrow range of emotion and experience."[2] Yet, despite *prima facie* resemblances, nothing could be more alien to Snyder's aims and achievements than the subjective impressionism of a poet like Arthur Symons, for instance, who in 1897 declared the "moods of men" to be the primary aim of his verse:

> There I find my subject . . . and whatever has once been a mood of mine, though it has been no more than a ripple on the sea, and had no longer than that ripple's duration, I claim the right to render, if I can, in verse.
>
> ("Preface" to *London Nights*)

In fact, it is exactly this "ego interference," as Snyder once commented, which "keeps someone else's poem from working" for him (S,IT,22). Like Olson, Snyder is deeply aware of "that peculiar presumption by which western man has interposed himself between what he is as a creature of nature . . . and those other creations of nature which we . . . call objects." And probably nowhere in contemporary American poetry has this dichotomy been overcome more convincingly than in Snyder's. Many of his poems seem like paradigmatic embodiments of Olson's notion that a poem ought to be a "field of force" in which man, including the speaker, becomes "himself an object" (O,W,24). As in "Beneath My Hand and Eye . . .," there is a general tendency, not to present nature in terms of man but to present man in terms of nature, both that of his body and his surroundings. For according to Snyder we enter this world, trailing not "clouds of glory," as we come from "God, who is our home,"[3] but

> slippery clouds of guts
> incense of our flowery flesh
> blossoms;   crusht;   re-turning
> knots of rose meat open out to—over—
> five-hued clouds—
> the empty diamond of all space.

> (S,C,93)

In an insightful interpretation of "Sixth-Month Song in the Foothills," Charles Altieri has shown how the poet, when speaking of himself, usually "refuses to supply explicit referents to the participles modifying his own actions, so that they appear as if freed from the limits of subjectivity." The effect of this, however, is not a "blend of subject and object,"[4] as in Romantic nature poetry, but a total elimination of that dichotomy:

> In the cold shed sharpening saws.
>   a swallow's nest hangs by the door
> setting rakers in sunlight
> falling from meadow through doorframe
>   swallows flit under the eaves.
>
> Grinding the falling axe
> sharp for the summer
>   a swallow shooting out over.
> over the river, snow on low hills
> sharpening wedges for splitting.

Beyond the low hills, white mountains
and now snow is melting.   sharpening tools;
          pack horses grazing new grass
bright axes—and swallows
      fly in to my shed.

                       (S,C,17)

The speaker or "subject" seems to be omnipresent in the poem. Yet, except for the last line he only refers to himself as an anonymous event amongst others, such as grazing horses or melting snow. Similarly, Snyder avoids the direct or indirect article to single out a phenomenon or event as an independent object, while presenting all phenomena, including himself, in terms of interrelated actions and movements. This is further enhanced by the frequent use of the gerund (e.g., "sharpen*ing*") which gives the descriptions a presentational urgency that draws the reader into the poem to make him become part of the "jewelled net" of nature's interconnectedness (S,E,129) embodied in the language. Nowhere, however, does the gerund create that momentary emotional intensity typical of the traditional post-Romantic lyric. Instead, as in other of Snyder's poems, it suddenly and for no specific reason, tends to switch into the present tense, as if to suggest that what is presented in all the immediacy of its here and now does—like

      the plank shutter
          set

Half-open   on eternity

                       (S,W,28)

—partake of the eternal round of being, of what has always been and always will be:

     —and swallows
     fly in to my shed.

Given the scope of this essay, I have mainly focussed on what seems to me Snyder's most outstanding contribution to Western poetry. Yet, just as the Eastern poets he translated cover a wide range of modes and tones, from the mystical luminosity of Chinese Han-shan to the mythopoeic deep imagery or colloquial satire of Japanese Miyazawa Kenji, so the poet's own work is by no means limited to the lyric mode of his "Flowers for the Void" (S,E,134) "going out into emptiness and into the formless which is the nature of pure joy" (S,IR,64). Snyder often speaks with a funny, self-ironical, satirical or outspokenly didactic voice, while a work like *Myths &Texts* (1960), hailed by Robert Bly as "one of the two or three finest books of poetry" of its decade (B,S,6,29), presents us with a subtly orchestrated structure, centered around specific symbols and myths that were inspired by "the happy collections Sapir, Boas, Swanton, and others made of American Indian folktales early in this century" (A,P,421). Julian Gitzen, in an extensive interpretation of the poem, has compared *Myths & Texts* with *The Waste Land*, though one may add that the "fragmental texture"[5] which in Eliot's poem expresses anguished spiritual chaos in the face of nothingness ("These fragments I have shored against my ruins") serves Snyder as a positive means for apprehending reality in its pre-conceptual suchness *(tathātā)* and as a medium for his poetic "re-enactment of [the] timeless dance: here and now, co-creating forever, for no end but now" (S,E,134).

> Intricate layers of emptiness
> This only world, juggling forms
>   a hand, a breast, two clasped
> Human tenderness scuttles
> Down dry endless cycles
> Forms within forms falling
>   clinging
> Loosely, what's gone away?
>   —love.
>
>   (S,M,34-5)

Another major poetic mode, that of his long poem in progress entitled *Mountains and Rivers without End*, at first seems to invite comparison with the American epic tradition from *Leaves of Grass* to the *Maximus Poems*. Yet as Snyder explained in 1959, it in fact emulates further models of Eastern literature and art. Its "dramatic structure follows a certain type of *Nō* play," while its overall structure (which "threatens to be like its title") was conceived "after a Chinese sidewise scroll painting" (A,P,421). In an even earlier statement to Kerouac recorded in *The Dharma Bums*, the poet jokingly anticipates that, just like the author of *On the Road*, he will be writing

> on and on on a scroll and unfold on and on with new surprises
> and always what went before forgotten ... I'll spend three
> thousand years writing it, it'll be packed full of information on
> soil conservation, the Tennessee Valley Authority, astronomy,
> geology, Hsuan Tsung's travels, Chinese painting theory, re-
> forestation, Oceanic ecology and food chains. (Ke,B,156)

It would be tantamount to splitting hairs to try to trace these various modes in terms of their successive evolution in the poet's life. Even in his beginnings, Snyder, unlike Robert Lowell or other poets of the "confessional" genre, for instance, displays none of the tormented, self-questioning, and often suicidal spiritual tendencies, so typical of post-Romantic poetry in the West. Instead, he seems to have evolved these several modes almost simultaneously and as from a common basis, and to have deepened, refined and elaborated them ever since. As Snyder points out himself, *Mountains and Rivers without End* (of which the first *Six Sections* were published in 1965) was begun as early as 1956, *Myths & Texts* (1960) "grew" between 1952 and 1956 (A,P,421), while the poems of the more "lyric order" as he calls them (S,IR,65), already dominate his first published collection of 1959 *(Riprap)*. Even earlier, in his diary of the years 1952-3, Snyder had begun to formulate the basic premises of his philosophy and poetics: his experience of *"no identity"* and "the void," his epistemological "love-making hovering between the void & the immense worlds of creation," his concept of form as "ellipse, is emptiness," the subsequent experience of linguistic disintegration ("my language fades. Images of erosion") and the attempt to reconstitute language after the model of Chinese poetry cross-bred with the primordial potential of the Anglo-Saxon heritage.[6] It was equally early in his career that Snyder assumed his clean-slate stance in favor of Primitive and Eastern mentality ("Let's be animals or buddhas," S,E,5,10,22,36) and against the Judæo-Christian world view:

> What use, Milton, a silly story
> Of our lost general parents,
>   eaters of fruit?
>
> .   .   .   .
>
>   In ten thousand years the Sierras
> Will be dry and dead, home of the scorpion.
> Ice-scratched slabs and bent trees.
> No paradise, no fall,
> Only the weathering land
> The wheeling sky,
> Man, with his Satan
> Scouring the chaos of the mind.
> Oh Hell!
>
>   (August 1955, S,R,7-8)

By 1955, Snyder had also entered his now well over 20 year old discipline of regular meditational exercises or *za-zen* and "like a blade which sharpens to nothing" (S,E,34), had started to gain insights which must have struck some of his early readers as being of an almost frighteningly staunch and inhuman rigor:

> Sky over endless mountains.
> All the junk that goes with being human
> Drops away, hard rock wavers
> Even the heavy present seems to fail
> This bubble of a heart.
> Words and books
> Like a small creek off a high ledge
> Gone in the dry air.
>
> A clear, attentive mind
> Has no meaning but that
> Which sees is truly seen.
> No one loves rock, yet we are here.
>
> (S,R,6)

To be sure, Snyder's early work shows traces of the confessional ("Bitter memory like vomit/Choked my throat") or romantically subjective mode, at times almost reminiscent of a poet like Matthew Arnold, stoically resigned to the cruelty of life, yet at the same time yearning for human compassion:

> In this burning, muddy, lying,
> blood-drenched world
> that quiet meeting in the mountains
> cool and gentle as the muzzles of
> three elk, helps keep me sane.

But far more forceful and ubiquitous is the impulse to negate all the "pointless wars of the heart" (S,C,34,46) and to come to terms with human suffering generally. Questioned about his attitude towards the confessional school of poets, Snyder replied: "I'm a Buddhist, which is to say you take suffering and impermanence for granted, as a base fact of the universe, and then proceed on from there" (S,IQ,50). Again, such an attitude is by no means new to Snyder and was in fact assumed even before the confessional poets made their first appearance in Anglo-American literature. As early as 1956, Snyder, age 26, concluded that there comes

> a time when the poet must choose: either to step deep in the stream of his people, history, tradition, folding and folding himself in wealth of persons and pasts; philosophy, humanity,

to become richly foundationed and great and sane and ordered. Or, to step beyond the bound onto the way out, into
horrors and angels, possible madness or silly Faustian doom,
possible utter transcendence, possible enlightened return,
possible ignominious wormish perishing (S,E,39).

By his subsequent creativity, personal development and indefatiga-
ble involvement in ecological, social, cultural and purely human
concerns, Snyder has left no doubt as to which of these two paths he
has chosen as his own.

[1]This, of course, may be an at least partly inauthentic statement. See Snyder interview p. 105.

[2]P. E. Lewis, "Robert Creeley and Gary Snyder: A British Assessment," *Stand* 13,4 (1972), pp. 42-7, 46.

[3]Wordsworth, "Immortality Ode," lines 65-6.

[4]"Gary Snyder's Lyric Poetry: Dialectic as Ecology," *The Far Point* 4,1 (Spring/Summer 1970), pp. 55-65, 61.

[5]"Gary Snyder and the Poetry of Compassion," *Critical Quarterly* 15,4 (Winter 1973), pp. 341-57, 347.

[6]See S,IQ,47: "Then, in terms of poetic craft, one must not only have an ear for daily speech, but the particularly poetic sense of refining, purifying, and compressing daily speech into the kind of compact utterance that a poem becomes. So first of all, in my poetry my craft has a sense of compression, a sense of ellipsis, of leaving out the unnecessary, of sharpening the utterance down to a point where a very precise, very swift message is generated, an energy is transmitted. In doing that, I have paid particular attention to the Anglo-Saxon or Germanic derived aspects of the English language, and have made much use of mono-syllabic words, of compactness and directness of the Anglo-Saxon heritage in the English language, which I have cross-bred with my understanding and ear for Chinese poetry."

Gary Snyder

Faas: The first thing I should like to discuss is your attitude towards Olson. You once called him "an apologist for Western culture" and his "trip from Sumeria to Gloucester a sort of justification for White-America."

Charles Olson

SNYDER: No, I never said "White-America," and altogether I don't think that's fair for me to say, really, because frankly I haven't looked at Olson that closely for a number of years; and when I first read Olson, I was feeling extremely partisan towards Eastern culture and my response to Olson was probably based on that excessive partisanship. So that all I can say in honesty is that I haven't studied Olson as deeply as I might have or should perhaps. And what I have read seemed to reflect a predominantly Atlantic and ultimately Occidental focus, which wasn't where my specific interests lay. My thinking comes together with Olson's direction when we come into prehistory and the Pleistocene.

Faas: You saw Olson's piece on Pleistocene Man?

SNYDER: Yes. And at this point I'm doing a lot more investigation of the Pleistocene horizon around the world than ever. Now, Pleistocene is before Eastern culture and Western culture diverge; your evidence would be from the artifacts that are essentially identical throughout the Eurasian landmass. And a number of other evidences coming right down to the upper Paleolithic give us in a sense a kind of international prehistoric culture. Olson's insights in this were interesting, but only point the way to some amazing possibilities that should be investigated further: prehistory.

Pleistocene Man

Faas: But then there also seem to be general points of affinity between Olson's poetic theories and your own.

SNYDER: Indeed! In intrinsic poetic theory: projective verse—I quote that right like everybody else as a starting point for thinking about the line's breath and the poem as a musical phrase or a *thala* (a rhythmic model). You know what a *thala* is? Well, you know the term *raga*.

Faas: Yes.

SNYDER: A melodic mode for an Indian piece. Every Indian piece is to a certain *raga* and also to a certain *thala*. And a *thala* is the rhythmic mode that goes with a certain melodic mode. [Chanting]: tatatatatatatata*ta* tetetete tatatata*ta*; the set-up for a *thala* should be reproduced on the drum. And so from Olson's notion and from other people's ways of seeing things, my sense of the form of poetry is analogous to the form of a *thala* which is a long thing sometimes, you know, completes itself and sets the tone, sets the rhythm and the style for a whole underlying poetic development.

Faas: It was interesting for me to find that a specific kind of Zen flute music is based on breath rhythm.

SNYDER: Shakuhachi.

Faas: Yes, I think that's it.

SNYDER: [Starts chanting]: and so forth. That's a Zen chant. Well, what I was doing last night [refering to a reading at the New York YMHA, early in 1974] in some of those poems, was based on *Nō*-drama chant which is also breath rhythm. My source of inspiration there is having attended many *Nō*-plays.

Faas: But are there any specific points where you differ from Olson?

SNYDER: I wish you'd told me you were going to ask these questions and I would have studied that. [Laughing]

Faas: On the whole, I think, there is much more affinity than difference.

SNYDER: There is actually a great deal of affinity and I'm fascinated by the way Olson's mind works. I think, as I said before, my direct teacher in these matters was Pound. I read Pound extensively. I did not read Olson extensively because I had already absorbed so much of that from Pound. I came to Olson a little later, somehow I didn't feel the need. I felt that Pound was my teacher already and that Olson had learned it from Pound. For that and for other reasons which are curious and which have to do with East and West coast differences. Like we did not read Olson very much on the West coast in the fifties. There was a remoteness there, and indeed it was Robert Duncan who was the West coast guru as Olson was the East coast guru. Duncan sort of shared West coast guru rites with Rexroth, and Rexroth never liked Olson at all. Actually, he put him down terribly.

Faas: I didn't know that.

SNYDER: He said he was a second-rate Pound, and as a human being he thought that Olson was too difficult. Of course, Rexroth was a difficult man in his own right. So, you know, I'm trying to think now what the actual facts were of those relationships between poets and

East and West Coast gurus

influences. In other words, thinking of Charles, I'm fascinated by the way his mind works, and he has a marvellous sense of phrasing and timing and a way of juxtaposing ideas which is, you know, absolutely brilliant. On balance, however, I find him too much of a head poet, over-intellectual, over-abstract, over-theoretical, his poems verging off too much and too often in the directions of reading lists to disciples and notebook jottings. I think he was rather indulgent of himself in that respect.

Olson too much of a head poet

Faas: Since we have started to talk about your contemporaries: How do you view the work of Robert Bly and his plea that American poetry will have to go through what he calls the "dark psychic woods of the unconscious," that is to say, through a period of Surrealism, before it will be able to become a really great modern poetry?

Bly and Surrealism

SNYDER: As I understand what Robert is saying, this is not necessarily a plea for Surrealism. I don't know if he would say that. What he has translated and praised in the way of, say, South American, American, Spanish and European poetry has not been really Surrealist poetry.

Faas: You mean not like early French Surrealism.

SNYDER: Well, it's been poetry of image. But Surrealism is another issue which I have questions about. It may not be fair, but I have a feeling that Surrealism skims off the top, it doesn't go deep enough into the unconscious, that it plays more with the subjective flow level of imagery which can be manipulated rather than . . .

Faas: Like automatic writing?

SNYDER: Yes, well, automatic writing or what we used to call stream-of-consciousness. And there's a deeper level that Bly is interested in, which is more . . . quiet, and which I'm interested in. Yes, I think we do have to go through that. I feel that American poetry probably will or should move further away from its rhetorical and rationalistic Anglo background, you know, Romantic Anglo background, and swing deeper into the mind. I would hope that my own poetry would do that.

Faas: You would hope?

SNYDER: Yes.

Faas: I always had the feeling that in a way you had bypassed that stage. Or, rather, what I mean is that with the advantage of a Buddhist education and years of meditational practice you did not have to pass through the Surrealist stage in order to get to the spiritual realms beyond that.

SNYDER: Oh yes, I don't mean I would wish to write like a Surrealist.

But I would like to work at deep sea levels, a little bit up from that absolute bottom transparency of the Chinese type poetry, a little more mythic, a little more archetypal. Well, I did that in *Myths &* *Texts*. That's the key poem in which I worked that kind of thing in. Actually, *Mountains and Rivers without End* is also where I'm writing that kind of poetry. Like that poem I read last night about the flowing, about the river mouth which finally just comes to a stop like that. I like that kind of work best right now.

Faas: À propos Surrealism, there is an interesting study by the German scholar Christian Kellerer entitled *Objet trouvé und Surrealismus* which tries to show that Surrealism is our Western access to a Zen Buddhist approach to life and art.

Surrealism and Zen

SNYDER: But there is one difference, there is a key difference, and the key difference is that the Surrealist conceived of that deep knowledge of himself as somehow still the ego.

Faas: Exactly. But then amongst the late followers of Surrealism you get artists like Jackson Pollock who are able to break through that ego barrier.

SNYDER: How does Existentialism fit in with that? Because Existentialism seems to me to have been working in the same direction.

Existentialism

Faas: I think the answer to that lies with a man like Robbe-Grillet whose essays *Pour un nouveau roman* in many ways read almost like a Zen Buddhist theory of the novel, although he doesn't seem to have been influenced by Eastern thought. One of Robbe-Grillet's starting points is the Existentialist notion of the absurd which to him is just the last form or rather inversion of our Western teleological concept of life and history—trying to find a meaning and a purpose in everything. To Robbe-Grillet, by contrast, reality is neither meaningful nor absurd: it is simply there.

SNYDER: It makes sense.

Faas: I find the same kind of "literal" understanding of reality in Creeley. He reports in an interview how he passed the same neon sign for weeks on end, read it every day and became so fixed on its literal *signifiant*—the words, the letters, the visual configuration—that it never occurred to him it contained an actual pun.

SNYDER: That happened to me yesterday in *Newsweek* magazine. There was an article about wildcat drillers in Texas. It quoted one of these wildcat drillers who had just begun to employ some young geologist, and this geologist came up to him as he was getting off his truck and the geologist said: "We have just gone through the Miocene." And then he came back a little later and said: "We are now going through the Eocene." And the driller said: "Well, young fellow, when you hit the kerosene let me know." [Both laughing]

Faas: Despite some obvious differences, you and other American poets seem to share the basic notions of a general open form poetics. Are we here dealing with a distinctly American phenomenon?

SNYDER: It seems to be. I don't know of anything like it in modern Japanese poetry, and certainly not in India. I'm telling you of places I know about.

American open form poetics

Faas: And yet there is at least one Japanese poet, I forget his name now, who began under the influence of European Dadaism . . .

SNYDER: Takahashi.

Faas: Right, and who now writes some kind of Zen Buddhist poetry.

SNYDER: That's because Zen Buddhism seems like the better tag to sell it by.

Faas: Speaking of world poetry generally, surely there are tendencies toward an open form poetics everywhere: Höllerer in Germany, Gustafsson in Sweden, but more at isolated points, whereas in the U.S. it seems to have caught on everywhere. Even with Lowell who, in his *Notebook*, went, I think, through an experience comparable to that of Williams when he found that he couldn't finish *Paterson*.

SNYDER: Lowell's *Notebooks* really were a change, a tremendous breakthrough, and a good one, mind opening.

Faas: Robert Duncan, during our recent conversations, jokingly said that you were a Marxist in disguise, and personally I find that there is a very strong sense of purposefulness and future-oriented pragmatism in you. Do you feel that Western teleological thought is compatible with Eastern philosophy?

SNYDER: Well, Buddhism does have a teleology, has a whole eschatology which is placed in a kind of mythic far future—a kind of Teilhard de Chardin vision of everything in the universe becoming finally enlightened together. Except for what do you do then? I suppose you start another universe, you will do it all over again. [Laughing] The Buddhist cosmic time span eschatology—you see the Bodhisattvas and the Buddhas all make vows not to achieve enlightenment until all sentient beings are saved. So all the Bodhisattvas and all the universes are working lifetime after lifetime for the salvation of all sentient beings. If Buddhism is doing its job, why then eventually all sentient beings would be saved. And then everything would be a Buddha. Zen mysticism says: well, wait it's already all a Buddha right now, if you can just see it, so that's ahistorical. It's the eternal moment. I think in those terms, but I also think in terms of organic evolution, and from that standpoint we have a critical time now in which decisions are

Buddhist teleology

being made which will have long reaching effects on the survival of many forms of life. All the time we are reducing biological diversity at a great rate with modern civilization. From that standpoint I don't know if I'm exactly a Marxist, but I'm committted to a biological Buddhist mystic defense of the diversity of life which I think is the work of poets as ancient shaman-poets and ancient servants of the Muse and the lady of wild things and non-human or extra-human realms. And I value the Marxist critique of Capitalism as throwing precise light on the economic reasons for the destructiveness of modern civilization.

Faas: But you have stood up for social progress as well, political progress.

SNYDER: Not if social progress was so narrowly construed as to move at the expense of other beings, that kind of simple-minded progress.

Faas: You once took a stand against the political apathy and conformism of institutionalized Buddhism.

SNYDER: Well, I don't think we can afford political apathy any more, I don't think it's impossible, and I think it's required that poets, Buddhists and everybody else be functioning beings aware of history, aware of economics, aware of ecology. And the understanding of these systems and how they work is another extension simply of the Buddhist understanding of interdependence which is poetical in the extreme if seen right. And it's the embracing of this kind of knowledge which I think is valuable right now.

political
engagement

Faas: I find that your concept of man leans heavily towards an almost Rousseauistic belief that "man's natural being," as you put it yourself, "is to be trusted and followed . . . and that in following the grain, one is being truly 'moral.' " On the other hand, you grant that "it is necessary to look exhaustively into the negative and demonic potentials of the Unconscious, and by recognizing these powers" symbolically act them out. Do you feel that your own poetry is doing that?

poetry and
the demonic

SNYDER: In a few poems I have tried to do that.

Faas: In fact, there is one poem which reminded me of Ted Hughes, I just can't remember its title, about the skinned . . .

SNYDER: . . . the skinned wolf.

Faas: Could you mention some of the others?

SNYDER: Yes, there is a poem called "Down," there's a couple of poems in *Myths & Texts*, in the third section called *Burning*, especially the one that has the line "*Maudgalyâyana* knew hell," and the poems in *The Back Country*, in the group called *Kālī*, a number of poems that deal with the goddess of death and destruction.

Faas: And yet you mentioned earlier that there were certain aspects of your life which you had excluded from your poetry, certain explosive potentials that you had never acted out in it—like the relationship with your mother which you said was very much like Allen Ginsberg's—and that perhaps you might even write your own *Kaddish* one day.

SNYDER: Well, I am still working some of these potentials out.

Faas: There is also your curious paraphrase or rather interpretation of a famous passage of the *Bhagavad Gita* which seems to bespeak an almost St. Francis-like mentality of love and compassion— quite in contrast to the *Gita's* life-affirming, yet fatalistic acceptance of eternal suffering and destruction.

SNYDER: Now, I don't know what you're referring to, actually. The most useful place where I quote the *Bhagavad Gita* is where I refer to "all created things rushing into Krishna's devouring mouth," and that's a total vision of the negative possibilities of the whole universe.

Faas: Let me see, I have got it jotted down somewhere. Here we are: "After the mind-breaking Void, the emptiness of a million universes appearing and disappearing, all created things rushing into Krishna's devouring mouth; beyond the enlightenment that can say 'these things are dead already; go ahead and kill   beyond them, Arjuna' is a loving, simple awareness of the abso-   emptiness lute beauty and preciousness of mice and weeds." Now, I felt that the emphasis here was on the "loving, simple awareness of the absolute beauty and preciousness of mice and weeds."

SNYDER: That is the final step, yes, the final step beyond the complete comprehension of the "emptiness" of the universe.

Faas: But in your interpretation that would point towards an almost Christian understanding of the universe.

SNYDER: No, I don't see it as particularly Christian. Today we take for granted via the atheistic scientific conception of the universe, its drift toward entropy, the emptiness of it, the meaninglessness of it.

Faas: I am thinking of how differently Hughes, for instance, might interpret this passage, probably emphasizing the suffering and the horrific whereas you emphasize the need for compassion and love resulting from such insight.

SNYDER: That is because the compassion is not what you would expect. You would not expect that the perception of the meaninglessness and emptiness of the whole universe would result in compassion for mice. That's one more step.

Faas: Do you feel that this is what's actually taught by the *Bhagavad Gita*?

SNYDER: It is not taught by the *Bhagavad Gita*. It is taught in other spheres. The way I phrased it there I was taking a step beyond the *Bhagavad Gita.*

Faas: At one point in the sixties, I have to quote you here, you expressed hope that a new society might within approximately three generations be formed "within the shell of the old," so to speak, and that "automation plus psychedelics plus a whole catalytic, spiritual change or bend of mind that seems to be taking place in the west" would produce a "vast leisure society." Yet, more recently, the future in 1970, I think, you drew a somewhat gloomier picture of mankind saying that at the moment a breakdown would be better and that probably there will be a transitional period with predatory tribes "living off the remnants of civilization." What are your feelings about all this right now?

SNYDER: Well, I can say very simply what the changes were which my thinking underwent between those two statements. The first about automation and a vast leisure society is what I call technological utopianism.

Faas: Like Fuller's.

SNYDER: Yes. There was an enthusiasm for that at the time—that was about 1965—that I got swept along with, without perhaps thinking very clearly. I should have known better, actually, because I had thought out these things once before. The problem with technological utopianism is shortage of resources, of energy. Where do you get the energy from to run such a technology? I turned away technological entirely from that as I studied resource availability. I read utopianism things like D. H. Meadows' *The Limits to Growth,* Jay Forrester's computer-based study of various potential curves for our society in the next century, which has received a lot of criticism but which is nonetheless, I think, pretty thorough. I read Gofman & Tamplin's book *Poisoned Power* on energy which sketches out energy resource supplies and contradictions in any future energy use. On the basis of that study I came to feel that there was not going to be a vast leisure society. On the contrary, there was going to be a vast peasant class if we are lucky, and that technological utopianism won't hold up. My second statement which is rather gloomy, is probably a more accurate prognostication, although you have to allow that modern culture is extremely ingenious, sometimes takes amazing bypaths, and pulls itself out of problems at the last minute.

Faas: So there is hope that it might fall on its feet.

SNYDER: Yes, there is some hope that it might fall on its feet. We'll see how Americans and this economy as a whole take this winter's [i.e. 1974/5] energy crisis. I mean if people take it in good spirit and are ingenious and adaptable, that would be a good sign. If it sparks off a lot of frustration, anxiety and anger and selfishness, then that would be another sign. [Laughing]

Faas: You once said that everywhere you go, you meet so many people who live in neo-tribal communities.

SNYDER: Less of them around now. It seems like most of those communes probably were never very stable, although people always talked about their own commune as though it were built on solid rock. But they have all evaporated, very few people are doing it. Like they had problems of men and women, and nobody agreed to wash the dishes. I guess I'm in kind of a depressed mood about the American national character right now, which seems _{communes} to be so intensely individualistic and selfish whether it's hip or straight, you know, long haired or not long haired, there is a streak of selfish individualism that the Chinese, for example, see as America's downfall. They look at the American character and they say: the Americans can't keep it together and they may be right.

Faas: A lot of the people living in neo-tribal communities seem to be in your area, Nevada County, California.

SNYDER: Well, it's everywhere, but the people that went out into the country five years ago from the city and started communes and things, went with very little idea of what they were doing. The first phase was sheer romanticism and sheer anarchy, and not in the good sense of the word. And that kind of thing failed, those people are all gone now. The survivors of that were the ones who became practical, so to speak, realized their limits and realized that they would have to do a lot of hard work and realized that they would have to get along with their neighbors. Those who did that are still there, and that element has become an extremely interesting new phase in American rural life. Formerly, urban and often college educated people establishing deep relationships and commitments in a rural area transformed themselves and in _{Chinese model} some sense their neighbors in the process. That is taking place in my area. My area is pretty well disciplined, actually, is really on top of it, and has no tolerance for this . . . One thing that we find very useful and shared with each other as much as Buddhism, has been reports on Chinese communities from People's China, as a model for what has to be done.

Faas: Mao's China.

SNYDER: Yes, the reports from a Chinese village, and other things like that which have given us a clue as to how to be cooperative and to work together without necessarily calling ourselves a community or a commune and banding together and so forth, and trying to hit a balance between American individualism and the need for cooperation. That's an interesting process. But I see how traditional run of the mill American individualism in this increasingly overpopulated, resource depleted world is a liability. It may have been a plus in frontier times, you know, because there was always some place to go to; the individual with no sense of cooperation would just go off by himself and do something else. That's not possible now, not even in the wildest countryside. So we have become like Europe and like China. We are now at the end of our resource and space freedom and we have to learn to live within the terms of what we've got. It will be interesting to see if we can do it.

Faas: From where do you get these reports?

SNYDER: I buy them at the Chinese Communist Bookstore, down in Berkeley.

Faas: And that works, what they're doing?

SNYDER: It really does work.

Faas: And do they keep up any of the old traditions?

SNYDER: Sure they do.

Faas: In an unofficial way, I suppose.

SNYDER: Well, some things are official, some things are unofficial. Some poets and thinkers are officially good, a few are officially bad, it's hard to get their works.

Faas: One biographical or rather semi-biographical question: What exactly did you do in Japan? I gather that you lived there from '56 to '57 and then again from '59 to '65, staying in a monastery.

Snyder   SNYDER: No, for the first time I was in Japan I was in a
in Japan   temple right through, and the second stay I was in Japan I was part of the time living in a monastery, doing *Sesshins* (intensive periods), part of the time out, doing research work, translating, work connected with Zen study, academic work in a Buddhist research library within the temple.

Faas: With other Americans and Europeans?

SNYDER: A couple of other Americans, one I'm going to see this afternoon, who is professor of Japanese at Columbia now, a Buddhist scholar, Zen Scholar, Philip Yampolsky. He translated the *Sixth Patriarch Sutra* and the writings of Hakuin. So I was leading essentially a layman's life, a Koji's life in Japanese terms, a lay disciple, keeping a close contact with my teacher, seeing him almost daily, and at the same time, out of necessity, earning a little money for my support, and doing research and scholarship, and a little gardening, a little vegetable gardening. My teacher then died, and I stayed on in

Japan for another couple of years, finishing up studies and researches that I wanted to pursue. Just before my teacher died I met Masa, and shortly after he died we got married.

Faas: And you practised regular meditation all those years?

SNYDER: Oh yes, of course. All through that time and I still do. We still get up in the morning and meditate.

Faas: Every morning?

SNYDER: Yes, and some of the people who live near us   meditation join us. When you were at Kitkitdizze we were meditating, weren't we?

Faas: No, not really, we had a kind of discussion.

SNYDER: Oh right, that was weekend. Saturday, Sunday we take off.

Faas: And you meditate in that little grove above your blockhouse.

SNYDER: Where we went up for the discussion, that was our morning meditation ground.

Faas: So you have been meditating for quite a while now?

SNYDER: I started when I was 22. Over twenty years.

Faas: I think I mentioned to you that in my own meditating I usually start to hallucinate after a while, I mean hallucinate in the sense of what Claudio Naranjo calls "vivid dreamlike sequences contemplated while awake with closed eyes."

SNYDER: You know, that's why we have sticks in the Zendo—

Faas: How do you notice that somebody is hallucinating? [Both laughing]

SNYDER: Oh, you know, they start giggling or fluttering their eyes, so you go whack!

Faas: I once told a Zen master about these experiences which to me are really the point at which I enter some sort of quietude, and he said: That has nothing to do with Zen meditation. You must be on the wrong track.

SNYDER: Yes. [Laughing] Well, if you don't get hung up on it, on hallucinating, it's all right. Don't make a career out of it. [Increased laughter] *Za-zen* has been an intimate part of my life since I first started in my early twenties, when I was a student at Berkeley. And sometimes I do more, and sometimes I do less. It's a practise which I find creative and stabilizing both.

Faas: How does it affect your creativity?

SNYDER: It moves me out of my daily-track mind, daily single-track mind, puts you in a large universe, and takes you away, gives you a perspective on the concerns and the work of the day and puts the work of the day in its own place and makes it a pleasure. It reminds you that the day's work is also your meditation and that the infinite

Buddha nature penetrates all things equally in multiple marvellous ways. And you live your life with more detachment and at the same time with more savor, which in a sense is what the whole Buddhist life is about: the detachment and selflessness which makes your life more rather than less.

Faas: Let me switch to your general interests. Do you read literary criticism?

general interests

SNYDER: Hardly ever. In fact, I probably haven't read criticism for 15 years. It isn't that I even look down on it, it's that I don't have time for it. That is to say if I make a choice of priorities of what I'm going to read, I'll read biology first, history second, anthropology third, poetry fourth and criticism somewhere at the end.

Faas: I seem to share some of your priorities.

SNYDER: Yes, I see you as a man of the history of ideas, and the history of ideas I'm very interested in, I respect highly. I just don't know what to do with it because there are too many ideas [laughter] and they keep getting out of hand. But it's not my business to try and figure out what we're going to do except as to simply make things work. Now, to put it in Buddhist terms, you study your own nature

tradition and the individual

deeply, you come to some understanding of your own nature, but your understanding of your own nature is not done in purely individualistic Romantic terms. The Romantic split between tradition and individual talent is no problem for the Buddhist. It's understood that you go to the tradition and study the lore handed down by men who have gone through the same process of meditation and study as yourself, and you respect and appreciate the accumulation of wisdom that they have brought forward. You tune that back into your study of yourself, you turn the soil over, and you actually work back and forth between absolutely naked self-examination and reference to a tradition that you respect.

Faas: Do we have any of that soil in our Western heritage?

SNYDER: Oh sure we do. It's called poetry. It's called the poetic tradition, that's the soil that we go back to.

Faas: I thought you were referring more to some definite framework of ideas in which the Chinese sages were able to live.

SNYDER: Ah, but the framework is the poetry, and the ideas come secondary to that. Maybe that's the way it should be. I would argue that experience, the experiential always precedes the ideology. And the experiential predecessor to Plato is Shamanism, mind expansion, the experiential predecessor to science is alchemy which is also mind expansion, and the experiential predecessors to other schools of thought are the instincts, emotions and experiences that we find most clearly manifested in the poetic tradition. Like it's after Provençal poets that we have what in the history of ideas is Romanticism. And it's in that sense that I look to poetry for the history of ideas. Poetry and magic, poetry and Shamanism, poetry and whatever it is generally, I think, manifest these things prior to their appearance in the world of formal ideas.

Faas: Unless you get poetry with a distinctly didactic or even propagandist bias like some of Eliot's, for instance.

SNYDER: People do that. You can subsume that under the heading of a special kind of experiential use of ideas, like taking ideas as experience and then recounting them in poetry. Yet, fundamentally it's the biological and physical life itself that provides the benefit of it.

Faas: But do you feel that in this way the *Cantos*, for instance, can be read for the same kind of benefit as, say the *Divina Commedia*?

SNYDER: I remember I was reading the *Divina Commedia* about the same time I was reading the *Cantos*. I had read it once through before because I was told to in College. And then I read it a second time through much more closely because I was told to by another poet. That second time was while I was working on a job in the mountains, it was after I had put in a full day's work: every night I sat by a candle and read it till I finished it. And then I went through Milton after that. Now reading both Dante and Milton was more an exercise in cultural history, reading the *Cantos* was not. Maybe it is now, but it wasn't at that time. And so this much misused or overused word "relevance," you know, comes in. We do live in our own times, and mayflies though we may be, we make the field around us that we can make, and so it's that sense of immediate usefulness, immediate manifestation that makes the difference. Like, I can read any number of things from the past and enjoy them and appreciate them and see them in their historical context, but there are few things that are still useful. Blake is still useful, Coleridge is not, although Coleridge's ideas are perhaps as good or better than Blake's. Now I don't know critically how to say that, except to think of it, you know, in terms of tools. I haven't really thought that out clearly. I find certain Chinese poets still useful, their thinking is alive to us, to me. What underlies my use of the word usefulness is an implied and assumed value which, I guess, is evolutionary in some sense. I feel that there is a line of development of the potentialities of human consciousness that we keep working at, and that some works, some poetry, is useful for a while, some poetry is useful for a longer time and keeps coming back to us.

the usefulness of poetry

Faas: This is what Duncan would presumably call your Marxist understanding of literary history.

SNYDER: Well, Duncan is very cute in calling it Marxist. I think of it as bio-classicism, because I really am curious about some basic paradoxes of evolution that are obviously still going on.

McClure put me on to one of the most interesting things, a book by a South African anthropologist, Phillip Tobias, entitled *The Brain in Hominid Evolution,* an historical and evolutionary study of brain size. What it all comes down to is that the average brain size of the human race was larger forty thousand years ago than it is now, and that the increase of brain size over the prior million years to that was the most striking feature of evolution—that the legs, the hands, the knees, the elbows all evolved more or less at their own rate, but that there was nothing physically that striking about it. The one single notable thing is the rapid increase of brain size. Now according to everything we think about evolution so far, if any one factor or feature of the body shows remarkable and swift change, it does so for an adaptive function. The shrinkage of the brain then must have also meant that that function was no longer necessary or was superseded by something else. What superseded the brain was society, social organization. Social organization, the computer—it is no longer necessary for everybody to be so sharp. So the organism was at its sharpest in terms of the individual members of the species about forty thousand years ago, and we are now witnessing a kind of decline. It does not have the appearance of a decline because society has its own life which enables it to maintain and transmit vast bodies of information, and so the information and the skills and survival techniques belong to society at large but they do not belong to us as individuals.

Faas: Do you find the theory convincing?

SNYDER: The argument seems to me plausible, and as such it should become part of our revolutionary, super-reactionary poetics, namely that we look back at that ground base of humanity forty thousand years ago again, refer ourselves back to that and ask the question again: Where were we going, where might we go?

Faas: At various points you have drawn attention to Rousseau, Blake, Whitman, Thoreau, Lawrence, Jeffers, Pound and Rexroth as the major Western influences on you.

SNYDER: Matthew Prior . . . everybody. [Laughing]

Faas: Yet in a programmatic statement for *Naked Poetry* you wrote that the "future can't be seen on the basis of the present."

SNYDER: Can't be *seen,* that's the emphasis.

Margin notes:
bio-classicism

influences

Faas: How do you see the role of D. H. Lawrence in the evolution of modern Anglo-American art and æsthetics?

SNYDER: Oh, I have a great respect for Lawrence, great respect, and he was certainly one of my greatest teachers. He was my first modern poetry teacher. It was in my early years of high school when my focus was essentially mountains and nature, when somebody was passing around a copy of *Lady Chatterly's Lover*—wow—so I read that, and I thought: I would like to read some more of this fellow. So I went to the Public Library and I found *Birds, Beasts and Flowers* listed in the catalogue. And I wondered: Is this a novel or what? I took it out of the library and it was poems. You   D. H. Lawrence
see, I grew up in a very poor, relatively uneducated rural background in Washington State, but I knew about the mountains and the trees. And so I read this book and I said: This man knows what he is talking about, and I was converted to the poetry right there, and to modern poetry.

Faas: Did you also read his essays?

SNYDER: Much later. When I say much later, I mean when I was nineteen. I was reading the rest of Lawrence by the time that I was nineteen but I was reading Lawrence's poetry when I was fourteen.

Faas: He really had it all together, and single-handed.

SNYDER: Really single-handed.

Faas: In Europe, a great many poets have been deeply affected by the language crisis to a degree you rarely find amongst American poets. Poets such as von Hofmannsthal or Ingeborg Bachmann virtually stopped writing poetry on account of the insights commonly associated with the name of Wittgen-   the language
stein. You, by contrast, told me that reading Wittgenstein   crisis
had turned you on to poetry.

SNYDER: Of course, because Wittgenstein himself was saying: This isn't philosophy, this is poetry. So it's not philosophy, then let's write poetry. [Laughing] I mean, maybe some of these European poets who quit writing, secretly wanted to be philosophers. So Wittgenstein disappointed them.

Faas: Concerning this whole issue, there is a curious point on which I can't understand Robert Duncan. He seems to have this belief in a Platonic, essentialist potential of language which appears to me almost like an escape from what has been happening in this whole area.

SNYDER: It's not like scientific theory for Robert. It's part of his feeling for poetry, that's all. Like, it's a poetic view of language, I think, a totally poetic view of language.

Faas: Did you actually read Wittgenstein?

SNYDER: I read the *Tractatus.*

Faas: Not the *Investigations?*

SNYDER: Yes, I read *Philosophical Investigations,* and then I read some papers about him by his disciples. This was years ago, shortly before I went to Japan. I had a friend in those days, Paul Wien-
Wittgenstein paul, who was a professor of philosophy at Santa Bar-
and Zen bara, and Paul was working with Wittgenstein and Wittgenstein switched him to Zen actually. And he came over to Japan and did Zen study for a while.

Faas: That's fascinating.

SNYDER: And then went back to Santa Barbara where he continued teaching and working in philosophy. He has written a couple of books about this, about the limits of language and moving into actual *practise,* one called *The Matter of Zen* and then another book since then about Zen.

Faas: Do you find them interesting?

SNYDER: They are very simple and very direct, yes. Quite interesting.

Faas: Have you read Whitehead as well?

SNYDER: I really have no knowledge of Whitehead. You see my intellectual theories and visions are not drawn from philosophers but inductively derived from reading history and anthropology and linguistics. I formulate my theories that way rather than
formulating by reading theoreticians, and that's what my reading has
his poetics been over the years. So my poetics are in a sense a kind of linguistic and anthropological poetics based on what human beings have done and extracting from that what the essence of poetry seems to be. So I use the shamanistic terminology of the magic of words and what that is, the mantric efficacy of sound, and the genres of poetry as derived from a Tribal concept: essentially work songs, power vision songs, love songs, courting songs, death songs, war songs, healing songs. That kind of terminology is what I feel comfortable with because that is how I see it.

Faas: There is some awareness of a language crisis in Williams and Pound with their experiments in fragmentation and the ideogrammic method. It has always been slightly puzzling to me
Whitman's how after all that poets of your generation could go
rhetoric straight back to Whitman and all his rhetoric.

SNYDER: We all wobble, I was going to say . . . we all swing back and forth, I guess, between that sense of needing to do the job with language itself, and occasionally thinking that the job can be done with emotions and ideas. Whitman is a great temptation, like it's the rhetorical temptation of just expressing yourself in big terms as against the work of doing it structurally. Convincing people with ideas is one system, the other is to change the structural basis. The structural basis is much less rewarding and much more time consuming, although if it works, it does the job. You see what I mean? But it doesn't have immediate results. So audiences don't respond well to poems which are structurally revolutionary, but they do respond well to poems which have a big rhetoric. This may be one of the dangers and temptations of the poetry reading circuit.

Faas: Also the dangers of a poem like *Howl?*

SNYDER: Well, *Howl* was also a structural innovation. Or not really an innovation, but nobody had done it well for a long time. Consequently that added something to the situation. It was people who imitated *Howl* afterwards that fell back into the old rhetoric. *Howl* itself for its time and place—I speak as one who saw and heard it read many times—was immediately appropriate and satisfying on many levels.

Ginsberg's *Howl*

Faas: Duncan told me about the impact the poem had on him so that he tried to write his own *Howl* the day the poem arrived.

SNYDER: Well that was actually something which you couldn't copy, although people tried.

Faas: Yet even a poet as different from Ginsberg as Galway Kinnell admits to the important influence *Howl* had on his poetry.

SNYDER: Oh yes, it had a lot of influence on people who at the time didn't admit it and didn't speak of it till years later. Yes, it undoubtedly is the most influential poem of the mid-century in America.

Faas: You'd really go as far as saying that?

SNYDER: Undoubtedly. And, perhaps, the only other single poem that has had that kind of impact is *The Waste Land,* in this century so far.

Faas: That implies a tremendous respect for somebody whom you once, I guess jokingly, referred to as a "transitional figure."

SNYDER: It's obvious. And we are all transitional figures. Ginsberg is not just a poet, he is a social force, and *Howl* is not just a poem, it's a social force. But the poem is intensely moving, intensely moving in the context of its own time. It made people weep who had never wept before. Quite an achievement.

Faas: I'd like to come back to modern philosophers and the influence they had on you. Were there any others besides Wittgenstein?

SNYDER: I really can't think of any others.

Faas: Or anthropologists? I noticed that Lévi-Strauss, for instance, assumes a more and more prominent place in your critical writing. And who were your main teachers when you did your B.A. thesis on *The Dimensions of Myth?*

SNYDER: On the whole, I feel, I was more influenced by cultural historians, such diverse figures as Frazer, Frobenius, the Americanist Franz Boas, people like that were shaping my thinking, and to some extent Jung.

Faas: Benjamin Lee Whorf?

SNYDER: Oh yes, very much so. But we haven't mentioned Jung before, and Jung was important for all of us, I'm sure.

Faas: So Duncan would probably call you a Jungian like Olson.

SNYDER: I called *him* a Jungian.

Faas: While he calls himself a Freudian, which is rather strange considering his concept of imagery and poetic creativity.

SNYDER: I guess one of the reasons why I say that Duncan is my favorite poet is because I can't figure him out. So I'm always fascinated by what he does and I'm always puzzled by his poetry and I come back to it. Whereas with a lot of other poets, I think I understand what they're doing, so I don't come back to them. So it's the fascination with difficulty and puzzle. And also it's a funny personal feeling I have about him. I even dream about him once every six months or so. I have sort of funny dreams about Duncan. Shall I tell you one of the dreams I had about Duncan?

dream about Duncan

Faas: Please do.

SNYDER: I've never been to Germany, but I dreamt that I was walking somewhere in Germany and I came down a steep grassy embankment, and there was Duncan standing there and he beckoned to me and said: Come right in, this way. And so we went into what was like a cave or an underground room, and we were under the ground and there was an earthen or stone wall that was entirely covered with breasts, and Duncan said: Drink from the one you like. And so I went up and like actually nursed on one of these breasts that were coming out of the wall. And Duncan was my guide.

Faas: Do you feel that there are any points of affinity between your work as a poet and recent developments in painting and music?

SNYDER: I'm really out of touch with that right now.

Faas: John Cage?

SNYDER: Cage's position I know, and I find that interesting.

Faas: And Pollock?

SNYDER: That also more like belongs to the early sixties as I understand it.

Faas: Oh sure, I didn't mean the last few years only.

SNYDER: Certainly, there was a period when quite a bit was coming together from Western avant-garde aesthetics and, what shall we call it, Zennist æsthetics. But that seems to have evaporated somewhat.

Like the whole field now is again wide open. Look at what's happening in every area: the population is exploding, economies are going up and down, more books are being published than ever before, and that kind of thing. So really everything seems out of hand, information overload. [Pause] It just occurs to me that I started talking about my kinds of reading and my inductive way of arriving at theories because I realized that I was being presented with questions about philosophers like Whitehead and Wittgenstein who are really not my intellectual direction. This is not to say that I can't comprehend them, but I don't find reading them as creative or productive as going to historical or anthropological facts or to direct experience. Now maybe that's a very modern thing.   the seventies

Faas: In fact, that in a way parallels my own change of interests in recent years.

SNYDER: It's a very interesting change of the mind. In my reading of Buddhist philosophy—here is a very interesting book concerning Gampopa I am studying right now—I switch back and forth between mythological poetic imagery statements and hard rational logical philosophical statements. Buddhism weaves in and out between those two areas in a very fascinating way. Plato does it a little bit when he invokes metaphors and mythical images like in *Phaedrus* or in the *Symposium*. Other philosophers generally don't. They don't use metaphors like the myth of the cave to talk about philosophical matters, they steer away completely from myth. But myth as a mode of intellectual dialogue is very interesting to me, because in a way it is able to deal with psychological complexities. And again the boundary line between psychology and philosophy is to me more interesting.   philosophy and myth

Faas: I mainly asked you those questions because I have dealt with the philosophers we mentioned in the context of a book I wrote on open form aesthetics, not because I expected you to have a very specific interest in them. Of course, I *am* interested in philosophy, and that is one of the things I found out about myself by coming to the U.S.

SNYDER: Just as when I went to Japan I found out who *I* really was. I found out that I was an American pragmatist. [Laughter]

Faas: In *Naked Poetry* you stated that we are not now looking for new forms and that what's needed is a totally new approach to the idea of form. Could you expatiate on this statement?

SNYDER: In stating that I was simply trying to break this thing of always saying: We are looking for a new form. And the question is:

Do we need any form at all, or, is there anything that is
everything not form anyway? It is more or less obvious that every-
has form thing has form, everything that we call a thing has form.
There is no formlessness in the world as we know it.
Faas: In the sense of Gestalt psychology.
SNYDER: Mm . . . like I discovered by practise that a lot of my poems
were each unique and represent each a different form of strategy.
Which is one way of looking at it. That the same form is never done
twice.
Faas: So that would be the totally new approach to form?
SNYDER: That would be one totally new approach to form which is to
see every poem as a different solution to a different problem.
Faas: When I read that statement I thought you meant a totally new
consciousness.
SNYDER: That would be on the way to a totally new consciousness. A
new consciousness is also very much part of our potentiality, one of
our future potentialities, hopefully. But so often we find ourselves
looking at the past, since we really haven't any ways of thinking about
the future that well. Now since I said that, Jerome Rothenberg has
brought out his books *Technicians of the Sacred* and *Shaking the
Pumpkin* in which all of this fascinating Primitive, pre-literate American Indian, Oceanic, African, Polynesian whatever, all this poetry
has been presented to us. And there are probably, you know, like
sixty different new forms that are possible, that have been brought
back to our consciousness by Rothenberg, forms that belong to our
own archaic past.
Faas: And you think that the kind of feeling needed in order to
really make these forms our own can be revitalized?
SNYDER: Sure, like we haven't used proverbs very well for several
centuries.
Faas: Also in *Naked Poetry* you say that each poem should grow from
an "energy-mind-field-dance" and that it has its own inner grain.
That, of course, reminds me of Olson, but also of the
the   Romantic concept of organic form as expounded by
Romantics Schlegel or Coleridge, for instance. Would you acknowledge the Romantics as predecessors along these lines?
SNYDER: I have nothing against it, although I don't feel the
influence on myself directly. Like I can't read Coleridge.
Faas: Not even the *Biographia Literaria*?
SNYDER: No, I can't even read Wordsworth, I really can't read him. I
find it tiresome. It's just tiresome.
Faas: And yet it seems to me that Coleridge's definition of the
imagination as "a repetition in the finite mind of the eternal act of

creation in the infinite I AM" was a first major step towards open form æsthetics, a definition he partly derived from Schlegel.

SNYDER: And where did he get it from?

Faas: As far as I can tell it was Herder who first modified Aristotle's mimesis theory in the direction of open form æsthetics by saying that the artist does not mirror nature, *natura naturata,* but imitates creation or *natura naturans.* And then Schlegel goes one step further by saying that the poet does not *imitate* cosmic creation, but repeats it, reenacts it.

SNYDER: That's beautiful.

Faas: And it's from there that Coleridge picks it up, I guess.

SNYDER: I think of form in terms of biological forms, like in the work of people such as Adolf Portmann, the biologist. Those people's work offers to me the most interesting information about what form is and how form changes. Form is always moving and adaptive and always has a function.   biological concept of form

Faas: How about the influence of Buddhism on your concept of form?

SNYDER: It's not very far from the biological sense of form.

Faas: Turning to your poetry, I noticed that you often tend to avoid articles or personal pronouns. For instance, instead of "*the* tree" you would just say "tree."

SNYDER: Really?

Faas: Not so much in the longer as in the shorter poems.

SNYDER: Well, I hope I haven't done it in any way that makes the poems obscure, because that's not my intention. My intention is just throwing off extra weight or what seems to be extra weight, and maybe in that I am influenced by my liking for Chinese poetry which has that stripped down feeling.

Faas: I also found that both your longer and shorter poems occasionally have an outwardly closed form. For example, you would repeat the first line of the poem at its end, or you conclude the poem with a kind of summary, or as in "It was when" (from *Regarding Wave)* would structure an entire poem around one long sentence. Do you feel that the open form impulse, as these examples seem to suggest, can include closed form devices?   closed form poetry

SNYDER: I don't see any objections to such devices and I have no antipathy as such to closed form. Like, anything that works, I'll use. I'm impressed by the fact that almost all the poems that I can remember by heart are poems with regular meters that rhyme and that it is very difficult to memorize poems that don't have these regular meters and rhymes. Right there, you see, there is an obvious function for that kind of form, that it's mnemonic, that it sticks in your mind.

Faas: That sounds like Ginsberg picking up on the old song traditions.

SNYDER: Exactly!

Faas: And taking poetry back to where it came from.

SNYDER: Right.

Faas: Yet that would be a slightly new use of rhyme and metrical devices.

SNYDER: But using ballad meter and using any of a number of easily available forms surely has its value, just as it's very difficult to sing songs that don't have these forms. You end up singing art songs, and art songs are the worst of all.

Faas: What do you mean by art songs?

SNYDER: Ah . . . I don't know how to describe art songs. Like if you set free verse to music it sounds like art songs. There is an area of the power of poetry that cannot be denied, which is the area of rhythm and structure, the area of drama.

Faas: Drama in what sense?

SNYDER: The drama of ballads, for example.

Faas: One of your critics claims that a main characteristic of your poetry is its lack of tension, its lack of drama. Is that because drama, along with tragedy, would be a specifically Western mode of literature to you?

poetry and drama

SNYDER: It's not really Western. Chinese poetry has the upper class literary style but then it has that huge body of folksong and ballad that belongs to the people, that's full of drama. And, of course, the poetry of India is all drama, all rhetoric. I don't use that strategy very often, but I respect it. And I would use it, you know. Whenever the time comes, I'll use it.

Faas: Isn't the Eastern concept of drama different from ours?

SNYDER: Well, I'm using it in the broadest sense of getting your interest aroused, keeping your interest up, and then fulfilling your interest. And also surprising it, and the surprises are the most interesting thing. It's like getting people going on something and then surprising them, that's the oldest literary trick of all. And it still works. And form is useful for that, just as *mantras,* the singing of *mantras* harmonizes with the rhythms of the breath rate of the body. The body is a closed form.

Faas: But then that particular body rhythm might open up into the rhythm of the whole universe.

SNYDER: The universe is a closed form.

Faas: Not a form of expanding boundaries?

SNYDER: But that's closed too, yes, expanding boundaries are closed, you're still talking about boundaries.

Faas: But they are open to the outside, to what surrounds them. Just like in Gestalt psychology you have one pattern or form, but it's expanding into, if not to say, constituted by all the surrounding patterns, and there is no end to it.

SNYDER: It's still form.

Faas: Oh yes, it's definitely form.

SNYDER: So all form is closed.

Faas: It's rather funny that I should be manœuvred into the role of an apologist of open form while you are defending closed form. [Laughter]

SNYDER: I'm not defending closed form. I'm just saying it's another strategy. And if you want to talk about empti- ness, the universe is not empty, the universe is full. And any concep- tion of the universe is still a conception that involves the nature of form.

Faas: And this is where poetry moves.

SNYDER: Poetry moves off the edge of that, that's where it is exciting.

Faas: And meditation would go beyond that.

SNYDER: Well, in and out of it. In Buddhist terms, the body is form, the mind has the potentiality of formlessness, and speech or lan- guage mediates between the two. It seems very accurate. But the mind is usually caught up in form because it is generally playing with linguistic tricks or replaying impressions that it has taken in. But the mind also has the possibility, like a mirror, of not necessarily reflect- ing anything, and that is the ground nature, the fundamental nature of consciousness. We tend to think of it as being full of forms because that's how we see it. Just as every time you look into a mirror you see something in the mirror. But a mirror need not necessarily have anything in it. It would still be a mirror.

Faas: At one point you speak of poetry as riding the razor's edge between the expressible and the inexpressible, and you criticize those poets who move too far into the realm of the inexpressible. Wouldn't you say that your own poems sometimes cross that border- line as well, moving into the realm of *mantra, koan*, etc., of those sacred magic genres which have usually evolved through generations and generations and derived their form from there?

SNYDER: Well, the borderline is probably something like this: When you are in a territory where there are no special expectations of your listener, you can still make a song, you're in poetry. If you have a request, ask a special practise from your listener, if you have to

[margin note:] all form is closed

[margin note:] the border- line to the ineffable

say:You must meditate two weeks before you listen to this poem and maybe observe some special diet, then you are in the specific realms of shamanistic or religious training. Now, messages are transmitted and things are taught and songs are sung within the shamanistic special realms of practise, but that's a very special world, it's a professional world almost. We bring poetry back from our special practises, so to speak, to the open realm of human dialogue where we can address it to anyone. That's the known international definition of poetry, after the fact. Otherwise it becomes like an esoteric tradition. There are poems that move in, so to speak, esoteric traditions.

Faas: In contemporary American poetry?

SNYDER: In some senses, yes. Poems that require special inside knowledge, special knowledge of the theories and so forth. That is not so interesting to me as public clarity.

Faas: Could you give an example?

SNYDER: Some kind of Surrealism perhaps. And even maybe the poems surrounding Olson and his group, in some ways, are a little bit esoteric. They require a certain amount of initiation. And, of course, this has been a charge which has been levelled at modern poetry generally, that it required special initiation. But that's in a much broader sense. Talking about the uses of language, there are ways we use language which are open to everyone, which *koan* and are public dialogue. There are private and esoteric ways *mantra* of using language which belong generally to religious traditions. There are other specializations today like the sciences which are again another question. But you see what I'm driving at. Like a *koan* functions in a very special realm that requires thousands of hours of meditation per minutes of utterance, whereas in the realm of poetry the proportion is less. [Laughing] And something like a *mantra* is a special use of language which requires repetition. There is a whole territory in which language gets its power by repetition. "Hail Mary, full of grace," and so forth. Poetry in "civilized" times does not use repetition as a device for gaining power, but it also is a method of gaining power.

Faas: Ginsberg talks about his use of *mantra*-like strategies.

SNYDER: He approaches that, yes, he fuses them with his poetry. And I involve similar things in a way in my poetry. What we're doing, I suppose, on that level, is that we're bringing back some territories of language use that belong to traditional and archaic cultures and that have been neglected in contemporary times quite a archaic uses bit. The "poetry reading" is what makes this possible. The of language fact that we do poetry readings means that we are led to using techniques which are extra-Western and in some ways archaic because we're using the voice, and we can sing, can chant *mantras,* create some special things around us, so that my poetics start with the voice, pure sound, and voice line melody, voice line rhythm possibilities, then explores mantric, that is, meaningless sound possibilities which I see in *mantras* and in various kinds of chants and in nonsense songs of children, and then move into rhythmic rhyme poetry of children..

Faas: Like yesterday at the YMHA.

SNYDER: Yes, I did some of that. That catches the minds of people and catches the minds of children, and then goes out into the trickier melodies that you get associated with open poetry, where you are steering between rather complex feelings and ideas on the one hand and ways of pushing language up against what it can say. It's a very paradoxical thing, poetry is in one way the finest use of language, but at that point it comes up to the very limits of language. In some ways it's the densest, the most concentrated use of language outside the technical scientific language. I mean by content analysis standards. But then it comes up against an end which is that razor edge boundary line. That's when I try to do some things with those silent poems, those quieter poems, because hopefully they do echo some non-linguistic, pre-linguistic, pre-verbally visualized or deeply felt areas. Like in that little bit of *haiku* æsthetics which says: The words stop but the meaning keeps going. That's another angle which is at work in Chinese poetry very much, in those little Chinese quatrains or double quatrains where the poem is very intense and very short.

Faas: Talking about the actual structure or texture of your poetry . . .

SNYDER: I like what Duncan says: that we are all writing the same poem.

Faas: Like weaving a big endless tapestry.

SNYDER: And in that sense no beginning or ending, just contributions.   poetic

Faas: But then there always is a beginning and an end the   closure
way the poem appears on the page typographically.

SNYDER: No, but the end goes on, it goes on in your mind. Like the end of the poem is just the beginning of whatever causal or karmic function it might have in the world, like what effect it has on people, like how it echoes.

Faas: William Stafford, talking about Olson's æsthetics, once said in an interview that he usually ends a poem when his powers to homogenize an experience come to an end.

SNYDER: I stop a poem when I feel it has been well enough begun that the reader can carry it from there. That the rest of it is for his mind.

Faas: You have rarely commented on your actual practises as a poet. Do you find that the order in which the poem appears on the page usually reflects the sequence in which its words and sentences occurred to you while you were writing it.

SNYDER: In short poems, yes. Short poems I write very quickly, very swiftly.

revision
Faas: And you don't revise them?

SNYDER: Not too much, because I don't write them down before I've got them more or less ready. I resist the impulse to write a poem down until I feel that it's fully matured. I keep poems in my mind for months.

Faas: Duncan showed me some of his manuscripts a couple of days ago. He says that he treats each of his revisions as separate poems.

SNYDER: I have thought about that. It's kind of charming. [Laughing] Except it takes more paper. The longer poems of *Mountains and Rivers* are real field compositions in which things do not belong according to chronology but according to place.

Faas: And that means rearranging, shuffling things around.

SNYDER: Yes. I've been doing twenty-five sections simultaneously over the last ten years, working a little on this poem, a little on this poem, a little on this poem, and, hopefully, like all the
field   sheep will be driven into the corral at the same time, and
composition then the poem will be done. I don't know anybody who is writing a poem like that, who's writing the whole thing at once clear out here, and trying to herd them all into the same gate at once finally.

Faas: Does one know anything about the writing practises of Zen Buddhist poets, like Basho, for instance?

Zen poetics   SNYDER: Pretty quick. You get that impression from reading Basho and the literature about Basho as a great *haiku* writer. Also, Basho was quite a critic, he had created a circle of disciples, and he was very quick in describing what were the shortcomings of various people. In fact, that's one of the most interesting things about the evolution of *haiku* with Basho and his circle: the importance that criticism played in it and how they made their living as *haiku* teachers. And as teachers their function was to be critics. They didn't make their living by giving poetry readings or by publishing poems. The money came from criticizing the people who studied under them.

Faas: Do you feel that a poem, if it doesn't have closed form, should at least have texture and coherence?

texture   SNYDER: I'm not convinced of that necessarily. But from my own poetry I noticed a tendency towards texture and coherence. But I can enjoy incoherent poems if there is

something else to it. I don't want to overstress coherence. Too much
texture and too much coherence leads back to that old trap of formal
perfectionism which cuts off the possibility of the idea and meaning
going on in the mind of the reader afterwards. So the kind of
coherence that I will strive for would be a communicative coherence
that liberates the reader to go on with it. You see what I mean?
Coherence in the sense of usefulness and relevance, and stimulation
and excitement and imagination, not coherence in the sense of: I
have shown you what I can do, I have now closed it up and now it's
done. I am a striver, not a finisher. [Laughing]

Faas: As opposed to a man like Yeats who felt that a poem was
finished when you could hear the clicking of the lid closing in on the
box.

SNYDER: Well, but I can't deny that some of Yeats's poems really do
that, beautifully, and yet they keep on going on in your mind.

Faas: Because Yeats being a great poet ever so often transcended his
own poetics.

SNYDER: Exactly. [Laughing]

Faas: In a previous interview you stated that your poetry tries to
explore the full landscape or architecture of consciousness from
contentless ground through the unconscious and conscious and on through sense perception and immediate   the scope
emotion to the realms of abstract scientific theorizing and   of his
pure mathematics. Yet it seems obvious that your poetry   poetry
inhabits some of these areas much more than others.

SNYDER: Obviously, my poetry does not occupy all of these niches,
and I don't even try to. The niches that I occupy, or that I hope to
occupy, are the warm humane mammal family niche, the archetypal
and mythic niche, and the transparent intuitive direct perception
niche.

Faas: Transparent, I guess, in the sense of form as emptiness, as
ellipse, leaving things out at the right spot, as you once put it.

SNYDER: At some points. The "form as emptiness" is not quite the
same as you understand it, I think. The quotation "form equals
emptiness" is from the *Prajñā Pāramitā Sūtra*, and it's a key term of
Buddhist metaphysics, *the* key term of Buddhist metaphysics, and it
has a whole history of ideas and traditions that fits around it for
Buddhists.

Faas: I'd now like to turn to your long poems. In which ways do the
strategies of fragmentation which you use in *Mountains and Rivers*
compare with Pound's? In fact, I see some even more   ideogrammic
striking similarities with Hart Crane's *The Bridge*.   method and
SNYDER: I haven't read that poem for a long time.   fragmentation

Faas: That peculiar kind of American fragmentation,

the juxtaposition of rhetorically unrelated bits of narrative, dialogue, dramatic monologue.

SNYDER: Yes, I really don't know. [Laughing] I haven't been thinking in those terms.

Faas: How then do you relate to Pound's ideogrammic method?

SNYDER: Well, the ideogrammic method was useful for us when we were young. Later, I went to study Chinese and I realized how little Pound or even Fenollosa understood about how Chinese works. I feel that as far as Pound goes, it's clear to me that I have more of a sense of clarity; I don't introduce things that are particularly obscure unless I can't help it.

Faas: Some of your poems in *Mountains and Rivers* seem to me extremely difficult.

SNYDER: You think so? I don't think so. [Laughing]

Faas: Especially "The Blue Sky" with all those names.

SNYDER: There's a lot of names, that's true. But hopefully when the whole thing is put together there will be enough reverberations and echoes from the various sections so that it will be self-informing. What I find is that every poem I do in *Mountains and Rivers* takes a different form and has a different strategy, and I have to let the strategy work itself out. When I get enough distance from it at some point I'll be able to understand more clearly what I've done. But like every poem has a very different strategy and they come in various ways from various quarries, many-faceted.

Faas: Is there any comparable technique of fragmentation in Chinese poetry?

SNYDER: No.

Faas: That's why I'm puzzled that you should go back to

two kinds
of consciousness   that kind of technique.

SNYDER: Doing what?

Faas: Fragmentation.

SNYDER: Well, that's because of this kind of poem. I'm writing two kinds of poetry.

Faas: But isn't a poetic mode always the expression of a specific kind of consciousness?

SNYDER: I have two kinds of consciousness. [Laughing] I don't know, I do *Mountains and Rivers* and then I do these other shorter poems.

Faas: So that would be your Western consciousness. [Laughter]

SNYDER: Perhaps. It's a mythic consciousness, myth fragments.

Faas: Have you seen the *Norton Anthology of Modern Poetry?*

SNYDER: Yes, I have.

Faas: In the introduction to your section, the editor speaks of your

relaxed, often cheerful acceptance of a world composed of fragments in contrast to Eliot's "These fragments I have
shored against my ruins" at the end of *The Waste Land.*   *Myths & Texts*
And that unlike Eliot "who juxtaposes cultures to point   and *The Waste Land*
up a disaster, [you see] in a pluralistic world of fragments
our salvation."

SNYDER: It's going in the right direction. But the next step would be
to understand that nothing is not related, that everything is interrelated. And that there really are no fragments.

Faas: The *shih shih wu ai* or what you called the "jewelled net of
interconnectedness."

SNYDER: Yes. It's different ways of connecting your network. The
Buddha says: "Bhikshu, you see this rice stalk. If you understand
this rice stalk, you understand the law of interdependent origination. If you understand the law of interdependent origination you
understand the *dharma,* if you understand the *dharma,* you know the
Buddha." A fundamental Buddhist position.

Faas: And how does Chinese poetry express that interconnectedness?

SNYDER: It expresses it in images, small images. "A high tower on a
white plane. If you climb up one floor, you'll see a thousand miles
more." [Laughing] That's why Zen as a training uses Chinese poetry
extensively, because they understand the uses of those images as
expressions of interpenetration.

Faas: And how do the images link up?

SNYDER: You just juxtapose two images.

Faas: With a gap of silence in between.

SNYDER: Sometimes. Well, what we're talking about now is very
interesting, but it's something I haven't really got clear enough
myself. If you want you can look up this book on the Buddhist
philosophy of interdependence by a man called Chang, entitled *The
Buddhist Philosophy of Totality;* it's a marvellous book, published by
Pennsylvania State University. It has many images that are used in
discussing interpenetration on many levels and how Chinese poetry
is doing that.

Faas: Do you want to discuss this issue of interdependence and
fragmentation any further?

SNYDER: Okay. There are two things. One is, say, a fragmented text
which appears fragmented and which is fragmented and which
leads nowhere. Another is ideogrammic method, a fragmented text
which appears fragmented but actually leads you somewhere because the relationships that are established between the fragments
express a deeper level of connectedness, which becomes clear to the

reader's mind if he is able to follow it. We have phony obscurity and we have obscurity which serves to communicate. Two differences. The ideogrammic method is intended as a method of communication in the sense of juxtaposing apparently unrelated things that show the connections automatically. That, of course, is what I'd have in mind in my work. Not that I want to make fragmented form but that I want to make a whole form.

Faas: But didn't you plan *Mountains and Rivers without End* as an open ended endless poem?

SNYDER: Endless? No, not really.

Faas: Do you remember what you told Kerouac, or at least what he claims you told him in *The Dharma Bums?*

a poem "without end"?

SNYDER: I said that as a joke. Yes, I was saying that facetiously. That wasn't really what my sense of it was. I was talking about *Mountains and Rivers without End* and I was tripping over the word "without End." But, obviously, what you do with "without End" is that you feed it back into itself and make a circle of it.

Faas: But you mentioned previously that your conception of the poem changed.

SNYDER: It has changed some, sure.

Faas: What were those changes? Say by comparison with open form poems like *Paterson* or the *Cantos*.

SNYDER: I would not like to get caught in between open and closed. If the universe is circular, which it is, does that not mean it is a closing world? We don't know. Actually something like the Möbius strip moves in and out of two dimensions; it is closed but it is also open. I'm not really worried about that. I would like to have the poem close in on itself but on some other level keep going.

Faas: What would be the other level? In the reader's mind?

SNYDER: Yes.

Faas: Or structurally, too?

SNYDER: Well, structurally in that each of the sections of the poem implies a direction that you can complete yourself. I don't do it, you know, once I have done it, I leave it, and people can play with that more if they want, do more with that if they want on their own.

Faas: But for you there would be a definite point where you leave off and think it's done.

SNYDER: Yes.

Faas: Do you have any idea right now when that's going to be?

SNYDER: Mm . . . a few years from now. I'm working on another book right now, about Japan, which is taking me away from writing poetry.

Faas: You told me that each of the 25 sections would center around a *ku* or key phrase.

"key phrases" in *Mountains and Rivers without End*

SNYDER: An image, a focal image.

Faas: Could you point one out, in "Bubbs Creek Haircut," for instance.

SNYDER: Well, the key in that is the third line in from the last, "double mirror waver." That shows you what the whole structure of it is.

Faas: I thought it would be "Goodwill."

SNYDER: That's another one. That runs through other poems, too. But "Goodwill" is more a content point. "Double mirror waver" is a structure point. Mutually reflected mirrors. Like, you see yourself many times reflected in a barber's shop. You look and you see yourself going that way and you see yourself going that way. It's a key image in *Avatamsaka* philosophy, Buddhist interdependence philosophy. Multiple reflections in multiple mirrors, that's what the universe is like.

Faas: So each poem would have that kind of central image or key phrase.

Buddhist interdependence philosophy

SNYDER: Yes, there is a key phrase in a sense. I'm not playing on it, but there is a place where I have the picture of what I'm doing somewhere in the poems. I was not always that conscious of it.

Faas: What exactly does *ku* mean?

SNYDER: A *ku* just means a little phrase. On page 20* in "Night Highway Ninety-nine" it's "—Abandon really means it/—the network womb stretched loose all/ things slip/ through," and then: "Dreaming on a bench under newspapers/ I woke covered over with Rhododendron blooms/ Alone in a State Park in Oregon." That again is the center of the structural principle in "Highway Ninety-nine" which is "slipping through." The "network womb" where all things slip through is a Buddhist image, the image of the *graha*, the great womb of time and space which intersects itself. And being sort of continually through that network. And then I put it again in the image of "Dreaming on a bench under newspapers" which is like waking up in another place, covered with blossoms. That's what I'm trying to show in "Highway Ninety-nine" as it moves across different space and time—paradigms again.

Faas: Do you come across these images in the process of writing?

SNYDER: Yes.

Six Sections from Mountains and Rivers without End Plus One. Writing 9. San Francisco: Four Seasons Foundation, 1970.

Faas: It's not that you have an image and organize a poem around it?

SNYDER: No, well, when I hit the image then I know what the poem is going to be.

Faas: It's not like James Dickey who once said that he always has any number of subjects ready in his head about which he could write poems.

SNYDER: Well now those, that's what you make the body, the meat of the poem. But this is the bones of the poem.

subject matter versus structure

Faas: But you don't have the latter as preconceived notions.

SNYDER: Well, when I see it, I know what I've got. I know what I'm doing, when I finally hit something like that. Until I hit that, I don't know what the poem is, so I haven't really begun to write the poem. I've just been doing some work with some images.

Faas: Would all that still be at the stage of thinking about the poem, of writing it in the mind as you say?

SNYDER: It's on the level of visualizing and re-visualizing and re-experiencing and projecting the images and then writing some of the images down and keeping a lot of it in mind.

Faas: Not like writing and rewriting the poem in your mind and then finally writing it down almost without corrections as in the case of your shorter poems?

the writing process

SNYDER: Well, *Mountains and Rivers* takes a little bit more replay than that. You have to do it because it's complicated. I have to go back, I have to re-look at it, I have to re-tune it, re-adjust it sometimes quite a bit, not too much but . . . You want to see some more of that?

Faas: Yes, please.

SNYDER: In "Hymn to the Goddess San Francisco in Paradise" on page 24, in the very first section there, starting with "—amazed to see under their clothes they are/ naked/ this makes them sacred/ & more than they are in their own shape/ free." I take that to be the center of what's being developed there. Going back to very ancient ideas of women and of goddesses which saw nakedness as a sacred state at the time of the pre-mycenaean mother goddess temples, when the priestesses only appeared occasionally but then they appeared naked. The nakedness was a sacred epiphany of itself. And the funny thing about nakedness is that it is the closest thing we have about ourselves, and yet it has this curious magic and always has had as far as we can tell. It evokes all in some curious way, and yet it's the plainest simplest thing on earth while having that awesome quality. That's what I was trying to evoke with the "Hymn to the Goddess." And the city is being contradictory in that way. [Pause] "The Blue Sky" which is all about healing and my ideas of language is a very complicated poem and I'm not sure that it hangs together exactly like that. But the most useful lines in it are (on page 41) "'Where'd you get the buttermilk?'/ I'd been looking all over for buttermilk. He said,/ 'At the O K Dairy, right where you leave town.'" That's the healing word in that. [Laughing]

Faas: That's more like "Goodwill."

SNYDER: Yes, that's like "Goodwill," it's a lot like "Goodwill." The other thing that's important in "The Blue Sky" is on page 42, that little comment on "[*comrade*: under the same sky/ tent/ curve]/ Kamara, Avestan, a girdle kam, a bent curved bow." I tried to imagine the poem arching like the bow of the sky, I didn't really do it very well, but I tried to think of the poem as going from one horizon over to the other horizon. It starts eastward from here, looking east, sunrise, and ends "Thinking on Amitatha in the setting sun" towards the center "where the Eagle/ that Flies out of Sight/ *flies.*" So the blue sky is the sky itself, the arch of the sky, the kam, the camber, it is the structure of the poem, starting from one end to the other and then going back to the center, and ties into the idea of bow and comrade. Let's see, we didn't do "The Market," eh? [Pause] It's weird poems, isn't it? [Laughing] Page 32. The pivotal point there is "when the market is closed/ the cleanup comes/ equals." Again, this is a poem about interconnections and exchanges, interchanges, and again I'm trying to lead to that with the last phrase about buying "bananas by the ganges." That's what happens when you break your customary set of equivalences, then where do you go? Which I hope will be taken up in another poem which will answer that. [Laughing] This poem essentially poses a question which is not yet answered in the body of the poems that are done. Just as "The Blue Sky" raises a question which is the Eagle, so I'll have to do another section which will clarify that.

Faas: So one important structural device in the framework of the whole work would be to raise questions in one poem and then, in a way, to answer them in another.

SNYDER: Yes, on many levels I hope to be doing that.

Faas: How do you see your poetry in relation to the reader or listener?

SNYDER: Well, poetry starts with breath, breath of life, spirit, voice, voiced, you know, breath voiced becomes voice, and then voice as a vehicle of signaling, which becomes language, lingua—lang—

tongue, all that physiological fundamental of it is very
the reader's   interesting to me. And then it moves out from there into
role   poetry as expression of inward states of being, fundamentally, but inward states of being which are more than
private, that invoke similar states of being in the hearer, that trigger
the same response, the same inward state, and in that triggering
establish a bond, a communication.

Faas: Eliciting some kind of creative participation?

SNYDER: Right. And the bond is established on a deeper level than
the intellectual front brain consciousness level of bonding. I'm talking biologically now, because this is really where I draw from, especially lately. Signaling and bonding is essential to a particular social
species like ourselves and the more complex and elaborate and deep
inward states of being are expressible, the higher level of
poetic com-   consciousness and higher level of evolutionary organiza-
munication as
"bonding"   tion you find in the organism. There is a book by Adolf
Portmann, the Swiss zoologist, entitled *Animal Forms and
Patterns*, which contains a very interesting theory about animals.
Now this is philosophy for me, this is my kind of philosophy. What
Portmann says is this: Catfish, squirrels etc., have no faces, they have
no facial expressions that signal to another animal. They signal with
their whole body. Their hair stands up, for instance. So moods or
states of feeling in animals are communicated by whole-body gestures, whole-body manifestations, also by sounds, the tone of the
sound. But as animals develop larger brains and higher biological
organization, the face and head become more important. Portmann
gives diagrams how the simple mammal forms have hair and fur
patterns that run right up and over their face and do not make any
formal distinction betwee the head and the body. With the higher
forms like tigers, the head gets a special patterning which accen-
tuates eyes and ears and which indicates that the head is the focus.
What that evolves into is the face. Now the face and its expressions
and the voice become the mode of expression of the inward state of
the animal. Wolves have a variety of expressions, as Konrad Lorenz
has pointed out. They communicate different states of feeling to
each other in that process, or rather by that means, and humanity
finally takes it another step, of course, to the capacity of communication. But the capacity of communication has many levels and the
most fundamental in a sense still remains the communication of
inward states of being.

Faas: So you establish communication by taking language back
from the purely conceptual, cerebral level to an animal body
physiological level.

SNYDER: Yes. And the more accurately the inward states of being can be expressed, the more remarkable it is. Like, sea urchins or sea slugs cannot see each other, they are completely locked in their own organisms. And in this sense there is a direction which is very beautiful, and that's the direction of the organism being less and less locked into itself, less and less locked into its own body structure and its relatively inadequate sense organs, towards a state where the organism can actually go out from itself and share itself with others. And poetry in language is of the greatest order of that sharing of the inner self with the outer, with the non-self. In a way, that's the whole value of poetry, in a way it's on the highest level of human bonding, that is to say that humans can share their real feelings with each other, which solves the need to be aggressive for one thing. That's the foundation of genuine communication and genuine love. Now, I'm no utopian. I see that working on some levels. So that's another angle which does not have to invoke magic.

poetry the highest level of human bonding

Faas: That reminds me of another question I wanted to ask you. Do you have any specific idea as to how you use myth in contrast to other poets?

SNYDER: I don't know how I use myth in contrast to other poets. I probably know as much about myth as anybody. Probably Duncan is the only other poet who has studied it as much as I have.

Faas: But his poetic use of myth is very different from yours.

SNYDER: I have a double sense of it: on the one hand myth in a way is our primary intellectual and poetic vocabulary, is the 50,000 year old international myth lore corpus, the world folklore motifs, world mythologies, world themes, world gods and goddesses, that whole thing is our fundamental vocabulary. Western literature uses its own myth vocabulary all the way through from Homer to James Joyce. India uses its own myth vocabulary all the way through in its literature and its thinking. That is a fundamental kind of human lore which as an objective study is fascinating in the extreme and has amazing historical connections and cultural connections, and so forth. That's the one side. The other side is the more Jungian sense of the collective unconscious and the archetypal images. According to Jungian thought the myths are simply the surface manifestations of things which are deep in the unconscious. But I know enough about mythology and its complexities to realize that you can't simply explain mythology by a Jungian principle. Mythology is an inner thing that is almost biological and in a sense almost pre-cultural. Mythology also is man's most archaic lore and one which culture by culture incontrovertibly

poetic use of myth

binds men together. It both liberates and binds. And you use those images as they come out of your own body. If you feel that a particular myth image or a particular god or goddess image is extremely attractive or interesting to you, then you have a relationship with it, and then you play that out from yourself against what is known about it in the world at large, in the external body of mythology. So that's what I do.

Faas: There is a kind of erudite mythological eclecticism in Pound.

SNYDER: I'm more interested in a poetical rather than a comparative mythological way, demonstrating what I think to be main strands in the world body of myth and how they relate to us today. I can only identify with what I consider to be main strands by a process of inner examination of those strands as well as by looking at them, you know, statistically. [Laughing] It's a dual process. "Bubbs Creek Haircut" is working all around that.

Faas: Some of your poetry is full of esoteric allusions which seems to call for something like Eliot's "Notes on the Waste Land."

SNYDER: But everybody knows about Shiva and Pārvatī, don't you think?

erudite
allusiveness
Faas: I really doubt it. [Both laughing] I would guess that amongst your listeners of last night about 10% would really know who they are.

SNYDER: Really? That's where I'm getting out of touch with my audience. [Laughing] Well, you know what I thought of, Ekbert? I thought, when I will have finished *Mountains and Rivers* to write a final poem section which would be footnotes and glossary all as one poem.

Faas: Number 26.

SNYDER: Or to break the page with a line here and write the footnotes as kind of another poem underneath. [Laughing] It would be fun to do something like that. It may be that that's necessary. As I say, I don't put any prime value on obscurity, it's not my intention to appear overly learned.

Faas: And then, of course, who would really enjoy reading a poem which needs too much learned documentation?

SNYDER: Sure, the reader reads it because it's interesting. That's why Pound fell down. That's why big sections of the *Cantos* aren't interesting. There are some very dry Cantos in the mid sections which don't hold up for that very reason. So, you know, like Pound dug a hole for himself there. I think I'm avoiding that, I think that the level of meaning, content, interest and music is going to be strong enough in *Mountains and Rivers* to sustain the reader through it. *Myths & Texts* has been very successful and *Myths & Texts* is a difficult poem, but it sells more copies per year now than it sold in 1959 when it was published. It has been in print steadily since 1959 and it sells a thousand copies a year—with no footnotes.

Faas: How do you respond to confessional poetry?

SNYDER: It's a work they have to do and probably it's work that has to be done. Also, certainly, there is an audience that benefits from it in some way. I read it, fine. I wouldn't consider that a main poetic stream.

confessional poetry

Faas: When I first met you in Kitkitdizze you said so nicely that nobody seems to take much notice of the number of establishment poets that are deeply neurotic, while on the other hand there were endless outcries against the supposed craziness of the Beat poets.

SNYDER: Yes, we have noticed that over the years. There was in many ways more tension and frustration and suffering and breakdown and alcoholism and so forth in the lives of the straight academic poets, at least as much and maybe more, than in the non-academic and supposedly crazier and freakier world. And the greatest model of sanity of all, of course, is that old madman Allen Ginsberg. [Laughter] Olson was a very sane man essentially, far stabler, say, than John Berryman or Anne Sexton. So it's very curious in a way, it's just that people don't notice it.

Faas: What do you think is the main reason for neurosis amongst establishment poets?

SNYDER: I suppose it's because when you're caught in the establishment, you are referring yourself to a set of expectations and trying to meet those expectations which are exterior to yourself. But when you step out of that you're only answering your own expectations and if you have high expectations for yourself, well, then you may get something interesting done. But you are not frustrated because you are not trying to please someone else. And whatever obscure demons there are in the white middle-class mind. I mean Berryman had some obscure demons since it's hard to locate why he should have had the difficulties he did really.

Faas: Duncan is reported by Bruce Cook to have said that your poetry is based on your "conception of the taste of the reasonable man."

SNYDER: I guess I must be a reasonable man because people keep telling me that. [Laughing] What I think I would be doing is trying to win the credibility of the reasonable man and then take him deeper. And I have to do that because I live in a very common-sense world. I always lived in a world where you had to be pretty straight because nobody would tolerate too much bullshit. I mean, who do you speak to? You speak to

the reasonable man

people who are fellow workers, and so you have to start off on some level of communication which they will listen to, then you take off from there. So in some senses maybe Duncan is right.

Robert Creeley

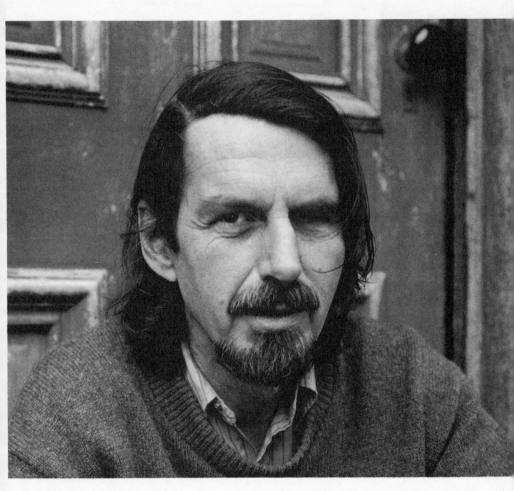

Photo: Gerard Malanga

ROBERT CREELEY (1926 -   )

"I've never felt that writing was fiction, that it was something
made up about something. I've felt that it was direct evidence
of the writer's engagement with his own feelings and with the
possibilities that words offered him . . . Wherever it is one
stumbles (to get to wherever) at least some way will exist, so to
speak, as and when a man takes this or that step—for which,
god bless him. Insofar as these poems are such places, always
they were ones stumbled into . . ."

One place Creeley, much against his natural inclination, has stumbled into all his life, is academia. He attended Harvard for a period
before and after a year in the American Field Service in India and
Burma during World War II (1944-45), but left the university just in
time to avoid completing his B.A.—which was later awarded him by
the rector of Black Mountain College. "Olson [in 1955] said, well,
you taught the courses, therefore you should have credit for
them—we'll give you a degree. It served." In 1960 he received his
M.A. from the University of New Mexico and subsequently taught at
various academic institutions before becoming a Professor of English at SUNY, Buffalo in 1966. Yet the unceasing restlessness of his
diversified existence seems to belie this *curriculum vitæ*: while in
Europe he became associate editor of the German Rainer Gerhardt's
Fragmente and the Japanese Katue Kitasono's *Vou* and ran his own
Divers Press in Mallorca; he edited the *Black Mountain Review* while
teaching at the college, tutored the children of a coffee finca owner
in Guatemala, or divided his life between Buffalo, New York and
Bolinas, California. The major turning point in his life came
through contact with Olson, with whom he conducted a four-year-
long (soon to be published) correspondence before the two poets
met in 1954. A poet (*Poems 1950-1965*, 1966; *Words*, 1967; *Pieces*,
1968; *The Finger: Poems 1966-69*, 1970; *A Day Book*, 1972; *Selected
Poems*, 1976), novelist (*The Island*, 1963), playwright (*Listen*, 1972),

short story writer (*The Gold Diggers*, 1954, 1965) as well as critic-æsthetician (*A Quick Graph*, 1970; *Contexts of Poetry: Interviews 1961-71*, 1973; *A Sense of Measure*, 1973), Creeley has also done important editorial work (*Mayan Letters* by Charles Olson, 1953, 1968; *New American Story*, 1965; *Selected Writings* by Charles Olson, 1966; *The New Writing in the U.S.A*, 1967, etc.).

Robert Creeley

By way of introducing his seminal review of Robbe-Grillet's first novel *Les Gommes* (1953), Roland Barthes remarks: "Above the entrance of Montparnasse station . . . there presently . . . is a big neon sign 'Good Mileage' of which several letters are usually extinct." This, he suggests, would be an ideal subject for the French novelist who tends to strip things of their anthropomorphic significations and to describe them in their literal, non-referential suchness. "All the artist's craft aims at giving the object a 'being there' and to deprive it of 'being something' " (Bs,E,29,31).

For Barthes, *Les Gommes* was a startling confirmation of his theory, mapped out in *Le degré zéro de l'écriture* (1953), that modern writers, ever since Flaubert and Mallarmé, had increasingly tried to strip language of the socio-ideological connotations tacitly inherent in its normal usage. After the Surrealists, after Camus and Sartre, it was Robbe-Grillet who had finally reached that "perfection dans l'imitation du réel" which before him had only been realized in a non-Western culture like the Chinese (Bs,D,33).

The work of Robert Creeley, whose artistic and intellectual career resembles an ontogenetic repetition of this development, could have provided Barthes with a comparable—and even earlier—confirmation of his thesis. Explaining the extreme "particularism and literalness" of his writing, the poet relates an anecdote oddly reminiscent of the neon sign in Barthes' review:

> I'm by nature and circumstance a very literal man. There was a sign over a diner as one drove from Albuquerque to Santa Fe, and it said: "Ly'n Bragg." For years I drove past that café and it never occurred to me that it was a pun. Lie and Brag . . . As far as being literal, I can be extraordinarily dumb in that way. (Pa,C,213)

If Creeley remained unknown to Barthes, there was a critic of comparable genius to help him turn this "dumbness" into one of the most astounding and puzzling achievements of contemporary American letters. Olson first wrote Creeley on April 21, 1950, and the long correspondence and friendship that was to follow helped Creeley, who in 1950 was still writing in the mode of Wallace Stevens, fully to come into his own as a poet, short story writer and novelist. But if the older poet started out as Creeley's mentor, Olson, in turn, became the younger man's beneficiary. Olson acknowledged having learned from Creeley "more . . . than from any living man," and called him "a subtle & beautiful man, worth more than all the rest of us" (N,C,46-7). And indeed, out of their correspondence grew the second part of Olson's essay on "Projective Verse," while Creeley's short stories, "the push beyond Lawrence" (N,C,41), as Olson called them, provided the latter with a heretofore unprecedented parallel in prose to his concept of poetry as a reenactment of Nature's forces. As Olson hurried to announce in his introduction to Creeley's *Gold Diggers* (1954), there are two apparently self-contradictory narrative "methodologies" to achieve this aim: "that the narrator stays OUT, functions as pressure not as interpreting person," or, alternately, as Creeley illustrated,

> the NARRATOR IN, the total IN to the above total OUT . . . the narrator . . . taking up the push of his own single intelligence to make it, to be—by his conjectures—so powerful inside the story that he makes the story swing on him, his eye the eye of nature INSIDE (as is the same eye, outside) a lightmaker. (O,U,127)

Creeley found in Olson—just as Robbe-Grillet did in Barthes—a critical intelligence to match his creative achievement, and he gladly yielded to Olson's advice. According to his bibliographer Mary Novik, he, for instance, revised "3 Fate Tales," so that the "narrator was allowed to intervene in all the ambivalence of his stance at the beginning of the first and second tale," and on further insistence by Olson, also "revised the ending of the first tale, putting the equivocal narrator fully IN," so that the tales, "previously separate exempla, are connected in the final draft by the qualifying presence of the narrator" (N,C,36). The result is a text which reads like *Dans le Labyrinthe* in miniature and can best be described in terms of *nouveau roman* theory or of the diverse statements, in which Creeley, following Olson, has paralleled, or even anticipated several of its major critical tenets.

Apparently unaware of post-Existentialist French fiction, Creeley found little in the modern novel besides D. H. Lawrence to presage the narrative mode he first developed in his short stories. The "divers techniques used to confront *time*" such as "[f]lashback, recall by certain of the characters, juxtaposition . . . of . . .'time' sequences" appear to him "ultimately makeshift" and of little use in his own attempt to portray a universe of "things shifting among themselves" (C,G,21-2), in which time and space have been reduced to their true nature of "qualifications" or what, using Whitehead's terms, Creeley might also have called "extensional and cogredient properties of events" (Wh,I,67). Equally inappropriate to him are the frequent digressions made use of by Joyce, Faulkner, Céline and others, because they only obscure or conceal the underlying symbolic pattern or "explanation" imposed on the material "anterior to the instance" of creation (C,G,43).

Creeley, like Olson, feels a "closeness of sympathies" with Existentialist writers like Sartre or Camus. For they, at least, were aware of the world in its simple "being there," underneath the anthropocentric projections of our thinking and language, aware of that "world *without appeal*" which Sartre's Roquentin discovers to his repugnance while looking at the roots of a chestnut tree. But Sartre's *La Nausée* or Camus' *L'Étranger* remain within the closed "universe of discourse" which their thinking repudiated. A scene such as Roquentin in front of the chestnut tree reads like an exemplum to prove the inadequacy of description, but staying in the descriptive mode itself, it becomes an ironic *reductio ad absurdum* of its message. In Olson's words it accomplishes nothing because it "does not come to grips with what really matters: that a thing, any thing, impinges on us by a more important fact, its self-existence" (O,W,56). In this way, Creeley felt that "the bulk of prose writing, 1930 to 50," including the Existentialist novel, and only excepting the work of D. H. Lawrence, was "of no consequence . . . in that it assumes, arbitrarily, a knowledge of event, of significance, which it does not make a means to in its own substance" (N,C,43).

Narratives like "3 Fate Tales" or Robbe-Grillet's novels, by contrast, are totally self-contained and non-referential to an exterior, "authentic" reality. As Robbe-Grillet puts it, "the work is not a substitute for an exterior reality, but is its own reality to itself" (R-G,R,166); or as Creeley declared,

> It's my own belief—any instance of the ASSUMPTIONAL knowledge of referents, which is to say, any case wherein the reader is referred to a *reality* not literally made a presence, given actuation, in the content, is a direct sapping of that writing's to-be-respected DEMAND on the reader's attention. (N,C,43)

This is most obvious in the use of ellipses or "holes" interrupting the narrative sequence. Robbe-Grillet, for instance, deliberately fails to tell the reader whether or not his voyeur Mathias has tortured and murdered the young girl that obsesses his imagination in *Le Voyeur*. As he comments himself, "Everything is told before the 'hole,' then again after the 'hole,' and there is an effort to bring together the two edges to eliminate this troublesome emptiness; but the opposite occurs, the 'hole' engulfs everything."[1]* Similarly, there is little to explain the fatal accident which forms the climax or rather anticlimax in Creeley's "First Fate Tale" (C,D,45-7):

> It is still quiet. But then out, it goes by me, and down. Stops. But I can't do anything, sit only for a moment, and then, jump, and look out, see there, down, the girl and the people already around her. Nothing of the woman until her head is just opposite mine, the mouth wide, scream, and someone I see the face of below, looks up and calls to her. It's all right. She isn't hurt. A miracle.

As the narrator emphasizes, the reason or motivation for all this "isn't known." If he is to "make . . . sense of it" it is exactly "that it isn't known, any of it. This woman or this girl or what has happened, and how I would have it, or my hand there." There is nothing even to set what happens into an analysable context of time and space. Everything seems to take place in an "eternal *now*" (R-G,R,134) in which time and space seem to annul each other: "I say time, to mean place," as Creeley's narrator puts it: "Any day of the week this could happen, to any, this girl, to others, me, you." And what may happen any day, may not have happened at all, not even to the narrator of the story. All he is able to affirm at the beginning of his narrative is that "[o]ne day, any day, there could be these people, or make them three people, this man and this woman and this little girl."

Unlike the traditional first person narrator reviewing the follies of the past from the armchair vista of maturity, Creeley's narrator, like Robbe-Grillet's, appears "*always* . . . engrossed in a passionate adventure of the most obsessive kind, to the point of frequently distorting his vision and of producing fantasies close to delirium." This is the "subjectivité totale" (R-G,R,148-9) of Robbe-Grillet's novels, or what Creeley, distancing himself from the Romantic "use of the *subjective* method as an excuse for emotional claptrap" calls "The subjective in a more basic character" (C,G,19), a concept which, after his controversy with Olson, came to amount to a total transcendance of the subject-object dichotomy.[2]

Even in his short stories, however, Creeley's subjectivity "in a

*Notes to this section on p. 164

more basic character" results in strategies of self-reduction similar to Robbe-Grillet's universe of disembodied abstractions, but alien to Olson's passionate ontological involvement with the world. The narrator of the "First Fate Tale" or *Dans le Labyrinthe* does not only invent his story in the very process of narrating it; in order to do so, he also has to invent himself—a "je néant" of guesses and speculations, circumscribed by the chimera of his own phantasizing. In other words, the story is not invented at all, but invents itself. Whatever happens, happens exclusively in the imagination of the reader, who through his creative participation becomes the story's real protagonist: "it is in his head that the whole story takes place, a story which he in fact imagines himself" (R-G,R,166). In imitation of the serpent swallowing its own tail, the line of systematic self-reduction comes full circle, and the story's final words return the reader to the introductory "I put it this way. That I am, say, myself," in which the narrator made a tentative, hesitating and unsuccessful attempt to posit his own identity: "Any day of the week this could happen, to any, this girl, to others, me, you. I suppose it is something, even, done with. As it turned out. Past, and even complete. I am left with it, made different, because of it. Or, am I? We are back to that" (C,D,47).

But how did a text like the "First Fate Tale" originate in actual fact? Both in the introduction to his short stories and in similar comments on his poetry, Creeley describes this creative process as the open-ended self-realization of a linguistic event. "[W]hat emerges in the writing I most value," he declared at an international poetry conference in Berlin, "is a content which cannot be anticipated, which 'tells you what you don't know'" (C,G,72). Even before he met Olson, Creeley had adopted this notion from modern jazz and abstract expressionism. In his interviews, reviews and programmatic statements he has again and again referred to Charlie Parker's uses of silence and rhythmical improvisation, or has quoted Pollock's famous statement about being inside the canvas, or Franz Kline's "I paint what I don't know" as models for his own sense of creativity (C,IR,174).

The particular use Creeley made of these influences is suggested by his belief that the true following of abstract expressionism is to be found in the "antithetically disciplined formalism of Frank Stella, and those akin to him as Neil Williams and Larry Poons" (C,G,349). Like Piet Mondrian before them, these artists are pursuing what Werner Haftmann calls the "active creation of 'nothingness,'"[3] trying to eliminate from their painting all reference, not only to exterior reality, but also to the very act of creativity.

According to Mondrian, this is achieved by opposing "the colour plane to the non-colour plane (white, grey, black), so that through this duality, the opposites can annihilate one another." "Line and colour must be composed *otherwise* than in nature,"[4] while (in Stella's terms) the painting becomes its own reality in which "only what can be seen there *is* there."[5] Or as Creeley himself put it, commenting on minimal art in general: "the painting is not a reference to another reality . . . but remains unequivocally its own occasion" (C,G,349). Stella himself has denied the reductionist approach to reality which critics have often imputed to him.[6] But it is clearly that "active creation of 'nothingness' " his paintings seem to reflect which explains the fascination they have for Creeley.

Creeley has often emphasized that there is "never a 'subject' *about* which one constructs an activity called 'poetry' "(C,G,72). Even T. S. Eliot's notion that the poet should embody emotions in "objective correlatives" seems to him a "disastrous mistake," since it proposes "that the thing for which there is an objective correlative is in some way a symbol of that object" (C,C,100), giving the poem the kind of referential meaning it should most try to avoid. If the work of art has any meaning at all, it must, as Olson says, "exist through itself" (C,G,54). What Olson's phrase suggests, of course, is a psycho-physiological "concrete," derived from a creative reenactment of nature which turns art into "the only twin life has" (O,W,61). Again, Creeley uses Olson's phrase in order to express a notion somewhat estranged from this original significance when he claims that art " 'means nothing,' [it] doesn't have a point." No wonder then that in this journey towards emptiness, the minimal artists gradually replaced Pollock and Olson as Creeley's main travelling companions, and that the "*zero* set" of an artist like Arakawa, "the real nitty gritty for any head-trip," as Creeley called it in a recent essay on "The Creative," has become a model for his poetic pursuits (C,Cr).

It is with a curious impatience that Creeley has inveighed against that "goddamn Zen" (C,B) which various friends keep drumming into his ears. Nonetheless, he admits to being "fascinated by Japanese writing, the haiku, and by people like Blyth in *Zen and English Literature*" (C,C,132-3), and he is as well aware as others that "the present attraction of the *Dhammapada*, or other Buddhist texts" is explained by the fact that they seem to offer a panacea for that hypertrophy of the ego, left to us as a burdensome legacy by Romanticism. As he seems to imply, this remedy has proved genuine for a poet like Gary Snyder, whose insights are the outcome of lifelong study and meditation in those fields. Yet if Creeley, as early as 1961, acknowledged Snyder's achievement as "a successful relation of hope" (C,G,209), there was little in his own work, written up to that time, to suggest that he might be headed towards a similar goal.

Like Snyder, Creeley was looking for ways to avoid the pitfalls of egocentricity, or what, after Lawrence, he calls *"sensationalism*, i.e., the repetition of a known sensation" (C,G,209). But the solutions worked out in their poetry up to 1961 were diametrically opposed. Unlike Snyder, who abandons his ego to the world of phenomena and action, Creeley tries to reduce it to zero. After its destructive raid on the universe, his "active creation of 'nothingness' " finally returns, like a boomerang, upon the creator—the poet, in Creeley's own words, working "towards a final obliteration of himself" (C,G,39): "[I] feel it [i.e., the poem] with the intensity of all the perception that I ... that the ego bit can recognize, and then destroy the ego by its own insistence" (C,C,39).

If there is truth in C. Kellerer's claim that many Western artists have moved closer and closer to a Zen Buddhist approach to reality during recent decades, it seems equally convincing that this gradual change of consciousness is resulting in what A. Ehrenzweig terms "the definite schizoid tinge of modern art."[7] Whereas the action painters, for instance, outdid Far Eastern *Sumi-e* artists in their emphasis on *ch'i-yün shêng-tung* (or the "resonance or vibration of the vitalizing spirit and movement of life," Si,A,21-2), filling every nook of their canvases with the turbulent psychographs of the unconscious, the minimal artists or their precursors seem to present us with the schizophrenic counterpart: final emptiness, the ubiquitous background in Far Eastern painting, becomes an aim of analytical demonstration to men like Mondrian, Stella or Flavin. The "automatic effusions" of Kerouac (in Creeley's words "a simplification of that chaos, familiar to us now in Zen teaching," C,G,249) versus the work of Robbe-Grillet or Creeley himself present us with comparable polarities in the world of literature.

In a more recent poem Creeley summed up his general approach to reality:

> All I knew or know
> began with this—
> emptiness
> with its incessant movement.
>
> (C,F,95)

This has been taken as Creeley's own testimony for the "continual threat of the void" at the center of his experience, stemming, as Charles Altieri has argued, "from his sense of isolation, of being cut off from all roots or grounds—in concrete experience, in tradition, and in his relationships with other people."[8] Yet instead of threatening him, the void seems to attract Creeley with the power of a religious mystery. His "mind locked" while watching "The Mountains in the Desert" as the light fades—"such geography of self and soul / brought to such limit of sight"—the poet is yearning for a state of mind which transcends the limitations of his ego:

> Tonight let me go
> at last out of whatever
> mind I thought to have,
> and all the habits of it.
>
> (C,P,166)

A similar abandonment to emptiness results from his insight into the futility of trying to describe our existence in this world:

> I keep to myself such
> measures as I care for,
> daily the rocks
> accumulate position.
>
> There is nothing
> but what thinking makes
> it less tangible. The mind
> fast as it goes, loses
>
> pace, puts in place of it
> like rocks simple markers,
> for a way only to
> hopefully come back to
>
> where it cannot. All
> forgets. My mind sinks.
> I hold in both hands such weight
> it is my only description.
>
> (C,P,190)

In the wooden sculptures of an unidentified artist Creeley found an embodiment of the mindlessness and quiet he is approaching here. The poem about these "Figures" reads like an indirect description of his own poetic aims:

> Did the man
> who made them find
> a like quiet? In
> the act of making them

it must have been
so still he heard the wood
and felt it with his hands

moving into
the forms
he has given to them,

one by singular
one, so quiet,
so still.

(C,P,147)

   Creeley is well aware that this artistic pursuit of the void must
itself result in artifacts of nothingness, and that the "poem supreme,
addressed to / emptiness" (C,P,29), as he called it, can be at best an
allegory of silence. Such a poem is "Waiting," in which through
certain stylistic devices, common to most of Creeley's earlier poetry,
a discussion of these very issues is turned into a *monumentum ære
perennius* to commemorate the self-annihilating act of creativity.
This is achieved by an almost totally abstract vocabulary, a frequently ungrammatical or deliberately nonsensical syntax, the re-
currence of certain phrases like the leitmotifs of a musical score, and
above all by the use of key words which through repetition are slowly
emptied of all the meaning they had in the context of their first
occurrence and which finally—like lights in the mirror cabinet of the
poem's total structure—fuse in a blinding glare of nothingness:

He pushes behind the words
which, awkward, catch
and turn him to a disturbed
and fumbling man.

What if it all stops.
Then silence
is as silence was
again.

What if the last time
he was moved to touch,
work out in his own mind,
such limits was the last—

and then a quiet, a dull
space of hanging actions, all
depending on some time
has come and gone.

God help him then
if such things can.
That risk
is all there is.

(C,P,167)

In the poem entitled "After Mallarmé," which deals with the
theme of quiet found in mindlessness (C,P,152), Creeley seems to
acknowledge that he is not the first and only poet who had the
courage necessary to take that risk. (See also C,P,29.) Despite many
formal dissimilarities of their verse, there are deep affinities between
the French and American poet. Of course, it was more than mere
courage that impelled Mallarmé to disclaim his allegiance to the
Christian God—"that creature of ancient and evil plumage"—and to
delve, before any other Western poet or artist, into the utter depths
of nothingness. The story of anguish and suffering, told in his
letters, describes how the first glimpse of the void, which Mallarmé
had while composing the *Hérodiade*, revealed an abyss that
threatened to engulf him in mental insanity. "My misfortune is," he
wrote to Henri Cazalis in March 1866,

> that, when I had polished my poetry down to this depth, I
> came upon twin abysses which drove me mad. The first was
> Nothingness, which I found without any prior knowledge of
> Buddhism.

This overwhelming vision of emptiness, both in himself and in the
world around him, soon became the conscious aim of all his artistic
endeavours. Henceforth his poems, those "Sumptuous Allegories of
Nothingness," as he called them, were created by an *"elimination"* of
all referential meaning and by methods of "self-destruction," rigorous to the point where Mallarmé had to look into the Venetian
mirror on his writing desk in order to preserve a sense of his identity.
"[I]f it were not in front of me here on the table," he confessed to
Cazalis,

> I would become Nothingness again. Which means that I am
> impersonal now: not the Stéphane you once knew, but one of
> the ways the Spiritual Universe has found to see Itself, unfold
> Itself through what used to be me.

Unlike Creeley, Mallarmé came to identify emptiness with a traditional concept of beauty, and adhered with painstaking assiduity to all the established rules of prosody. Yet, common to both poets is an autotelic, music score-like use of language, and Mallarmé's discussion of this characteristic culminates in a brilliant feat of critical synthesis that Creeley has often tried to formulate: "[O]ur principal aim," Mallarmé wrote on December 5, 1866, "should be to make the words of a poem self-mirroring (since they are sufficiently autonomous to begin with and need no outside impression) to such an extent that no one of them will seem to have a color of its own, and all of them will be merely the notes of a scale" (M,E,88,92-5). Here we have Creeley's frequently repeated plea for a non-referential use of language, to be achieved by techniques such as "feed-back" or "repetitive relocation of phrasing" (C,C,88). These will reduce the communicative meaning of words to the minimum or rather non-existence of "existing through themselves" where "they [i.e., the words] speak rather than someone speaking with them," returning them "to an almost objective state of presence," and will thus engender a poetry or "complex of sounds and rhythms, which move in a parallel to music" (C,G,55).

Of course, Creeley has also remarked that he does not wish "to confuse poetry with music" and has repeatedly drawn attention to the emotion underlying and informing "the order and movement of *sound*" (C,G,53,131) determining the form of his poems. And naturally there are several poems, even amongst his earlier work, which do not reach, or even approach the etherealized purity of the "poem supreme, addressed to/emptiness." Yet until the early sixties nearly all of them seem to revolve, as if drawn by a mysterious force, in an ineluctable orbit around nothingness. Take a poem like "The Pool." In terms of description that can be visualized, and of narrative that can be summed up, it far exceeds the limits which usually keep the scope of such mimetic features down to a very minimum. But what actually do we see and hear?

> My embarrassment at his nakedness,
> at the pool's edge,
> and my wife, with his,
> standing, watching—
>
> this was a freedom
> not given me who am
> more naked,
> less contained

by my own white flesh
and the ability
to take quietly
what comes to me.

The sense of myself
separate, grew
a white mirror
in the quiet water

he breaks with his hands
and feet, kicking

There is the speaker and his wife with another man and probably the latter's wife. The speaker feels embarrassed, "less contained/ by [his] own white flesh," maybe jealous, contemplating his alienated self in the water, until the other man, by diving into the pool, breaks the reflection "with his hands/ and feet, kicking." Yet even a bare outline such as this tacitly fills in gaps in the narrative and provides us with circumstantial description or psychological motivation which the poem itself stubbornly withholds from the reader. It also evokes a scenic authenticity totally lacking in the labyrinthine world of isolated details and unrelated emotions created by the poem. Conversely, the outline fails to render the poem's real impact on the reader: the aura of total elusiveness conveyed by the fragmented geometry of surface description and the faltering staccato movement of utterance—that "graph of indeterminate / feelings" which "despairs of its own / statement, wants to/ turn away, endlessly / to turn away" (C,P,159,184). Mainly through repetition of certain key words, self-reflecting and mutually self-effacing, this vagueness finally condenses into an ideograph of nothingness, and the poem goes on to end in a thematic statement, expressing the speaker's yearning for a state of quiet, silence and emptiness, reached by "the risk" of his self-annihilating creativity:

pulls up to land
on the edge by the feet

of these women
who must know
that for each
man is a speech

describes him, makes
the day grow white
and sure, a quietness of water
in the mind,

lets hang, descriptive
at a risk, something
for which he cannot find
a means or time.

(C,P,141)

In the "Boogie-Woogie" series, painted during the years shortly before his death in 1944, Mondrian started to fill the static configurations of his former style with bands of variegated color and to infuse them with the throbbing rhythms characteristic of his early work under the influence of Van Gogh and the Fauves. Sometime after 1960, a similar change seems to occur in the poetry of Robert Creeley. As early as 1962, the poet felt that he had begun "to relax," to feel "more settled, more at ease in [his] world" (Os,A,60). But the real change must have occurred at a level far deeper than that. Thus, most of his recent poetry seems to have been written by a man who, after emerging from the depths of mystic experience and still blinded by the glaring vision of emptiness, has come stumbling back into reality, groping for a hold in the bewildering chaos of a world, deconceptualized by his former quest for the void. After a ten-year-long effort to write the "poem supreme, addressed to / emptiness," we find him wondering around 1960: "then what / is emptiness / for." And his own answer: "To / fill, fill" (C,P,178) announces the earthbound drive of his new poetic idiom, and the direct thematic concern of several of his subsequent poems. There is the old fascination with "infinite emptiness," but now there is also a yearning for concrete reality and life, as expressed in the poem entitled "Joy":

I could look at
an empty hole for hours
thinking it will
get something in it,

will collect
things. There is
an infinite emptiness
placed there.

Even if the marmoreal stillness of the earlier work has turned into a "broken silence,/ filled with screaming," Creeley seems unperturbed in his new programmatic belief that "There is / a silence / to fill," because "It is possible, in words, to speak / of what has happened—a sense / of there and here, now / and then" (C,W,106,107,113,122).

An "absolute failure as a 'visual artist'" (Pa,C,210), Creeley had to relearn reality's alphabet and to return to his childhood's most primal cognitive gesture of simple enumeration in order to achieve this aim. "A Piece," Creeley's best known and most controversial poem since 1960, is the odd, but at the same time most direct expression of this effort.

> One and
> one, two,
> three.
>
> (C,W,115)

As he once pointed out in conversation, "the first way I could know that the world existed was in my ability to count it." Only from here could he proceed to register the "Small facts / of eyes, hair / blonde, face / looking like a / flat painted / board" or to tentatively posit his identity: "Here I / am. There / you are." This anxious questioning of himself in relation to others—"You are not / me, nor I you" (C,F,43-4,56,61)—finds an affirmative answer in the poet's discovery of the female principle. A creature of veritable flesh and blood, but also of mythic dimensions, comprising the polarities of light and darkness, she suddenly arises from the maze of lifeless abstractions that form the world of Creeley's earlier poetry:

> She was largely warm—
> flesh heavy—and smiled
> in some deepening knowledge.
>
> .   .   .   .
>
> She laughed and turned
> and the heavy folds of cloth
>
> parted. The nakedness
> burned. Her heavy breath,
> her ugliness, her lust—
> but her laughing, her low
>
> chuckling laugh, the way
> she moved her hand to the
> naked breast, then to
> her belly, her hand with its fingers.

A symbol of everlasting life, she embodies all that humans want or need to know,—"her eyes / the depth of all one had thought of, / again and again and again" (C,F,50-2). And the poet who follows her turns into the Yeatsian fool who has recognized the essential oneness of all being, yet also knows about the unending flux of creation, life and death:

> In secret
> the out's in—
>
> the wise
> surprised, all
>
> going coming,
> begun undone.
>
> Hence the fool dances
> in endless happiness.
>
>   (C,F,55)

Thus none of his former vision has been lost, but the poet has learned to approach reality from a realm "beyond despair" (J.-P. Sartre), bringing to it the insights gained in his earlier quest for the void. It was obviously understating the case when Creeley declared only a few years ago that he had recently tried to develop a writing "that simply says: the road is going this way down the hill and there are trees here." No doubt it was new for him "to make a statement of what seems to be physically actual" in a specific place (Pa,C,210). But his poetry in no way limits itself to such phenomenological transcripts of reality. Like Rilke before him, he not only records, but celebrates existence: "I love water, I *love* water— / but I also love air, and fire" (C,B). And while formerly he had conceived of his poetry as an uncommunicative way of talking to himself (C,IR,173), he now feels a need to speak to others, even at the risk of having to be "descriptive":

> a *description,*–hey!
> see the dog
> walk—
>
>   (C,B)

The most obvious outcome of this whole development is that Creeley, in abandoning the attempt to write the "poem supreme, áddressed to / emptiness," tends to consider his more recent poems as one continuous testimony to his own life experience. In this sense his 1963 description of The Cantos or A as "a day book or journal," which "attempts to deal with reality over a man's life" (C,C,17) seems to anticipate the impulse behind his lyrical output since Pieces (1969). However inappropriate when related to Pound's and Zukofsky's poems, the statement also shows the poet's recent tendency to re-define his position within the tradition of American poetry. Asked if he considered Pieces as an open poem like the Cantos, Maximus and Paterson, Creeley described his work as

> a kind of open writing in the sense that it was composed in a journal as daily writing . . . I wanted a mode that could in-clude, say, what people understandably might feel are in-stances of trivia . . . in the same sense that Williams says—"the total province of the poem is the world"—something of that order in Paterson somewhere—the sense that poetry isn't a discretion, that it is ultimately the realization of an entire world. (C,C,192)

As his most important overall achievement, however, Creeley's recent poetic idiom can rise to a totally new vibrancy and transparent clarity evoking a world of concrete sensual detail while retaining the mystical luminosity of the "poem supreme, addressed to / emptiness." Such are the qualities to be found in a poem like "The Moon" which, without abandoning its Creeleyan tone and diction, is reminiscent of Chinese poetry, and equal to the best of Snyder's work in that mode:

> Earlier in the evening the moon
> was clear to the east,
> over the snow of the yard
> and fields—a lovely
>
> bright clarity and perfect
> roundness, isolate,
> riding as they say the
> black sky. Then we went
>
> about our businesses of the
> evening, eating supper, talking,
> watching television, then
> going to bed, making love,

and then to sleep. But before
we did I asked her to look
out the window at the moon
now straight up, so that

she bent her head and looked
sharply up, to see it.
Through the night it must
have shone on, in that

fact of things—another
moon, another night—a
full moon in the winter's
space, a white loneliness.

I came awake to the blue
white light in the darkness,
and felt as if someone
were there, waiting, alone.
. . . .

(C,F,59-60)

[1] Quoted by B. Morrissette, *Alain Robbe-Grillet.* Columbia Essays on Modern Writers, No. 11 (New York: Columbia University Press, 1965), p. 19.

[2] See above, p. 25.

[3] *Painting in the Twentieth Century,* 2 vols. (London: Lund Humphries, 1965), I, 202.

[4] Quoted by H. L. C. Jaffé, *De Stijl* (New York: Harry N. Abrams, Inc., n.d.), pp. 120, 189.

[5] Quoted by G. Battcock, ed. *Minimal Art, A Critical Anthology* (New York: E.P. Dutton & Co., Inc., 1968), p. 158.

[6] Ibid., p. 159.

[7] See C. Kellerer, *Objet trouvé und Surrealismus* (Hamburg: Rowohlt Verlag, 1962), passim; A. Ehrenzweig, *The Hidden Order of Art* (Berkeley: University of California Press, 1971), p. 66.

[8] "The Unsure Egoist: Robert Creeley and the Theme of Nothingness," *Contemporary Literature* 13, 2 (Spring, 1972), pp. 162-85, 162.

Robert Creeley

Faas: In the introduction to Olson's *Selected Writings* you say that Camus "may speak of a world *without appeal*, but the system of discourse he makes use of is still demonstrably a closed one." All he accomplishes is a *description* of reality, which in Olson's words "does not come to grips with what really matters." One finds a similar critique of Existentialism in Robbe-Grillet.

Robbe-Grillet

CREELEY: There is a lovely joke à propos Robbe-Grillet. We have some old friends in New Mexico, a young French architect and his wife, and apparently Robbe-Grillet came travelling through the country, and stopped there to give a lecture or something, and they introduced themselves, and asked him if he knew Robert Creeley. And he said: Robert Creeley, that's me. [Both laughing]

Faas: I find there are extraordinary affinities between his and your work, and I wondered if you are familiar with Robbe-Grillet.

CREELEY: I know him somewhat, but the insistent abstraction in his writing is really distracting to me. I mean by that the frame of the writing. *Last Year in Marienbad* is an obvious instance. When I saw the film, I was really depressed incredibly, but very impressed also.

Faas: Have you read *Pour un nouveau roman*?

CREELEY: No.

Faas: Do you know if he is acquainted with your work or Olson's?

CREELEY: I don't know if he is or isn't, because these friends said he really became so comically involved with the play on the names.

Faas: So probably it was just a pun. Did you ever meet him yourself?

CREELEY: No, I happened to be away at the time. I briefly met Michel Butor and I liked him very much as a man. But when he was talking about the opera he was then trying to design as a chance operation, it really turned out that the parts of the opera, the very segments of it, were highly defined. You know, it was sort of "three acts." He was only using chance factors for the way in which one act would follow another, and I felt that doesn't really do it.

meeting
Michel Butor

Faas: That's like early Stockhausen.

165

CREELEY: Yes, that's still too didactic.

Faas: Of course, Robbe-Grillet goes much further than that.

CREELEY: Yes, Michel Butor really seemed like the classic Frenchman, but a very pleasant man.

Faas: Did D. H. Lawrence in any way anticipate your own techniques as a short story writer?

CREELEY: I read Lawrence intensely when I was a younger man.

Faas: Of course, in general philosophical terms the resemblances seem obvious but when it comes . . .

CREELEY: . . . to the actual writing, there are two writers: Lawrence and Joyce. When I was a junior at high school about a year away from graduation, the *Dubliners* really hit me. That's perhaps the text of Joyce's that hit me most, that whole sense of the epiphany where there was a moment of incredibly intensive consciousness that flooded the whole context, that kind of focus, that really fascinated me, whereas I remember reading again and again and again *The Turn of the Screw*, and truly not getting anything out of it, I was very frustrated by it.

Joyce, Lawrence and Dostoyevsky

Faas: Also by James's theory of the novel?

CREELEY: Yes, I love James, I mean, but when it's used as a text for writing, it curiously leaves me cold. Whereas with Lawrence, it was the intense revelation, that highly charged situation of emotion created. What I most remember reading decisively of his work is *The Fox* and *The Captain's Doll*—the so-called novellas which I thought were extraordinary, and the short stories. I was also reading a lot of Dostoyevsky, the novels, the shorter novels and the short stories. All three of them, Dostoyevsky, Joyce and Lawrence, are, I think, writers that use intensive emotion as revelation, moments of extraordinary intensity.

Faas: But your own style of writing is so different from theirs.

CREELEY: Oh yes, but then I read a lot of Williams' short stories, *Life along the Passaic River*.

Faas: Do you feel that he anticipated your actual prose style?

CREELEY: Well, in the forties, my stories were felt to be sketchy. Williams in turn would call my stories sketches, very interesting sketches. [Laughing]

stories without a plot

Faas: So you must have taken it one point further than him.

CREELEY: Yes. I remember one time when one story was accepted for publication in the *Kenyon Review*, the editor John Crowe Ransom was really nonplussed by it. He said he didn't understand it, and he sent it to Robert Penn Warren. Anyhow, to make a long story short,

Robert Penn Warren's comment was that he found it without plot and he couldn't truly understand a story that didn't have a plot. He said that he was constitutionally in favor of plot, as he put it.

Faas: By hindsight all this seems so ludicrous, of course.

CREELEY: But then it was like being the awful kid at school who was doing something irrevocably wrong.

Faas: Even Cid Corman sometimes commented negatively on the short stories.

CREELEY: Although Cid without question was the person who found them good enough to publish. But he also was confused by them, I think.

Faas: You have commented negatively on the so-called Modernist treatment of time, on devices such as flashback, recall, juxtaposition, etc.

CREELEY: Yes, I think all that's very limited.

Faas: By contrast, you say that one should treat time and space as mere "qualifications" of the narrated events or, as you call it, "the things shifting among themselves." That term "qualifications" reminds me of Whitehead describing time and space as "cogredient or relative properties of events." Did you derive your own notion from him?

CREELEY: I didn't get it from him. I finally bought a copy of *Process and Reality* about a week ago. [Both laughing] Yes, it seemed ridiculous not to, you know, have read it. But I had so much of that information from Olson and friends like Duncan. Personally, I never read texts of that kind decisively.

Faas: In "The Creative" you write that recently in Berlin you were delighted to discover that Heisenberg "has fallen upon the arts as though upon a blissful bed of flowers, *knowing*, in his age, as Gregory Corso would say, that the *conceptual* dilemma of the sciences leads them round and around the careful maze of their various *contexts*."

CREELEY: Yes, that's from Arakawa who was in residence at Höllerer's Literarisches Colloquium. Arakawa is a very interesting painter, a man using incredible situations of speech and linguistics, similar to the kind of things I'd like to say with images and words. He is fascinated by Heisenberg and said that Heisenberg, according to the men working with him, had come to believe that the assumptions in the sciences were disastrously romantic and that the formulations of the premises were so assumptive that the information derived from them was becoming more and more arbitrary.

Faas: In a way that has been his general trend of thought all the way.

CREELEY: Unhappily I never read him. The book of Arakawa's that I

Whitehead and Heisenberg

really like is *Der Mechanismus der Meinung (The Mechanism of Opinion)*. It's a very curious book, it's a continuous text and it doesn't have any stated end in view.

Faas: I find the closest parallel to your short stories in Beckett.

CREELEY: I had the honor once of meeting Beckett and dug him entirely. Thanks to John Calder who is a publisher in England, and thanks really to Mrs. Bettina Calder. One day in London, Bettina said to me: later tonight John is going to see Sam in Paris and they'll be talking a lot, so why don't you fly over to Paris: he's going to meet him at the Café de Lille. So bring a bottle of Irish whiskey and introduce yourself and I'm sure things will go well. And so I went and we stayed talking from about eleven at night till six in the morning. It was incredible!

meeting
Beckett

Faas: Did he know your work?

CREELEY: Yes, he did, and he really liked it and I was enchanted. He is an extraordinarily generous and humble man. The things he was saying were so energized that I did what one does as a child when the energy is so concentrated that all of a sudden you giggle or blurp, sort of making aha. And he thought that I was, not mocking him, but that I was laughing. And suddenly he said: you find that funny? And I said: heavens no. But I was just so concentrated that I had to relieve the tension. And he was describing or stating what he had as an imagination of a word that would be entirely autonomous in its creation and existence. It was his dream to realize one word that was absolutely self-created. And he said it's about this big [indicating a height of about seven inches, both laughing] and it has the situation of stone. And then later I was reading in Jung or somebody about the phallic stone, and it was very much the same. I don't know if Beckett was aware of Jung's image, but it was very similar to it. Beckett literally said it was that high and he wasn't being metaphoric. Somehow he had the imagination that this word would physically take place.

the self-
created word

Faas: Which of your works had he read?

CREELEY: My stories, I think, and possibly the novel. I know that mainly through Bettina who's a close friend of his and I knew that *she* had read them and talked to him about it.

Faas: What did you talk about with Beckett?

CREELEY: For a time John discussed the plays which had just been put on in the Place de l'Odéon, which was mainly to make Beckett relax enough so that he simply talked about senses of language and the imagination of reality. He spoke in this very, not tentative way, but at times there'd be pauses, he'd begin to say something and then he'd sort of test it in his mind, then return to its continuance, say a little more, check it out, you see. He spoke, not haltingly as though he were impeded in some physical way, but constantly checking what he was saying so that I had no idea what time it was. I mean I realized finally it was six in the morning, so the thing I most specifically remember is that extraordinary creation of a word that should have no other cause but itself.

Faas: Did you know Beckett's work by the time you wrote your short stories?

CREELEY: I first heard of him, I believe, through Alex Trocchi and a group of expatriates living in Paris in the early fifties, who ran this magazine called *Merlin*, which published Beckett's first French writing in English.

Faas: That was in the early fifties. But you had already written some of your short stories by that time.

CREELEY: Yes, I'd written a lot of them by 1954.

Faas: I was just wondering if Beckett could have had any direct influence on you.

Beckett's influence

CREELEY: Not really. *Waiting for Godot* I reviewed in the *Black Mountain Review*. But by that time it was already sort of wide information. But I must have gotten a lot of equivalent information from the so-called Existentialists whom I certainly read. Now, I remember a story by Beckett that really blew my mind, called "The End." It's a story in which a man simply recedes, to where he is finally lying in a boat, in a boat-house. He has a whole contrivance of physical realities so that he manages to exist, and he defecates by shifting his body this way and that way a bit. He's a beggar and has this drop-board that permits the patron to give money without actually touching this awful person, so that he can beg but in no way offend the donor. It's kind of a classic Beckett trip. So I can't truly date when I first read his work but I remember that story vividly. And I wrote stories after that, but I'd already written quite a few before that.

Faas: You had already written some before 1950.

CREELEY: Right.

Faas: When did you write the "3 Fate Tales"?

CREELEY: I wrote those in New Hampshire, so that's previous to 1950.

"3 Fate Tales"

Faas: They seem to me the most interesting and the most extreme, in a way.

CREELEY: That comes out of a kind of wild blend of Dostoyevsky and Stendhal.

Faas: Stendhal?

CREELEY: I mean the way that Stendhal would substantiate some attitude in reality by giving you an instance of it.

Faas: While telling the story becomes its very subject.

CREELEY: Yes, exactly, which I really loved in his writing.

Faas: How about the influence of Existentialist writers?

CREELEY: My generation, the group of friends I had at college, grew up flooded with them. But I finally broke down trying to read Sartre's sequence of novels.

Existentialist
writers

Faas: *Les chemins de la liberté*.

CREELEY: Yes, I got through one or maybe two, but I just got bored. Equally, *The Stranger* always irritated me. Years after I read it, Bert Almon, a student of mine who had done research on it, pointed out that the first draft of the novel was in the first person, was proposed as a personal narrative, and then Camus began to abstract and objectify it to the point where I felt that he kind of blew it. I mean I would have been very curious to have read it as a personal narrative. But then Ionesco was a great relief, I thought he was terrific.

Faas: Let me switch to Hart Crane. In 1954 you wrote: "We know, we know, we know, etc., that *The Bridge* was a 'failure'—though why, and how, we are not at all quite so sure of." This was obviously stated in reaction against the New Critics.

Hart Crane

CREELEY: And particularly the teachers of the forties that I had for instructors, who very smugly felt that the structure of *The Bridge* didn't arrive at any coherence. And demonstrably, I suppose, they are right: there isn't any great realization of a coherence finally in the poem. But I don't know. It's very hard for me to speak objectively about Crane, I was so moved by what he was trying to do. His incoherence to me is really attractive.

Faas: Crane once said that *The Bridge* might be published like *Leaves of Grass*, every new edition incorporating new additions. So at some point he did conceive of it as an open-ended poem.

CREELEY: I think that the people who were sympathetic to Whitman at that time were primarily sympathetic to him for "sociological or historical purview." They really weren't interested in the structure at all, and those who considered his structure were Williams and Pound. Williams thought it was too amorphous, and Pound, I think, intuited that it was really useful, this sense of an expanding center, and really recognized that Whitman was one of the basic keys to the possibilities of the long poem. Williams was funny, he shifted back and forth on the subject of Whitman. At one point he is calling him America's greatest poet, at another point he's saying that he is too blowzy. I

Whitman

think Williams tacitly is also responding to his homosexuality. Williams was very Puritanical, I mean, he was a very double man. I don't know if he is a Gemini, but he sure feels like one. He led this crazy diversity of lives.

Faas: Would you say that *The Bridge* fails mainly because Crane tried to fit it into some alien concept of unity?

CREELEY: Well, it doesn't fail. I had the experience of teaching it, like they say, last spring, sort of leading these tender students into this incredible chaos. What's—what does this mean? It's like walking through the sky or something. What are all these clouds doing here? [Laughing] And then we'd refer to Crane's sense of his purpose, you know, either his plan for Otto Kahn or some such text, and, you know, forget it. Yes, I think, had he let it move on impulse and trusted that impulse, he would have had an extraordinary thing, instead of trying to fit it into a pattern. In fact, Williams rather comes across in the same way, with his concept of the order of *Paterson* in four books.

Faas: But he finally broke through that, didn't he?

CREELEY: Yes, with *Paterson V*.

Faas: Which Crane never did. Of course, that was much later, so Williams had a much better chance, with the model of the *Cantos*.

CREELEY: No, Crane really had a bleak life.

Faas: At one point Robert Bly accused Olson and the Black Mountain School of a positivist Objectivism which tries to evade the human psyche.

CREELEY: I don't think he'd say that today. It's akin to Gregory Corso calling me an intellectual gangster. [Laughing] I suppose, that was probably because of Charles' kind of intensive razzle-dazzle vocabulary. It must have been intimidating if you a) don't understand what he is talking about and b) see what the authorities implicit were. Again Bob Bly's sense that a whole spectrum of European literature was being ignored was a little in error, simply that for various reasons a number of us had read that writing pretty widely. As a younger man I had, happily, Rainer Gerhardt as a friend and he made me aware of many European poets, in particular Trakl.

Faas: Do you like Trakl's work?

CREELEY: I was very moved by it, he is really haunting. There must be innumerable translations of "Grodek" but I never saw one that really got it.

Faas: The other poet whose criticism of Olson has always puzzled me is Gary Snyder.

CREELEY: I think Gary, being a Buddhist, has the usual
Snyder and Westerner's distrust of the Easterner, and he is also fear-
Olson ful of a situation which is continuous in the European
tradition, or Western world in that sense. Gary is an extraordinary
intellectual actually, but he has a lot of distrust of head-trips, and
Charles is a fantastic head-tripper. I remember talking to Joanne
Kyger about it, who had been married to Gary for a time, and she felt
that Gary literally never understood Olson. So there was some of
that resentment and confusion with the texts. I think he just hasn't
really centered on it.

Faas: The same I think is true of Robert Bly.

CREELEY: Yes. I don't think it has been a key situation for their own
interests.

Faas: But I think there is some truth to Bly's contention that Objectism to some degree evades the psyche.

CREELEY: What Olson is trying to do is break a condition which is
possibly much more disastrous the closer you are to the European
tradition, not sentimentally, but growing up, you know, on the East
Coast. Neither Bly nor Snyder really have the onus of Eastern
intellectual European thirties, forties kind of thinking. And what
Olson is, I think, most involved in doing is trying to find an alternative to the heavy humanist tradition. I mean, it's all very well to speak
of the human psyche and its value to human experience, but Olson
was trying to work, not just towards an attitude, but towards an
experience of humanness that would be as explicit, say, as any other
physical event in the world. Going back to Whitehead, he is trying to
"clear out the gunk," as Olson says, that gave the psyche that peculiar
"soulful" state—the "center of the sinful earth," etc.

Faas: I recall that in 1951 you had a controversy with Olson about
Objectism versus, what you termed, "the *subjective* in a
controversy more basic character."
with Olson CREELEY: Olson's Objectism, that's the way he puts it in
the "Projective Verse" piece, means to be as clean, to be as
specific, or to be as actual, as actualized, not as realized, but as
actualized, to be as substantively the case, to be as "firm as fish is," as
he says in one of the *Maximus Poems*: that the poem should be as firm
as fish, like a physical event, as actual as that, not metaphorically but
substantively it should be an issue of a physical condition—that true.

Faas: So in other words you gave in to his position?

CREELEY: Not entirely. I was really charmed, at the University of
Connecticut last weekend, seeing Charles Olson's literary executor
and George Butterick, who both told me variously that Charles was
at times intimidated by me. I was so intimidated by him that it never

occurred to me he was having anything of the like feeling. And they said that the letters would really reflect that.

Faas: But don't you feel that your creative impulse does essentially derive from the unconscious?

CREELEY: Sure, I mean, I couldn't think where else it should come from. As a writer I am possibly the one among my own friends and immediate companions, like it or not, who uses books least. I can't work from books, I paradoxically can't work from literature except through absorption in some very obvious and simple ways.

creativity and the unconscious

Faas: Yet you have few Surrealistic, dreamlike or hallucinatory images in your poetry.

CREELEY: What's interesting to me is the inability to rewrite. That has fascinated me all my life, that I basically can't rewrite so I'm stuck with what I first get. And that I don't really have much design or determination except that I attempt, when I'm writing, to let it be as accurate as possible. I mean I have very little predetermination as to what literally is going to get said. I used to feel kind of glib, saying, like, I wrote "off the top of my head" or on impulse. It sounds a little jazzy and presumptuous. But it has been so specifically the case over the years that now it just is the case. And writing a novel, for example, I had some sense of the area of experience and the factual events otherwise that I wanted to discuss, wanted to bring in as material, in some very vague sense of, not plot, but sequence of events, that I found I might involve. But other than that what I used as a context was the number of chapters. *That's* the plot. And I do the same thing in a text that's to be published by Scribner: a collaboration between myself and the sculptor Marisol, a number of images of her work, reproductions of her sculptures interweaving with a sequence of prose pieces. And that at moments becomes markedly surreal. Duncan, thank God, is very impressed by the Marisol text, because I really use him as a close reader. I think he is the closest reader I have.

Faas: In a letter, published in *Origin* (1953-4), Duncan makes a statement concerning his "entirely differentness" from Charles Olson, defining poetry as "a revelation of language not personality." Similarly you have often stated that you are "frankly and selfishly interested in words," that writing to you is "primarily the experience of language" and that you believe in poetry "determined by the language of which it is made." Yet there seems to be a crucial difference between Duncan's concept of language and your own. When Duncan says "I follow the word," "the word takes over" or "the word for me is the living flesh"

concept of language

he really speaks of language in a deeply neo-Platonic and Orphic sense.

CREELEY: Yes.

Faas: Or he calls poetry the ground on which we participate in the "cosmic language." Do you share any of these notions?

CREELEY: I don't feel as comfortable with them. I feel awkward with that terminology. I would feel closer to Wittgenstein's "words are all acts," that the structure of words that one composes, that one comes to compose, constitute reification rather than revelation, and reification of some specific situation of the human. I mean they bring news of that order. That's why I said, selfishly: my writing constitutes a revelation of myself to myself in ways that I find otherwise very awkward to attain.

Faas: And yet all that is at the center of Duncan's poetics.

CREELEY: Yes, he's got this incredible "cosmic consciousness." Probably it was the West, those very vast sunsets and so on. I mean Duncan can move in the largesse of that Romantic temper.

Duncan's largesse

Faas: Yes, it's deeply Romantic.

CREELEY: He is like Victor Hugo in that respect. I remember Olson saying towards the end of his life that Duncan has become, not the Man of Letters, but the Master, that he had really become possessed of that power, and that it was extraordinary. I've always felt that Duncan's ability to realize an incredible compass of reality was frankly more expansive than Charles'. I don't know, it's hard for me to judge. Charles' insights, in their depth of perception, are to me extraordinary. Robert's are really more like exfoliating this extraordinary *extending* world, like Whitman's.

Faas: So when *you* talk of language as something which reveals itself or unfolds in the process of creation you mean it in a sense closer to Wittgenstein.

CREELEY: Yes. You know that extraordinary piece of Wittgenstein's, I've got it here, it's a recollection of a lecture on ethics and religion, and at the end of it he makes a statement that's just dazzling, which I believe so deeply, he says:

> Now I am tempted to say that the right expression in language for the miracle of the existence of the world, though it is not any proposition *in* language, is the existence of language itself. But what then does it mean to be aware of this miracle at some times and not at other times? For all I have said by shifting the expression of the miraculous from an expression *by means of* language to the expression *by the existence* of language, all I

have said is again that we cannot express what we want to express and that *all we say* about the absolute miraculous remains nonsense. Now the answer to all this will seem perfectly clear to many of you . . .

And then at the end he says:

that is to say: I see now that these nonsensical expressions were not nonsensical because I have not yet found the correct expressions, but that their nonsensicality was their very essence. For all I wanted to do with them was just *to go beyond* the world and that is to say *beyond* significant language. My whole tendency and I believe the tendency of all men who ever tried to write or talk Ethics or Religion was to run against the boundaries of language. This running against the walls of our cage is perfectly, absolutely hopeless.

[Laughing]
Faas: And it is so nice to see that Wittgenstein was kind of a mystic.
CREELEY: Right. I remember the first time I read that, I had taken some acid, and I read that thing hour after hour and it just glowed.
Faas: Have you known Wittgenstein's works for a long time?
CREELEY: The person who turned me on to him was Zukofsky: "a point in space is a place for an argument."
Faas: When was that?
CREELEY: Fairly early, in the fifties. I don't read Wittgenstein in any heavy didactic sense, though.
Faas: You mean, you read him for pleasure.
CREELEY: Yes. [Fetching a book] That's the most recent I read, *Zettel*. Look at this one!
Faas: Looks like a *maṇḍala*.
CREELEY: Yes, it's very much like Jasper Johns. You see this pattern over here. [Pointing to a grouping of numbers on a piece of paper stuck on the kitchen wall] These are figures that come of numbers being written on top of one another. I really like that. I am fascinated by the experience one has of words saying things. I realize as I get older that one's experience of that activity is increasingly subjective. Especially in the relation with Bobbie, for example. We have lived so long together that the assumption as to what the other means becomes so didactic. It's almost impossible for us not to hear what we hear in our own heads if the other says something.
Faas: Being aware of the language as language.
CREELEY: Yes.
Faas: Rather than as meaning.

CREELEY: Yes, right, [laughing] we leap entirely to the quote, to the words.

Faas: Ted Hughes makes an interesting statement to that effect saying that conversations between people to a large extent are like the twittering of birds, and the liking one develops for another person's talk usually depends on certain rhythmic and melodic structures rather than on the content and meaning of what is being said.

CREELEY: Yes, again the evening with Beckett was so delightful because of listening to him *physically* talking. It was only a few, you know, very intensive things said otherwise that I really remembered.

Faas: Let's move on to a related question. At one point you say "I feel poetry as a complex of sounds and rhythms, which move in a parallel to music." What exactly is your position on that?

poetry and music

CREELEY: I suppose it's something like Schwitters', where there was a strong intent to have poetry be a pure structure of sounds and rhythms. Like he really got bugged when some Czech told him that he'd used the Czech word for bread, he really hated that somebody should say, you have a word there or sound that means something apart from its physical event. But then it's linked up with the whole question of semantic meaning. It can't be gainsaid, I mean, that music does not have that situation to pay attention to. I hate programmatic music, music that sounds like something.

Faas: Late nineteenth century music.

CREELEY: Yes, and the kind of blowzy trip of the 1950's, Prokofiev and so forth. That just bored me out of my head, or that kind of interpretation music, you know, some kind of groaning voice telling you you hear the wind through the forest.

Faas: So, analogously you want pure language?

CREELEY: Yes, not even "pure" language, but language that never forgets that it is language.

Faas: Is there any modern music which you feel moves in directions you follow in your poetry?

CREELEY: Well, sure, Cage is fascinating to me, for example. I've been fascinated by re-qualifications of senses of "serial order." I was reading a text called *The Psychology of Communication*, by George A. Miller. For example, the human situation has difficulty regaining the context if there is something interpolated, like; "That man, whom you saw yesterday, is my father." "That man is my father" is the basic statement— "whom you saw yesterday," is the element that's being inserted. This is also applicable to computer structure. If you keep putting in

serial order in psychology

statements into the basic statement, after about three or four such insertions, the hearer or witness gets very, very confused. The human attention apparently is not recursive and tends to be always where it is, so the more there is interpolated in that fashion the more difficult it is for the human to regain locus. And Miller points out that we can usually pick up where we left off in a simply physical context. Painting a fence, for instance, we know where we stopped because there is the new paint, physically it is. Poetry obviously is a way to regain a situation in the recursive that is to remind us where we are constantly by a structure. Now I am   Cage fascinated by what happens when we aren't so reminded, when we break and move into different patterns to locate the experience of being somewhere, and that's what I find extraordinary with Cage: the attempt to requalify the experience of serial order, which to me is really crucial.

Faas: Could you give me an example of something analogous in poetry?

CREELEY: Say, you write a poem about "a day at the beach" or a poem in a certain meter, or a poem having rhymes of this or that order. All of these elements could be variously used to locate the reader, to give him a reassurance that he knows where he is. If he can't understand what's happening in the third verse, then the very structure of the fourth verse relocates him and lets him continue. Williams towards the end of his life was fascinated by what he called measure, because the nature of experience apparently began to alter, senses of location in life began to yield, began to give up the sense of overall purpose, became increasingly secular. What does it all mean? That's the kind of crisis that occurred in the forties with the Existentialists, just one long individual intelligence trying to find a place in a world that seemingly has no recognition and no response. I am fascinated by how one thing can follow another, and how diverse that pattern can be. Bill Eastlake is a very pleasant friend and novelist and in one of his books this Navaho lady is saying that she knows the TV story is over when she sees the lady hand another the box of soap. That's the end of the story. It's like: *and so they all went home* or something.

Faas: Or your four pages.

CREELEY: Yes, exactly. I am fascinated by what can be used as a mode of coherence in that way.   coherence

Faas: But it is coherence after all.

CREELEY: Yes, because without that coherence it's like Williams' contention that it all simply spills on the page without a particular condition.

Faas: But it's a totally arbitrary containment.

CREELEY: Yes, but it still is a containment. And Cage to me was its most clear exponent.

Faas: At the moment he seems to move in a kind of weird paradise of mathematical abstractions, a profoundly happy man; I met him in New York the other day, such an impressively gentle man in the best sense.

CREELEY: Isn't he? That's a picture of him over there. [Showing Cage picking mushrooms]

Faas: Yes, that's exactly like him.

CREELEY: I really dig him. He's an extremely sweet man.

Faas: There is one statement of yours which has always puzzled me, namely that the follow-up of abstract expressionism is to be found in the "antithetically disciplined formalism of Frank Stella and those akin to him, as Neil Williams and Larry Poons."

CREELEY: That probably comes of my friendship with Neil Williams and to some extent with Larry Poons. I suppose what I was saying was that those artists who most saw the experience of abstract expressionism, its completions or its successes, tended therefore to move towards alternatives, instead of continuing its situation, instead of making it a tradition, moved on from its containments to areas that hadn't actually been used. Neil, for example, pointed out to me that Frank Stella had really moved away from Robert Motherwell, in particular from the kind of anthropomorphic shapes that Motherwell had used. I don't really know anything about Neil's own really early paintings.

minimal art

Faas: Werner Haftmann talks of an "active creation of 'nothingness'" in artists like Mondrian, and I think the same would apply to painters like Stella.

CREELEY: I don't think that's quite true.

Faas: Frank Stella, of course, doesn't agree with it either. But you have said yourself that a painting of Stella "is not a reference to another reality . . . but remains unequivocally its own occasion." So you would grant that he tries to obliterate referential reality.

CREELEY: That's for sure. The thing in Stella I was fascinated by was the paintings of the middle sixties which would influence reality with extraordinary impact. He worked with these shaped canvases just using line grids and it changed scale entirely around it, so that people walking by would be getting constantly smaller and larger.

Faas: And then his non-referential use of paint.

CREELEY: Yes, wanting it to be the thing in itself.

Faas: Like you with language.

CREELEY: Or like Williams, for example. The heteroclite and the diverse and the specifically common. That's particularly interesting to me, especially in Chamberlain.

Faas: I'm not too familiar with Arakawa's work and I wondered what you meant by "*zero* set," "the real nitty gritty for any head-trip," in talking about him.

CREELEY: Let me get that book I talked about previously. [Fetches book] *The Psychology of Communication* by George A. Miller. He's speaking about grammar situations [reads]: "Our college students seemed unable to reinvent the concept of zero . . . In [the] linguistic context, it simply did not occur to most people to use the perfectly familiar concept of zero in order to simplify their classification scheme . . . In a numerical context they thought of zero, but in a linguistic context they did not." That was the point that really got to me. "*Zero* set" is really a fascinating place to be. [Both laughing] It's like the ultimate imagination. I don't know what "*zero* set" is obviously, but as I understand it, it would be the concept of something that neither is nor is not. It wouldn't be less than and obviously it wouldn't be either more or less. It would be nothing. Zero.

> Arakawa's "*zero* set"

Faas: Not unlike Sanskrit *śūnyatā*, I guess, "the void of inexhaustible contents," as D. T. Suzuki paraphrased it.

CREELEY: Yes, how you could state that which by being is not, you know, that which by being is not is not by being. A curious paradox. And Arakawa was talking to me about "*zero* set."

> *śūnyatā*

Faas: What particular work of his are you referring to?

CREELEY: I'm referring to this book *Mechanismus der Meinung*. I wish the hell I had it here.

Faas: But all that is exactly what, using Haftmann's terms, I mean by "active creation of 'nothingness.' "

CREELEY: Yes, trying to realize something that doesn't have, that isn't more or less, or isn't something added or something subtracted. The invention of zero was the greatest step forward in the history of mathematics. Zero is a fantastic concept.

Faas: All throughout your earlier poetry I find a yearning for destruction not only of outward reality but also of yourself, a striving for

> some time beyond place, or
> place beyond time, no
> mind left to

> say anything at all,
> that face gone, now.

At some point you say that in your creative efforts you are working
"towards a final obliteration" of yourself. I feel the poem,
self-   you write, "with the intensity of all the perception that I
reduction   . . . that the ego bit can recognize, and then destroy the
ego by its own insistence." Is that kind of experience a
pleasurable or an anguished one?

CREELEY: I have some insistent pattern in my own nature that makes
me extremely restless and, not so much bored, but just that the
moment something becomes familiar to me, known to me and relax-
ing to me, I simply tend to reject it, I don't know why. It just really is
insistently the case. Presently I almost feel a delight in that way. For
example, I was in New York last weekend in the company of a friend
I have there, a girl I really enjoy and like to be with, and we were at a
club, I mean a place that frankly isn't literally my kind of interest nor
is it suitable to my age, so to speak, to be there. But there I was
nonetheless and at one point I realized that she was splitting with this
other fellow and I thought, wow, that's really heavy. So she says, I'll
call you tomorrow or something. [Both laughing] In the meantime
I'm stoned out of my head in this mad place, the Club 800 which is an
old time apparently transvestite bar that's now a rock and roll scene.
It's about 5 o'clock in the morning and the vibes are up to 80,000
whatever, two, three hundred people dancing like mad in this place.
And I don't know where the hell I've got to. But again on some kind
of weird persistent intuition I find my coat, I hit the street and it's
raining, a kind of nice gentle spring rain and I feel like wow, isn't the
world sweet, and I think: What in the name of heaven makes me so
pleased? It's as though I'm stepping out onto the earth again, not
sentimentally but it's all beginning again. And somehow the kinds of
That's all   anticipation, the responsibility, not responsibility, but the
fallen apart,   kinds of assumption and argument, and the plot, let's say,
what's next?   it's broken again, thank God. I love the excitement of
something like: here it is, that's all fallen apart, what's
next?

Faas: It seems similar to the kind of experience I have had in the
past of somehow getting drunk, until you finally don't quite realize
any more where you are going and where you are, and then wake up
next morning: and here are walls, furniture, curtains, a window you
have never seen before, and it makes you laugh.

CREELEY: I love it.

Faas: And of course one goes around deliberately looking for these
experiences.

CREELEY: Once as a kid in New York I was like in some boredom and loneliness. I saw these five guys get into a car and just got in line with them and got into the car with them, and thankfully they didn't turn out to be offended. I mean that would be characteristic.

Faas: But in those quotes I read to you, you were saying something very specific about the act of poetic creativity as being an obliterating of your ego.

CREELEY: Yes, like turn the ego into material. So again with a bad relationship like last weekend, the ego was instantly offended like: how dare you leave me? But then the situation became so immediately more interesting to me, and now I was a far more real person to myself than I had been even moments before, you know. It's like I was back in business, whereas even moments before I knew all too well where I was: I was an older man with a younger woman, in that kind of old time familiar place.

Faas: So the act of creativity would be breaking away from the old familiar ego.

CREELEY: Yes, so that all the condition of the material has to reveal itself, has to pertain, because there can't be any assumption. Finally, that evening, I was very stoned and I couldn't find my way to where I stayed, so finally I asked a bum who walked me all across the city, and it was terrific. [Laughing] I mean I felt that this was a weird and unexpected blessing that other kinds of containment would sadly never be able to stop for. I don't mean to be sentimental about it but I mean the world breaks open in a beautiful way when there can't any longer be assumptions about it.

Faas: And writing a poem somehow helps you experience the same thing.

CREELEY: Yes, somehow.

Faas: So it's really a kind of self-transcendance.

CREELEY: Well, whatever, self-revelation more than self-transcendance.

Faas: You describe that experience in "Figures." Who was the artist in that poem?

CREELEY: A really moving New Mexican, sadly but lovely drunken sculptor named Patrocinio Barela, and he lived in Taos and used to peddle these little santos figures. He'd peddle them mainly for drink, and he finally burnt to death. There are pictures of his work in the *Black Mountain Review*.

Faas: The sense I got from that poem is that these figures gave you the same feeling of self-obliteration and quiet.

CREELEY: Right.   Mallarmé

Faas: There is a poem of yours entitled "After Mallarmé."

CREELEY: It turns out it's Jouve. [Both laughing] Somebody told me he couldn't find that poem in Mallarmé, and it's actually a poem by Jouve, and it was quoted to me by Philip Guston.

Faas: Really! Nonetheless, there are striking resemblances between you and Mallarmé.

CREELEY: I have read Mallarmé, but only in a very kind of scattered way.

Faas: Have you read his letters?

CREELEY: No.

Faas: It's just a few I am referring to, from around 1866, describing his mystical insights into nothingness.

CREELEY: Rexroth once referred to me as the corn-fed Mallarmé. [Both laughing] It's kind of sneering but still.

Faas: Charles Altieri has argued that "at the center of [your] experience is the continual threat of the void" stemming from your "sense of isolation, of being cut off from all roots or grounds—in concrete experience, in tradition, and in [your] relationships with other people."

CREELEY: I think he is unwittingly a little sentimental, I think he is overstating it.

the void

Faas: And interpreting you too much in humanistic terms.

CREELEY: Yes, the void can be at moments like the whole of creation or something in an almost punning sense, you know. When younger I felt probably fearful that everyone was going to go away through the fact of being a kid whose father died young, and various other realities thus, losing an eye and whatnot, having very few people as family to relate to and feeling awkward in the social milieu.

Faas: When did you lose your eye?

CREELEY: When I was two, and my father died when I was four, and then our social habits changed because of losing him. But I don't find myself presently particularly threatened by the void. A poem like "The Hole" is curiously positive.

Faas: You also talk of "The poem supreme, addressed to/ emptiness."

CREELEY: Yes, I don't think it was an awful word.

Faas: I have the impression, perhaps equally overstated, that the void, instead of constituting a threat, represents some kind of *fascinosum* to you, something compellingly attractive almost, in an Eastern or mystical sense.

CREELEY: I was really struck when I read that sequence of poems called *Numbers* in Texas a few years ago and there was an

Numbers

Indian novelist that New Directions publishes, I think his

last name is Lal, and he came round afterwards and told me charmingly that that sequence of poems— particularly "Nothing," the zero poem—were fantastic, realizations of Indian, you know, Buddhist theosophy, I guess he'd call it. And really dug it. The delight in zero. and Buddhist theosophy

Faas: Why then did you inveigh against that "goddamn Zen"?

CREELEY: That's the Zennies. You know, I'm teaching here, and I've just got a large cluster of papers, and one or rather several of the students are really and understand- ably washed away with contemporary, generalized Buddhist thought, and they are very boring. It has nothing to do with friends like Gary who have made it a very distinct part of their own condition. the "goddamn Zen"

Faas: Gary to me has this almost frightening kind of sanity and balance which doesn't seem to leave much loophole for the ordinary neurotic.

CREELEY: Oh he's not that sane, really, he's very healthy, so things that would occur in a patterning of the neurotic for others of us or me, for example, would occur in Gary in a completely uninvolved straightforward condition of health. When he was here, I suddenly realized that I've lived here for six years, and one of the students comes back and I sleep with her. And then I get all these neurotic echoes of it in my own head: like what have I betrayed—X, Y or Z [both laughing], what's happening? Gary has really worked to rid himself of all that.

Faas: I must admit that I tend to feel more like you, too.

CREELEY: Of course, I am at times obviously hooked on the tensions and energies I get from irreconciliations, so to speak, and I am obviously much more attached to the tensions than he is, he doesn't like them at all. Snyder

Faas: Have you known him for a long time?

CREELEY: I've known him since '56.

Faas: Has he always been like that?

CREELEY: When I first met him he was a markedly shy fellow.

Faas: The way Kerouac describes him in the *Dharma Bums*.

CREELEY: Never pompous, never careful particularly, but serious. He was more tender and more serious than others were, in a very deliberate sense. Then I didn't see him for a long time, when he was in Japan and when he and Joanne were married. And then the next time I saw him at all was when Don Allen and he came up to stay with us in New Mexico, when he and Joanne had just broken up, and that was a heavy time in his life, that really hurt him and confused him, 1965. He didn't really know what happened. It was like a sadly incongruous marriage, although both of them were extraordinary. But Joanne has a level of nervous energy which just frustrates Gary. And Masa, his present wife, has a crazy wry particular humor. We had a lovely conversation with her, where she is describing to Bobbie all of Gary's twelve pairs of shoes which he has for every condition of weather and terrain [both laughing] and she is like kind of wryly describing all these shoes with Gary sitting next to her. At first it was almost flattering, but then it got obviously pretty ironic.

Faas: What most impressed me when he came to New York was the complete ease with which he conducted himself in front of a huge audience.

CREELEY: He feels very at peace in the world. His reading here was of the same order, and the one impression which everybody seems to have literally taken away was this sense of an extraordinary peacefulness. It wasn't that he told them to be that, but they really felt completely relaxed and well used.

Faas: Duncan seems to share some of your impatience with Westernized Zen. When I talked to him in 1973 he called Snyder some kind of Prussian officer—said in a joking way, of course, but still . . .

Duncan and Snyder

CREELEY: And it's Duncan that Gary is paying homage to. [Laughing] Robert loves all the double-edged, the double-faceted, the double-faced, he sees as I see "the underside turning" and the double nature of reality, due to the condition of his eyes etc., etc. And there is something about the will to purity that really bores him. Robert's life has been incredibly intensive and diverse and I think both of us in various ways at first had difficulty, I know I did, hearing the rhythmic structure of Gary's writing. He has moved very much from Rexroth, and I missed the sensual texture, I missed an experiential kind of intensity, I felt that its physical skill was very interesting but . . .

Faas: What do you mean by experiential intensity?

CREELEY: In contrast, say, to Allen. To me Allen was terrific, just that he moves so directly to the personal center of his own reality whereas Gary would tend to always be at some distance, I wouldn't really know who Gary was at all. But then his later poems would have some beautiful sensual texture, like "Wash in the Sun."

Faas: Or "The Bath."

CREELEY: But it's still a curious objectifying of the body state.

Faas: I sometimes feel its simplicity may be just beyond my understanding.

CREELEY: His health seems to speak for him at this point. It would really need some weirdly perverted or distorted sense that would want to question where he is at.

Faas: I told Snyder: I find it very difficult to write about you because there are no problems.

CREELEY: Right. Yet it seems that his early life was anything but easy. Something seems to have really freaked him as a younger man, possibly the relationship with his mother.

Faas: So your insight into emptiness or what the Indian novelist called your "realizations of Buddhist theosophy" are a direct outgrowth of your own individual development?

CREELEY: Yes.

Faas: No direct influence of Buddhism itself?

no direct Buddhist influence

CREELEY: No, not really. Like Lawrence Ferlinghetti really spent so much of his life on the West Coast, and last summer we were down at his place in Big Sur and he was saying that despite his long friendships with many people who are decisively involved with Buddhism—Gary, for instance—his own sort of American East Coast upbringing made him, not wary of it, but it wasn't where the center of his own experience seemed to find its place. In a like sense I would just feel that I am very interested in it, much like Thoreau or someone like that, but the reification of that experience would occur to me in a very different vocabulary, that's all.

Faas: In 1961 you said that Gary Snyder's work presented "a successful relation of hope."

CREELEY: Gary has an incredibly strong will, resourceful, extremely, yes, not serious in a heavy sense, when younger it did seem so, he just eschewed the whole anxiety head trip which was so familiar in the East. This part of the country uses it so much, you know,· as an energy turn on.

Faas: And you think he eschewed all that.

CREELEY: Or he worked through it. That long long time in Buddhism must have had a lot to do with it. At least my understanding is that Zen is a formal practise to break that kind of consciousness among other things.

Faas: Let's turn to your more recent development. I got the impression that sometime in the '60's your work and your sense of yourself underwent a profound change.

CREELEY: Yes.

Faas: I'll briefly mention some of the things I noticed. A couple of years ago you said that all you had recently tried to achieve was a kind of writing "that simply says: the road is going this way down the hill and there are trees here," and that you were now simply trying to make a statement

development since the sixties

"of what seems to be physically actual" in a specific place, which obviously is the opposite of your earlier poetry where you are trying to say . . .

CREELEY: . . . what I feel . . .

Faas: . . . and also trying to write "the poem supreme, addressed to / emptiness."

CREELEY: Right.

Faas: I wonder how this change occurred.

CREELEY: We'd moved here in the middle sixties. Almost always my changes have to do with relationships or with people, and mainly with Bobbie. Also, in a book like *Words* I began trying to think of ways in which I could break habits of writing and composition. Using long hand instead of typing, even something as simple as that, had a profound effect. And then I think the key book is *Pieces*, that really is where the decisive change occurs, where the concept of poems as set instances of articulate statement yields to a sense of continuity. I was fascinated by my friends' ability to continue, and I realized that I didn't have a thematic proposal for that situation. I'd written a novel but that seemed to me something else and I'd seen Duncan work with *Passages* and Allen with various texts of his, or Olson's *Maximus Poems* or Zukofsky's *A* or whatnot, and I wondered what kind of modality would really give me something that could also in a sense continue as a situation of writing, that wouldn't each time contain itself in a singular statement, so I'd really just write it as a common audit of days.

Pieces the decisive step

Faas: But doesn't this new concern with reality and things contradict what you said about your autotelic use of language?

CREELEY: Yes, it's like easing oneself down into the physical world.

Faas: To me it almost seems like the poetry written by a man who has been blinded by a glaring vision of nothingness and now comes stumbling back into reality.

CREELEY: Yes, and starts to see that there are real things here. In the sixties there also was that extraordinary experience of acid for the first time, and that had a large impact on ego-structures. I mean that doesn't *solve* the question, for the previous habit structures are very, very tenacious and recur soon afterwards. But in any case it stays as true information. So I was trying to think of ways in which the statement could include the diversity and variousness of experience rather than always choosing these moments of intensive crisis which tend to be singularizing and thus contained.

taking acid

Faas: So there is a whole new sense of the real which seems to go hand in hand with a new sense of language.

CREELEY: Yes.

Faas: Ginsberg recently told me that your poem "Oh No" provided him with an illustration of his new concept of space which he developed under the influence of Chögyam Trungpa. You know the poem I mean:

> If you wander far enough   "Oh No"
> you will come to it
> and when you get there
> they will give you a place to sit·
>
> for yourself only, in a nice chair,
> and all your friends will be there
> with smiles on their faces
> and they will likewise all have places.

CREELEY: Oh no! That's kind of ironic, the poem itself is meant as a kind of awful irony.

Faas: Isn't it! [Both laughing]

CREELEY: It's like Wittgenstein's "A point in space is a place for an argument." How one can transform it into beatitude, terrific! It's like the pie in the sky, forget it. That's funny. [Laughing]

Faas: Was it at the time of the Vancouver poetry conference in 1963 that these changes in your development came to a fulfillment?

CREELEY: It was rather the beginning of it. In fact, it was Allen who said to me one night: You don't really have to   Ginsberg's worry about writing a good poem any more, you can write   advice what you want to. We talked of modes of composition and how constricted I felt by how I had developed as a writer, and we really went into that, that's the text of "Contexts of Poetry." I had recognized increasingly how modalities of saying things had become ends in themselves, and their use otherwise was getting more and more impeded. So I was trying to think of ways to break out, and partly it was thinking of other modes of transcription which would change the experience literally. And then shifts in senses of what the occasion, I suppose, of the writing really was. Like I respect Galway Kinnell and like him as a person, and yet   Galway feel some distance from his writing, not criticism in some   Kinnell awful sense, but I really don't turn on to the way he writes, and I keep on wondering why. And perhaps what happens is that in his writing there is such an intensive signal of its occasion, there is such an insistent program, that I'm really bored.

Faas: Yes, he so loads his poetry with all kinds of poetic, symbolic or allusive imagery, that in the final analysis it all seems a little tenuous, paradoxically.

CREELEY: Yes, he overworks it in a funny way. And so whatever could be called the impulse is curiously smothered, and the program of the purpose overrides the actual writing. So he is like a very skilled workman, like putting all this stuff on.

Faas: So your own development involved a getting away from this notion of poetic creativity as a conscious craft.

CREELEY: Yes. The real breakthrough begins just about the end of *Words*, and then it really is manifest with *Pieces*. That's the key book for me. In some ways I tried to continue the information of that into *A Day Book*. But I tend increasingly to believe like Duncan that the formal situation of *A Day Book* is possibly too arbitrary and that the conjoinment of prose and poems in that book doesn't really mesh in the way that I'd hoped it might. It really is too hard, and the congruence of one to the other is not particularly informative. So I really ought to do what Duncan reminds me I should do anyhow: put together three prose situations of thirty pages each as a cluster, a new version of the three tales, like Flaubert's, which has been weightily in mind for years. I have been fascinated by that sense of three tales like "3 Fate Tales." That sense of the three is really insistent.

Faas: Personally, I can't quite understand your fascination with numbers.

fascination with numbers   CREELEY: I can't really tell you why that's the case, it's not in some symbolic sense. When I was a kid preparing to go to college my rating in some mathematical skills was way above everything else. I love patternings that can be situated in numbers. I don't have any sophisticated information in numbers but I'm fascinated by conditions in which numbers can be used either to demonstrate or to describe.

Faas: Your more recent poetry also shows a marked impatience with imagery and in particular with "the damn function of simile, always a displacement of what *is* happening." By contrast there are a lot of similes in your earlier poetry which almost reads like John Donne's very often.

imagery

CREELEY: Yes? He was a heavy influence, of course, at one point.

Faas: Of course, Donne's conceits and similes, although they are cryptic, always contain a solution, whereas your early poetry offers the same kind of riddles, but without solutions.

CREELEY: Yes. Contemporary. [Both laughing]

Faas: So Donne was a direct influence?

CREELEY: He and the whole cluster of poets of his period. Wyatt, Herrick, although they are much different, no not so much Marvell, but Vaughan, and, oh God, Crashaw, I was trying to remember the edition of metaphysical poets, edited by Saintsbury?

Faas: Grierson?

CREELEY: Yes, Grierson. That was really a heavy book for me.

Faas: There is a final point concerning your more recent development. Up to some time ago you conceived of your poetry as of an uncommunicative way of "telling something to yourself."

CREELEY: Yes. Now I just write it because I enjoy writing it. I don't think I have any greater sense of purpose, except in those instances where there is a kind of very shy or minimal commission or sense of occasion, like for a birthday, yes. Right now I'm working on prose.

Faas: *Mabel*?

CREELEY: Yes. I'm off poetry for a bit, not in the sense that I don't like it or something, but at the moment I'm just too emotionally hung up. I mean I'm not Gary and I'm just too questioning of my own life at the moment to find the kind of, yes, it's funny, it's a blend of relaxation and intensity, I don't know. The last time I felt myself really writing poetry in the way that I love it, was at the very end of *Pieces*, that whole section "Mazatlan: Sea." That to me is the last poetry that I have written in a body state, I want to say, or at least in a conscious state of experience that was to me absolutely delicious. Subsequently poetry has been like stabs and seizures and fits and irritations and explanations and bullshit. I mean I liked it, wrote a whole book of it, so to speak, but I felt too little in it, and too much practise. The most moving poem to my own imagination would be the poem for my mother's death which is a kind of attempt to realize what had happened and to honor her, you know; and one or two things of that order that I have done. Those weren't poems of any human ease, they were deeply compulsive and painful. And I haven't felt at home in poetry for about four years, I guess, which is an awkward and difficult thing to say, but it doesn't particularly worry me because I've gone through periods of that nature before. I mean it worries me like hell, but . . .

Faas: Are you aware of any reason for all that?

CREELEY: Duncan again has been very useful: like body changes, emotional changes one goes through in one's late forties. Senses of boredom with previous conduct, ah, senses of questions about going on, doing it. Just to do it seems a kind of random way. Really being tempted to move off entirely, but questioning as to what that means. Thinking of Gary, who is a good friend, I don't see that constantly changing the place and subject is really going to do anything at all. I don't really feel depressed but it's like: is this poem necessary? I'd

really like to write prose in this way because it lets me move out . . .
Faas: Anyway I find your short stories really fantastic.
CREELEY: I'd better write some more, yes.
Faas: I like them much better than the novel.
CREELEY: Yes, I do too. I think the short stories are singular, whereas the novel, I wrote it just to have written a novel. But it didn't really get to anywhere.
Faas: Let me just read a couple of lines from a more recent poem, "The Finger":

"The Finger"   She was largely warm—
flesh heavy—and smiled
in some deepening knowledge.

· · · · · · · ·

Her heavy breath,
her ugliness, her lust—
but her laughing . . .

and so forth. What was the actual circumstance that prompted these lines?
CREELEY: This was in this house we were staying at in Gloucester and Bobbie was sitting by the fireplace; we had taken the acid quite late, about two o'clock in the morning, and we'd started a fire. Bobbie shifted to some lighter clothing so she had on this lovely kind of orange velvet wrapper, just lounging in front of the fire, like this incredibly beautiful woman, this firelight and this velvet and this chuckling woman, it was just incredible.
Faas: Of course, in the poem she also has these demonic, threatening aspects.
CREELEY: Right, you don't fool around with that, no no, she is not at all to be tickled, as Olson would say. [Both laughing] What's fascinating to me is how these states of experience, however they are gathered, may be obviously simple recollections unwittingly of a whole context of information that's been got, but has been forgotten.

I remember at one time talking to my eldest son—he's a
mystical   classic New England fellow, he's at Harvard, a graduate
experience   student in art history, and has been brought up largely by
his mother from whom I've separated. We do get on without question, but he finds it very awkward to propose anything that has any "magical" situation in his life. So Bobbie and I were talking to him once about thinking, and he obviously loves to think. And I asked him if he had ever found while he was thinking any kind of transformation occurring in it, physically or otherwise. So he said, once he'd been working late at night in the stacks and concentrating upon some text when suddenly, unexpected by himself entirely, he

experienced that the light around him seemed to alter. There, all of a sudden, was kind of a magnesium blue permeation of light all around him, and a humming, a distinct sense of humming, not like birds' wings but like a vibrating, a very curious vibrating sound that he could hear distinctly as a hum, and that the light wasn't just like a light-source but that it seemingly permeated the air, this intense whitish blue light. And this went on for a few seconds and then dissolved, and he felt very confused and thought he'd possibly fallen asleep and dreamed it. But he said he felt very high—of course, he doesn't use words like that—but curiously untired. And I said: Well you know, friend, you've described one of the classic trips. [Laughing] I mean, we don't have the books in the house, but you could go and check them out yourself. Now whether it's obviously a physiological state or whether it's some mystic state is up to you to determine, but I mean that's it. So he was pleased to know that.

"The Moon"

Faas: Do you feel that there is a comparable new mystical dimension to your recent work? I'm thinking of poems like "The Moon."

CREELEY: I feel that my danger in such situations is that I become coy about them. Like last night I was lying in bed, still affected by this flu and I'd been watching TV and reading variously, and suddenly I was aware of this intense light from the window. And when I looked out of the window I thought: full moon. But I couldn't see the moon actually. So I went out and saw it sure enough and then I checked the calendar and it was full moon. And I was really feeling depressed the last week and the full moon really excites me and pleases me and reassures me. And so I thought: well, that's just what I needed, that moonlight. And to suddenly get it so specifically through the window. It was really good news to know that moon hadn't forgotten me somehow. [Both laughing] But you see I can't get off and be easy about it and say: isn't it sweet and it has such affection for me. It's like a Jewish puritanism, sort of.

Faas: Your recent attempts to write a long poem have been compared with *The Cantos*, *Paterson* etc.

CREELEY: I came upon a quote of Thoreau's talking about what he calls a "day book" in which he collects the events of the day and so on, and then he translates them into some information and judgment of his own. I'm interested in the phrase "a day book" where he uses it for notations of what happened. But the point is that I don't transfer or translate, but let it stand. It's interesting as a form but I don't have any impulse to continue it, no. *Pieces* was really the success of that sequence.

the long poem

Faas: Yet I don't really see any kind of resemblance to *The Cantos* or *Paterson*. Maybe Zukofsky's *A*?

CREELEY: But then *A* is a different pattern also. *A* has a very diverse and specific sense of structure. I mean Louis has a very formal composition among other things, with a number of things in mind to accomplish. So he would have pieces of it ahead and backwards and he has a very strict sense of formal composition that he is working to realize whereas I was fascinated to know what happened if you accumulated rather than designed and determined, that is, if you made the accumulation the crux of the situation rather than the moment to moment determination, let that collect rather than say: this is a good poem, this is a bad poem.

coherence   *Faas*: And which would be the element of coherence?

CREELEY: That it was written. I mean that could be coherence.

Faas: Ginsberg says that the coherence is dependent on the concentration with which you observe the movement of the mind while writing, in other words that the coherence would dissolve as soon as the concentration slackens. So the poem would reflect some kind of inner coherence of mind experience. Again when he talks about the beginning, middle and end of a poem he uses these terms in a totally non-Aristotelian sense, so the beginning, middle and end of a poem would be determined by the beginning, middle and end of a thought process and the poem would leave off when the thought process . . .

CREELEY: . . . reaches a stasis . . .

Faas: . . . or a decisive turning point. Does that make sense to you in terms of your own work?

CREELEY: It does make sense to me in terms of his but not too much of mine. You see, Zukofsky speaks of writing as a way of getting to or realizing or arriving at that which gives the hardened piece, and I could certainly believe in that, or do believe in that; to write in order to realize what brings you to rest, you know.

I don't   I don't certainly try any longer to do something that
write to   will be simply extraordinary or brilliant or whatever, as I
resolve   don't write to win prizes any longer. Again Allen's sense
the world.   from a few years ago: You don't have to write good poems
any more. In any case, I don't see any point of stasis in any human situation that to me would be more than temporary, I don't mean this pessimistically, but I don't see how the experience of being human can be in any point a stasis, I just don't see how it can be. It can arrive at a containment but I don't see how that containment can be more than a momentary situation even though that moment may last for twenty years. So that I write now primarily to recognize and

thus to register states of consciousness, of feeling that are in various ways constantly changing and constantly in flux. I write to see what stays the case and what changes, that's all. I don't write for peace, I mean I write for peace in the sense that writing these things gives me peace, but I don't write to resolve the world. What we were saying earlier: using art to reify all the states of human consciousness that do occur in all the states of human experience, to give, not simply a record but a reification of all those diversities. It sounds pessimistic, I assume, to say that each one of us dies so that that resolution in itself seems ample and sufficient. You know, I was extremely moved by Williams' late poems, simply that they continued an information that was to me extraordinarily valuable. And the one or two times that I had a chance to talk to him, he said: You hear a lot about old age being a time of fruition, that you feel you have accomplished X, Y and Z and that you can relax and enjoy the world and realize that you have done things in it, etc., etc. But actually it's an awful drag, you know. There is no rest in that way ever apparently, and what works to accomplish it, is always defeated by the very physical experience we have as people. So I think of myself much more like Burroughs' lone telegraph operator. I am simply a re- the lone telegraph operator cording instrument. That's what I really love in Bur- roughs, where he says: I'm merely a recording instru- ment and I'm not here, you know, to make plots or . . . I would far more feel that I'm here simply to write it down, don't mind me if the news is good, bad or otherwise. [Both laughing] I'm not here to bring enlightenment or a resolving of human ills, I am here to tell you what happens as best I can. Not at all to insist on myself but just to give manifest of that one consciousness among myriad others, and the information can be as desultory or insignificant as proves the case. So the only act that's valuable is that which is used to articulate these states, you know. I think that's probably where Duncan and myself would sheer off from Gary who wants the poems to realize a state of beatitude and to work to that purpose possibly. To me that's an indifferent object. I mean it isn't that I don't care about human suffering or the human dilemma, but I don't particularly care about it as an artist.

I personally find extremely valuable those poems which make manifest human states of consciousness, physical states and various experiential states at all points of age and condition. And the resolu- tion is fine, but the resolution, as Jess Collins would say, curiously throws out the baby with the bath water. I mean, I want the full condition of the experience not so much so that I can make a judgment but so that I can compare. I know, for example, that in points of my own despair or even delight it's been extremely useful to me to be able to read Williams' poems written when he was in his forties. I find them valuable simply because they give me information about where I'm at. They don't teach me but they give me companionship. Perhaps I'm simply tired of endless plans to tidy up the world. Phil Whalen tells me charmingly that there are a lot of young kids crashing on the Zen Center, some of whom have to be relegated to the steps because they are rather obstructive in the Center itself, and I mean Zen just ain't gonna save them.

Faas: Many people just aren't aware of the fact that Zen involves very rigorous discipline.

CREELEY: It's the ability to yield your ego and your will to an authority. You see, to an American that's almost unthinkable, you spend all your life getting out of it and here you have to give yourself back to your father.

Faas: Does the term "open form" make sense to you?

open and closed form

CREELEY: It's confusing to me. What is it, *Naked Poetry*, that whole stupid thing. You know, this country has had such a bleak battle between "free verse" and so-called classically, conceptually formal verse or previous senses of metrical pattern. I keep wishing there was a word that was more accurate. I mean, projective verse is one sense, but that too is a kind of final cliché, it doesn't really locate very much. Closed and open I guess. I don't know. Open form? Yes. What's your sense of it?

Faas: Generally speaking there seems to be a tendency now to incorporate closed forms into open form æsthetics. In various ways you find that in Duncan, Snyder and Ginsberg, for instance.

CREELEY: I certainly use closed forms with very decisive patterns that are very familiar.

Faas: And you don't feel that closed form relates to one type of experience, and open form relates to another?

CREELEY: The thing that really made more sense to me was, years ago, Pound trying to inform me by letter about ways in which a magazine might be edited—trying to make me back off my heavy-handed seriousness in various respects. He said, first of all, get three or four people you really dig, and depend on them and publish them, let them publish anything they want and that will be your core, your constant, so to speak. On the other hand, he said, let about a quarter or a half of the magazine run hog wild so that any idiot thinks he can get in. And he said, verse consists of the

the constant and the variant

constant and the variant. Any element that stays decisive in the context can be used as the variant, any element that stays decisive in the context can be used as the constant.

It's like Duncan's sense of enclosing the closed in the open. Pound's presumption was that in order for the situation to have a coherence there must be an element that stays sufficiently stable to offer measure for the remainder of the activity. For example, if you have a strong rhythmic situation, use that as the constant and keep it factually persistent. Or Kenneth Koch, well, he simply uses a very steady heroic couplet, and into that he can literally pour anything, throw in all this lovely garbage. He uses a contained, reasonably stated line of bullshit and you can read on and on and on despite the fact that it's obviously going nowhere.

Faas: So you think there is an absolute necessity for *some* kind of coherence, rhythmical or otherwise?

CREELEY: I tend to, yes.

Faas: In 1953 you spoke of the poem as a whole defined by a "relevant and actual tension between diverse parts." That almost sounds like Cleanth Brooks.

CREELEY: Yes, Brooks and Warren was a text I used as a kid.

Faas: Would you consider that statement as dated now?

CREELEY: I would still regard it as interesting. I mean, I would now tend to read it as the situation of words energizing one another. I mean Kenneth's writing, for instance, gets too flaccid for me. He's a funny guy, I saw him like last weekend.

Kenneth Koch

Faas: What did somebody call it? Transcendental high camp, yes.

CREELEY: It *is* high camp. Restoration wit carrying a handkerchief in his sleeve or something. It can be very charming and very funny, and one poem of his that hits me very much is "Sleeping with Women" where there is a crazy curious sound pattern.

Faas: But then that kind of funniness often conceals so much aggressiveness against anybody who is not trying to be witty, any kind of seriousness being taken almost as a threat that has to be diminished, run down and ridiculed.

CREELEY: That's very much a New York scene, you can understand that situation when you are still very young, when you are feeling very questioning and threatened by the authorities surrounding you, then there is almost sadly a physiological paranoia before you have any sense of situation that gives you any place to be.

Faas: That's what I liked about Robert Bly, that he was almost apologetic about what he'd written about Olson, expressing an attitude very much like the one you're describing right now, just as he's very relaxed about this whole controversy with James Dickey.

CREELEY: Bob Bly is such an easy man to get along with, I like him. He is just like the old time classic Minnesota farmer. It's so lovely that he should be the great defender of the Great Mother, being like the old time patriarch himself, a lovely paradox. [Both laughing]

Faas: Somewhere you have stated that the "pace of [your] writing is concerned with the speed with which [you] can type" and that with two fingers you "type actually as fast as [you] can talk."

the writing process

CREELEY: I just write it down, I mean, I could show you notebooks and stuff, it's just physically writing. I mean I think a lot, I think endlessly with a consciousness of trying this on and trying that on. That really is attractive to me in Wittgenstein, that constant preoccupation with thinking.

Faas: But are you aware of observing your mind process while writing?

CREELEY: Oh yes.

Faas: So it would not be altogether different from Ginsberg's graphing the movement of his mind?

CREELEY: No, because writing gives me that curious detachment.

Faas: I have always been puzzled by the fact that Ginsberg frequently adduces Gertrude Stein as an antecedent for his own way of writing whereas to me she seems to have been propelled by language . . .

CREELEY: Right.

Faas: . . . while Allen Ginsberg is really concerned with the dynamics of the mind. And in that dichotomy, I think, you would be much closer to Gertrude Stein.

CREELEY: Yes, I agree. I am fascinated with what words say and how that saying stimulates one to move in them. I feel like I'm moving in words.

Faas: Although you don't seem to go quite as far as Gertrude Stein in letting the language take its own course.

CREELEY: She was more syntactically oriented than I am.

Faas: When does a poem come to a close?

poetic closure

CREELEY: When the energy drops. It's like Pound's law of discourse: say what you have to say and then just shut up. Sometimes when I was younger I tended to overwrite, that is to write beyond the impulse. And then I would frequently find that I'd go back and cut off the last verse and the center of the poem was clear.

Faas: So there is a kind of center related to the impulse of creation.

CREELEY: Right.

Faas: William Stafford once said that his poems usually come to a close when his powers to homogenize an experience come to a close.

CREELEY: In what *I'm* doing I certainly don't know that I am homogenizing. My wife has a recollection of that movie in which you see the doctor arriving through the pouring rain, coming home, and he says: Tonight history was made, I've just delivered Louis Pasteur. [Both laughing] That kind of trip, yes.

Faas: What are your criteria for evaluating your own work? I mean what makes you decide whether or not you are going to publish a poem. You have often emphasized that you never revise. *evaluating his own poetry*

CREELEY: The important thing is that they should *feel* right. If in reading them, what's getting done, seems to me moving, appropriate and revealing, then I tend to trust them.

Faas: Revealing in terms of content?

CREELEY: Things that I respect are high energy states and/or some situations where the words are so relating that that constitutes an interest. It could be like a pun or a sing-song or some very minimal event possibly in that way. I use myself as the only measure that way and I will, as I said, use friends, like Duncan specifically, I'd use his advice. But usually if it feels right, then I trust it. I mean at times I've thrown away poems which later were published. For instance, I'd written a poem called "The Name" and threw it away, and then my wife happily asked me what I was doing and I recovered it from the waste basket and she said: That's really a moving poem. I don't know what caused me to throw it away, because now I can't quite see why I was dismayed by it.

Faas: Does concentration play any role in all that?

CREELEY: Yes, just physically, I'll show you one of my notebooks. [Fetches notebook] Like this is the poem on my mother's death. [Shows a manuscript without corrections, with very clean spacing and in beautiful handwriting]

Faas: It looks like a transcript.

CREELEY: No. That's the initial composition. That's primarily how a text will look. I remember when I sold the manuscript of *The Island* to Washington University one of the people there wrote me: We would like to know whether this is a copy of the actual manuscript or the actual manuscript. But that's truly the way I write. I must practise in my head in ways that I'm not quite able to articulate and to apprehend. There must be a lot of this going on in my head . . .

Faas: . . . before you write it down.

CREELEY: Yes. Not so much even the text itself, but it must be like playing chess games in your head endlessly.

Faas: But you wouldn't go ruminating on the lines, like Lowell or Snyder.

CREELEY: No. It's really written right there. [Shows further poems]

Here's a drunken night in a bar. [Both laughing] I don't rush *these* into print! And this is a poem that's really funny. I have a photographer friend, Walter Chappell, who told me he would like a poem to preface a collection of his photographs and he wanted it so it would fit on two pages, so I had two columns of twice four verses each, so it adds up to sixteen. [Laughing] So this poem is not only written straight out, man, but I'm counting as I go. [Laughing] Perhaps I should sit on a sidewalk and write poems to order.

Robert Bly

Photo: Layle Silbert

ROBERT BLY   (1926 -   )

There we go again! The Olsonite poets are always approaching poetry through technique; Creeley is a perfect example
. . . When I have fought against what was weak in my own
poems, I have often found myself fighting the American longing to lie down in technique and rest. . . I think Gary Snyder is
right when he says that wherever we are is not where we're
heading: we're going somewhere else. Talk of technique
"throws light" on poetry, but the last thing we need is light. St.
John of the Cross said, "If a man wants to be sure of his road,
he must close his eyes and walk in the dark."

Of Norwegian descent, Robert Bly was born in Madison, Minnesota,
a state he has lived in nearly all his life. He graduated from Harvard
in 1950 and received his M.A. from Iowa University in 1956. Married since 1955, he started his turbulent literary career with the
founding, in 1958, of the magazine *The Fifties* (later *The Sixties* and
The Seventies), attacking American poets for their "elegant
isolationism" and for failing to absorb the impulse of Surrealism like
poets in Europe and South America. His translations of Trakl, Vallejo, Ekelöf, Neruda, Tranströmer, Rilke, Lorca, Jiménez and
others, many of them published by his own Sixties Press, began to
remedy these deficiencies long before his own poems. The first
collection, *Silence in the Snowy Fields* (1962), shows little kinship with
French or Spanish Surrealism, an impulse which, reinforced by the
poet's political involvement, only became fully apparent in *The Light
Around the Body*. This collection was published one year after Bly, in
1966, had taken the occasion of a reading at Reed College to launch
American Writers Against the Vietnam War. Awarded the National
Book Award for his second volume, he handed over the prize money
to help young Americans "defy the draft authorities." A belligerent
individualist all his life, his more recent involvement with Eastern
mysticism seems to have brought Bly and his work *(The Morning
Glory,* 1969; *Sleepers Joining Hands,* 1973) into closer contact with
what he formerly saw as his opponents amongst the Beat poets and
"Olsonites."

Robert Bly

An owl on the dark waters
And so many torches smoking
By mossy stone
And horses that are seen riderless on moonlit nights
A candle that flutters as a black hand
Reaches out
All of these mean
A man with coins on his eyes

The vast waters
The cry of seagulls.

("Riderless Horses," B,L,58)

Poetry such as this gives Robert Bly an almost unique position in Anglo-American literature. With the possible exception of Philip Lamantia, one has, I think, to go back to *The Waste Land* to find lines that capture the phantasmagoria of the subconscious with comparable convincingness and magic:

A woman drew her long black hair out tight
And fiddled whisper music on those strings
And bats with baby faces in the violet light
Whistled, and beat their wings
And crawled head downward down a blackened wall
And upside down in air were towers
Tolling reminiscent bells, that kept the hours
And voices singing out of empty cisterns and exhausted wells.

("What the Thunder Said")

Even in Eliot's work, however, *The Waste Land* stands out as a unique and mysterious creation. Not surprisingly, it grew more and more alien to the author, to the point where he felt called upon to deprecate the poem as a "structureless" "piece of rhythmical grumbling" (E,IR,54) and a mere "relief of a personal and wholly insignificant grouse against life" (E,F,1). And there is little else in Anglo-American poetry which, like parts of *The Waste Land,* compares with the work of poets such as Éluard, Lorca, and Neruda.

Among the minor poets, David Gascoyne has (before Bly) made the most energetic attempt to launch a Surrealist movement in the English-speaking world. But his poetry at best offers examples of the consciously manipulated dream-imagery that Breton himself had condemned as a pseudo-form of automatic writing. And the theoretical position stated by the 19 year old poet in his *Short Survey of Surrealism* (1935) was abandoned two years later in favor of the programmatic intent to narrate in poetry "the contemporary Zeitgeist of Europe" (Ra,M,167f.).

Among the major poets, Wallace Stevens welcomed "The Irrational Element in Poetry" and predicted its absorption into the mainstream of Western literature. But he was both too rational and too traditional a poet to contribute much to that tendency himself (Ra,M,309). William Carlos Williams praised the Surrealists as well as Gertrude Stein for their linguistic experiments, but he could hardly sympathize with their psycho-ideological claims and programs while propagating a philosophy of "no ideas but in things." Ezra Pound, after 1922 increasingly absorbed by socio-economic issues, was blind to the poetic and epistemological achievement of Surrealism and incensed by its later Communist orientation. In an ill-tempered diatribe he accused "The Coward Surrealists" (1936) of ideological escapism and compared their revolutionary stance with the "dim ditherings of the æsthetes in 1888" (Ra,M,185). If such party prejudice could do little to stop the influence of Surrealism in England and America, Eliot's well-informed controversy with its claims and theories, conducted over a period of several years, was considerably more successful in doing so.

After all, Eliot himself, while under psychiatric treatment in Lausanne, had produced, in a spurt of semi-automatic writing, some of the greatest and deservedly most famous Surrealist poetry in world literature. But *The Waste Land,* written after a serious nervous breakdown, was largely an efflux of that unconscious which Eliot, when in better control of his psyche, tried to exclude from poetic creativity. Poetry, he stated as early as 1919, "is not a turning loose of emotion, but an escape from emotion; it is not the expression of personality, but an escape from personality" (E,E,21). After composing *The Waste Land,* he, of course, had to admit that there were periods in his life, mainly during "some forms of ill-health, debility or anæmia," when poetry had come to him like a mere "efflux . . . approaching the condition of automatic writing" (E,U,144). On principle, however, he had "no good word to say for the cultivation of automatic writing as the model of literary composition" (E,E,405). When asked whether he had ever felt the need for a new language to express the experience of his night mind, he answered with a definite *"no,"* and added: "I am not, as a matter of fact, particularly interested in my 'night-mind'" (Ra,M,185).

It is tantalizing to speculate what might have happened to the life and poetic career of Hart Crane if he had ever come into contact with the Surrealist poetry of France, Spain, or South America. Instead, it was *The Waste Land,* as seen through the distorting lens of its academic interpreters, which became the much admired model for *The Bridge* (1930), and it is tragically ironic how the critical dictates of its author, disseminated by the New Critics, came to cripple a creative impulse which came closer to Surrealism than that of any other of the major Anglo-American poets, with the possible exception of Dylan Thomas. Crane dreamt of a poetry that would "express its concepts in the . . . direct terms of physical-psychic experience," raising "the entire construction of the poem . . . on the organic principle of a 'logic of metaphor,' which antedates our so-called pure logic." But despite the precedent of Whitman's *Leaves of Grass,* which, as Crane himself put it, was issued in a "number of editions, each incorporating further additions,"[1]* he felt compelled to fit *The Bridge* into the Procrustean bed of an obsolete unity concept. Analogously, his imagery and syntax, which occasional exercises in automatic writing could have infused with greater ease and naturalness, were all too often bogged down in the over-elaborate convolutions of a self-conscious rhetoric and in a willful striving after symbolism, meaningfulness, and complexity.

It is with these examples in mind that Robert Bly had reason to claim in *The Fifties* that unlike Europe and South America, England and North America have practically "had no bold new poetry since the astounding daring of *The Waste Land,*" because the "other poetries have passed through surrealism; we have not." And in both Eliot and Pound, "the mind won over the unconscious without too much struggle—the old Puritan victory." The result was that after the "rather dry flurry of leftist poetry in the thirties . . . poetry has been getting older every year" (B,F,3,7-9). According to Bly, a genuine rejuvenation of Anglo-American poetry must gain its impulse from the model of foreign poetries, from a return to the "fertile internationalism" of early Pound and Eliot (B,IJ,38) which their very followers among the New Critics had sacrificed to an "elegant

*Notes to this section on p. 222.

isolationism" (B,S,6,22). To be sure, Pound as well as Eliot, when drawing on the French tradition, had neglected the poetry with Surrealist elements (e.g., Rimbaud's "Le Bateau ivre") in favor of a more Objectivist kind of poem (e.g., Rimbaud's "Au Cabaret-Vert"). But it was their undeniable achievement to have drawn attention to poets such as Nerval, Lautréamont, Baudelaire, Rimbaud, and Laforgue, who were the first to adopt underground passages of association, to dare enter the "dark valley" of the unconscious and thus prepare the advent of a new imagination which finally, around 1910, began to appear "all over the world" (B,F,1,36). To Bly, this is the "jerky," "jumping," or "leaping" imagination, swiftly passing from the conscious to the unconscious and producing a poetry in which images become the very content of the poem. "It seems to me," he wrote in *The Fifties,* "that the greatest tradition of all modern poetry, and the *avant-garde* for a century has been the heavy use of images" (B,F,2,14). Bly tends to avoid the term "deep image," which Robert Kelly and Jerome Rothenberg coined in 1961 and which has since become the most common label for the kind of poetry written by himself and other poets under his influence. On the other hand, there is little in his critical writings which yields a clearer and more accurate description of the term "image." We can only guess that Bly may mean something like the "expression of psychic force which suddenly becomes language" (G. Bachelard), which thinks *for* the poet (P. Éluard) (Ra,M,49) and which is close "to the psychological archetype of Jungian analysis" (R. Duncan,D,C,29). Bly himself has repeatedly referred to Freud and Jung as the fountainheads of the new imagination and has criticized Imagism for its lack of psychological depth: "The Imagists were misnamed," he wrote in *The Fifties,* because "they did not write in images from the unconscious" (B,F,3,8). An image such as Pound's "Petals on a wet, black bough" is a mere picture, whereas true images like Lorca's "death on the deep roads of the guitar" (B,F,1,37-8) bring "together different thoughts by inexplicable means" (B,S,5,81).

Even if Bly was right in claiming that American poetry had failed to traverse the "dark valley" of the unconscious, there was little in his first volume to suggest that he would make this journey himself. Granted, the poems in *Silence in the Snowy Fields* (1962) frequently mention the wind with its numinous afflatus, or death and darkness in which man has to immerse himself for his psychic rejuvenation; and there are the ubiquitous assertions that we "want to go back, to return to the sea," dive "into the sea of death," "go back among the dark roots," that we are "returning now to . . . the depth of the darkness," or are "falling into the open mouths of darkness."

But such language is at best reminiscent of D. H. Lawrence, whereas the imagery which poets like Lorca and Neruda have gathered from these archetypal depths hardly disturbs the almost idyllic *Silence in the Snowy Fields*. Instead, there are similes such as "The bare trees more dignified than ever, / Like a fierce man on his deathbed"; images which tell a little story or fairytale (e.g., the snowflakes "like jewels of a murdered Gothic prince / Which were lost centuries ago during a battle"); or, even more elaborate, the conceit-like expansion of an initial image that determines the structure and meaning of an entire poem, such as "Waking from Sleep":

> Inside the veins there are navies setting forth,
> Tiny explosions at the water lines,
> And seagulls weaving in the wind of the salty blood.
>
> It is the morning. The country has slept the whole winter.
> Window seats were covered with fur skins, the yard was full
> Of stiff dogs, and hands that clumsily held heavy books.
>
> Now we wake, and rise from bed, and eat breakfast!—
> Shouts rise from the harbor of the blood,
> Mist, and masts rising, the knock of wooden tackle in the
> sunlight.
> Now we sing, and do tiny dances on the kitchen floor.
> Our whole body is like a·harbor at dawn;
> We know that our master has left us for the day.
>
> (B,Si,13)

This is not to deny the aptness, beauty, and vividness of some of these images, or the mythopœic power of a stanza like the following:

> The strong leaves of the box-elder tree,
> Plunging in the wind, call us to disappear
> Into the wilds of the universe,
> Where we shall sit at the foot of a plant,
> And live forever, like the dust.
>
> ("Poem in Three Parts," B,Si,21)

However, there is little that is genuinely Surrealistic here, and even where Bly comes close to it, he is reminiscent less of Dali's minutely detailed hallucinatory psychographs than of Arnold Böcklin's late nineteenth century Romanticism with its weird, apocalyptic animals and statuesque mythic creatures inhabiting a crepuscular landscape of death:

> I know these cold shadows are falling for hundreds of miles,
> Crossing lawns in tiny towns, and the doors of Catholic
>   churches;
> I know the horse of darkness is riding fast to the east,
> Carrying a thin man with no coat.
>   ("The Clear Air of October," B,Si,52)

This seems like the world of a man in love with death, and indeed no other theme is more central to the poet's early work. However, there is none of Böcklin's sickly fascination with a death that is terrifying, but instead an almost Zen-like acquiescence to death as an inevitable part of life which the poet has learned to fear and love as much as life itself. "Through our dark lives," we read in one of his poems, "Like those before, we move to the death we love" (B,Si,32). What at first seems full of darkness and gloom is finally revealed as a world of serene happiness which Bly expresses in the most direct and simple terms. For at its basis lies the conviction that our human life is embedded in the larger life around us, and that despite death, it will continue there:

> Oh, on an early morning I think I shall live forever!
> I am wrapped in my joyful flesh,
> As the grass is wrapped in its clouds of green.
>   ("Poem in Three Parts," B,Si,21)

The final aim of Surrealism was a heightened level of consciousness from which "life and death," as Breton put it in the *Second manifeste du surréalisme* (1930), "le réel et l'imaginaire, le passé et le futur . . . cessent d'être perçus contradictoirement" (Br,M,76-7). The French Surrealists never reached that goal themselves. But they hewed a path through the obscure psychic woods of the Western subconscious from which later artists such as Jackson Pollock, Charles Olson, and John Cage have been able to emerge towards a new understanding of reality similar to that which Buddhist artists, for instance, have for centuries embodied in their music, painting, and poetry.

Before he began to publish his poetry, Bly spent several years in solitary self-confinement and analysis, a time he frequently remembers in his interviews and more recent poetry: "When I was alone, for three years, alone . . . in New York, in that great room / reading Rilke in the womanless loneliness" (B,Sl,58,59). It was here that he first found "the inward path I still walk on," and where one day he lost himself in the "curved energy" of an all-pervasive Godhead which "makes grass grow," "gives food to the dark cattle of the sea,"

or, as a kind of double, frequently invoked in Bly's poetry, shares the
poet's own personality:

> There is another being living inside me.
> He is looking out of my eyes.
> I hear him
> in the wind through the bare trees.
> ("Water Drawn Up into the Head," B,Sl,65)

Bly's first volume, *Silence in the Snowy Fields,* seems to show the poet
emerging, as if from a shamanistic journey, into the light of this new,
joyful consciousness. However, one poem, entitled "Unrest," stands
out from the rest like an open wound, foreshadowing the world of
Bly's future poetry. Here we have his first vision of the "strange
unrest [hovering] over the nation" that was to become the central
theme of his second volume, and which led him in 1967 to found,
with David Ray, American Writers Against the Vietnam War. And
here, for the first time, in a poem about his nation's society and
politics, we find the Surrealist imagery absent in the poems about
himself. Viewing the psycho-political disorder around him, the poet
retreats into the *selva oscura* of the unconscious he was personally
about to leave behind.

> A strange unrest hovers over the nation:
> This is the last dance, the wild tossing of Morgan's seas,
> The division of spoils. A lassitude
> Enters into the diamonds of the body.
> In high school the explosion begins, the child is partly killed.
> When the fight is over, and the land and the sea ruined,
> Two shapes inside us rise, and move away.
>
> But the baboon whistles on the shores of death—
> Climbing and falling, tossing nuts and stones,
> He gambols by the tree
> Whose branches hold the expanses of cold,
> The planets whirling and the black sun,
> The cries of insects, and the tiny slaves
> In the prisons of bark:
> Charlemagne, we are approaching your islands!
>
> We are returning now to the snowy trees,
> And the depth of the darkness buried in snow, through
>   which you rode all night

With stiff hands; now the darkness is falling
In which we sleep and awake—a darkness in which
Thieves shudder, and the insane have a hunger for snow,
In which bankers dream of being buried by black stones,
And businessmen fall on their knees in the dungeons of
    sleep.

(B,Si,25)

In using such images while writing about the outer world rather than about himself, Bly seems to depart from the original Surrealist impulse. And indeed, he has little interest in automatic writing. Breton's or Aragon's poetry appears to him "drab and squeaky" beside that of Lorca or Neruda, whose collection *Residencia en la tierra* he considers the "greatest surrealist poems yet written in a Western language." For Aragon and Breton "are poets of reason, who occasionally throw themselves backward into the unconscious, but Neruda, like a deep-sea crab, all claws and shell, is able to breathe in the heavy substances that lie beneath the daylight consciousness" (B,N,3) and at the same time he never loses his hold on concrete reality.

Bly himself heavily revises his own poetry, claiming that the approximately 1,000 lines of a recently published book, for instance, are based on about 100,000 actually written (B,IJ,30). Such conscious sifting and correcting, he is convinced, can probe deeper into the subconscious than any direct outpourings of the ego, while the process of creativity remains as open and unpredictable as in automatic writing. As he said in an interview, he often starts with a somehow striking line, "and then the unconscious keeps putting things in one after another that you were not quite aware of and at the end of the poem you feel amazed" (B,IL,63).

This process is reflected in the halting staccato of Surrealist images which in Bly's second volume, *The Light Around the Body* (1967), provide us with a nightmare vision of the American psyche. The fairy-tale world of his earlier work with its Arthur Rackham-like lyricism, Romantic oddity, and occasional cuteness (e.g., "This new snow seems to speak of virgins / With frail clothes made of gold, / Just as the old snow shall whisper / Of concierges in France," B,Si,16) has been transmogrified into the schizophrenic phantasmagoria of a painter like Richard Dadd. The bankers and businessmen who made their first appearance in "Unrest" are now part of a proliferating host of famous political figures, of types and characters from all walks of modern life, inhabiting a world of grotesque disfiguration, horror, and death, side by side with "strange plants," "curious many-eyed creatures," and other monsters. And all this is portrayed with such graphic precision and vivid plasticity that it evokes the illusion of a Surrealist wax figure cabinet.

Bly obviously had to sacrifice his hard-won personal serenity to achieve this vision. As he claims in his essay "On Political Poetry" (*The Nation,* April 24, 1967), the "life of a country can be imagined as a psyche larger than the psyche of anyone living," yet only the poet who has "such a grasp of his own concerns that he can leave them for a while" is able to penetrate into this socio-political unconscious and come back with a truly political poetry which (like Yeats's or Neruda's) transcends the mere versification of political opinions found in, for example, the works of Kenneth Fearing or Edwin Rolfe. As in "The Great Society," this Surrealist vision of contemporary life and politics ironically inverts the accepted image of that society, thus offering a critique of its actualities as powerful as any poetry of a directly polemical and propagandist orientation:

> Dentists continue to water their lawns even in the rain;
> Hands developed with terrible labor by apes
> Hang from the sleeves of evangelists;
> There are murdered kings in the light-bulbs outside movie
>   theaters;
> The coffins of the poor are hibernating in piles of new tires.
>
> The janitor sits troubled by the boiler,
> And the hotel keeper shuffles the cards of insanity.
> The President dreams of invading Cuba.
> Bushes are growing over the outdoor grills,
> Vines over the yachts and the leather seats.
>
> The city broods over ash cans and darkening mortar.
> On the far shore, at Coney Island, dark children
> Play on the chilling beach: a sprig of black seaweed,
> Shells, a skyful of birds,
> While the mayor sits with his head in his hands.
>
> (B,L,17)

Of course, a poem like "The Great Society," except for the irony of its title. is not political in any exclusive sense. That aim is part of the much larger attempt to change the general bourgeois consciousness which Bly, not unlike the French Surrealists, holds responsible for our destructive politics and general life style. Just as the establishment culture is dominated by hypocritical moralizing, pragmatic reasoning, and future-oriented ideology, the new consciousness and the poetry which is its medium should be characterized by a non-moralistic, pre-rational, and a-teleological outlook.

It was in this sense that Bly defended his friend James Wright against the attacks levelled at *The Branch Will Not Break* (1963) (B,S,8,59 ff.). Thom Gunn had criticized Wright for deliberately excluding "the operation of the discursive reason," and Larry Rubin had attacked his "willful refusal to enter into the business of inter-preting experience . . . and attempting to show relationships." In his retort, Bly simply questioned the validity of these criteria. What Gunn and Rubin posit as absolutes, he argued, boils down to the demand that Wright should "relate what he is describing to the great ideas of the Western World." "This is called 'giving meanings'" whereas the demand for "discursive reasoning" in poetry more often than not results in the handling of "accepted ideas" and "moral platitudes." Such "poetry of 'relationships'" may still dominate the English-speaking world, yet Wright and himself, Bly argued, are far from alone in their refusal to impose rational order and meaning on reality. After all, Chinese poets have written in this way for 3000 years, and amongst his contemporaries there is "the generation of '62 . . . Creeley, Wright, Snyder, etc., [which] represents a watershed in American poetry."

The fact that James Dickey, whom shortly before Bly had hailed as a fellow traveller and the "exact opposite of the fashionable 'my healthy limitations school'" (B,S,7,55), is not mentioned as a member of this group was a portent of what was to follow. For shortly after his article on Wright, Bly launched a blistering attack against *Buckdancer's Choice* (1965) (B,S,9,70-9), whose author he called "a huge, blubbery poet, pulling out Southern language in long strings, like taffy, a toady to the government, supporting all move-ments toward Empire, a sort of Georgia cracker Kipling." For a man pretending to advocate a poetry free from the platitudes of Western ideology and moralizing, the attack seems curiously self-defeating.

Echoing his article on Wright, Bly grants that "a true work of art . . . moves into deep and painful regions of the memory, to areas most people cannot visit without wincing." When Dickey, in "The Firebombing" and "Slave Quarters," portrays feelings of self-protective apathy and gloating joy over Western racial superiority and the destructive power provided by our technology, he not only, it seems to me, fulfills that function but extends it into the realm of his nation's psyche. And though his method is non-Surrealistic, it is no less truthful than Bly's in poems such as "Unrest" and "The Great Society." Bly criticizes Dickey's poetry for its "easy acceptance of brutality" and concomitant repulsiveness. Yet how could Dickey's poems be considered more repulsive than Bly's? And where in "Unrest" or "The Great Society" do we find "the real grief . . . [the] masculine and adult sorrow" which, according to Bly, can alone redeem that repulsiveness? It is the very absence of any such philanthropic attitudinizing which saves these poems from the "kitsch" Bly has attributed to "Slave Quarters," and which gives them the terrifying and cathartic power they possess.

The issues at stake here are as old as the genre in which Dickey's poems are composed. It is true that the speakers in "Slave Quarters" and "The Firebombing" are not as clearly individualized as the personæ of Robert Browning, and that it is often difficult to dissociate them from the author. Yet even Victorian dramatic monologues, as nineteenth-century critics were the first to realize, are characterized by a strange amalgam of "subjective objectivity." Just as the most confessional of poets has to resort to some "oblique, objective, or dramatic way of expression,"[2] so Browning, giving words to a murderer and sexual psychopath like Porphyria's Lover, could only do so by transmogrifying, through his empathetic imagination, what was part of himself into the character of his poem. Although he was far more concerned than Dickey to invest his personæ with all the trappings of an autonomous individuality, there were enough critics who identified these characters with the author and accused him of the cynicism of Bishop Blougram or the dissoluteness of Fra Lippo Lippi.

The confusion persists, and Bly, while making fun of the "jabber about 'personæ,'" hardly clarifies the issue by declaring that in "Slave Quarters" "the umbilical cord [between author and speaker] has not been cut. Mr. Dickey is not standing outside the poem." It is far more convincing when Dickey, in an indirect answer to these charges, points out that

> Every poem written—and particularly those which make use of a figure designated in the poem as "I"—is both an exploration and an invention of identity. . . . A true poet can write with utter convincingness about "his" career as a sex murderer, and then in the next poem with equal conviction about tenderness and children and self-sacrifice. As Keats says, it is simply that the poet "has no personality." I would say, rather, that he has a personality large enough to encompass and explore each of the separate, sometimes related, sometimes unrelated, personalities that inhabit him, as they . inhabit us all. (Di,S,155,161)

To be sure, Bly's criticism, if taken *cum grano salis*, is not entirely irrelevant. For a poet using personæ without the techniques of multiperspective fragmentation developed by Pound, Eliot, and Williams, or without the self-transcendence achieved by D. H. Lawrence, somehow remains caught within a closed ego system. In other words, it seems doubtful whether anybody writing in the second half of this century can adopt a genre as obsolete as the dramatic monologue without falling into patterns, clichés, and sentiments typical of a previous age and alien to our literary sensibility as well as to our understanding of man in our time. And indeed, if poems such as "Slave Quarters" avoid these pitfalls by the compelling urgency of their subject and sheer technical brilliance, there are other poems by Dickey which sound like unintentional parodies of Browning. Keats' prophetic notion of the "chameleon poet" without a personality found an embodiment, appropriate for its time, in the Victorian poet and the proliferating multitude of "men and women" he projected in his dramatic lyrics. But modern man has learned to see his ego as immersed in Jung's collective unconscious, as only another object or event in Whitehead's open-ended universe of interrelated forces, or even as the final emptiness of Eastern philosophy. And it is possible that no great poetry can be written now which precludes an awareness of such insights.

In "The Teeth Mother Naked at Last" from a more recent volume of verse, *Sleepers Joining Hands* (1974), Bly attempts a solution for some of these problems. A combination of Neruda's Surrealism with Ginsberg's Whitmanesque rhetoric and Pound's techniques of fragmentation, the poem in its indictment of the Vietnam war reads like an indirect answer to "The Firebombing" and its "easy acceptance of brutality." "The Firebombing," Bly had written, "has no real anguish. If the anguish were real . . . we would stop what we were doing, we would break the television set with an axe, we would throw ourselves on the ground sobbing" (B,S,9,74). Yet it is exactly where it translates these gestures into verse that "The Teeth Mother" has the least effect on the reader:

> If a child came by burning, you would dance on a lawn,
> trying to leap into the air, digging into your cheeks,
> you would ram your head against the wall of your bedroom
> like a bull penned too long in his moody pen—
>
> If one of those children came toward me with both hands
> in the air, fire rising along both elbows
> I would suddenly go back to my animal brain,

I would drop on all fours, screaming,
my vocal chords would turn blue, so would yours,
it would be two days before I could play with my own children
   again.

                                        (B,SI,25)

My anguish is far more real when I consider the diabolic destructiveness in the following lines from "The Firebombing," regardless
of whether the speaker voices the poet's own feelings or not. For if he
does, it is only to Dickey's credit that he portrayed himself with the
unflinching objectivity even poets frequently reserve for the more
attractive aspects of their personality:

> All leashes of dogs
> Break under the first bomb, around those
> In bed, or late in the public baths: around those
> Who inch forward on their hands
> Into medicinal waters.
> Their heads come up with a roar
> Of Chicago fire:
> Come up with the carp pond showing
> The bathhouse upside down,
> Standing stiller to show it more
> As I sail artistically over
> The resort town followed by farms,
> Singing and twisting
> All the handles in heaven kicking
> The small cattle off their feet
> In a red costly blast
> Flinging jelly over the walls
> As in a chemical war-
> fare field demonstration.
> With fire of mine like a cat
>
> Holding onto another man's walls,
> My hat should crawl on my head
> In streetcars, thinking of it,
> The fat on my body should pale.

                                        (Di,P,184-5)

Bly must have come to recognize some of the contradictions pointed
out when he declared, in 1972, that he "didn't criticize [Dickey] on
moral grounds," and granted him the rank of an "extraordinary
man, almost a genius" with "this quality of thinking about these

negative things and trying to write about them." And it is easier to agree with Bly when he limits his criticism to the fact that Dickey's "imaginative form starts to collapse" and that "in terms of metaphor and action [he] has stopped going through the skin," which, according to Bly, separates Western man from his inner spiritual life (B,IL,59-60).

This change may partly be due to Bly's increasing immersion in Buddhist philosophy, which largely confirmed—but also deepened and modified—the beliefs he had held from the very beginnings of his poetic career. "In the last eight or nine, ten years," he confessed in 1972, "the thinking I've learned most from has been Buddhist" (B,IL,50). Buddhism also seems to have given him a maturity which is reflected not only in the softening of his attitude towards Dickey and others but in the greater complexity of his more recent poetry. Bly sounded convincing enough when in his earliest collection he wrote lines such as

> through our dark lives
> Like those before, we move to the death we love.
>
> (B,Si,32)

And his acceptance of death as well as the Zen Buddhist-like serenity derived from it may well have evolved from a long spiritual struggle. It is all the more admirable that Bly was ready to repeat, on the level of our socio-political consciousness, the journey through the "dark valley" of the subconscious, which he had personally already brought to a resolution. And the results speak for themselves. In lines like the following, which, in a fusion of his early and middle styles, seem to expose his hard-won serenity to the horror and suffering of the world around him, a new tone of harassing self-analysis and genuine sorrow emerges:

> I decide that death is friendly.
> Finally death seeps up through the tiniest capillaries of my
> toes.
> I fall into my own hands,
>   fences break down under horses,
> cities starve, whole towns of singing women carrying to the
> burial fields
>   the look I saw on my father's face,
> I sit down again, I hit my own body,
> I shout at myself, I see what I have betrayed.
> What I have written is not good enough.
> Who does it help?

I am ashamed sitting on the edge of my bed.
("The Night Journey in the Cooking Pot," B,SI,62-3)

Buddhism also must have brought Bly a clearer understanding of his own philosophical and poetical position and to some extent transformed his attitude towards those American poets who are engaged in a similar quest. In the past, for instance, he has often reprimanded Ginsberg for his obscenity, "unkindness," and "fear of the unconscious," or for giving up "all hope of imaginative precision and delicacy" (B,S,4,38;5,70;6,40). But more recently, he has hailed him as "the rebirth of a very powerful spiritual man" and as a fellow traveller in a common pursuit who, unlike Gary Snyder and himself, has gained his access to a new consciousness "not through the Tibetans and Japanese—but through the Hindus." With obvious approval Bly quotes Ginsberg's remarks about the psycho-physiological basis of poetic language, that "as soon as you have a new syntax," for instance, "you have a new way of breathing and as soon as you have that you have a new consciousness" (B,IL,54,59).

These, of course, are insights closely akin to, if not inspired by those of Olson. Yet, ironically, it is the latter's position, above all, which seems to have eluded Bly in his search for a new poetry and poetics. Bly's accusation that Olson embodies the "formalist obsession" of American poetry hardly needs refuting, while his contention that both form and content are "expressions of a certain rebellious energy rising in the psyche" (B-M,P,163-4) is not too far a cry from Olson's (or rather Creeley's) famous dictum that "form is never more than an extension of content" or that "if one taps, via psyche, plus a 'true' adherence of Muse, one does reveal 'Form'" (O,W,16,29). And in the light of Buddhist philosophy it should be easy to understand that Olson's Objectism does not imply a positivist approach to nature or an evasion of self, but a quest complementary rather than opposed to that of Bly or Surrealism generally.

To Bly, however, Objectivism is no more than the theoretical formula for a failing more widespread than any other in American poetry—for the absorption in things, which, as he wrote in *The Sixties*, "is shared by almost all the poets in America today... It is the quality that the poetry of Lowell and of Merwin has in common with that of the Beats, as well as with the poetry of the Black Mountain group, who after Charles Olson and William Carlos Williams emphasize 'objects' and 'objectivism'" (B,S,4,39). All this may be true, though even Williams, the most famous and uncompromising practitioner of such thingyness in verse, at least *strove* for the inwardness Bly finds lacking in his poetry. "A life that is here and now is timeless," he wrote in 1939. "That is the universal I am seeking: to embody that in a work of art, a new world that is always 'real'" (W,E,196). Such timelessness reached by an absorption in the *hic et nunc* has, of course, been the universal aim of mystics of all traditions and is a notion central to most Eastern philosophies. The Zen Buddhists, for instance, call it *ekakṣaṇa*, which in Suzuki's paraphrase is the "eternal Now" or "absolute present" (Su,W,268) reflected in the "momentariness of *sumi* paintings and *haiku*" (Wa,W,199) as well as of most Sino-Japanese art and poetry. In this way the famous Chinese poet Tu Fu, whom Bly quotes as a model for real inwardness (B,S,4,39), might well have preferred Williams' poetics to the Surrealist manifestoes or to Rimbaud's plea that the poet should "par un long, immense et raisonné *dérèglement* de *tous les sens*" try to immerse himself into the unknown of "l'âme universelle" (R,W,306-8). And where, one might ask, does a lyric like the following by Tu Fu differ markedly from any of Williams' shorter "Objectivist" poems?

> The catkins line the lanes,
>   making white carpets,
> And leaves on lotus streams
>   spread like green money:
>
> Pheasants root bamboo shoots,
>   nobody looking,
> While ducklings on the sands
>   sleep by their mothers.[3]

Yet, granting the ultimately mystical orientation of Williams' poetic aims, there remains the more serious question of whether he or any of his Western peers can, like some Eastern poets, reach this goal by a mere empathetic immersion in objective reality. It is the very model of Zen Buddhism which has led many of his followers to the erroneous belief that such a shortcut to a new consciousness is generally accessible.

Zen teaches its disciples to ignore and avoid hallucinations and dreams and instead to focus on the pre-conceptual suchness of reality. Yet such a seeming rejection of the unconscious is the outcome of a struggle that lasted more than two millennia, so that the "participation mystique" (Lévy-Bruhl) with the subconscious, which may be a matter of painful and strenuous therapeutic effort for a Westerner, has long been a readily available experience for the Buddhist. And even Suzuki, a more recent exponent of the doctrine, defines *ekakṣaṇa* as "the awakening of consciousness out of the darkest recesses of the unconscious" (Su,W,268); while the pre-Christian

Lankavatara Scripture, the most important of the Sutras for the evolution of Zen Buddhism, reads like a running commentary on what, in Jungian terms, we would now call the collective unconscious—that "memory of . . . discriminations, desires, attachments and deeds [which] is stored in Universal Mind since beginningless time, and is still being accumulated," that "habit-energy" which "like a magician . . . causes phantom things and people to appear and move about" (Go,B,300 ff.). The "intuitive mind" which is able to penetrate beyond the conscious and unconscious world helps us understand the dream-like emptiness of both: "The discriminating-mind is a dancer and a magician with the objective world as his stage. Intuitive-mind is the wise jester who travels with the magician and reflects upon his emptiness and transiency. Universal Mind keeps the record and knows what must be and what may be." Yet, again and again, it is emphasized that the final insight into the unruffled quietude of Universal Mind can only be reached by traversing the unconscious to the point of a sudden " 'turning about' at the deepest seat of consciousness."

It is only beyond this stage that all dichotomies of good and evil, past and future, inward and outward, and, above all, the duality of subject and object cease to be seen as opposites—not, however, by an extinction of the mind but by its tranquilization. Just as the "old body" continues to operate, so the "mind-system, because of its accumulated habit-energy, goes on functioning." To talk of the egolessness of either the self or the non-self would therefore be as pointless as to assert their essentiality. Both are "neither real nor unreal," so that their relationship, as one Zen expert puts it, "becomes a real relationship, a mutuality in which the subject creates the object just as much as the object creates the subject. The knower no longer feels himself to be independent of the known; the experiencer no longer feels himself to stand apart from the experience" (Wa,W,120).

Modern quantum mechanics teaches a similar lesson, and it was from its combination with the Eastern philosophy he knew through reading Jung that Olson derived his theory of Objectism. According to Heisenberg's Indeterminacy Principle, which the poet repeatedly invokes in his writings, "it is impossible to measure the simultaneous place and speed of a nuclear particle with absolute exactitude" for (in Olson's paraphrase) "a thing can be measured in its mass only by arbitrarily assuming a stopping of its motion, or in its motion only by neglecting, for the moment of measuring, its mass" (O,W,61). As Heisenberg points out in more general terms, we can only gather knowledge about our relationship to nature, never about nature as separate from the observer, so that rigid dichotomies such as internal versus external, soul versus body, and subject versus object lose their validity.[4] Objectism—which in his "Projective Verse" essay of 1950 Olson defined as "the getting rid of the lyrical interference of the individual as ego, of the 'subject' and his soul"—is a reinterpretation of Williams' and Zukofsky's Objectivism in the light of these insights. In contrast to Objectivism, Objectism is not conceived of as the opposite of subjectivism, nor is man seen in contrast to nature. For man, as Olson says, "is himself an object" (O,W,24).

Analogously, Olson, in his lifelong concern with the poetic image, held a position not at all unlike Bly's. Needless to say, Olson opposed "the suck of symbol which has increased and increased since the great Greeks first promoted the idea of a transcendent world of forms" (O,W,61) and he tried to limit the use of that term to what he believed to be its original meaning: "Greek *symbolon*, 'a sign by which one knows or infers a thing'" (O,M,11). In this way, Olson was fond of quoting a slightly altered sentence from the Taoist treatise *The Secret of the Golden Flower* as the sum total of what he "had to offer": "That which exists through itself, is what is called meaning" (originally: "the Way [Tao]") (O,T,61).[5] Meaning, in other words, is identical with, not referential to, pre-conceptual reality or suchness—identical with things viewed (as Shao Yung, another Taoist put it) "not subjectively but from the viewpoint of things" (Ba,C,451). A Western poet in search of such reality, however, must first traverse the "dark valley" of the unconscious, and then, in the attempt to express himself, contend with the final incommunicability of such insight.

Olson, albeit vaguely, seems to have been aware of both these problems. He knew that it was only by using images, and avoiding allegory, symbolism, and discursive logic, that the poet could stay close to the suchness of things, and that his images, in order to express this "meaning," have to be imbued with both the world of the conscious and of the unconscious. This, I think, is the meaning of a cryptic note Olson jotted down in 1955: "An image is truth, not image, except as without image it is impossible to present truth (An image may be defined as any proximate object to which there is a flow of feeling) The conversion of archetypes to working images."[6] In insisting on the fluidity and dynamism of such imagery, Olson again almost seems to anticipate Bly's plea for a poetry that evokes "that swift movement all over the psyche, from conscious to unconscious, from a pine table to mad inward desires" (B-M,P,163). To Olson an image should not be a static picture, but a "vector." "As the Master said to me in the dream, of rhythm is image / of image is knowing / of knowing there is / a construct" (O,U,121).

Of course, it is one thing to explicate Olson's poetics and another to evaluate its general influence. And no doubt it was the latter which inspired and, to a degree, justified Robert Bly's criticisms. In this way, his single-minded and sometimes over-aggressive attacks on Olson and the "elegant isolationism" (B,S,6,22) of American poets generally, have performed a salutary function. The image of Bly as the Surrealist opponent to Objectivism may therefore soon come to be replaced by that of the poet who helped relate American open form poetics back to some of its European origins.

[1]See Hart Crane, *The Letters*, ed. B. Weber (Berkeley: University of California Press, 1965), p. 239; *The Complete Poems and Selected Letters and Prose*, ed. B. Weber (London: Oxford University Press, 1968), p. 221; J. Unterecker, *Voyager: A Life of Hart Crane* (New York: Farrar, Straus and Giroux, 1969), p. 590.

[2]See E. Faas, *Poesie als Psychogramm* (Munich: W. Fink Verlag, 1974), pp. 11, 143 ff.

[3]"Wandering Breezes: 8," *Li Po and Tu Fu*, ed. A. Cooper (Harmondsworth: Penguin Books, 1973), p. 205.

[4]*Das Naturbild der heutigen Physik* (Hamburg: Rowohlt Verlag, 1972), pp. 18, 28.

[5]See also *The Secret of the Golden Flower*, ed. R. Wilhelm (London: Routledge and K. Paul, 1972), p. 21.

[6]Quoted by R. von Hallberg, "Olson, Whitehead and the Objectivists," *boundary 2*, 2:2 (Fall 1973 - Winter 1974), 85-111,107.

Robert Bly

Faas: To what degree do you acknowledge Philip Lamantia and David Gascoyne as predecessors for your own attempts to introduce Surrealism into Anglo-American poetry?

BLY: My view of Surrealism came entirely from Spanish and South American Surrealism.

Faas: It seems to me that in your earlier poetry collected in *Silence in the Snowy Fields* you are influenced by D. H. Lawrence.

BLY: No. *Silence in the Snowy Fields* looks back to Synge; and a couple of translations that Frank O'Connor made of medieval Irish work which moved me greatly; and then there is Antonio Machado. He is the father of that book.

D. H. Lawrence

Faas: And you hadn't read D. H. Lawrence at all at the time?

BLY: I had read a few poems, but among the English, Wordsworth is a much deeper influence.

Faas: But then there is all that imagery of going into the depths, into the dark and into the sea of death, etc., which seems exactly like Lawrence.

BLY: No link. I never read much of D. H. Lawrence's poetry until someone gave me the three-volume edition four or five years later. The only one I knew well was "Bavarian Gentians," which I think is a great great great great poem.

Faas: That's the poem I was thinking of, actually.

BLY: I still learn much from Lawrence, not from his poetry, but from the motion that he made from the intellect and down into the body.

Faas: So you do respect him.

BLY: Oh tremendously. The essay in the middle of *Sleepers Joining Hands* is full of mad generalizations for which I first saw the possibility in *Fantasia of the Unconscious*. Why not? A book of unsupportable generalizations about things that interest us. I don't think my essay would exist without *Fantasia of the Unconscious*.

Faas: There is an interesting book about Surrealism by C. Kellerer,

who claims that Western art, after a transitional period of Surrealism, or after crossing the "dark psychic woods of the
Surrealism   unconscious," as you would call it, is moving closer and
and Zen   closer to a Zen Buddhist approach to reality. Does that
kind of general overview make sense to you? Kellerer
describes Pollock as approaching Eastern calligraphic painting
techniques, for instance.

BLY: We could imagine a poetry in which a great "flowing" consciousness is present, and the outer world is also present. In ancient
Buddhist art the world is very very very very present. The artist is
aware of it all the time. Such an artist would never do as Pollock does
and scatter it around like this, because in doing so he has dissolved
the world, he has returned to the state of the infant in which the
world is not clear. I respect Pollock a great deal, but I would think he
is the *end* of a Western tradition and that he has nothing to do with
the calligraphers, because the calligraphers are dealing with content.
When they are doing a calligraphy, every one of their curves to them
has the shape of a mountain or a moon in mist.

Faas: And you don't think that the impulse of action painting could
finally incorporate that concreteness?

BLY: I don't know. The tendency now is for everything in art to
break the link with the adult energy of the unconscious, if you can
say such a thing, and instead to proceed back towards the crib. The
baby is also spontaneous. So you have two movements
here, which appear alike, but are not. There is a very
infantilization   interesting book entitled *Man-Child: A Study of the Infantilization of Man* by David Jonas and Doris Klein. It is an
impressive book. If the infantilism continues, all the things Lawrence stood for will be destroyed. I've just translated a poem by H.
Martinson about D. H. Lawrence:

> You waited for the hour when all things would take on soul
>   again,
> and taste, feeling, and soul would touch them,
> as the day of inwardness came.
>
> But the world was extroverted.
> Only misunderstanding really thrived.
>
> The new deep communion you sang of did not happen.
> The interior table was set,
> but only a few came
> and only a few of those were capable of eating.

The rest came out of a meaningless curiosity.

The church in the body had to be locked up.
Now it stands open to the storm of steel, given over
to the demons of extroversion.

It's a good poem, and it gives another way to understand pop art.
Pop art makes sense to me in terms of infantilization. The sense of
adulthood is weak with us; it is stronger in the European psyche, and
even more so in the Chinese. They imagine adulthood as the ability
to balance *yin* and *yang*.

Let's return to Surrealism and open form. Both are launch
points into the unknown. We launch out, and go away
from patriarchal form, and then what happens? There is
a powerful magnet over there, not far away, near the wall.
It is the magnet of the crib, or the cradle, or "the Primitive
man." It is too strong in America; it's too strong! It pulls art down
into the crib, it pulls it backward. The "New York School" of recent
years in art and poetry has not gone forward into the union of *yang*
and *yin* as the ancient Chinese art and poetry did. Chinese artists
moved for a thousand years into adult minglings of *yin* and *yang*, of
mist and discipline. We go a little way away from the patriarchal and
start to curve down. The lethargy in the colleges is a form of infantilism.

Faas: You once said that "the road to the new brain goes through the
forest." That, in a way, seems to summarize what you have been
talking about right now.

BLY: Yes, following that imagery, what we do is we find a gingerbread house in the forest and stay there. We never bother to put the
witch into her own oven. We just ask for more cookies.

The Sufis and the Buddhists leave the gingerbread house and
aim for an adult consciousness. But in order to reach that, the soul
has to go through the mammal brain, which means it has to go into
human suffering and into the body, into a deep sexual life. Lawrence says a man, like a flower, is "fertilized" by a strong sexual
experience.

As Americans, we have to go through the mammal brain, but we
don't want to do that. We went into the Vietnam war and did all that
reptile killing and we now refuse to go through the mammal grief. I
ended the reading last night with poems of Kabir, and the students'
faces lit up all over the room. It was beautiful. That ecstasy is what
they want more than anything, but they don't want to or know how to

go through the mammal brain in order to get there.

Faas: Of course, that's an impression that one frequently gets in America, that people think they can take a shortcut to the new consciousness.

BLY: And one has to say in favor of Ted Hughes that he goes through the mammal, though he may not arrive at the new brain . . . The new brain is not so prominent in him. As Marie Louise von Franz would say, he is a little "caught" by black magic, and black magic hates the new brain. He's a little "caught" there. That's expressed by the crow, which is black. He wants someone to take him and bring him out, someone to bring him out of that. But there is nobody that's that far in, so nobody can help him. I see him as a suffering mammal, a great suffering mammal.

Faas: Are there any contemporary artists whose work parallels what you are trying to achieve in poetry?

BLY: I feel a strong kinship with Morris Graves, Max Ernst, de Kooning, Jean Arp, and with some work of Rauschenberg. To me Max Ernst is great, inexhaustible. I don't know any recent Surrealist poetry that comes near his *Une semaine de bonté.*

Surrealist art

Faas: But isn't that still deep "in the forest"?

BLY: Certainly, oh yes.

Faas: But do you see any glimpses of light from the open country on the other side?

BLY: There is something luminous about his paintings, the open country is floating all through them. The open country lives in Jean Arp's sculpture also.

Faas: But I was thinking of more recent art.

BLY: Well, Rauschenberg, I think, is a genius—sometimes!

Faas: But how about your criticism of pop art?

BLY: Rauschenberg is not only a pop artist.

pop art

Faas: I remember your saying that pop art—in Lawrence's terms—is putting the umbrella up again where Surrealism had taken it down.

BLY: Did I? Lawrence said that when you look up, in most centuries, you do not see the black sky with stars, but instead an opened umbrella on which artists have painted some stars. Humanity prefers that, it is less scary. A strong artist will tear holes in the umbrella so you can see the stars again. Eliot did that, so did the Surrealists. The whole Andy Warhol school is just putting the umbrella up again. I like Lawrence's image—it explains a lot to me. None of Warhol's movies tear open anything, just as pornography never tears open anything, it closes instead. The point of commercial pornography is to prevent you from experiencing. This is only my opinion; most people don't agree with me.

Faas: No, I wouldn't either.

BLY: Most people think Andy Warhol is part of the avant-garde, I don't.

Faas: To me, your poetic development shows a curious reversal of the development we talked about in relation to Kellerer's book. In this way, *Silence in the Snowy Fields* seems to have been written, not by a man "deep in the forest" of the unconscious, but by one who has traversed that forest and has come out the other side. You have often referred to a period of depression, solitude, and self-analysis, in New York, I gather, before you began to write poetry, and I wondered how that period relates to your first collection of poetry and what kind of experiences you went through during that period. poetic development

BLY: I'd rather not talk about that very much. But you're right in your sense of the order. I did write some Surrealism before *Silence in the Snowy Fields.* I didn't put it in because I didn't want to break the tone of *Silence.*

Faas: So biographically speaking your development doesn't really reverse the general historical one in which Surrealism seems to precede the kind of consciousness which must have inspired *Silence in the Snowy Fields.*

BLY: But then there is no reason that Surrealism cannot return later. At any point it may be necessary for you to return to the confusion of the unconscious again.

Faas: But you don't want to talk about that period in New York.

BLY: I describe it in the autobiographical poem in *Sleepers Joining Hands* as well as I can. I was simply living in a small room, very poor. [Pause] Anyway it wasn't a period in which I did much writing. I understood Sartre's *Nausea* very well in those days. I didn't care for Sartre at all until I had been there for about two years, until I picked it up. I read the first five pages and I felt weak, almost fainted.

Faas: Most American poets seem to bypass the crisis described in *Nausea,* I mean the whole consciousness and language crisis which had such a devastating effect on many European poets—actually destroyed them as poets. Like Hugo von Hofmannsthal, for instance, who was probably the first to undergo that experience. He wrote all his greatest poetry before he turned 24, then suffered the crisis he describes in his the language crisis famous "Lord Chandos Letter" (1902), and after that just stopped writing poetry. Of course, what Gary Snyder says concerning this whole problem makes sense to me: that a poet like Hofmannsthal really wanted to be some kind of philosopher-magus.

BLY: That language crisis involves the emotion of disgust. "You are defiled by what comes out of your mouth."

Faas: That's like the phrase Hofmannsthal uses in the "Lord Chandos Letter": that words seemed to disintegrate in his mouth like mouldering mushrooms . . . What I'd like to discuss is the your concept of the image.

"deep image"   BLY: I'm not fond of the term "deep image."

Faas: Yes, I noticed that you avoid it in your criticism. But you have never given a detailed description or definition of what you mean by image.

BLY: Let's try to make a distinction between "projection" and "image." Pound and Eliot both believed that a feeling is best kept fresh in art by being "projected" onto the outer world. "Smells of steaks in passageways" becomes an objective correlative of a certain feeling of mingled fatigue and despair Eliot experienced when he entered rooming houses. The substances "smells," "steaks," and "passageways" can all be taken out of the work of art and re-inserted back into the world. So they are "objective." Eliot doesn't use projection exclusively, he uses it mostly. Then, if "smells of steaks in passageways" is a projection of an inner fatigue out onto objects, what is an "image"? I'll quote some lines of Lorca, and then of Trakl:

> I want to sleep for half a second,
> a second, a minute, a century,
> but I want everyone to know that I'm still alive,
> that I am the little friend of the west wind,
> that I am the elephantine shadow of my own tears.

Somehow the psychic energy has remained inside the psyche, and there it created a new substance, "the elephantine shadow of my own tears." Trakl says:

> On silver soles I climbed down the thorny stairs, and I walked into the white-washed room. A light burned there silently, and without speaking I wrapped my head in purple linen; and the earth threw out a child's body, a creature of the moon, that slowly stepped out of the darkness of my shadow, and with broken arms dropped over a stony waterfall, fluffy snow.

You notice that the psyche is in a state of great energy. Moving with its own immense energy, it becomes equal to the world. Instead of depending on the outer world for support, it begins somehow to create a third world, neither "physical" nor "inner."

It's as if a human being and a badger together would give birth to an angel. Or as if an angel and a tree give birth to a bridge. It's as if a bull woke up one day with so creating a third world much energy, he ignored the fence-posts and barn-door of his pasture and created Assyria instead.

We're so used to "fence-post and barn-door poetry" we don't recognize what Lorca is doing. We all write barn-door poetry. Most political poetry is barn-door poetry, and most love poetry now.

The phrase "deep image" suggests a geographical location in the psyche. It misses what the bull does. So I didn't feel that Robert Kelly caught the physicalness of the image in his "deep image" essay. Kelly has a wonderfully strong mind, but it's not especially physical. Rothenberg's mind is more physical.

Faas: I spent a day with Rothenberg several months ago, and liked him a lot.

BLY: He and I were friends, and still are, and we had conversations and planned magazines in which we tried to bring forward ideas of this sort. He did "Poems of the Floating World" . . .

Faas: Let me quote a few phrases by Duncan, who says that the image should be "close to the psychological archetype of Jungian analysis" or that it should be an "evocation of depth . . . not unrelated to the neo-Platonic images." Also he Duncan on image says that the image should be a "received sign of the great language in which the universe itself is written."

BLY: I like the last one best. I get sick of hearing Plato's name spoken of in every discussion of the image. I agree an image can be "close" to an archetype, but the way to ruin a poem is to put in a lot of archetypes. I insist the image is a physical thing, and Plato doesn't know a thing about that.

We don't have to work on this. [Pointing to his brain] We become "successful" through *this*, but the mysterious thing is that art is created with this. [Pointing to his heart] What was the last one again?

Faas: The image is a "received sign of the great language in which the universe itself is written," which is really an Orphic concept.

BLY: And Orpheus, as you know, decided to go down here. [Pointing to his body]

Faas: The first one makes most sense to me.

BLY: They all make "sense," but it's a question of tone.

Faas: So you would hesitate to formulate a phrase or definition like that.

BLY: I would try to avoid it.

Faas: Like associating the image with Jungian archetypes and so forth.

BLY: I hate the word archetype.

Faas: Can you make any statement as to how images originate in your consciousness?

BLY: No.

Faas: Why not?

BLY: I don't *want* to make any statements on that. If I do, in this rapid tone, I'd make it with my thinking function. It wouldn't be just to the experience to describe it with one-fourth of the brain!

Faas: Did you know that Duncan has criticized Imagism in almost the exact same terms you use?

BLY: I'm not surprised.

Faas: How does your admiration for Chinese poetry relate to all this? After all, there don't seem to be many images like "death in the deep roads of the guitar" in Chinese poetry.

BLY: On the contrary, there are lots, and we can't get them through the English language, because the translators are used to "projection" poetry and they translate the poems into the barn-door poetry they know. Until Trakl's and Lorca's true image poetry penetrates to the minds of the scholars who translate Chinese, until that happens, we will be blind to Chinese poetry. In the meantime we have A. C. Graham's translations of *Poems of the Late T'ang.* In Li Ho you'll see images almost too wild to be disguised.

Chinese Sur-
realist poetry

Faas: So you would say that there is a very strong element in Far Eastern poetry of what in Western terminology we'd call Surrealist imagery?

BLY: Oh yes, very strong. Another way of talking about their sophistication would be to talk of the union of the senses. Here is a little poem of Bashō's. He is listening to the temple bells in his garden.

> The temple bell stops,
> but the sound keeps coming
> out of the flowers.

Bashō has taken a sound and changed it into an odor. That's someting that an Imagist couldn't do, or at least has not, to my knowledge, done. This art belongs to the whole area of changing of substances and transforming them. The ancient Chinese and Japanese poetry is far ahead of ours. American students in the poetry workshops have a hard time bringing an odor in its natural form into a poem, so we smell it as an odor. It's rare to hear a sound that's not a language sound in an American poem! It's rare to see green in a poem! Imagine being so at home in them that you could transform them!

Faas: How do you relate to Breton's concept of automatic writing? Do you think it's a useful exercise?

BLY: No.

Faas: My feeling is that exercises in automatic writing, even if they wouldn't have produced the actual poetry, could have had a very liberating effect on Hart Crane, for instance.

automatic writing

BLY: Automatic writing to me has more to do with Freud than with poetry.

Faas: That's more or less how T. S. Eliot felt about it, although he had to admit that parts of *The Waste Land* were composed in an efflux of poetry approaching the condition of automatic writing.

BLY: That's probably why it doesn't hold together as a work of art. Automatic writing evidently comes from fragmented parts of the psyche; and they are not connected to the whole and they are just like men at the edges of the raft crying, trying to make one realize that they're out there; and he brought too many of them into *The Waste Land;* the result is that it falls apart as a work of art. Its victory was a human victory, of compassion and listening.

The Waste Land

Faas: Of course, later he became almost ashamed of his poem, calling it a mere piece of rhythmical grumbling.

BLY: That's so typical. What he's gone through he feels obliged to deny to others. But there are real images in *The Waste Land:* "bats with baby faces in the violet light / Whistled, and beat their wings / And crawled head downward down a blackened wall . . ."Bats with baby faces in the violet light cannot be inserted into the universe or taken away. The are something insane, from another world.

Faas: At the beginning of my essay I compare these lines with some of yours.

BLY: I'd like to see it. I love that passage, love it, love it.

Faas: I'd like to come back to your concept of creativity for a moment. In my studies of Chinese æsthetics I found that the ancient literati talk a lot more about painting techniques than about poetic creativity.

Chinese æsthetics

BLY: It's not really worth investigating maybe; it would be different for every poet.

Faas: Whereas the painter calligraphists seem to be talking about the same thing most of the time: a kind of gestural automatism, a complete fusion with the subject matter, etc.

BLY: Lovely, but I don't think we are advanced enough to do that.

Faas: I wondered if there might be any analogue to that in poetic creativity.

BLY: Probably.

Faas: And I thought it was Olson's great contribution to have rediscovered this physiological basis of poetic creativity, this genuine spontaneity in contrast to the fictitious spontaneity of Romantic nature poetry.

Olson BLY: On the other hand, there are no real objects in Olson's poetry, perceived without the intrusion of the intellect or the ego.

Faas: That's exactly what he criticized in Pound.

BLY: It's a problem with intuitive types. There are no cows, a cow is a symbol for some part of his psyche. There are no horses, every horse is a symbol of part of his psyche. In a way, Jung is like that.

Faas: And Surrealism would avoid that, in your opinion.

BLY: Although in *most* Surrealism the author is again using only the intuitive part of his intelligence. It's possible that a great work of art cannot come out through using only one of our "functions" or "intelligences." It's as mistaken as Yvor Winters' trying to use only his thinking function. In good Spanish or South American Surrealism the world is often present, as well as the inner impulses from the unconscious. I'm not sure where Breton is in this. I don't feel "the world" so much in his poems. His younger impure followers evidently feel that the Surrealism is more in-Surrealism tense and daring and more genuine if the world itself is left out. That is one reason they hate Neruda. Several American Surrealists have written me letters attacking me for translating Neruda. Some Surrealists feel also that if the Vietnam war appears in a poem otherwise Surrealist, it is a violation of the ideals of Surrealism. The Puritan wishes to control the interior of his world, the American Surrealist wishes to control the interior of *his* world. Neruda is wise to call for "impure poetry." I think a Surrealist who tries to shut off in his own poems political comment is involved in Puritanism. Of course, he sees his point of view as wildly anti-Puritanical. But we all have many surprises for each other.

Faas: But is there any principle as to how *you* make images interconnect?

BLY: There, you are doing it again. I don't *make* images interconnect. If they don't and I notice it, I throw the poem away.

Faas: And how do you notice it?

BLY: Reading the poem.

Faas: So again you wouldn't like to make an analytical statement about that?

BLY: No.

Faas: In an interview from the year 1972 you stated that the thinking which in the last eight or nine years you have learned most from has been Buddhist, and I wondered if Buddhism has also influenced your writing and creativity.   influence of

BLY: You are asking questions in a pre-Lawrence way,   Buddhism
you are trying to fragment the psyche too much, and you
are forcing me to think of myself as a third person. It's wrong to try and pin down religious influence. Perhaps an intelligent theory of meter could be discussed. But Buddhism, if it has influence, influences the entire psyche, it has to do with the integration of previously disconnected parts of the psyche, therefore you can't point to any one thing.

Faas: I was mainly thinking of my own comparison between action painting and Chinese calligraphy, that in both cases the artist abandons himself to the autonomous movements of his body.

BLY: Buddhism doesn't do that, Buddhism is very disciplined, they hate that kind of stuff.

Faas: I would speak of disciplined spontaneity.

BLY: Mu Ch'i made an ink wash of five pears. They are done with ink, I take it, and so could not be corrected. I suppose it took maybe 35 seconds.

Faas: Quite.

BLY: But this is preceded by fifteen years of this discipline. In the West we want to have "autonomous movement of the limbs" before the fifteen years are over.

Faas: I couldn't agree more. One can see some of that disciplined spontaneity in the work of Peter Brook and Jerzy Grotowski when compared with most Happenings.

BLY: Happenings belong to the history of infantilism, in
my opinion. I repeat that I feel a danger in your ques-   disciplined
tions, namely that you are drawn to the work of Lawrence   spontaneity
and after, but approach it in a pre-Lawrence way.

Faas: But how does one avoid that?

BLY: How would Lawrence ask a question?

Faas: But you know, I'm not Lawrence. I'm just a University-trained European intellectual. [Both laughing]

BLY: Oh, now don't give me that modesty stuff!

Faas: I'm not really trying to be evasive. I know the shortcomings of what I'm doing, or rather of the way I'm doing it, only too well.

BLY: I don't mean shortcomings. I mean that you have a responsibility to Lawrence if he is one of your heroes. He says it is important to approach a problem from the point of view of the whole psyche. He opposes his new approach to the old fragmented or intellectualist approach. You're asking me for intellectualist formulations of various experiences which are bound to fragment the experience. I like your intellectual energy. But you might try to ask the questions in a Lawrence or post-Lawrence way. You might have to interpret the answer. I don't know what it would be like. But I sense it's harmful to your own psyche to ask intellectualist questions.

the new critical approach

Faas: As a motto for one of your books you use those beautiful lines by Bashō:

> The morning glory —
> another thing
> that will never be my friend.

I think that's an example of what one can learn from Zen Buddhism or Eastern philosophy generally.

BLY: I agree.

Faas: In one of his interviews Ginsberg explains how the gaps between his images make the concrete world of the poem transparent for the final emptiness of the Absolute, the "blissful empty void" or *śūnyatā*, as the Buddhists call it. Does that notion make sense to you?

BLY: What makes me vomit is that last thing, the "blissful empty void" or *śūnyatā*. We are all tourists of the East, all Westerners are, and we take their concepts and we misuse them constantly because of our crude psychological development. I've done it many times myself, I'm sure, I misuse them crudely, but somewhere there's a line which one shouldn't pass, and *śūnyatā* is an extremely serious concept or state. I think no Westerner has ever experienced it except perhaps San Juan de la Cruz or Santa Teresa de Avila. Now to have this dragged over and stuck into a little passage about poetry is revolting. I feel the same way about the phrase "Dharma Bums," can't stand it. It's exploitation not different from what the American soldier did in Vietnam, and Ginsberg doesn't realize, in my opinion, that when he uses a phrase like this he is violating the Buddhist religion in the same way that American marines violated a village.

the tourists of the East

Faas: Would the same apply to Gary Snyder as well, in your opinion?

BLY: No, no. Once in a while, maybe. It applies to me too once in a while. But Gary has worked on the problem, he has worked hard, very hard. And these concepts need to be brought in, they are very valuable, but somehow the concepts are being destroyed. The poet's job is to keep language fresh, and Ginsberg is aware of that. And yet he takes a word like *śūnyatā* and throws it in any old place; he's cheapening language. Why does he do that?

Snyder

Faas: You've often attacked Ginsberg.

BLY: I don't attack him.

Faas: At least there are various critical remarks throughout your prose writings. You spoke of his "lack of gentleness."

attacking Ginsberg

BLY: Where did I say that?

Faas: Somewhere in *The Sixties,* I think, I could find it for you.

BLY: Ginsberg's lack of gentleness?

Faas: Yes. Then you criticize him for his use of four-letter words and shocking subjects.

BLY: That must have been in 1958, in *Fifties* No. 1.

Faas: And then you accused him for giving up "all hope of imaginative precision and delicacy."

BLY: When was that?

Faas: I don't have the exact reference here, but somewhere in *The Sixties,* I think. I could quote a lot more. [Both laughing]

BLY: That's interesting.

Faas: But recently you have called him the "clear rebirth . . . of a very powerful spiritual man" and have approvingly quoted his remark that "as soon as you have a new syntax, you have a new way of breathing and as soon as you have that you have a new consciousness." Has there been any change in your attitude towards Ginsberg?

change of attitude towards Ginsberg

BLY: There has. I wrote an article for *The American Poetry Review* recently giving examples in poetry of the "four intelligences" Jung talks about. They are thinking, feeling, grasp of the senses, and intuition. I gave Louis Simpson as an example of a thinking man basically. I mentioned that the hostility early on that thinking types felt towards Ginsberg was connected with the perception that he was urging them to develop their weak feeling function. I think that's true of my early hostility to Ginsberg.

Faas: So you're really saying your *peccavi* here.

BLY: Yes, of course . . . But at the same time we all notice that Ginsberg's spiritual gift is mingled with some sort of sloppy language. I mentioned that earlier. You see the problem. I feel two people in him. One is spiritual, one not. Recently I have been able to

separate those two more. One part of Allen urges you on to develop
your feeling areas, and since feeling is open on one side to the spirit,
he is actually urging you to develop spirit. Then there's another
being in him urging you to remain content with clutter. I'm thinking
of the poem in his new book from a meditation retreat in Colorado
describing his breath going out over the country to Lowell, Mass.,
then to Kyoto, Vietnam, etc. It is a sort of tourist poem, with a couple
of anecdotes of each place. The poem loads us down with memory
clutter so the poem somehow misrepresents meditation. One half of
him is the grandmother, and the other half is the wolf! But the
grandmother is so amazingly generous. It comes out in his singing,
too.

Faas: So you have become friends.

BLY: Oh yes. Yes. We read together whenever we can. Once in my
house, he saw a group of anthologies in a bookcase, and said, "Well,
Robert, when we're both in all those anthologies, then what?" That's
how wise the grandmother is.

*[I next read Bly the passage from my essay dealing with his attack on James
Dickey. This led to a long and fascinating discussion of "The Firebombing"
and "Slave Quarters" which Bly, however, preferred to delete from the
typescript of the interview, saying there is too much criticism of others here.
(E.Faas)]*

Faas: In your criticism you have mainly drawn attention to the
poetries outside the Anglo-American tradition. Occasionally, but
not very often, you mention Wordsworth, whom you compare with
the Chinese poet Tao Yuan Ming, or Yeats as having the sense of
"Gott-Natur," or Blake, who took a first step into the psychic forest.
Are there any other English or American poets with whom you feel a
deep affinity?

BLY: Besides Yeats and Blake—Chaucer, certainly. Even more the
Grail poets, the Tristan poet, and the author of *Gawain and the Green
Knight.* To me they are contemporary.

medieval poetry

Faas: Duncan and, before him, Pound have argued that
it was during the period of the "romances" that the Western mind, for a short phase at least, began to recuperate
some of the energy and imagery repressed by Christianity.

BLY: I'm just beginning to think of the possibility of the Grail poems
being reworkings of Sufi literature. I have instead seen them as
vigorous attempts to bring forward the feminine in man, in the male.
Shortly after the Grail work, the movement was entirely crushed.
The church moves in after the fourteenth century A.D. Respect for
the feminine doesn't rise again until the Romantic age, but it appears
once more in our time. Pound touched on Troubadour poetry, but

Pound doesn't seem involved in the spirit—or the link between the spirit and the feminine. What the Grail poems discuss even more is some strange creature who is wounded. He has a bit of steel or iron in his testicles, and he can't be healed; this wound remains unhealed century after century. So there is such a thing as   wound literature "wound literature." It is ignored through the whole eighteenth century. The European psyche knows it is wounde.¹ It's a profound wound which will not heal, and in the eighteenth century people did not discuss it. They put a plaster or a bandage over it. In the nineteenth century, writers live out the agony of the wound. But they still will not investigate it, and it's only in our time that the wound is beginning to live and be lived again—also in words—

Faas: The Waste Land brings it up.

BLY: I think so.

Faas: Ted Hughes once described the poem to me as a love poem for this degraded and desecrated female spirit.

BLY: He's right surely. [Pause] Aristotle caused a wound and the Grail legends talk about that wound, now no work is of any value that does not face the wound . . .

Faas: You take Aristotle as being representative of Greek rationalism, I guess.

BLY: That kind of thing, yes. The Middle Ages centered around Aristotle, the whole mentality that led to the Ph.D. as well as to secularism. And I personally think that the Aristotle mentality is related to the mass-man also. Ortega y Gasset's *Revolt of the Masses*— what a powerful book! Underneath, Aquinas and Aristotle are much alike. One is the religious version, the other the secular version. The Grail legends describe the wound made by the Catholic Church that foolishly adopted Aristotle.

Faas: Ernst Topitsch has described how this fusion of Greek and Christian thought leads right up to Hegel and Marx . . .

BLY: . . . and leaves out an entire world, which is the world hinted at in the "romances." They are still secret literature, secret literature for a small group.

Faas: Duncan links that to Gnosticism, neo-Platonism, Hermeticism, and all the other heretical movements.

BLY: Yes. Bosch also. Centuries later Dürer appears with his great femininity, his combination of femininity and precision. In the twentieth century Antonio Machado. In between the two there is Blake. Blake talks about the wound in "Oh rose, thou art sick."

Faas: So you feel that Romanticism initiated Modernism.

BLY: I do surely.

Faas: Do you find that American poets of the last two decades have responded to your plea, made in the late fifties, that they must traverse the dark psychic woods of the unconscious before they will be able to write a truly great modern poetry?

BLY: I don't believe that it's possible to write post-Lawrentian poetry or "wound-poetry" or however you want to describe it without solitude; and when people in the universities try to write such poetry they often find the style without the way of life; it sends them off on just another sidetrack. I think that's what's happening. The style has been picked up but I don't see much deep change. I underestimated how much a style is a part of a way of life. Rilke is right at the end of his Apollo poem where he says that in order to write differently you have to change your *life.*

Faas: You have often criticized Olson for embodying the "formalist obsession" of American poetry. On the other hand, I find that your own position is not at all antagonistic to Olson's. I see it as complementary . . .

BLY: Sure, why not.

Faas: . . . rather than antagonistic to him. But why then did you have to attack him for something which is not even at the center of his poetics? I mean there is so much more to Olson than his concern with breath rhythm, prosody, and so forth. For instance, his concern with the physiological autonomy of the creative process.

controversy with Olson

BLY: Several times—maybe those remarks are in interviews or essays you haven't seen—I've said about Olson that I respect his intellectual speculations tremendously.

I started my magazine to clear ground for myself and for other poets. By 1964 the ground was absolutely and entirely covered with Charles Olson bushes. There was not a spot of ground that was not shaded by a Charles Olson bush. Creeley, after a long correspondence with Charles Olson, formulated the dogma "form is never more than an extension of content." Olson praised it, and most writers since find it self-evident. But I don't think the statement is true at all.

form not an extension of content

I have the feeling that I sense Bach's mathematical form with one part of myself, and his ecstatic freedom with another part. That implies there are two separate forces meeting in a third body.

Field published a weird essay recently by Donald Hall, in which he suggested that some of the oral or breast sensuality of infancy goes into sound in poetry, and so into form. He suspects that poetic form is linked with archaic layers of the pleasure instinct, experienced first with depth in infancy. I add that some of the adult grasp of "the world" goes into content. We can see that such a visualization is incompatible with the accepted idea Olson has praised. Far from form and content being extensions, one of the other, it is more likely they are distinct and opposite forces, opposite in charge.

I wrote a letter to *Field* commenting on this issue, and I'll read you a couple of paragraphs:

> Charles Olson wonderfully understood that American poetic form could not be an imitation of English form, and that the roots of form go back to the body and its breath, not to English metrical habits. It seems though that he wanted the form to be adult—he was interested in the time after the invention of the typewriter, rather than the primitive time before the baby or the aborigine has ever seen a typewriter.
>
> His essay on projective verse makes the whole problem of form technical, post-industrial, needing ingenuity and a typewriter with a good spacer. I'm unjust to his intellectual liveliness, but there is some Puritanism, that is, dislike of childhood, in his essay. Russian poets don't seem to have that.

Faas: Even Duncan would partly agree with that, I think.

BLY: Suppose a work of art is a container of energy, a sort of battery, then bland formulations of the unity of form and content merely mislead young poets as to what a work of art is. There is something bland in much Black Mountain poetry.

Faas: You know, that at the Berkeley reading, being obviously quite drunk and stoned, he said that he was really in love with our lady of Christ.

BLY: I think he must have been a lively man. As a person, as a teacher, he was evidently extremely warm, with a fantastically big mammal brain. He taught Creeley an amazing number of things. But to go back, suppose we use open form. The sound sensuality question is how do you bring infantile pleasure or sound sensuality into an open form poem?

Faas: Snyder is very concerned with that.

BLY: Is he?

Faas: Oh yes. How do you get that rhythmic sensuality back into open form poetry?

BLY: Sensuality seems the right word to use.

Faas: You once said that Objectivism—and I don't think that's fair to Olson's Objectism—is an evasion of self. I feel that both you and Olson are rather more interested in a kind of self-transcendence.

BLY: Yes, yes.

Faas: You achieve it by delving into the unconscious, whereas Olson achieves it by trying to abandon himself to some kind of autonomous, automatic process of creativity akin to what Werner Haftmann calls the gestural expressionism of action painting—a physiological process which is larger than himself and in which he fuses with the flux of nature.

BLY: Absolutely right.

Faas: So I don't understand why you object . . .

BLY: When he says that we must try to avoid "the soul getting between us and the objects," I agree, and yet, what does it mean? It's a secular statement, an Aristotelian statement. So therefore I find him coming from two sides; he makes Aristotelian statements and yet he struggles against the Aristotelian box. By an Aristotelian I mean someone who encourages a naked confrontation between "mind" and "object," with the "soul" left out. That's vague, I know. But it's possible we *share* soul with objects. How could we then leave out soul as we try to get near objects? It's possible we're not the only beings who *have* soul!

Objectism

I do like the way he thinks from scratch. "I go down and look at the Mayan tombs and no one has ever looked at them with a fresh eye as I have." Pound looked at economics that way. The American apparently longs to be the amateur discoverer. It's a great weakness and a great strength. I do it too. I try to throw off the European mind background, and then I have to become an amateur psychologist if not an amateur archaeologist. You understand that impulse? It's very American, very American. It's all through Hemingway. Hemingway says: "The Europeans don't know anything about style. I found a style. I found it in the woods." That impulse is in all of us.

the American amateur discoverer

Faas: Talking about the form of a poem, you once spoke of its "mysterious arbitrariness." You also said that it is obsolete to consider form as the most inportant thing about a poem. And finally, in a statement reminiscent of Pound and Lawrence, you said that a great work of art often has at its center "a long floating leap around which the work gathers like steel shavings around a magnet."

BLY: Magnetic energy gives so many possibilities for understanding art. In the leaping sentence I'm thinking of content. The substance of a poem arranges itself round the center leap. In the *Odyssey* the poem first leaps into the Great Mother, and

poetic form

then all the scenes such as visiting Circe, visiting the Cyclops, going down to the dead, center themselves naturally around the initial leap. The poem takes its form that way without mind-intervention.

Faas: Creeley claims that he usually writes a poem in one stretch, so that the order in which the words appear on the page reflects exactly the chronological sequence of creativity. Or Snyder told me that he often completes a poem in his mind and then just transcribes it onto the page. By contrast you once said that you wrote about 10,000 lines for the poem catled "Sleepers Joining Hands" and only published about four hundred. Do you   revising
revise just by throwing things away, like Creeley, while leaving the rest untouched?

BLY: I revise by magnetics, see what holds on. In that poem, I didn't know what the poem was about so I worked in confusion for four years.

Faas: In a totally open process of creative discovery.

BLY: Evidently, that's why I wrote so many lines.

Faas: Of course, Snyder, likewise, uses a totally different way of writing in composing the various sections of *Mountains and Rivers without End.*

BLY: Yes. There must be other ways, too.

Faas: Last night you spoke of three levels of consciousness. In the lowest level there is a great deal of repression, violence, and isolation. On the second level the man or woman—you gave D. H. Lawrence as an example—moves out past his ego into creatures and trees. Then you read Kabir's ecstatic poems as   open form
an example of work on the third level. How does "open form" relate to these three levels?

BLY: I haven't thought this over myself.

Let's say first that writing a good rhymed and metered poem means that the man or woman has learned how to repress successfully. Repressing well is a valuable art in civilization, as important as knowing how to build with wood. We repress constantly. When Breton, for example, allows angry lobsters with hair to come up, at the same second he is repressing tenderness. The problem is that when we're young, we don't choose what to repress. We repress firmly, but not wisely. In other words the material stays down. Poets who write a great deal of rhymed verse in their twenties have trouble growing, because their literary self-respect becomes associated with successful repression. We all know examples of that. Frost is one, on a wide scale.

Let's try to relate that idea to states of consciousness.   repression

and   The man or woman in the lowest stage—where we are
projection   most of the day—experiences constant projection. The
American man is not angry, other people are. He is not feminine,
Marilyn Monroe is. The American woman says: "I am not dark
inside, the blacks are dark." She is not obsessed with force, the
Russians are obsessed with force. But the marvellous discovery
Freud and Jung made is that only energies already pushed out of
sight are projected out onto others' faces. We can't get hold of our
energies, only see them on the faces of others. As a man, I can't get
hold of my female side, I can only see it on the faces of women. This
inability to get hold of our energies is an experience in the lowest
stage of consciousness. We have all had those experiences thousands
of times.

To return then to rhymed and metered poems . . . The poet
says, "I am not orderly inside, the poem is." This projection, like all
projection, is dangerous when it becomes a habit. Frost's life got
more and more disorderly as that *habit* took hold.

"Free verse" or "open form" then is not a literary technique—
that's why I dislike Olson's essay "Projective Verse"—that's odd—
Projective Verse!—but it is a step in growth. It is a way to encourage
us to let up a little in repression, ease up the projection, and move out
a bit from the lowest stage of consciousness. It doesn't always succeed, and those who write rhymed and metered poetry today don't
always stay in the lowest stage of consciousness, by any means. We're
dealing in tendencies, possibilities, only. Richard Wilbur did not stay
there.

As a person moves from the first to the second level of consciousness, he or she allows some repressed material to rise—just as
you are allowing it to rise in your hallucinations.
Faas: That's right.
BLY: Here's a possible visualization of it, that I see. Each time we
enter the second level there may be three sudden movements taking
place at the same instant. Energy pushed down rises up towards you
from below; then the brother of that energy sent off to live on the
faces of others descends down to you . . . at the same moment your
feminine soul appears as a speck on the horizon rushing toward you.
If a woman is writing the poem, or experiencing the second stage,
the movements are identical except that her masculine soul is what
the need for   appears far away hurrying towards her. There is a lot of
a new cycle   swift and vigorous motion, as of dancing, involved . . .
of repression   What "open form" and Lawrence's "we have come
and release   through" and Marianne Moore's intuitive joinings of dis-
parate material without "classical form" and Neruda's jumble in the

Residencia poems mean is not that repression is bad, but that we need a different cycle of repression and release than we have had.

From what I've said about release, we can guess what the third stage would be like. I suspect the idea of "open form" falls away in the third stage—the man's feminine side would be close to him, I think, and he would feel light for the first time. The woman's male side would be close to her—as the male side of Marie Louise von Franz has come very close to her. You feel in her prose that she's projecting very little. But some. We cannot enter paradise, we cannot in this life, we cannot have all the exiled material returned. Marie Louise has said that over and over—

Faas: You think that some of Gary Snyder's poems reach that stage?

BLY: Certainly.

Faas: Would you identify the new brain with this third level?

BLY: No, not really when I come to think of it . . . I don't think so. I would guess we need all our brains at that stage.

Faas: I was a bit puzzled that you called Creeley a poet of "the steady light," who tended to remain in one brain when he writes. To me it seems that he is a poet fascinated by the void, like Mallarmé: "The poem supreme, addressed to/ emptiness."

BLY: I don't know how to answer that. He has a weird   Creeley
path of his own. I don't really understand it, but I respect it. I feel very close to him—I kiss him when I see him—

Faas: I am going to see him up in Buffalo in a couple of weeks.

BLY: Then please tell him from me that I think his new poem about his mother in the hospital is marvellous.

Allen Ginsberg

Photo: Gerard Malanga

ALLEN GINSBERG (1926 -)

> The problems confronted in attempting to graph the opera-
> tions of the mind in language and the problems confronted
> historically at this apocalyptic-end-of history time are so com-
> plex and so new and previously unexperienced by any culture
> ... that no previous models of speech forms ... just as no
> previous models of life style within memory are sufficient, and
> we're going to have to out of our own native genius invent our
> own, out of our own imagination, as Blake and Whitman
> proposed.

Ginsberg's deliberate efforts to destroy his charisma are, paradoxically, part of his personal magnetism. While forever paying homage
to his masters (Williams, Pound, Burroughs, Kerouac, Trungpa), he
has turned into the figurehead of a whole generation as America's
most internationally acclaimed poet since Whitman. The major data
of his life, many of them already shrouded in legend—his Blake
vision in Harlem, the reading of *Howl* at the San Francisco Six
Gallery, his reign and public arrest as King of the May in Prague, and
his involvement in numerous trials—seem to focus the literary as
much as culturo-political history of an entire era. A "Buddhist Jew
with attachments to Krishna, Siva, Allah, Coyote, and the Sacred
Heart," Ginsberg was born in New Jersey, the son of poet high-
school teacher Louis Ginsberg and his wife Naomi, a Communist
radical, whose death he lamented in *Kaddish* (1961). Educated in the
public schools of Paterson, New Jersey, he there made the acquain-
tance of Williams who taught him to listen to the rhythm of his own
voice. After temporarily suspending Ginsberg in 1945, Columbia
University finally granted him a B.A. in 1948. But his real education
was provided by older poet mentors like Burroughs and Kerouac. A
prolific poet since his teens (see *Empty Mirror,* 1961; *The Gates of
Wrath,* 1972), he found his own voice of "Hebraic-Melvillean bardic

breath" in *Howl*, a lament for his "generation destroyed by madness," dedicated to Carl Solomon, whom Ginsberg, in 1949, had met as a patient in the Columbia Psychiatric Institute. Widely known after an obscenity trial in which Judge Clayton Horn granted *Howl* "redeeming social importance," he began a life of global pilgrimages through South America, Europe, Israel, India, Japan and his own country. Much of his work published since *Kaddish* (*The Yage Letters*, 1963; *Planet News*, 1961-1967, 1968; *Indian Journals*, 1970; *The Fall of America*, 1972; *Mind Breaths*, 1977) gives an account of this ceaseless quest. For several years now, Ginsberg has been associated with Chögyam Trungpa's Naropa Institute where he is co-ordinator of "The Jack Kerouac School of Disembodied Poetics," teaching "poetics and meditation in the whispered transmission school of Milarepa (12th century Tibetan Buddhist yogi-poet)."

Allen Ginsberg

But at the far end of the universe the million eyed Spyder that
    hath no name
spinneth of itself endlessly
the monster that is no monster approaches with apples, per-
    fume, railroads, television, skulls
a universe that eats and drinks itself
blood from my skull.

(G,K,86)

This evocation of the horrific aspect of Nature or the "Great Being" from Ginsberg's poem "Lysergic Acid" has many parallels, not only in the poet's own work, but in contemporary literature and art as a whole. Here, for instance, is a passage from Burroughs' *Naked Lunch* describing a scene from the blue movie shown at "A.J.'s Annual Party." What begins as a straightforward pornographic film à la *Deep Throat* suddenly turns into a Surrealist orgy of sadism and murder, in which Mary, the female participant, assumes the role of a bloodthirsty Ogress:

> She bites away Johnny's lips and nose and sucks out his eyes with a pop . . . She tears off great hunks of cheek . . . Now she lunches on his prick . . . Mark walks over to her and she looks up from Johnny's half-eaten genitals, her face covered with blood, eyes phosphorescent. . . .

Among the passages charged as "brutal, obscene and disgusting" in the Boston trial of 1962, this one is probably the most "offensive" in the entire novel.[1]* Yet it is hardly more so than much that for millennia has been an accepted part of the artistic canon of many non-Western cultures. Tantric, Hindu or Taoist art provides examples of the almost total absence of sexual tabus in specific cultures of ancient Tibet, India or China, while a few quotes from Heinrich Zimmer's *Myths and Symbols in Indian Art and Civilization* could have easily convinced Burroughs' judges that a gruesomeness

*Notes to this section on p. 268.

comparable to *Naked Lunch* is a common attribute of many Eastern divinities and, in the case of Black Kālī, of "the most cherished and widespread of the personalizations of Indian cult." "Innumerable representations of the devouring Black Kālī," Zimmer writes, "depict [the] wholly negative aspect of the Universal Mother." In a sculpture reproduced in the book, for instance,

> she appears as an emaciated, gruesome hag of bony fingers, protruding teeth, unquenchable hunger . . . [feeding] upon the entrails of her victim. And who among beings born is not her victim? She cleaves the belly and draws out and gobbles the intestines—that is what she is fond of—steaming with the last breath of expiring life.

Other representations show her "adorned with the blood-dripping hands and heads of her victims, treading on the prostrate, corpse-like body" of Shiva, her spouse and lover.[2]

Moreover, such monstrosities are by no means a specific obsession of one particular religion. The Great Mother in her "negative elementary character"[3] is common to many of the world's mythologies and her archetypal attributes are clearly evident when we compare Black Kālī with, for instance, the Aztec Coatlicue whose monumental sculpture, now in the Anthropological Museum of Mexico City, miraculously survived the destruction of Montezuma's Holy City at the hands of the Christian conquerors. Like the Indian Goddess, Coatlicue is adorned with the blood-dripping hands and torn-out hearts of her victims. In this she also resembles Vishnu, supreme deity of the Hindu pantheon, as depicted in the celebrated 11th chapter of the *Bhagavad Gita*. Like the latter's "Universal Form" as "Time," "the Destroyer of the worlds" equipped with many faces, eyes, arms, bellies, legs, terrible teeth and devouring mouths (B,G,229), the Mexican Earth Mother and mother of all the Aztec divinities has myriad eyes, multiple serpent faces and devouring jaws, several bodies and claws as well as fearsome arrays of tusks.

Western culture proves to be different from most others in excluding such notions from the accepted part of its religious consciousness. Here, Heraclitus was both the first and last of the great philosopher prophets (before Blake or Nietzsche) who, in his famous proposition that "war is the father and king of all," affirmed the horrific as an intrinsic part of the divine. But such wisdom was obscured by the advent of Greek idealistic philosophy and Judæo-Christian eschatological thinking which reinforced each other in "the illusion that good may exist without evil,"—either in a Platonic realm of ideas or in a heavenly hereafter in which "there shall be no more death, neither sorrow, nor crying" (Wa,G,48). Evil was explained as an incomplete self-realization of the ideal or was relegated to the infernal region of the fallen angels, while on the level of secular religion the Great Mother was gradually replaced by "Frau Welt" whom Chaucer's contemporary, the preacher John Bromyard, describes as a beautiful lady with her back full of worms and festering sores.[4] By the late Middle Ages this image, which also adorns the outside of many cathedrels, had acquired the ubiquity of a literary *locus communis*.

What to most religions is an unalterable part of the divine is explained by Christianity as the result of man's sinfulness. Thus God assumes the role of a judge to whom the horrific, by a further twist of the same cosmological notion, becomes the justification for punishing man for the evil which is an inherent part of all creation. As if modelled on this scheme, the segregating, torturing and exterminating of large groups of people for their sinfulness, unorthodox beliefs, impure race or ideology has been one of the most obvious hallmarks of Western spiritual history. Ironically, the most frightening excesses of this kind have tended to occur in periods of enlightened ideologizing such as our own which, coincident with the breakdown of traditional values, has witnessed the total unleashing of the demonic forces ignored or suppressed by idealistic philosophy and Judæo-Christian religion. The concentration camps of this century may thus be seen as a secularized extension or psychological enactment of the horror world which Dante and others have portrayed with such zestful detail and ingenious precision.

The actual holocausts of recent decades were paralleled and often heralded by an unprecedented emergence of the horrific in art. It is the final irony of our tragic misconception of evil that such art was denounced as decadent and corrupt by the very ideologists who began to stage its imagined horrors in the barbed wire infernos of the German and Russian concentration camps. Of course, there were others who clearly recognized the function of this artistic phenomenon in the spiritual development of our time. Not long before the Nazi exhibition of decadent art in Munich opened its gates to innumerable visitors from Germany and abroad, a large Picasso retrospective in Zurich and the stir it had created caused C. G. Jung to write an essay about the artist (1932). To the psychiatrist it is a symptom of the general emergence of the "antichristian and Luciferian forces . . . in modern man" that Picasso follows "the demoniacal attraction of ugliness and evil," thereby dissolving the "accepted ideals of goodness and beauty" into "fragments, fractures . . . [and] disorganized units." Despite its obvious schizophrenic tinge, the painter's work (just like Joyce's *Ulysses*) complies to the fullest extent with the "social significance of art" in its time. For the latter, as Jung had written as early as 1922,

> is constantly at work educating the spirit of the age, conjuring up the forms in which the age is most lacking. The unsatisfied yearning of the artist reaches back to the primordial image in the unconscious which is best fitted to compensate the inadequacy and one-sidedness of the present.[5]

Eastern literature showed Jung that the images emerging in this process often resemble the symbols of various non-Western mythologies. As he found in 1938, the sequence of events described in *The Tibetan Book of the Dead*, for instance, "offers a close parallel to the phenomenology of the European unconscious when it is undergoing an 'initiation process,' that is to say, when it is being analysed" (BT,xlix). Even Jung, however, might have been surprised to see how closely a description such as the following of the "blood-drinking wrathful deities" which the soul encounters on her journey after death comes to paralleling the horrific in the art and literature that began to emerge towards the end of his life (1875-1961):

> from the south-east, the Red Pukkase, holding intestines in the right [hand] and [with] the left putting them to her mouth . . . from the north-west, the Yellowish-White Tsandhalî, tearing asunder a head from a corpse, the right [hand] holding a heart, the left putting the corpse to the mouth and [she then] eating [thereof]; . . . from the north-west, the Black Crow-Headed One, the left [hand] holding a skull-bowl, the right holding a sword, and [she] eating heart and lungs. (BT,142-3)

For although Jung's insights were preceded by artistic developments originating with "the Romantic Agony,"[6] it was only after World War II that the horrific began to dominate modern art. The full extent of this phenomenon and of its origins is as yet uncharted, but it is sufficient to mention names such as Francis Bacon or Edward Kienholz, Ted Hughes or William Burroughs to remind us that the horrific, far from being the subject matter of outsider visionaries such as Bosch, Goya or Blake, now holds center stage in the imaginative world of present-day art and literature. Among North American poets, Allen Ginsberg no doubt has had the strongest impact in this realm, and it may contribute to our understanding of modern art in general to follow the poet through his arduous struggle with the demons which loom so frighteningly in our contemporary consciousness.

The fourth book of *Paterson* reprints a letter which Ginsberg sent Williams, along with some poems, shortly after his release from a New York mental hospital. One of the poems, later published in *Empty Mirror* (1961), has the mysterious title "The Shrouded Stranger." As Ginsberg explained to Williams, it was based on a real dream about "a classic hooded figure" and "the void," a dream which had "become identified with [his] own abyss" (W,P,205). Thus inspired, the poem not only seems to prefigure a more than fifteen year long search for the hidden divinity, but to anticipate some of its ultimate fulfillment:

> I dreamed I was dreaming again
> and decided to go down the years
> looking for the Shrouded Stranger.
> I knew the old bastard
> was hanging around somewhere.
>
> I couldn't find him for a while;
> went looking under beds,
> pulling mattresses off,
> and finally discovered him
> hiding under the springs
> crouched in the corner:
>
> met him face to face at last.
> I didn't even recognise him.
>
> "I'll bet you didn't think
> it was me after all," he said.
>
>   (G,M,46-7)

Before Ginsberg, fulfilling his own dream prophecy, could face up to the "Shrouded Stranger" in real life, he had to subject himself to shamanistic rituals of self-destruction and learn to accept his bodily self in a "universe that eats and drinks itself" (G,K,86). What launched him on this fearsome journey was his 1948 Blake vision which Ginsberg, like a latter-day Ancient Mariner, has told and retold ever since. Even in this first of many hallucinatory experiences, the attainment of "cosmic consciousness," the exhilarating awareness that "existence itself was God," is overshadowed by dread and doom. As the poet recalled in 1965,

> I experienced "The Sick Rose," with the voice of Blake reading
> it, as something that applied to the whole universe, like hear-
> ing the doom of the whole universe, and at the same time the

inevitable beauty of doom. I can't remember now, except it was very beautiful and very awesome. But a little of it slightly scary, having to do with the knowledge of death—my death and also the death of being itself, and that was the great pain.

The experience left Ginsberg with no doubt that he "was born to realize . . . the spirit of the universe." But in his repeated attempts to fulfill this mission he more and more came to resemble Dr. Faustus who yearns to see God, yet only succeeds in conjuring up the devil. Shortly after the Blake vision, when once again he tried to invoke the "Great Spirit," it did indeed appear to him, but in the shape of "some really scary presence, it was almost as if I saw God again except God was the devil." And although Blake seemed to urge him on "To find a Western Path / Right through the Gates of Wrath," Ginsberg "got scared, and thought, I've gone too far" (Pl,W,304,305,308,311).

None of these early visions found direct expression in the poet's published verse, and to judge from their actual descriptions there was, in fact, little visual detail to record. Subsequent drug experiments, however, not only brought back the hallucinations, but filled them with an eerie phantasmagoria of archetypal images embodied in the concrete realities of modern life. Such a fusion is documented in Ginsberg's report of an experience which inspired the second part of *Howl*:

> I had an apt on Nob Hill [San Francisco], got high on Peyote, & saw an image of the robot skullface of Moloch in the upper stories of a big hotel glaring into my window; got high weeks later again, the Visage was still there in red smokey downtown Metropolis. (A,P,416)

But how could such visions be turned into poetry, without "thought of transcription," as Ginsberg put it later, "haz[ing his] mental open eye" (G,H,25)? From about 1945, when the 19 year old poet wrote "big long poems about a last voyage looking for Supreme Reality" (Pl,W,301), up to the composition of *Howl*, it took Ginsberg an entire decade to find a satisfactory answer to this question. The early poems, collected in *Empty Mirror* (1961), *Reality Sandwiches* (1963) and *The Gates of Wrath* (1972), many of which discuss the writing of poetry itself, bear witness to the formal ingenuity Ginsberg unfolded in this search as well as to the many impasses he encountered along the way. One such poem records how he abandoned the concentrated precision of his early manner under the influence of poets like Wyatt or Williams:

I attempted to concentrate

the total sun's rays in
each poem as through a glass,
but such magnification
did not set the page afire.

                                      (G,M,18)

As if to ensure himself of a possible alternative, Ginsberg gave the
poem a motto culled from Thomas Hardy's introduction to *Poems of
the Past and the Present* (1901). "The road to a true philosophy of life,"
it reads, "seems to lie in humbly recording diverse readings of its
phenomena."

Yet neither Hardy nor any contemporary poet seemed to
suggest a satisfactory medium for such recording. Instead, Cézanne
(to whom he was introduced by his Columbia University teacher
Meyer Schapiro) gave him the exact effect of "a catalyst to visionary
states of being" he tried to achieve in poetry. Looking at the paintings Ginsberg "got a strange shuddering impression," a "cosmic
sensation" resembling his Blake vision, as if he "could see *through*
[the] canvas to God" (Pl,W,291ff.). He immediately set about to
investigate the painter's techniques and found several which, he felt,
were directly transferable to poetry. Instead of using perspective,
Cézanne simply juxtaposed one color against another, for instance,
or instead of *imitating* reality, he *recreated* it by processes of reduction
and reconstitution:

> So, I was trying to do similar things with juxtaposition like
> "hydrogen jukebox" . . . Cézanne is reconstituting by means of
> triangles, cubes, and colors—I have to reconstitute by means
> of words, rhythms . . . phrasings . . . The problem is then to
> reach the different parts of the mind, which are existing simul-
> taneously, the different associations which are going on simul-
> taneously, choosing elements from both, like: jazz, jukebox,
> and all that, and we have the jukebox from that: politics,
> hydrogen bomb, and we have the hydrogen of that. (Pl,W,206)

Somewhat later, Ginsberg found that this method of compressing "basically imagistic notations into surrealist or cubist phrasing"
(Kr,G,166) is related to the poetics of Fenollosa's *The Chinese Written
Character as a Medium for Poetry*, and that his use of dashes, the most
obvious hallmark of this method, can be seen in the light of *haiku*
technique which, in Pound's terms, is characterized by "a form of
super-position . . . one idea set on top of another" (P,G,89). In
Ginsberg's own words, a dash or ellipse—"the hair-raising awareness
in between two mental visual images"—can give us a glimpse of
śūnyatā, of the "blissful empty void" of Buddhism "to which the Zen
finger classically points" (Pa,C,57).

With these issues solved, there remained the more difficult problem of embodying his prophecies in an adequate new prosody and texture. Unaware of Olson's "Projective Verse" essay (1950) at the time, Ginsberg again found little that was of help in this search. Not even Williams' prosodic experiments, let alone the "ridiculous limited little accent or piddling syllable count" of traditional verse seemed to offer a satisfactory model. There was nothing Ginsberg felt sure about except that he was "sick of preconceived literature and only interested in *writing* the actual process" (Kr,G,170). But by 1951 Kerouac had settled down in front of a typewriter fed by a stolen role of U. P. teletype paper, to venture on an almost non-stop marathon of automatic prose composition, later published as the novel *On The Road* (1957). This gigantic effort of "the new Buddha of American prose" (G,H,3), who also trained Ginsberg's sensibility to the "eccentric modulations of long-line composition displayed by Smart, Blake, Whitman, Jeffers, Rimbaud, Artaud & other precursors" (B-M,P,221), taught the poet how to graph the movement of his mind in disregard of literary, grammatical and syntactical inhibitions. This was achieved by a physiological automatism close to Olson's breath rhythm poetics. As Kerouac protested in a 1968 interview, he "formulated the theory of breath as measure, in prose and verse, never mind what Olson, Charles Olson says, I formulated that theory in 1953 at the request of Burroughs and Ginsberg" (Ke,IR,83).

By 1955, all these methods, which Ginsberg had been testing and evolving over the years, finally fused in the poet's imagination to produce his first major poem and one of the most influential works of twentieth century literature. *Howl* itself, in an indirect homage to Cézanne, speaks of "the use of ellipse," or of the poet

> who dreamt and made incarnate gaps in Time & Space
> through images juxtaposed, and trapped the archangel of
> the soul between 2 visual images and joined the elemental
> verbs and set the noun and dash of consciousness to-
> gether jumping with sensation of Pater Omnipotens
> Æterna Deus.
>
> (G,H,16)

In the second part of the poem, this "Pater Omnipotens Æterna Deus" is also portrayed in his negative aspect, the "robot skullface of Moloch," as Ginsberg had visualized it from his apartment window in downtown San Francisco:

Moloch whose mind is pure machinery! Moloch whose blood is

running money! Moloch whose fingers are ten armies!
Moloch whose breast is a cannibal dynamo! Moloch whose
ear is a smoking tomb!
Moloch whose eyes are a thousand blind windows!

(G,H,17)

One of Ginsberg's most detailed and revealing self-interpretations explains how here, for the first time, he succeeded in capturing one of the visions which ever since 1948 had been haunting his imagination with a sense of doom and destruction. To sum it up in terms of the poet's general concept of creativity, the vision is turned into poetry by a rhythmical articulation of the feelings it engenders in the body. By arranging themselves around this "definite rhythmic impulse" the words may, to the poet's own amazement, take their own illogical and unexpected course.

> The poetry generally is like a rhythmic articulation of feeling
> . . . At best what happens, is there's a definite body rhythm that
> has no definite words, or may have one or two words attached
> to it . . . And then, in writing it down, it's simply by a process of
> association that I find what the rest of the statement is . . .
> [B]efore I wrote "Moloch whose eyes are a thousand blind
> windows," I had the word, "Moloch, Moloch, Moloch," and I
> also had the feeling DA de de DA de de DA de de DA DA. So it
> was just a question of looking up and seeing a lot of windows
> . . . So Moloch whose eyes—then probably the next thing I
> thought was "thousands." O.K., and then thousands *what?*
> "Thousands blind." And I had to finish it somehow. So I
> hadda say "windows." It looked good *afterward*. (Pl,W,289-90)

In his introduction to *Howl*, Williams expresses surprise at Ginsberg's "ability to survive," for literally, as he remarks, Ginsberg, "from all the evidence, [has] been through hell." Yet the worst was still to come. To assure his survival, the poet, only 29 at the time he screamed out his "howl of defeat" (Williams), could either flee or accept the demons he had summoned from his subconscious. In this archetypal situation he resembled the soul in the *Bardo Thödol* who is advised not to fear or flee the Wrathful Deities it is about to encounter. Because met in the right spirit of self-abandonment, they are recognized to be no other than the Peaceful Deities in disguise, and like those, mere emanations of one's mind:

> the fifty-eight flame-enhaloed, wrathful, blood-drinking
> deities come to dawn, who are only the former Peaceful Deities
> in changed aspect . . . the least of the least of the devotees of
> the mystic *mantrayāna* doctrines, as soon as he sees these

blood-drinking deities, will recognize them to be his tutelary
deities, and the meeting will be like that of human acquain-
tances. He will trust them; and becoming merged into them, in
at-onement, will obtain Buddhahood. (BT,131-2)

As if following such advice, Ginsberg decided to face the demons.

The crucial event in what followed was the death of the poet's
mother. In and out of mental hospitals for most of Allen's childhood, she had turned into a living incarnation of the awesome
divinity he later was to encounter in his vision—into the "fatal Mama,"
the "old woman of skulls" (G,K,27,31), whose traumatic impact on
the young boy finds expression in a ruthlessly realistic anecdote
from *Kaddish*, the elegy on Naomi's death:

> One time I thought she was trying to make me come lay
> her—flirting to herself at sink—lay back on huge bed that
> filled most of the room, dress up round her hips, big slash of
> hair, scars of operations, pancreas, belly wounds, abortions,
> appendix, stitching of incisions pulling down in the fat like
> hideous thick zippers—ragged long lips between her legs—
> What, even, smell of asshole? I was cold—later revolted a little,
> not much—seemed perhaps a good idea to try—know the
> Monster of the Beginning Womb— (G,K,24)

The hold which this and similar experiences had on Ginsberg was all
the stronger since he knew himself to be closer to his mother than
any other member of his family. Her "mad idealism," her visions of
God, her very insanity prefigure or even parallel ("I was in bughouse
that year 8 months," G,K,24,25) the poet's own experiences. Yet
given his willingness to face evil and destruction, this "madness" now
becomes the very means to redeem the media-perverted consciousness and Moloch-inspired violence which caused it and which, like
many others who "suffered death and madness," had

> murdered my mother
> who died of the communist anticommunist psychosis . . .
> complaining about wires of masscommunication in her head
> and phantom political voices in the air
> besmirching her girlish character.
> ("Wichita Vortex Sutra," G,N,132)

In this way *Kaddish* can celebrate "the Monster of the Beginning
Womb" in her positive aspect of the "holy mother" whose "world is
born anew" and thus becomes the source of the poet's inspiration:

> O glorious muse that bore me from the womb, gave suck

first mystic life & taught me talk and music, from whose
pained head I first took Vision—

Yet such acceptance of suffering is still far from the abiding
equanimity of the "devotee of the mystic doctrines," and in the very
passage that follows, the redemptive power of the poet's visions is
again called in doubt:

> Tortured and beaten in the skull—What mad hallucina-
> tions of the damned that drive me out of my own skull to seek
> Eternity till I find Peace for Thee, O Poetry.
>
> (G,K,29)

So the search for the hidden divinity becomes ever more frantic
and self-destructive. In the footsteps of William Burroughs,
Ginsberg visits Peru to try the hallucinogenic Ayahuasca in the
company of the natives. His visions, recorded in the descriptions and
drawings of the *Yage Letters* to his older friend, were the strongest
and most frightening since his "Merry Visions of Blake" in Harlem.
Still ruminating about his mother who died "in God knows what state
of suffering," the poet experiences "the Great Being, or some sense
of It, approaching [his] mind like a big wet vagina," and during a
subsequent session

> got nauseous, rushed out and began vomiting, all covered with
> snakes, like a Snake Seraph, colored serpents in aureole all
> around my body . . . like a snake vomiting out the universe—
> or a Jivaro in head-dress with fangs vomiting up in realization
> of the Murder of the Universe—my death to come—
> everyone's death to come—all unready—I unready. (G,L,52)

Ginsberg tried to preserve his sanity by somewhat artificially treating
these hallucinations as a "temporary illusion," but the "fearful" and
"almost schizophrenic alteration of consciousness," caused by the
drug, proved to defy such psychological self-persuasion. "I don't
know if I'm going mad," he reports to his friend. "I hardly have the
nerve to go back, afraid of some real madness; a Changed Universe
permanently changed." Burroughs' reply to Ginsberg's plea for help
ultimately turned out to be the right advice: "There is no thing to
fear. Vaya adelante." Yet for Ginsberg such acceptance of the Wrathful Divinities was not to be achieved before several more years had
gone by (G,L,53-64, see also Ginsberg's drawings of "The Great
Being" and "The Vomiter" reproduced below).

The poems inspired by the Peruvian adventure read like one
agonized howl of yearning, fright and despair. ":[R]eady for [the]

disintegration of [his] mind," the poet throws himself at the mercy of the "Creator and Eater of Mankind," imploring him to "devour [his] brain," to "attack [his] hairy heart with terror" and to "transfigure [him] to slimy worms" ("Magic Psalm," G,K,92,93). Yet though the "Ever-Unknowable" fulfills the poet's longing for self-sacrifice, doom is his ultimate answer, and the shamanistic journey never penetrates beyond the valley of death and destruction:

> No refuge in Myself, which is on fire
>> or in the World which is His also to bomb & Devour!
>> Recognise His might! Loose hold
> of my hands—my frightened skull
>>> —for I had chose self-love—
> my eyes, my nose, my face, my cock, my soul—and now
>> the faceless Destroyer!
>> A billion doors to the same new Being!
> The universe turns inside out to devour me!
> and the mighty burst of music comes from out the inhuman
>>>> door—
>>> ("The Reply,"G,K,97-8)

Ginsberg's journey through India (1962-3), which he had hoped would prove to be his "promised land," only led him into the lowest region of this inferno. Though it was reassuring for him to note that the *Bhagavad Gita* representation of Vishnu in his negative aspect of "world-destroying Time" resembled what he had "seen often on LSD, etc.," he was only too well aware that "fearful Allen" had never lost his fear "in the face of that monster."

Because I am still clinging to my human known me, Allen
Ginsberg—and to enter this thing means final, complete
abandonment of all I know of my *I am* except for this outer-
seeming otherness which requires my disappearance.
(G,J,28-9)

Tantrism, a religion devoted to the worship of the Great Mother
in her negative elementary character, teaches that this self-
abandonment can only be achieved through a detached, though
fully sensual, acceptance of one's physical passions and desires. "A
whole series of India holy men" Ginsberg consulted on his journey
gave similar advice, directing him "back to the body—getting *in* the
body rather than getting out of the human form." Such words
turned the tip of the scale. Years of shamanistic self-destruction led
Ginsberg into an ever deepening despair in which, bereft of love,
hope, even "sacred poetry," the meaningless suffering of himself
and those around him seemed to provide the only sense of existence:

> Skin is sufficient to be skin, that's all
> it ever could be, tho screams of pain in the kidney
> make it sick of itself, a hollow dream
> dying to finish its all too famous misery
> —leave immortality for another to suffer like a fool,
> not get stuck in a corner of the Universe
> sticking morphine in the arm and eating meat.
>
> *Bankok - May 28, '63*
> Chinese meats hanging in shops— . . .

This is the state reached at the end of the Indian journey—a state of
despondency so complete that it could transcend its proper bounds
and reach out into a new realm beyond despair. This aloneness, as
Ginsberg himself observed, "is like a returning home" (G,J,208-10).

It also marked the turning point in his quest of the "faceless
Destroyer" who, elusive and threatening in his cosmic aloofness till
then, is now forced to reveal himself in his own creation. This
epiphany was recorded in "The Change: Kyoto - Tokyo Express,"
dated 7/18/63, on a subsequent journey through Japan.[7] "Seeking
the Great Spirit of the / Universe in Terrible Godly / form," the poet
still sees himself and the rest of mankind as the Destroyer's victim:

> O suffering Jews
> burned in the hopeless fire
> O thin Bengali sadhus adoring

> Kali mother hung with
> nightmare skulls O Myself
> under her pounding
> feet!

Yet accepting his own body and suffering, the poet, like the enlightened soul of the *Bardo Thödol*, recognizes such phantoms as mere projections of his agonized self:

> Who is, who cringes, perishes,
>   is reborn a red Screaming
> baby? Who cringes before
>   that meaty shape in
>   Fear?

> In this dream I am the Dreamer
>   and the Dreamed I am
>   that I am.
>   (G,N,59-60)

And the "Destroyer of the World" who several years before had answered his "Magic Psalm" with a "Reply" of doom now appears as the "sweet lonely Spirit" who, eager to follow the poet's conjurations, seems ready to reveal himself in his own creation, forceful yet benign, with a gesture of "fear not" and ultimate peace:

> Come, sweet lonely Spirit, back
>   to your bodies, come great God
>   back to your only image, come
>   to your many eyes & breasts,
>   come thru thought and
>   motion up all your
>   arms the great gesture of
>   Peace & acceptance Abhya
>   Mudra Mudra of fearlessness
>   Mudra of Elephant Calmed &
>   war-fear ended forever.
>   (G,N,61)

The epiphany on the Kyoto - Tokyo express left Ginsberg a man "in mid-age, finished with half desire / Tranquil in [his] hairy body" ("A Vision in Hollywood," G,N,106):

> Joy, I am I
> the lone One singing to myself
>   God come true—
>   ("Wichita Vortex Sutra," G,N,113-4)

As if by miracle, all monster visions vanished from the poetry written after "The Change" and even failed to reappear when Ginsberg decided to resume his drug experiments. While in his 1965 *Paris Review* interview he claimed to have renounced all use of hallucinogenics, a footnote to this statement, added in 1966, reports that subsequent LSD experiments had produced no "monster vibration, no snake universe hallucinations" (Pl,W,312). Another such experiment inspired the "Wales Visitation" which Ginsberg describes as his "first great big Wordsworthian nature poem" (Kr,G,22). Here, the multiple million eyed "Monster of the Beginning Womb" has been replaced by the Great Mother of creativity and harmonious balance:

> O great Wetness, O Mother, No harm on thy body!
> Stare close, no imperfection in the grass,
>> each flower Buddha-eye, repeating the story,
>> the myriad-formed soul
>
> . . . .
>
>> & look in the eyes of the branded lambs that stare
>> breathing stockstill under dripping hawthorn—
> I lay down mixing my beard with the wet hair of the mountain-
> side,
>> smelling the brown vagina-moist ground, harmless,
>> tasting the violet thistle-hair, sweetness—
> One being so balanced, so vast, that its softest breath
>> moves every floweret in the stillness on the valley floor,
>> trembles lamb-hair hung gossamer rain-beaded in the
>> grass,
>> lifts trees on their roots, birds in the great draught
>>> hiding their strength in the rain, bearing same
>> weight.
>
> (G,N,141)

The lines, of course, bespeak an eagerness to proclaim the newly found happiness which belies the serenity they profess. But such exuberance is easily understood considering what preceded it, and nobody more than Ginsberg himself was aware of this self-defeating over-assertiveness. So "Autumn Gold: New England Fall" from *The Fall of America* (1972) completely reverses our expectations of another "Wordsworthian nature poem" and, instead, gives a humorous self-portrait of the poet as the self-complacent saint and quester after "the spirit of the universe":

> I thought I was my body the last 4 years,
> and everytime I had a headache, God dealt me
>> Ace of Spades—

I thought I was mind-consciousness 10 yrs before that,
and everytime I went to the Dentist the Kosmos disap-
peared,
Now I don't know who I am—
I wake up in the morning surrounded
by meat and wires,
pile drivers crashing thru the bedroom floor,
War images rayed thru Television apartments,
Machine chaos on Earth,
Too many bodies, mouths bleeding on every Continent,
my own wall plaster cracked,
What kind of prophecy
for this Nation.
(G,F,50-1)

Ginsberg's recent development resembles Robert Bly's to the point where they could join hands in a common cause. Having come to terms with their psycho-religious problems, both began to devote more and more time to public issues, such as fighting the Vietnam war or the socio-political consciousness which caused it. The latter is the central theme of *The Fall of America*, in which the poet seems to refocus his concern with the horrific by directly analysing the destructive forces in our time. "Earth pollution," as Ginsberg put it in one of the poems of this "epic containing history,"

identical with Mind pollution, consciousness Pollution identical with filthy sky,
dirty-thoughted Usury simultaneous with metal dust in water courses
murder of great & little fish same as self besmirchment
short hair thought control.
(G,F,142)

Such new concerns also demanded a new language—a language which could oppose the corrupt rhetoric of politicians and public media. A reader of Wittgenstein, Fenollosa and Eastern philosophy, Ginsberg had always been keenly aware of the insufficiencies of human language generally and of the fallacies of Platonic essentialism and Aristotelian rhetoric in particular. Language to him is "a vehicle of feeling . . . itself [it] doesn't mean anything—Wittgenstein and the Diamond Sutra agree on that" (G,R,7). And such a purely emotive medium was the "language-inner-thought-monologue-abstraction" or "mental-image-mathematical-abstraction" in which he had expressed his cosmic visions. But even that had degenerated into a sterile and "fixed habit" and as such into "a block to further awareness." Thus by 1961, the poet finds himself unable to compose anything but dream notations and diaries and, again inspired by Wittgenstein, wonders if perhaps "we've reached point in human or unhuman evolution where art of words is oldhat dinosaur futile, & must be left behind" (G,R,10).

In this quandary Ginsberg consulted his friend William Burroughs who in the meantime had devised his "cutup" method based on the model of ideograms and hieroglyphs. In contrast to Aristotelian logic—"one of the great shackles of Western civilization"—this technique, as Burroughs explained in an interview, tries to juxtapose "what's happening outside and what you're thinking of," thereby recording a "psycho-sensory process that is going on all the time anyway" (Pl,W,154-7). Of course, Ginsberg was unlikely to adopt the actual scissors-pasteboard dissections and remodellings of human consciousness involved in this pursuit, and as if to confirm this fact, Burroughs rejected his former disciple, disclaiming the bond of their previous friendship. As Ginsberg wrote after his visit to Burroughs in Tangiers following the Peruvian adventure, the novelist

> was cutting up [his art] with a razor as if it weren't no sacred texts at all, just as he was cutting up all known human feelings between us, and cutting up the newspapers, and cutting up Cuba & Russia & America & making collages; he was cutting up his own consciousness & escaping as far as I can tell outside of anything I could recognize as his previous identity.
> (G,R,8-9)

The only result Ginsberg gained from his visit was the additional fear of perhaps being a mere "degenerate robot under the mind-control of the mad spectre of Burroughs" (G,R,10), an image which continued to haunt him during his journey through India.

Yet while the spiritual change which finally culminated in the Kyoto-Tokyo express epiphany was still germinating, Ginsberg already began pondering "radical means" towards a new poetic breakthrough such as "Composition in Void: Gertrude Stein," "Association: Kerouac & Surrealism," "Random juxtaposition: W. S. Burroughs" and "Arrangement of Sounds: Artaud, Lettrism, Tantric Hantras" (To P.O.—July 8, 1962, G,J,39). To explore the relations "between poetry and mantra chanting by means of the yoga of breath" (G,IS,12) has proved to be the most fruitful of these propositions for Ginsberg's subsequent development. As he announced in "Wichita Vortex Sutra," his first major poem after "The Change,"

> I search for the language
> that is also yours—
> almost all our language has been taxed by war.
>
> . . . .
>
> I lift my voice aloud,

> make Mantra of American language now,
> pronounce the words beginning my own millennium,
> I here declare the end of the War!
>
> (G,N,125-7)

Not being a musician himself, Ginsberg found models in the rock music of Dylan and others, music which to him marks the full re-entry of a physiologically determined poetry into Western art. It can thus be related to Pound's principle of the "tone leading of vowels" or to Artaud's discovery that "certain rhythmic frequencies of music or voice might alter molecular patterns in the nervous system" (G,B) as well as to a system as ancient as Sanskrit prosody which to Ginsberg is based on "patterns of physiological reactions built into the language" (G,P,20). As the poet formulated it on September 10, 1966,

> Mantra repetition—a form of prayer in which a short magic formula containing various God names is chanted hypnotically—has entered Western consciousness & a new Mantra-rock is formulated in the Byrds & Beatles.
> (B-M,P,221)

Where previously Ginsberg had exorcised his private demons by accepting his bodily self, his new body-mantra-poetics was devised to dispel the public demons controlling our present-day consciousness. And Blake who had launched him on his long quest

> To find a Western Path,
> Right through the Gates of Wrath,

was also there to welcome the quester upon his return. It was "The Sick Rose" which 21 years earlier—"with the voice of Blake reading it" to him in his Harlem flat—had brought about Ginsberg's first cosmic vision.

> O Rose, thou art sick!
> The invisible worm
> That flies in the night,
> In the howling storm,
>
> Has found out thy bed
> Of crimson joy:
>
> And his dark secret love
> Does thy life destroy.

Ginsberg immediately recognized that the poem "applied to the whole universe." Yet it took him one and a half decades to make Blake's vision—which, in a way unique for the West, portrays the horrific as an unalterable part of all life—an accepted part of his own experience. Similarly, he had always felt that his "physiologic ecstatic experience had been catalysed in [his] body by the physical arrangement of [the] words." Yet only much later did he recognize that "The Sick Rose" represents an example of "pure Mantra" within English poetry—"as penetrant & capable of causing Transcendental Knowledge as any Hindu Hare Krishna or Hari Om Namo Shivaye." To make this impact complete, Ginsberg, by way of an exercise for his future creativity, finally set about to reinvent the unrecorded melodies to which Blake himself used to sing his *Songs of Innocence & Experience* "unaccompanied at friends' houses." As the poet-composer explains on the blurb of his album:

> The purpose in putting them to music was to articulate the significance of each holy and magic syllable of his poems . . . I hope that musical articulation of Blake's poetry will be heard by the Pop Rock Music Mass Media Electronic Illumination Democratic Ear and provide an Eternal Poesy standard by which to measure sublimity & sincerity in contemporary masters such as Bob Dylan, encouraging all souls to trust their own genius Inspiration.
>
> For the soul of the Planet is Wakening, the time of Dissolution of Material Forms is here, our generation's trapped in Imperial Satanic Cities & Nations, & only the prophetic priestly consciousness of the Bard—Blake, Whitman or our own new selves—can Steady our gaze into the Fiery eyes of the Tygers of the Wrath to Come. (G,B)

Have his past shamanistic experiences provided Ginsberg with the Bodhisattva consciousness necessary for this task? His poetic testimony leaves little doubt as to how to answer this question, although the poet seems to be well aware of the fact that human achievements, and especially those of the spirit, are rarely final or absolute. Asked to sing "The Tyger" at a Blake Poetry Class in 1971, Ginsberg replied:

> I've worked on "The Tyger"—the rhythm is the same as heartbeat—but that's like revolution, or the total wrath to come, so I'm not quite capable of looking it in the eye yet. (G,A,23)

[1](New York: Grove Press, 1966), pp. viii, 97; punctuation as in the novel.

[2]Ed J. Campbell. Bollingen Series VI (Princeton, N.J.: Princeton University Press, 1972), pp. 212-3, 215.

[3]See E. Neumann, *The Great Mother. An Analysis of the Archetype*, Bollingen Series XLVII (Princeton, N.J.: Princeton University Press, 1974), pp. 147-208.

[4]*Summa Predicantium*, 2 vols. (Venice, 1586), II,90v-91.

[5]*The Spirit in Man, Art, and Literature*. Bollingen Series XX (Princeton, N.J.: Princeton University Press, 1972), pp. 82-3, 138-9.

[6]The title of the well-known study by Mario Praz.

[7]See G,IR,6-7: "My poem *The Change* is a renunciation of this first vision, as I'd got hung up on it abstractly, and it had become an obsession. So I'd had to remove it into my own body again. The realization that the whole visionary game was lost came to me on a train leaving Kyoto—at which point I started weeping and sobbing that I was still alive in a body that was going to die. Then I began looking around on the train and seeing all the other mortal faces, 'with their noses of weakness and woe,' and I saw how exquisitely dear they all were—we all were—so I pulled out my notebook, while the illumination was still glowing in my body, and, while my breath was still fitted to weeping, scribbled everything that came into my thought-stream—all the immediate perceptions of the moment in the order in which I could record them fastest. Later on, that becomes known as a poem. The mind supplies the language, if you don't interfere. That's something I learnt from Jack Kerouac,—how to let the mind supply the language."

Allen Ginsberg

Faas: Did you write "The Shrouded Stranger" before or after your Blake vision?

GINSBERG: I think that's after. The concept came before though.

Faas: It was based on an actual dream, wasn't it?

GINSBERG: Well, I had a series of related dreams since I was three.

Faas: About the Shrouded Stranger?

GINSBERG: Yes. Kerouac had a very similar thing in *Dr. Sax;* that in fact was *his* Shrouded Stranger.

Faas: I haven't read that novel.

GINSBERG: Well he talks about the Shrouded Stranger there too. And we'd discussed that book quite a bit, discussed how to end it and everything like that. That was one of my favorite books, because he enlarges on the Shrouded Stranger.

Faas: A similar figure occurs in the *Waste Land.*

GINSBERG: Yes, it's an archetype, the boogie man, the Hooded Stranger.

Faas: In *Empty Mirror* you have one stanza beginning "I attempted to concentrate the total sun's rays" and so forth, with the motto from Thomas Hardy . . .

GINSBERG: . . . which suggests doing the opposite.

Faas: Yes, quite. I assume that these lines are referring to a particular style you practised before you started publishing your poetry.

GINSBERG: They refer to the poems in *The Gates of Wrath,* and particularly to the poem that begins "I cannot sleep, I cannot sleep." I was just trying to arrange and rearrange sort of symbols of mystical experience, like the words "light," "skull," which were really very vague. They referred to something Gnostic, but they didn't really describe anything seen. So it was "reference" rather than "presentation." I thought at the time that I would be able to write a poem that was so dense and would have so much symbolic significance that it would be able to penetrate anybody else's consciousness.

Faas: In the way the New Critics taught people to write.

GINSBERG: Yeah, well, I didn't have that in mind, but it was influenced by that kind of practise.

Faas: Were there any poets and artists besides Cézanne, Kerouac and Burroughs who helped you develop the mode of expression used in *Howl?*

GINSBERG: William Carlos Williams.

Faas: But didn't you have to go beyond Williams in order to write that poem.

GINSBERG: No, I only expanded on his style and then got to work from there. The poem I read tonight [March 28, 1974] "Transcriptions of Organ Music," was really basically Williams's practise. What Williams presents is facts, which I put together in a Surrealist way, but they are still facts, like "hydrogen jukebox."

Williams' influence

Faas: The image you discuss in the *Paris Review* interview.

GINSBERG: It's the most obvious as "Surrealism." But at the same time it is jukebox, hydrogen bomb and so forth.

Faas: What inspired your notion of ellipse, of the gap between two images which gives you a flash of awareness of *śūnyatā* or the final emptiness of the absolute?

GINSBERG: That comes from the *haiku.* You know the books by Blyth on the *haiku,* that's the best sample, the work in four volumes. That's the book Kerouac and Gary and I used, the basic text to study to get an idea of what was possible.

Faas: And Cézanne?

GINSBERG: Well, the Cézanne stuff was actually [pause] '48. The model for *Empty Mirror,* the first book of my earlier poems I published, was Williams. And the models for *The Gates of Wrath,* those are rhymed poems, was Andrew Marvell.

Faas: Thomas Wyatt—

GINSBERG: Yes, and Raleigh, Christopher Smart. And my father.

Faas: How about the influence of Walt Whitman?

GINSBERG: I knew Whitman before I wrote *Howl,* but I didn't really sit down and read his entire poetic output, all through *Leaves of Grass,* until *after* I had written *Howl,* and then I saw that it was important.

Whitman's influence

Faas: And yet everybody seems to take it for granted that *Howl* was directly inspired by Whitman.

GINSBERG: No, it's more a combination of Williams and Hart Crane—and Shelley. The Moloch section—"Moloch whose eyes are a thousand blind windows"—the Moloch section which is the strongest thing in *Howl,* I think, is more like that dizzying dance foot that you would get in Shelley's [pause]—

Faas: Epipsychidion?

GINSBERG: Yes, "One life, one death, one heaven, one hell, one immortality and one annihilation," which I knew from my father as a kid, or from Poe or from Hart Crane's "Atlantis" or from Shelley's "Ode to the West Wind" or from the end of "Adonais" or from some Wordsworth like "A sense sublime of something far more deeply interfused"—that long breath which continues. A lot of that I got from Kerouac, that sense of a long breath in a builded rhyme, in a builded rhythm.

Faas: Lawrence, too, you began to study *after* the completion of *Howl?*

GINSBERG: I didn't study him, I just read him. You see , after picking up on what Williams was doing, I read his contemporaries and poets generally that were writing in a kind of open form. So I went and looked up works by Louis Zukofsky and Pound and later by Charles Reznikoff and the Objectivists and the Activists and the Imagists and Marsden Hartley and Lawrence, and then Christopher Smart and anybody that wasn't writing just rhymed stanzas, I just started reading anything that would apply—the Bible—

Faas: Did you have any personal contact with Olson in those years?

GINSBERG: No, not until 1958. Met him in '57, knew of him in '55 through Black Mountain people. I didn't meet Creeley or Duncan until '55.

contacts with Olson

Faas: That was in San Francisco, wasn't it? But the real coming together happened at the Vancouver poetry conference in 1963, I guess.

GINSBERG: Well we'd met and we knew each others' work but till then we didn't actually have a convention, so to speak.

Faas: You have described how everything seemed to join at Vancouver, how Olson said to you: "I feel I am one with my skin" and Creeley: "I am in my place" and how you yourself had, as it were, returned to your own body.

GINSBERG: And now, I think, for the same concept I would use the word "space," which I get from Chögyam Trungpa. I'm taking the language from Trungpa because it means the same thing as all the others and, yet, it doesn't have the hang-ups of body or body-mind, and at the same time it's the classical yogic and Buddhist term for appreciation of the actual space, and the emptiness of space, the infiniteness and the emptiness. That's what the mantra "Ah" is. "Ah" before the place or space, that we breath into, "Ah." So it's almost literal appreciation and use of space. And traditionally it is the seed syllable mantra for purification of speech, as well as the appreciation of space like the color blue of the sky.

Faas: I don't quite understand that yet.

GINSBERG: Okay, let's see. You can understand Creeley's use of "place," as "we'll all get to heaven and everybody will have a smile on their faces."

Faas: That's right, and we also will have "beautiful chairs to sit in"—

GINSBERG: "And we'll likewise all have places." To come back to the place meaning as Williams, to come back to *this* place to see what is here rather than wandering off with the imagination. So you could also say, interchange the word, come back to *this* space here in the apartment and the space in which the apartment sits and the space through which the planet moves, and the space into which we breathe, as being the one common element that holds all of us together, and also the one element that is open and free which does not stop us; to which we can speak, into which we can breathe. It's sort of the womb of being. They say *dharma-kāya* is space and at the same time the host which holds us all together and the place where we exist. So an appreciation of that space place means an awakenedness to the fact that we are here and that there is no paranoia closing down and imprisoning all of us.

Faas: It seems to me that Creeley has only found that kind of space more recently.

GINSBERG: He always used the word "place" in that way, I thought.

Faas: But then in his early poetry you find this almost obsessive pursuit of emptiness, this reduction of self and of all concrete things to a zero. And more recently he has suddenly started to grope around for objects, counting them . . . But let's go back to Lawrence for a moment. Has he had any major influence on your work?

Lawrence's influence

GINSBERG: I think I am indebted to Lawrence more indirectly through Kerouac and Burroughs. At one point I read a lot of his poetry, and some of his prose.

Faas: His critical writings as well?

GINSBERG: Well, his thing on Whitman in *Studies in Classic American Literature* is interesting.

Faas: I find him to be one of the greatest pioneers of open form poetics and philosophy.

GINSBERG: Except, you see, one problem with what we call open form and that's one problem with Lawrence's poetry, is that it is completely open and completely loose, but because he's got a literary mind in his head and he thinks he's writing poetry, he has a tendency to be slightly pompous or artificial, a little bit deliberative in his statements rather than accidental or inadvertent or caught or embarrassed or funny or Surrealist on account of that's the way the mind is, you know, putting things together fast without realizing why or how. And then there is also not too much interest in the musical part, not too much interest in balancing lines like in Pound or Williams, not much interest in the measure of the line. And in open form poetry there still is an interest in measuring the line, open form or free poetry, spontaneous poetry.

Faas: In 1961 while discussing Wittgenstein and Burroughs' cutup method you wondered whether perhaps we have "reached a point in human or unhuman development where art of word is oldhat dinosaur futile and must be left behind." How do you feel about that now?   Borroughs' cutups

GINSBERG: It seemed like an apt perception for that time because it did seem to me that Burroughs' cutup things are very similar by hindsight now to regular mindfulness meditation procedure. That is, in *vipassana* meditation where what you do is switch attention to the breath going out of your nostrils thus interrupting and cutting up thought forms and so taking a distance from thought forms rather than getting entangled in them; and thus observing thought forms comma anger comma sleepiness comma discursive fantasy and finding, paying attention to the gaps between two thoughts and mixing mind with space. Actually the traditional explanation by Gampopa, so I'm told, is mixing breath with space, mixing mind with breath, mixing mind with space, which is very similar to Burroughs' proposition of "all out of time and into space." So the exercises that Burroughs was using to cut himself out of language, which is to say out of the conceptual prison or projection, or projective fantasies, fantasy projections—out into space, is very similar to the description of meditation by both Zen and Tibetan teachers, in particular, Chögyam Trungpa. I was taking it at that time perhaps a little too literalistically, in a little upside down way.

Faas: Yes, you said that Burroughs was cutting up his art with a razor just as he was cutting up all human feelings between you, and then a little later that you feared you might be a mere robot under the mind control of the mad spectre of Burroughs.

GINSBERG: There was a certain amount of humor in that, I mean. [Laughing] It was one of the possible fantasies of the situation which I was able to deal with objectively by putting it on paper and saying: "I'm a robot under the mind control of the mad spectre of Burroughs." It's in that kind of voice, I mean, that's comedy also.

Faas: Did you really have a break with Burroughs at that point?

GINSBERG: Yes, I did, I mean somewhat of a break, nothing permanent. I had known him already for fifteen years, and I was to know him for another fifteen years, so   break with Burroughs

it was just like in any relationship, a temporary disequilibrium. Because for one thing he was really going into something very radical in terms of introspection of his consciousness and something which I didn't get myself into until many years later, though at the time I saw the relation between what he was doing and what I understood ideologically of Tibetan practise. I even had a dream about this which is somewhere in my journals [Grove Press (New York, 1977), pp. 154-7]. Burroughs is almost a Tibetan Lama *sangha* type, but working independently.

Faas: I got the impression that you were repelled by his coldly analytic approach to language and experience, dissecting everything.

GINSBERG: That was one aspect of my thought about it. The other was, like, a great deal of interest in it and preoccupation which I carried around for several years.

Faas: You mentioned that your "monster vibrations" completely disappeared after a certain point—1966, was it?

GINSBERG: Yeah.

Faas: How do you explain that?

monster visions   GINSBERG: Well there was always a shadow over me of the recollection of the mystical experience I had in 1948 connected with hearing Blake's voice. There was a series of visionary moments of intermittent sort of cosmic perceptions relating to Blake's *Songs of Innocence and of Experience,* and the last one was scary, as traditionally it's described sometimes: there are, you know, hellish visions as well as heavenly visions. And then I had the idea that what I was seeing was my egoless death state and it scared me. The monster vibration is described in the *Yage Letters.* There is even a symbolic picture I drew, the equivalent of the "Vomiter" or the "Blind Eye" or something, that little *maṇḍala* in the book. And it's similar to the horrific deities of the Tibetan pantheon. So I was getting vibes like that. But rather than seeing their function I was seeing them as a threat; or actually I was seeing them as representative of a divine order, but feeling that I was too afraid to go into it, and afraid to accept that, afraid to accept that as part of myself or something. But I was in the wrong relation with them. And I simply came into a better relation with that aspect of nature later on, probably because I had been sort of insistently imposing on myself an ideal of a state of consciousness that was ecstatic and celestial, and I was looking for that. And because I was pushing that so hard (and it was only a figment of memory really, an imagination), I was coming up with the opposite side of that, which was non-celestial and murderous.

Faas: But don't you feel one has to live with these monsters permanently?

GINSBERG: They are just little *māyā* day-dreams. Even Buchenwald is a little *māyā* day-dream.

Faas: Why then are they worshipped in India and Tibet, for instance?   all *māyā* day-dreams

GINSBERG: Because people think they are real. Well, it's very complicated, the practise of relating to these deities goes through various stages, some is worship, but then the other is annihilation of them and mastery of them. Some of the Tibetan practises include becoming them. And then after becoming them, realizing that they are just creations of your own mind and that they are like little fantasy doggies, too, say, but that they are illusory in the sense that both heaven and hell are illusory, aren't they? I think it was at a certain point around '67, when I stopped seeking a divine vision in acid, that I ceased getting demonic visions. And it's the same thing, I think, in Zen or in Tibetan practise, if you stop seeking *satori,* stop seeking illumination, you've sort of arrived at the end of the search.

Faas: In other words you can't find *satori* as long as you are consciously looking for it.

GINSBERG: In other words there is no *satori.* Just to put an end to it, there is no *satori.* And there is no hell. Or if you want, you could turn it around and say that *satori* consists in the realization that there is no *satori.* So you don't have to seek any further. So everything is complete and everything is perfect then.

Faas: You have often described your Blake vision but never really given a detailed account of what happened to you on the Kyoto-Tokyo express.   "The Change"

GINSBERG: Well, it was just about as much as I could remember, it wasn't anything quite as full, it was simply a realization that I had been pushing it too hard to regain my "vision," pushing myself too hard to go into the demonic, thinking that it was real, in order to get to some kind of *satori.* And pushing myself too hard with guilt, thinking that I should be taking acid to really cleanse out my soul, and making too much strain and effort in order to seek for some kind of illumination. I began realizing that the very effort I was making was a burden, and was preventing me from being present in my own mind.

Faas: When you look back on the years of depression and creative sterility which preceded that experience . . .

GINSBERG: That would be from about '61—

Faas: —to '63?

GINSBERG: Yeah. What I actually finally did was cut up my own illumination as Burroughs recommended. I finally abandoned or cut up or cut out of my obsession of becoming the divine center of the universe.

Faas: You don't feel that you repressed anything instead of absorbing and accepting these former visions.

GINSBERG: Well, I don't think we're really understanding each others' language yet. There is still a hang-up. I had some sort of a mystical experience, the nature of which I don't understand, which was both heavenly and hellish, okay. Then I kept trying to recapture those experiences while still being afraid of experiencing the hellish ones. But I was hung up on getting a heavenly experience, and then I used the acid for that purpose. And the more I strained to have a heavenly experience the more I'd get a hellish experience, because the hellish experience was the fear of being left out of heaven.

the demons
non-existent

Faas: Like Dr. Faustus trying to conjure up God and instead conjuring up the devil.

GINSBERG: No. [Laughing] It's too Romantic you're making it. It's something much simpler. The hellish experience existed in the fear of not making it into heaven. But, there is really no heaven. So that I was trying to get to somewhere that didn't exist. And because I failed, I kept feeling I was in hell. So I had imagined a heaven, so to speak, or was in the process of imagining a heaven, or trying to remember a heaven which is the same thing: to synthesize a heaven by my thought or my effort or my activity. And because I could not successfully do that I kept thinking then that I was in hell and doomed. Once I realized that there was no heaven to strain for then there was no hell to fall into, to be worried about. I realized I wasn't missing anything. So it's not a question of absorbing the demons, but it's a question of realizing that the demons don't really exist, in a sense, that they are self-created, out of a fear of missing the big event.

Faas: In the sense of the *Bardo Thödol . . .*

GINSBERG: Anyway, I have never been there, it's just a book. [Laughing] Oh, I am sorry, go on, "in the sense of the *Bardo Thödol . . ."*

Faas: I meant, in the sense of the *Bardo Thödol* which teaches the soul to just accept these wrathful divinities as projections of the mind . . .

GINSBERG: Right.

Faas: . . . and as unreal.

GINSBERG: Yes. I found a tremendous number of people who freaked out on acid; they freak out because they think that what they see on acid is real, and then try to incorporate that into their everyday life.

Faas: What was Gary Snyder's reaction to that? You mentioned that he went through a similarly horrific experience.

GINSBERG: I think once in a while or so when younger before he went to Japan, he visioned a little bit, though he had a long period of meditation and so, according to his Snyder traditional Zen understanding, he was probably a lot freer than I was of that kind of preoccupation. Actually it's only, I think, last fall [i.e., of 1973] that I finally got over the whole, really got completely through with the whole process by simply renouncing any idea of obtaining *satori* or illumination. I gave up on trying to get into heaven entirely. In the course of attending this Buddhist seminary and sitting ten hours a day and having a chance to examine every single minute thought that I was having about the idea of getting illuminated, I realized that I wasn't getting any more illuminated than the fact that I was sitting. And once I gave up substituting an imaginary heaven for the present reality, then heaven and hell were off my shoulders like a weight fallen off.

Faas: And that occurred a few months ago?

GINSBERG: Half a year ago. It occurred in stages, it was progressive. I'd had some sort of a brain seizure, "frantic light does seize my brain"—writ by Blake when he was fourteen. I had some sort of a hallucination perhaps when I was young, 22, and clung to that as a reality, because it seemed so complete and heavenly, it was only after renouncing heaven that you can be where you are. I wouldn't even want to say that you only have to renounce heaven and you get to heaven, because again that would be deceptive.

Faas: That's a new way you put it now. Previously you used to speak about getting back to the body.

GINSBERG: Yes.

Faas: But then, I suppose that would be a kind of simultaneous process.

GINSBERG: Yes, although I was too involved in a false dichotomy between mind and body. In my experience, let's see. My awareness and understanding of the process of self or non-self changes over the years. I'm sorry I have led people up blind alleys. [Laughing] I finally led people up as many blind alleys as Burroughs' I've been up. So that what Burroughs recommended at advice the end of *Yage Letters,* his telegram or his letter to cut out completely, cut up the Word, cut up my own Word, was very good advice. But it took me about fifteen years to finally realize how or what or why. Because I didn't want to cut out because I was sentimentally attached to the idea of being a saint in heaven, or something. It was just "a projection of my own ego."

Faas: But even now your own mode of expressing all that is quite different from Burroughs's, isn't it?

GINSBERG: Well yes, because it's a different situation, a different person, a different set of experiences that we're dealing with.

Faas: Can we switch to your attempt "to make *mantra* of American language." In *Improvised Poetics* you say that one shouldn't take that statement too literally.

GINSBERG: I forgot why I said that. Oh yes, because somebody else was taking it too literally. I don't know, there was an essay on it by Paul Carroll.

mantra poetics   *Faas:* In *The Poem in its Skin?*

GINSBERG: Yes. I have a lot of correspondence with him in that book about that. So *Improvised Poetics* is probably referring back to that. Yes, look at that, because we had a real correspondence about what I meant by that.

Faas: But you're still pursuing that path, I gather.

GINSBERG: Yes.

Faas: Robert Bly writes that a poet who wants to write a true political poem has to have such a grasp of his own psyche that he can leap up from it into the higher sphere of the national or political psyche. Does that notion make sense to you?

GINSBERG: Well, not entirely. If the grass and narcotics police try to set me up for a bust, my personal private life and my house is connected quite directly with the police bureaucracy, and so there is no disjunction between the political and the personal, there, in that case. Ah, so, as I am, so to speak, a cocksucker, there are laws about sex which are political and therefore personal to the extent that they impinge on my private life.

Faas: Yet would it make sense to you to speak of a national psyche? I recall several passages in your poetry where you treat a nation as if it had a psyche.

the national   GINSBERG: Yes, I think it's possible to do that, especially in
psyche   an electronic age where everybody is subjected to continuous bombardment with the same images and thought forms. Like, I'll give you an instance, right this minute [March 27, 1974]—the idea current in U.S.A. that "the war is over in Vietnam" seems to me just like an individual suppressing realization of a conflict going on around the house. It's like, you know, his mother and his father having a deadly battle around the house and they might shoot each other, and the son didn't want to recognize it. So right now there is this vast war going on in Vietnam which we are funding and which we are completely responsible for and which everybody is acting as if unconscious of, and which is not referred to

in polite political discourse or private life as it *was* three, four, five years ago. Everybody is pretending it's over, so to speak, but they know it's not over. So in that sense there is a national psyche, in the sense that the electronic network of communications is not bringing that war up into front page, front-brain, picture consciousness right now, but is relegating it to third and fourth page, and only with stories that are neutral and not charged emotionally. Or, for instance, see the Cambodian bombing was much more violent and illegal than any of the Watergate stuff. And yet everybody, the whole national consciousness—I should say, national media consciousness—is concerned with Watergate wire tapping on that slight level and has not yet been willing to confront this real heavier violence of the Cambodian bombing and the illegality of that which was just as illegal as the plumbers' activities—much more illegal!— mass murder, violation of the Constitution, violation of the tradition and everything, violation of what's supposed to be the tradition. So by nation-psyche I really mean, I suppose, the accumulated composite consciousness formed by all the interlocking mass media and their effect on people's everyday conversation and thought forms.
Faas: Including their own private thoughts.
GINSBERG: Well, thought forms inside the brain couldn't be more private.
Faas: I have tried to figure out some of the changes in style and content your poetry has undergone since "The Change."
GINSBERG: Yes, I've gone through quite a few since.
Faas: I wondered if you could make any comments as to how your style has changed.

development since "The Change"

GINSBERG: Well, I would say "The Change" is prophetic of a more literal change later on, say in the last year. A final abandonment of the pursuit of heaven, of—I should be more literal— final abandonment of the attempt to reconstruct the Blake vision I once had, and live by that. Because, finally, the memory of the Blake vision left such a strong impression of universal consciousness that it didn't seem right to abandon it. In fact, my first thought when it happened to me was "I must never forget this." But it sort of now appears by hindsight to be somewhat, say, like the Temptation of St. Anthony. You know, if you get a vision of heaven you might get hung up on that, and meanwhile, you know, you don't feed the beggar next door or don't feed your cat, or whatever. You see, theoretically a complete universe of consciousness would be total attention to "minute particular" detail around you, complete present attention. Wouldn't that be so?
Faas: In a Zen Buddhist sense.

GINSBERG: Well, when you look at all the descriptions of religious experience there is really always an absorption in seeing the universal in the particular. I mean it's always "No ideas but in things" finally. Not only in Zen but even in Christian mysticism I think you find it.

Faas: One finds that mystical attitude in William Carlos Williams.

GINSBERG: Well, but a Zen type mystical attitude.

Williams'   Faas: Quite.

mysticism   GINSBERG: In which the mysticism is "No ideas but in things." So, what I'm trying to say is that clinging to a memory of a mode of consciousness that I wanted to obtain or attain prevented me from obtaining that very mode of consciousness, because I was substituting memory for present attention, and constantly referring every perception I have now or had back to 1948, and what would that look like *sub specie æternitatis*, so that finally the vision, the memory of the vision became a hang-up. And now I'm even beginning to wonder, but maybe I should just say that I just had a freak out hallucination, to get rid of it, you know.

Faas: Your poetry since "Wichita Vortex Sutra" seems to be characterized by a more rhythmic *mantra*-like language which at the same time is more fact-oriented.

GINSBERG: Yeah. I suppose, I haven't really figured that one out. Yes, ideally it would be interesting to be able to compose rhythmic articulation, a sequence that would be exciting rhythmically, yet contain nothing but the facts, and at the same time have a kind of subtle interconnectedness and harmony that would appear from the outside to be divine, so to speak.

Faas: Do you feel that *The Fall of America* is a completed poem?

the end of   GINSBERG: No, well, I have a lot of fragments and long
The Fall of   poems since then, that connect with that. I don't think it
America   will ever have a completed form unless it arrives by accident. But a sort of completed form did arrive to the *Cantos*, simply by Pound pursuing to the end his preoccupations and registering his changes of sensibility. Maybe the end of *The Fall of America* will be: What the fuck am I getting so hung up on symbols of war and politics, I want to go back and sit on a mountain. [Laughing] I mean that might be the end for all I know. I mean I might finally realize that that's the point where—what it's all about. Or maybe I can go into exile or something like that. I think the police state is going to get worse and worse, I can't see how it's ever going to improve, because it's so built-in now.

Faas: I really can't see you doing that.

GINSBERG: Well I can't see it either. But what if the police came round knocking on my door? Well I can't see myself hanging around and going to jail forever. But I'm saying that the police state in America is really getting badder and badder, you know there's a hundred million dollar budget, the most right wing military people are now in control of the army and intelligence agencies, and they are not at all affected by the whole Watergate scandal. In fact, it's almost like the scandal itself will make people feel that they have done something to purify the government, while in fact the entire police bureaucracy and intelligence-military-industry are stronger than ever and more vicious than ever, and they are getting interconnected up by computers, so everybody's got dossiers, so the end of *The Fall of America* might be the abandoning of America finally.

Faas: You have recently propagated a poetry whose "root lies in neolithic tribal earth knowledge."

GINSBERG: A lot of that I get from Gary Snyder, it's like adaptations of his language, because I'm very imitative in that way.

Faas: One also finds these notions in D. H. Lawrence who in part derived them from the North American Indians.

GINSBERG: I don't think necessarily one will have to go back to . . .

Faas: Lawrence?

GINSBERG: No, to the Indians, something may emerge out of this situation here. I mean it might wind up with people of East Tenth Street where I live with no more heat, no more light, living in the ruins, and gathering in the streets every night for community block consultations and people meditating, singing, dancing and prophesizing on the brick and stone ruins of New York.

Faas: What criteria do you have for evaluating your own work? Somewhere, you say, for instance, that in a poem each syllable should have a place and a purpose; or you claim that each poem should have an emotional feeling center.   evaluating his own poetry

GINSBERG: Well, I write a great deal, and my habit of writing is to write in journals and notebooks, generally, not all the time, but that's the general habit. And then I cull from the notebooks things that seem to be complete poems.

Faas: And what's a complete poem?

GINSBERG: Well, something that seems to have a beginning, a middle and end. [Laughing] Or something that embarrasses me because of the truthfulness, or something that seems quite clear and hard, the images seem hard in the sense of precise and not abstract, not generalized, but composed of "minute particulars"; or if the sound is coherent, the vowel structure is clear. Since each poem has a different form more or less, there is no way of knowing it in advance. But by hindsight I can look at a piece of writing and say: That's interesting. But for criteria very specifically, almost the highest criterion I know is, if I weep while writing it's generally good writing—weep for the truthfulness of what I'm writing. And if I'm embarrassed by it, it very often turns out to be a really good poem, in which I'm reclaiming areas of my awareness which I hadn't admitted to myself or others.

Faas: That, I suppose, is what you call "present temporary form," which, you say, is all that form can ever be.

GINSBERG: I'd rather qualify this by saying: for this kind of writing. For instance, I've been doing a lot of blues lately and that has a very regular form of three lines, there are twelve bars and an aaa rhyme.

Faas: It seems that just like Duncan or Snyder, you seem reluctant to use the term open form.

open form   GINSBERG: Well, no, it's a usable phrase. It's just that I don't think I heard it until when? I don't know. When did it come into circulation?

Faas: Maybe with books like Umberto Eco's *L'opera aperta*, that is to say in the early sixties.

GINSBERG: Well, I had done most of my work in what you might call "open form" from 1950 to 1960 so I went into the habit of using that phrase, but I didn't think of it in those terms.

Faas: What were the terms in which you thought of "open form" in the '50's?

GINSBERG: "Spontaneous poems . . . scribbles . . . writings . . . ditties . . . Williams modern . . . Kerouac free style . . . free verse . . . etc."

Faas: You spoke of your poems as having a beginning, a middle and an end.

GINSBERG: Yes, where the thought process begins, where there's a middle, and where [laughing] I don't know, well, beginning, middle and end. I'm thinking of a poem I wrote recently, a description of breathing, and I have the breath go over the Grand Teton Mountains to Northern San Francisco into Hawaii and Australia and Saigon through the Indian Ocean and Africa and Marseille and on top of the Eiffel tower and then through the Atlantic to New York to Paterson, N.J. onto the Midwest finally arriving back in Teton village where it first began breathing. So [laughing] it had a beginning, a middle and an end. And that's a pretty good poem because it had that much clarity. But it's just the beginning of a series of thoughts and an end of a series of thoughts, a definite emotional end I guess and conclusive.

Faas: So it's really the beginning and end of a thought process.

GINSBERG: Right.

Faas: William Stafford says that his poems usually come to an end when his powers to homogenize an experience come to an end. beginning, middle and end

GINSBERG: I don't quite know what that means. I don't mind it actually, if I knew what it meant.

Faas: I think it means to impose some kind of order upon an experience or reality, to make an experience shapely.

GINSBERG: But then I don't know what that means either. In other words the experience one has while writing is the experience of one's own mind and to *put* order into it wouldn't that mean to rearrange one's normal sequence of thought-reflection?

Faas: Anyway, I didn't mean to defend that statement.

GINSBERG: No, but I don't even know what it means because, well, I'm saying quite literally, I don't know what it means. I would also put order into my thoughts if I knew a way of doing that without violating the nature, the natural structure of the thought. I do feel that thought has a natural order of its own, so it's a question of transcribing the thought in its own order, and in that sense a beginning, a middle and an end.

Faas: But of course it would be very difficult to describe that kind of . . .

GINSBERG: Not too hard. For instance, you know my book called *Empty Mirror*. There is this little poem that begins "How sick I am!" called "Marijuana Notations." So I got high and thought ahah at the beginning of a thought feeling sensation, and then made several ruminations about it, "does everybody feel this way?," and then suddenly switched the mind from that kind of introspective self-persecution to: "It is Christmas almost and people are singing Christmas carols down the block on Fourteenth Street." So that was the end, shifting the mind the thought process completely to something more real. It was a lot of subjective thought about my being sick or not being sick, very vague really, representative of a twenty year old or a twenty-four year old talking to himself. But then suddenly the mind comes down, suddenly I realize, you know, it's hopeless, and switched the thought like a cutup almost, or like you switch back to the breath attention in mindfulness meditation. Suddenly I switched back to observing something real at the outside of myself, outside of my subjective babbling. So in that sense it has a beginning, a middle and an end. In almost like ah . . .

Faas: But always in terms of actual experience.

GINSBERG: Well in terms of the experience of the mind.

Faas: Of actual thought process.

GINSBERG: Yeah, I would think that would be the criterion. Like one poem that does not have a beginning and an end is at the beginning of *Planet News*, a long poem called "Journal Night Thoughts" which is just sort of discursive free association. It's almost not a poem, but I included it because it's a specimen of that poetical mode, I mean it's very intense language, but at the same time it doesn't have any subject at all except the thoughts of the moment of that day, the thoughts at the moment of writing, recollecting all the thoughts of that day.

Faas: It seems that you avoid the term automatic writing, preferring to speak of spontaneous writing.

automatic versus transcriptive writing

GINSBERG: Well, automatic writing has to me the association that you are not completely conscious of what you are writing.

Faas: Not completely conscious of what you are writing?

GINSBERG: Yes, just the hand moving and just the unconscious coming out as if dictated by voices or from the unconscious but, you know, the hand moving and creating words that the mind is not aware of.

Faas: So graphing the movement of the mind, as you understand it, would imply a high degree of consciousness.

GINSBERG: Yes, depending . . . the process would be observing what is going on in the mind and writing it down, as simple as that, rather than to attempt to separate yourself from awareness of what your thought forms were. I would speak of spontaneous writing as writing down your thought forms as they occur. Automatic writing, I think, is a technical term which implies that you don't know what you're writing at the time. You really don't know, it might be ghost voices, and I think certain Surrealist practices were attempting to approach that.

Faas: With the assumption that if you have a poetic genius whatever comes out might be a great poem, I suppose.

GINSBERG: I would have the same assumption about recording the thought forms of spontaneous mind and really if you are a poetic genius, if your mind is shapely, then what comes out will be shapely. In other words if you see clearly into your mind, if you remember and recollect clearly what you were thinking, it would be thoughts in minute detail, thoughts of minute detail, it will have objects and it will have real describable things in it. It won't be sort of vague moods, it will be actual buses passing by, yellow street signs, those of Tenth Street.

Faas: I am puzzled by the fact that you frequently mention Gertrude Stein as a model for your technique of graphing the mind-movement. At one point when a well-known

Gertrude Stein

psychiatrist wrote that she was doing automatic writing, she replied that the man was wrong.

GINSBERG: We are still having this confusion about automatic writing. I didn't say she was doing automatic writing, I said that she was writing down the sequence of verbal sounds.

Faas: Exactly, like an unfolding of language . . .

GINSBERG: . . . that occurred to her during the time of composition.

Faas: But I don't think she graphed the movement of her thoughts the way you do.

GINSBERG: No, she wasn't interested in memory, she wasn't interested in the future, she had a specific subject which was a few sentences like "Napoleon ate ice cream on Elba" and then she would recombine the words over and over again in the normal order that they came to her. Actually "the graph of the mind-movement," that poetry is a "graph of a mind moving" is not my phrase, it's Philip Whalen's from his poetics statement at the end of Don Allen's anthology. Philip Whalen once read Stein's "Composition as Explanation" to me aloud about ten years ago and it seemed exactly on the line of what I was interested in. Gertrude Stein made a lot of different kinds of art experiments, but her experiments were all with the present consciousness during the time of composition.

Faas: I would distinguish between two kinds of automatic writing.

GINSBERG: You keep calling it automatic writing, I don't see anything automatic about it. If I am recalling what I am thinking, that's not automatic, it's very deliberate. I would say transcriptive more than automatic—stenographic transcription of mind thought, of how the mind thinks.

Faas: All I was really trying to say was that Gertrude Stein wasn't interested in "graphing the mind-movement."

GINSBERG: I think in certain compositions she was. That's what I was saying, she made a great many different kinds of experiments in present consciousness, experiments in present consciousness during composition. She was interested in the present consciousness during composition, would we agree on that?

Faas: Well, I don't know Gertrude Stein's work *that* well.

GINSBERG: You have to read her aloud.

Faas: When does a line break? It wasn't clear to me what you say about that in your *Improvised Poetics*. Sometimes you say it's determined by the page . . .

GINSBERG: That's Creeley's method . . . Basically breath-stop. the line break

Faas: . . . or that the thought breaks.

GINSBERG: Well, when you talk and then after a while like you run out of thought and words, and then you're gonna stop and take a breath and continue. So that's when you have your breath-stop. Breath-stop and the thought-division could be the same.

Faas: Which would imply a new kind of thinking, wouldn't it?

GINSBERG: No, only an *observation* of your thinking. Same thing as usual, except you're observing it, and see where it stops, and there's a gap, and where a new thought begins. Because if you observe thought, it actually does stop and there are gaps in between. It's like a movie, it looks continuous, but actually it's a lot of different frames. And thought is the same way.

Faas: Graphing the movement of the mind, while, I suppose, standing back from your own stream of consciousness.

GINSBERG: Observing it or recollecting it.

Faas: I just don't have any personal experience of graphing the movement of my mind, so it's difficult to understand.

graphing the mind movement

GINSBERG: Well, I'll show you. Really, it's very simple. Sit up with your back straight. Now, the primary attention could be on the breath coming out of the nostrils, so that—keep your mouth closed so there's no air pocket, and instead of thinking about the conversation or about me, or looking at me or anything like that—look toward *there* maybe [pointing to the kitchen wall]—so we don't get tangled in some kind of subjective thing, pay attention to the flow of breath out through the nostrils for maybe five breaths. Can you do it for five breaths just on the out-breaths? Forget about what's going on inside you on the in-breaths or any other time. And really sit up straight—Yeah, now—Okay. [Pause] Now are you able to put your complete attention on your breath going out . . . or do thoughts interrupt?

Faas: I have an image of the hair in my nose.

GINSBERG: Okay, so pay attention to breath after it leaves your nose and the space in front of your face, into which the breath flows, for five breaths.

Faas: Pay attention to the air coming out? and flowing into space?

GINSBERG: Yeah, into space and dissolving in space, or identify with the breath going out and dissolving.[Pause] Okay now, you're paying some attention to that.

Faas: Yes.

GINSBERG: What else were you thinking about?

Faas: Sort of an image of a balloon coming out of my nose as in comic books, and then I was also thinking about telling you about it.

GINSBERG: Okay, so there's three separate things going on. Now can you pay attention to the invisible space not in the form of a balloon. [Pause] I don't mean invisible but transparent. [Pause] Now during the last few breaths, what other thoughts came into mind? Anything about Frankfurt or anything like that?

Faas: No, you see, when I meditate I usually try to concentrate on one image: a clock outside the town gate of Eibelstadt, a German medieval town I used to live in, and that sort of came into my mind.

GINSBERG: Okay, fine. Well, try one more time, and when the clock rises, switch your attention to your breath again. [Pause] So your thought is separated between the clock and the breath, and it's really discontinuous. There is a gap in between.

Faas: I see. [Both laughing]

GINSBERG: Just literally speaking, there is a moment of shift, that's almost a fraction of a second. So if you do meditate and continue to practise attention to breath, you never can stop your mind from thinking and wandering and travelling in space, but you keep interrupting it, bring it back to the breath and the space in front of you.

Faas: I suppose that's what I'm trying to do with the clock.

GINSBERG: Yeah.

Faas: I mean I can never stay with that image for any longer than say thirty seconds.

GINSBERG: Okay, so that in that sense thought is discontinuous, I mean there are jumps and gaps in between the thoughts, and there are actually complete gaps in between for only a micro-second, but . . .

Faas: And that's where you talk about *śūnyatā*.

GINSBERG: Well, a gap is—that is Chögyam Trungpa's terminology—that gap in which we are just sitting in space or in just empty space. Now, if you practise that kind of thing either for meditation or just trying to recollect what you were just thinking about when you are writing you notice you get a *writing a line of Ginsberg poetry* lot of different thoughts with gaps in between, and in that sense thought is discontinuous, like movies, in the sense of the cinema, you know with twenty-four or fifteen frames a second. So you might have like three or four thoughts a second, or maybe one thought a second, but in between—and the thoughts jump around, so obviously you were thinking of a clock, but then you might think from a clock to the . . . Beats, your paper or your nostril. So that's all I mean when I say remembering or recollecting. So the process of writing for me is remembering and recollecting the thoughts I was just having while writing.

Faas: And the writing is a kind of stepping back from that.

GINSBERG: Well, the mind steps back, and the writing registers it fast, you just scribble it fast. The first words that come to your mind, the first flashes of what it was, your clock, a hand, a gingerbread hand, iron letters, roman numerals, roof, grey tiles, those were the first things . . . So that's "clock roman numerals iron letters roof grey tiles," and you've got a line of Ginsberg poetry. That's exactly it, you see. It's the first thoughts, whatever you can get. I have a whole scene of clocks and roofs and whatever I remember from Munich or wherever I saw a clock, just picking up, you know, like when you sketch very fast.

Faas: Yet these are still only fragments. How do you put them together? The way they come out?

GINSBERG: Like a *haiku*: "clocks iron letters."

Faas: No, I mean once you have written a line.

GINSBERG: You move on to the next.

Faas: Add them up, just in the order in which they came out?

GINSBERG: Move on to . . . yes.

Faas: And never shift them around.

GINSBERG: No no no no no. No you couldn't—then you'd be stopping the whole process.

Bibliography & Abbreviated References

A,P Allen, D. M. *The New American Poetry.* Edited by D. M. Allen. New York: Grove Press, 1960.

Ab,M Abrams, M. H. *The Mirror and the Lamp. Romantic Theory and the Critical Tradition.* New York: Norton, 1958.

Ab,S ———. *Natural Supernaturalism. Tradition and Revolution in Romantic Literature.* New York: Norton, 1971.

B,F Bly, Robert, ed. *The Fifties.* (Journal)

B,IJ ———. "An Interview with Robert Bly." *Tennessee Poetry Journal,* 2, No. 2 (Winter 1969), pp. 29-38.

B,IL ———. "Interview." *The Lamp in the Spine,* 3 (Winter 1972), pp. 50-65.

B,L ———. *The Light Around the Body: Poems.* New York: Harper & Row, 1967.

B,N ———. *Neruda and Vallejo: Selected Poems.* Edited by Robert Bly. Boston: Beacon Press, 1971.

B,R ———. "Reflections on the Origins of Poetic Form." *Field,* 10 (Spring 1974), pp. 31-36.

B,S ———, ed. *The Sixties.* (Journal)

B,Si ———. *Silence in the Snowy Fields.* Middletown, Conn.: Wesleyan University Press, 1962.

B,Sl ———. *Sleepers Joining Hands.* New York: Harper & Row, 1974.

Ba,C Baskin, W., ed. *Classics in Chinese Philosophy.* Totowa, N.J.: Littlefield, Adams & Co., 1974.

Bi,A Birch, C., ed. *Anthology of Chinese Literature.* New York: Grove Press, 1967.

Br,M Breton, André. *Manifestes du surréalisme.* Paris: Gallimard, 1972.

Bs,D Barthes, R. *Le degré zéro de l'écriture.* Paris: Éditions Gonthier, 1970.

Bs,E   ____. *Essais critiques*. Paris: Éditions du Seuil, 1964.

Bu,L   Bush, S. *The Chinese Literati on Painting. Su Shih (1037-1101) to Tung Ch'i-Ch'ang (1555-1636)*: Harvard-Yenching Institute Studies XXVII. Cambridge, Mass.: Harvard University Press, 1971.

BG   Anonymous. *The Bhagavad Gita As It Is*. With Introduction, Translation and Authorized Purport by A. C. Bhaktivedanta Swami. London: Collier-Macmillan Ltd., 1969.

BT   Anonymous. *The Tibetan Book of the Dead*. Edited by W. Y. Evans-Wentz, with a Psychological Commentary by C. G. Jung. London: Oxford University Press, 1960.

B-M,P   Berg, S. & R. Mezey, eds. *Naked Poetry: Recent American Poetry in Open Forms*. Indianapolis: Bobbs-Merrill, 1969.

C,B   Creeley, Robert, *A Day Book*. New York: Scribner, 1972.

C,C   ____. *Contexts of Poetry: Interviews 1961-1971*. Edited by D. Allen. Bolinas, Cal.: Four Seasons Foundation, 1973.

C,Cr   ____. *The Creative*. Los Angeles: Black Sparrow Press, 1973.

C,D   ____. *The Gold Diggers and Other Stories*. New York: Scribner, 1965.

C,F   ____. *The Finger: Poems 1966-1969*. London: Calder and Boyars, 1970.

C,G   ____. *A Quick Graph: Collected Notes and Essays*. Edited by D. Allen. San Francisco: Four Seasons Foundation, 1970.

C,IR   ____. "Interview." By L. Wagner and L. MacAdams, Jr. *Paris Review*, 44 (Fall 1968), pp. 154-187.

C,P   ____. *Poems 1950-1965*. London: Calder and Boyars, 1966.

C,W   ____. *Words*. New York: Scribner, 1967.

Ce,B   Coleridge, Samuel Taylor. *Biographia Literaria*. Edited by G. Watson. London: Dent, 1965.

Ch,C   Chang Chung-yuan. *Creativity and Taoism: A Study of Chinese Philosophy, Art, and Poetry*. New York: Harper & Row, 1970.

D,A   Duncan, Robert. *Audit/Poetry*, IV, No. 3 (1967). Featuring Robert Duncan.

D,C   ____. "The H.D. Book," II, 2. *Caterpillar*, 6 (January 1969), pp. 16-38.

D,F   _____. "Ideas of the Meaning of Form." *Kulchur,* 1, No. 4 (1961), pp. 60-74.

D,I   _____. *An Interview.* By George Bowering and Robert Hogg. Toronto: Beaver Kosmos Folio, 1971.

D,S   _____. "The H.D. Book," 1, 5. *Stony Brook,* 1/2 (1968), pp. 4-19.

D,T   _____. *The Truth and Life of Myth: An Essay in Essential Autobiography.* Fremont, Mich.: The Sumac Press, 1968.

D,W   _____. "Changing Perspectives in Reading Whitman," *The Artistic Legacy of Walt Whitman.* Edited by E. H. Miller. New York: New York University Press, 1970, pp. 73-101.

Di,B   Dickey, James. *Babel to Byzantium: Poets and Poetry Now.* New York: Farrar, Straus, and Giroux, 1968.

Di,P   _____. *Poems 1957-1967.* New York: Collier Books, 1967.

Di,S   _____. *Sorties.* Garden City, N.Y.: Doubleday and Co., 1971.

E,E   Eliot, T. S. *Selected Essays.* London: Faber and Faber, 1966.

E,F   _____. *The Waste Land: A Facsimile and Transcript of the Original Drafts etc.* Edited by V. Eliot. London: Faber and Faber, 1971.

E,IR   _____. "Interview." *The Paris Review,* 6, No. 21 (Spring-Summer, 1959), pp. 47-70.

E,P   _____. *On Poetry and Poets.* London: Faber and Faber, 1969.

E,U   _____. *The Use of Poetry and the Use of Criticism.* London: Faber and Faber, 1967.

E,W   _____. *The Sacred Wood: Essays on Poetry and Criticism.* London: Faber and Faber, 1969.

F,C   Fenollosa, Ernest. *The Chinese Written Character as a Medium for Poetry.* Edited by E. Pound. San Francisco: City Lights Books, 1968.

G,A   Ginsberg, Allen. *Allen Verbatim: Lectures on Poetry, Politics, Consciousness.* Edited by G. Ball. New York: McGraw-Hill, 1974.

G,B   _____. *Songs of Innocence and Experience.* By William Blake; tuned by Allen Ginsberg. MGM Records: FTS-3083.

G,F   _____. *The Fall of America: Poems of These States, 1965-1971.* San Francisco: City Lights Books, 1972.

G,H ———. *Howl and Other Poems*. Introduction by William Carlos Williams. San Francisco: City Lights Books, 1971.

G,IO ———. "Interview." *Unmuzzled Ox,* iii, No. 2 (1975), pp. 14-25.

G,IR ———. "Mystery in the Universe" (1965). *Rogue,* 10, No. 3 (June 1965), pp. 1-9.

G,IS ———. "Interview." *Spectrum,* 21, No. 34 (20 November 1970), pp. 5, 12.

G,J ———. *Indian Journals: March 1962-May 1963*. San Francisco: City Lights Books, 1968.

G,K ———. *Kaddish and Other Poems, 1958-1960*. San Francisco: City Lights Books, 1961.

G,L ———. *The Yage Letters: William Burroughs and Allen Ginsberg*. San Francisco: City Lights Books, 1971.

G,M ———. *Empty Mirror: Early Poems*. Introduction by William Carlos Williams. New York: Totem Press-Corinth Books, 1961.

G,N ———. *Planet News, 1961-1967*. San Francisco: City Lights Books, 1968.

G,P ———. *Improvised Poetics*. Buffalo, N.Y.: Anonym Press, 1971.

G,R ———. *Prose Contribution to the Cuban Revolution*. Detroit: Artists' Workshop Press, 1966.

Go,B Goddard, D., ed. *A Buddhist Bible*. Boston: Beacon Press, 1970.

G-R,W Goedl-Roth, M., ed. *Weltkulturen und moderne Kunst*. München: Verlag Bruckmann, 1972.

K,L Keats, John. *The Letters*. Edited by M. B. Forman. London: Oxford University Press, 1952.

Ke,B Kerouac, Jack. *The Dharma Bums*. New York: Viking Press, 1958.

Ke,IR ———. "Interview." *Paris Review,* 11, No. 43 (Summer 1968), pp. 61-105.

Kh,S ———. Kherdian, D. *Gary Snyder: A Biographical Sketch and Descriptive Checklist*. Berkeley: Oyez, 1965.

Ko,N Kornbluth, J., ed. *Notes from the New Underground*. New York: Viking Press 1968.

Kr,G Kramer, J. *Allen Ginsberg in America*. New York: Random House, 1970.

L,B   Lowell, Robert. Review of R. P. Warren's *Brother to Dragons. Kenyon Review,* 15 (1953), pp. 619-625.

L,IR   ———. "A Conversation." *The Review,* 26 (Summer 1971), pp. 10-29.

L,W   ———. "William Carlos Williams." *Hudson Review,* 14 (1961/62), pp. 530-536.

La,A   Lawrence, D. H. *Apocalypse.* With an introduction by R. Aldington. London: Heinemann, 1972.

La,C   ———. *Selected Literary Criticism.* Edited by A. Beal. New York: Viking Press, 1956.

La,E   ———. *Selected Essays.* Harmondsworth: Penguin Books, 1968.

La,F   ———. *Fantasia of the Unconscious and Psychoanalysis and the Unconscious.* Harmondsworth: Penguin Books, 1971.

La,M   ———. *Mornings in Mexico and Etruscan Places.* Harmondsworth: Penguin Books, 1971.

Li,T   Liu, J. J. Y. *Chinese Theories of Literature.* Chicago: University of Chicago Press, 1975.

Lv,P   Levertov, Denise. *The Poet in the World.* New York: New Directions, 1973.

M,Œ   Mallarmé, Stéphane. *Œuvres complètes.* Paris: Gallimard, 1951.

M,E   ———. *Selected Prose Poems, Essays, & Letters.* Edited by B. Cook. Baltimore: Johns Hopkins Press, 1956.

N,C   Novik, M. *A Writing Biography and Inventory.* Unpublished Doctoral Dissertation on Robert Creeley. University of British Columbia at Vancouver, 1973.

O,I   Olson, Charles. *Call Me Ishmael: A Study of Melville.* London: J. Cape, 1967.

O,L   ———. *Letters for Origin: 1950-1955.* Edited by A. Glover. London: Cape Goliard Press, 1970.

O,M   ———. *Maps,* 4 (1971). Featuring Charles Olson.

O,P   ———. *Proprioception.* San Francisco: Four Seasons Foundation, 1965.

O,R   ———. Review of E. A. Havelock's *Preface to Plato. Niagara Frontier Review* (Summer 1964), pp. 40-44.

O,T   ———. *Poetry and Truth: The Beloit Lectures and Poems.* Edited by G. F. Butterick. San Francisco: Four Seasons Foundation, 1971.

O,U   ____. *Human Universe and Other Essays.* Edited by D. Allen. New York: Grove Press, 1967.

O,V   ____. *The Special View of History.* Edited by Ann Charters. Berkeley: Oyez, 1970.

O,W   ____. *Selected Writings.* Edited by R. Creeley. New York: New Directions, 1966.

Os,A   Ossman, D. *The Sullen Art. Interviews with Modern American Poets.* New York: Corinth Books, 1963.

O'C,P   O'Connor, F. V. *Jackson Pollock.* New York: Museum of Modern Art, 1967.

P,B   Pound, Ezra. "Epstein, Belgion and Meaning." *The Criterion,* 9 (Oct. 1929-July 1930), pp. 470-475.

P,G   ____. *Gaudier-Brzeska: A Memoir.* Hessle, East Yorkshire: Marvell Press, 1960.

P,L   ____. *The Letters: 1907-1941.* Edited by D. D. Paige. New York: Harcourt, Brace & World, Inc., 1950.

P,P   ____. *Selected Poems.* Edited by T. S. Eliot. London: Faber and Faber, 1964.

Pa,C   Packard, W., ed. *The Craft of Poetry.* Garden City, N.Y.: Doubleday and Co., 1974.

Pl,W   Plimpton, G., ed. *Writers at Work: Third Series.* New York: Viking Press, 1967.

R,W   Rimbaud, Arthur. *Complete Works: Selected Letters (English and French).* Edited by W. Fowlie. Chicago: University of Chicago Press, 1966.

Ra,M   Ray, P. C. *The Surrealist Movement in England.* London: Cornell University Press, 1971.

Rg,A   Rothenberg, J. & G. Quasha, eds. *America a Prophecy. A New Reading of American Poetry from Pre-Columbian Times to the Present.* New York: Random House, 1974.

Rg,T   Rothenberg, Jerome., ed. *Technicians of the Sacred. A Range of Poetries from Africa, America, Asia, & Oceania.* Garden City, N.Y.: Doubleday and Co., 1968.

Rn,P   Robertson, B. *Jackson Pollock.* New York: H. N. Abrams, 1960.

R-G,R   Robbe-Grillet, Alain. *Pour un nouveau roman.* Paris: Gallimard, 1963.

S,C	Snyder, Gary. *The Back Country.* New York: New Directions, 1967.
S,E	——. *Earth House Hold.* New York: New Directions, 1969.
S,IA	——. "Interview." By N. Tarn. *Alcheringa,* 4 (Autumn 1972), pp. 104-113.
S,IG	——. "Interview." By D. Kozlovsky. *Modine Grunch,* 3 (January 1970), pp. 21-25.
S,IQ	——. "Interview." By L. Bartlett. *California Quarterly,* 9 (Spring 1975), pp. 43-50.
S,IR	——. "Interview."*Road Apple Review,* I, No. 4 and II, No. 1 (Winter 1969-Spring 1970), pp. 59-68.
S,IT	——. "Interview." By G. Fowler. *Literary Times,* IV, No. 2 (December 1964), p. 22.
S,M	——. *Myths and Texts.* New York: Totem Press in association with Corinth Books, 1960.
S,R	——. *Riprap, & Cold Mountain Poems.* Writing 7. San Francisco: Four Seasons Foundation, 1969.
S,T	——. *Turtle Island.* New York: New Directions, 1974.
S,W	——. *Regarding Wave.* New York: New Directions, 1970.
Sc,P	Scully, J., ed. *Modern Poets on Modern Poetry.* New York: McGraw-Hill, 1969.
Si,A	Sirén, O. *The Chinese on the Art of Painting.* New York: Schocken Books, 1971.
Su,M	Suzuki, D. T. *Mysticism: Christian and Buddhist.* World Perspectives. Volume Twelve. Planned and edited by R. N. Anshen. Westport, Conn.: Greenwood Press, 1975.
Su,W	——. *Selected Writings.* Edited by W. Barrett. Garden City, N.Y.: Doubleday, 1956.
Su,Z	——. *Essays in Zen Zuddhism. First Series.* New York: Grove Press, 1961.
W,E	Williams, William Carlos. *Selected Essays.* New York: New Directions, 1969.
W,P	——. *Paterson.* New York: New Directions, 1963.
Wa,G	Watts, Alan W. *The Two Hands of God. The Myths of Polarity.* New York: Collier-Macmillan, Ltd., 1969.
Wa,W	——.*The Way of Zen.* New York: Random House.

Wh,I   Whitehead, A. N. *The Interpretation of Science: Selected Essays.* Edited by A. H. Johnson. Indianapolis: Bobbs-Merrill, 1961.

Wh,S   ———. *Symbolism, Its Meaning and Effect.* New York: G. P. Putnam's Sons, 1959.

Wn,L   Whitman, Walt. *Leaves of Grass and Selected Prose.* Edited by J. Kouwenhoven. New York: Random House, 1950.

Y,B   Yates, F. A. *Giordano Bruno and the Hermetic Tradition.* New York: Random House, 1960.

Y,S   ———. "Magic in Shakespeare's Last Plays." *Encounter,* 44, No. 4 (April 1975), pp. 14-22.

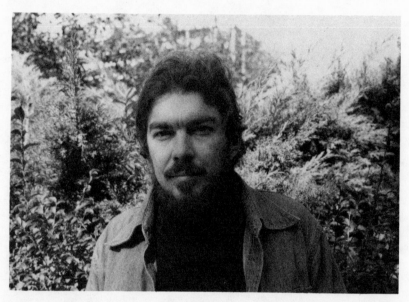

Ekbert Faas was born in 1938 in Berlin. He studied in Munich, Paris, Madrid and London and holds a Ph.D. (1965) and a Dr.habil. (1971) in English literature. Besides articles, interviews and translations, he has published books on Renaissance literature, post-Romantic poetry and, more recently, on Modernist and non-Western æsthetics. At present he is writing critical studies of Ted Hughes and Robert Duncan. A writer as well as a teacher by profession, he has held appointments at European and North American universities and presently teaches at York University in Toronto.

Printed May 1978 in Santa Barbara & Ann Arbor
for the Black Sparrow Press by Mackintosh and Young
& Edwards Brothers Inc. Design by Barbara Martin.
This edition is published in paper wrappers;
there are 1000 hardcover trade copies; & 125 copies
have been handbound in boards by Earle Gray & are
numbered & signed by the authors.